AFTER EDGEWATER

DAN LARGENT

BLG PUBLISHING

DEDICATION

This book is dedicated to all of my fellow dreamers.

ACKNOWLEDGMENTS

I would like to thank every person who has encouraged me during my journey as an author. To my wife, April, and children Brooke, Grace, and Luke, I hope you know how much I appreciate your support. To my editor, Nancy Gulden, I cannot sing your praises enough. To all of the media outlets that have given me a platform to share my work, you will never know just how grateful I am. To my friends, family members, and strangers that read my first book, THANK YOU from the bottom of my heart.

Dream BIG

Prologue

Cooper Madison stared at the four-inch scar located on the inside of his right elbow. He always felt that it was a cruel irony how the scar from his Tommy John surgery resembled a smiley face when he cocked his right arm upward at a ninety-degree angle.

Ulnar Collateral Ligament reconstruction, named after the former Major League pitcher that first underwent the procedure in 1974, is typically completed by taking a tendon from the patient's forearm and inserting it where the UCL once was.

Dr. Craig Mueller, Cleveland's team surgeon, had just finished examining Coop's range of motion and was now seated across from his patient on a stool.

"When did you start to feel the discomfort?" Dr. Mueller asked.

"About halfway through a round of batting practice yesterday," Coop replied.

"Any guess on how many pitches you threw before you felt it?"

"Not sure... Fifty or so, I suppose..."

"Did you warm-up properly before throwing?"

"Yeah..."

"Any other factors that you can think of that might have caused the pain?"

"No, sir..."

"How would you describe the pain when it occurred? Did you feel a pop like when you originally injured the elbow?" Dr. Mueller asked.

"No sir, it definitely wasn't anything like when it popped. This time it was just a dull pain that got worse with each pitch," Coop answered.

"Well, that's a good thing then. My guess is that you have some tendinitis in your elbow, which is not uncommon given how long it has been since your surgery."

"Will it go away?" Coop asked.

"It can, but you'll need to rest and ice. Lots of ice."

"How long? We have the playoffs coming up in two weeks. The team is going to need me to be able to throw."

"Old habits die hard, don't they? You're not a young man anymore, Cooper, so things like this can take some time to heal properly."

"Don't remind me…"

"I would say to take the next week off completely in regards to throwing, and make sure that you're icing at least four times a day. After a week, test it out and see how it feels. If there's no pain, then you can ease back in slowly. However, if the pain is still persistent, come back and see me."

"What happens then? I mean, if the pain's still there?"

"Well, we can do an MRI to rule out any tears and then come up with a game plan to get you back into shape."

"Ugh, this sucks, Doc. The boys are really counting on me to be able to throw, especially with the playoffs approaching…"

"They'll understand, Cooper. I'm sure that they'd rather you take it easy for a week or two so that you're hopefully able to throw once the postseason arrives. They'll survive without your arm for a while."

"I know… but it still sucks, Doc…"

"Welcome to being over 40 years old, Cooper. Speaking of

playoffs, have you been to any games recently? Tito sure has the boys hitting their stride at the right time, as usual. Kind of reminds me of the 2016 World Series squad. Hopefully this season we'll finally get that ring!"

"To be honest, Doc, I haven't been to a game in person since the World Series run. You're about my only connection to the club anymore," Coop responded.

"Well, I suppose that's because being a team surgeon is about the safest job in professional sports. Plus, we are a hell of a lot cheaper than the players to keep around," Dr. Mueller chuckled as he gave Coop a pat on the knee and stood up to leave the examination room.

"I'm not gonna argue with you there, Doc. Thanks again for fitting me in today."

As he was about to exit the room, Dr. Mueller turned around and looked at his patient, who despite being four decades old still looked like he could toe the rubber in a Major League uniform.

"Don't be a stranger, Cooper, and I'm not talking about visiting me. This town still loves you, and even if the faces in the clubhouse are different now, I can assure you that they would love to see you too."

"I appreciate that, Doc…"

After Dr. Mueller left the room, Coop glanced down again at the scar that had brought him to see the man who made the incision all those years ago. So much had happened since then, but the memories of that evening in 2006 were still fresh in Coop's mind.

1

Cooper Madison had just made it back to the big leagues in October of 2006. So much in his life had changed in the past few weeks, and for the first time since the death of his father, Jeffrey, he felt like his life was right back where it should be.

His arm felt lively and strong during warm-ups in the bullpen, and he was determined to make his limited pitch count stretch as far into the game as possible. After his final warm-up pitch he made sure to seek out the two people that he made sure were seated behind home plate.

Clarence Walters, owner of CW Security Solutions, was easy to find. Not only was he noticeable due to his massive frame, but he was also holding up the oversized gold key pendant and necklace that Coop had given him as a gift earlier that day when Clarence drove him to the ballpark.

"Coop, you really shouldn't have, man…" Clarence had said earlier when he opened the velvet box that contained the thick gold chain and shiny key pendant.

"Normally, this is where I'd make a joke and say that it's really fake gold or something stupid like that to avoid being sincere. But, that was the old Cuppah Madison, Clarence. Ever since our talk, I really have been trying to work on that. It's because of you, man. You're one of *my* keys, Clarence Walters," Coop said in his still-present drawl, referencing the day that Clarence had called him out for always trying to deflect whenever conversations became too real.

"I… I don't know what to say, other than thank you, Coop."

"There's an inscription on the back of the key; flip it over."

Clarence removed the large pendant with his thick fingers and flipped it over before reading the tiny engraved words out loud.

"Being honest may not get you a lot of friends, but it'll always get you the right ones… John Lennon."

"That was one of my daddy's favorite sayings, and your talk about certain people being 'keys' in our lives made it a no-brainer to put on there for you. I needed that brutal honesty from you that day, and I'm better because of it, Clarence."

"I truly appreciate it, Coop. I'm so proud of you, and not just because of today. Your daddy would be proud of you too, you know. He's watching…"

Coop gave Clarence a nod from where he stood just outside the pitcher's mound and turned his gaze one seat to the right.

Cara Knox, the girl that came into his life just weeks prior, was beaming with pride as she mouthed the word that said so little, yet meant so much.

"Nothing…"

Coop smiled, winked, and then silently answered.

"Nothing…"

"You ready, big guy?"

The words brought Coop's mind back to where his body had remained during his brief acknowledgement of Cara and Clarence. They came from his catcher, Chaz DeLisio, who was a ten-year veteran in "The Show".

"You better believe it, CD…"

"Atta boy! Training wheels are off tonight, brother. Let's go right after these guys with that fastball that I used to hate trying to hit when I was with the Cards…"

"Yessir… lots of hard stuff tonight, I only have so many to use and don't want to waste any," Coop said, referencing his strict pitch limit. Aside from a couple of minor league relief appearances, this was Coop's first start on the mound in over a year.

It was the final game of what had been a disappointing 2006 campaign for Cleveland, but the news that Cooper Madison was starting on the mound brought a playoff-like atmosphere to the sold-out Jacobs Field.

"That's what I like to hear, baby! Let's get after it," Chaz said as he trotted back to his spot behind home plate.

Coop toed the rubber for the first pitch of what many were calling the second act of his prolific career. He took the sign from his catcher, rocked back into his wind-up, and delivered a fastball.

"Striiiike one!" the umpire growled as the leadoff man for Tampa Bay, Frankie Rositano, watched a 96 mph fastball catch the outside corner of the plate.

The capacity crowd exploded in a raucous cheer as if it was the final out of a playoff game. Amongst those screaming the loudest were Cara and Clarence, who leapt out of their seats as soon as they heard the call by the umpire. Also cheering loudly were the guests in the Owner's VIP Suite. Cara's family and her best friend, Lucy Eckert, were there, along with Coop's agent, Todd "T-Squared" Taylor. They joined Coop and Cara's friends from the Westcott Hotel where he lived, and they were all going nuts. Even Rahul Ansari, the Indian-born limousine driver who was witnessing his first baseball game ever was jumping up and down as he high-fived Grace Brooks, who also worked for Clarence as a private security guard.

"Atta boy, Coop!" Chaz yelled as he made the return throw to his pitcher.

Coop took a deep breath and delivered another fastball, this time towards the inside part of the plate. The batter took a hearty swing, but the ball zipped past the barrel of his bat for strike two. The cheers seemed to double in size as those in attendance could feel the stadium shake.

Chaz gave Coop the sign for a slider away, nearly an impossible pitch to hit when executed properly with two strikes. It starts out like a fastball and then dives away from the batter with a sharp break. As good as Coop's fastball was throughout his career, his slider was far more devastating as an "out pitch". Big league hitters will often say that it is a tall task to make contact with a dominant slider - even when they know one is coming.

Coop rocked and fired a perfect slider that started at the strike zone and ended up six inches off the plate after its break. The right-handed Rositano didn't stand a chance as he tried to check his swing.

"Striiiike three!" yelled the umpire as he extended his arm and punched the batter out.

"That's one, baby!" Chaz yelled as he fired the ball down to the third baseman to throw it "around the horn" - a baseball team's way of celebrating an out when nobody is on base.

Cara and Clarence each had tears of joy as they jumped up and down while cheers of "Coooooop" filled the stadium.

Coop felt the adrenaline flowing through his veins as he toed the rubber to face the second batter, Carter Cheney, a speedy left-handed outfielder who had a reputation for going to the opposite field.

Chaz, sticking to the game plan, signaled for a fastball on the inside corner. In the event that Cheney would try and drag bunt for a hit, which he was also known to do early in games, he would have a harder time getting the barrel out on the inside heater.

Coop started his wind-up, feeling as good as he had ever felt on the mound, and reached back to deliver the pitch before his arm began its violent motion towards the target.

Then he felt it.

As he came through on the delivery, Cooper Madison felt a pop in his elbow that would alter his career, and life, forever.

2

"I don't get it, Doc... Everything felt great... In fact, I haven't felt that good in years. Why'd this happen now?" Coop asked Cleveland's general team physician, Dr. Nicholas Shaia, as the two sat in the training room of Jacobs Field.

Minutes earlier, Cooper Madison's MLB comeback came to a crashing halt due to the pop he felt on only his fourth pitch of the game. The injury made him scream and drop to the ground in pain and immediately silenced the 40,000 plus fans in attendance.

"That's hard to say, Cooper. In fact, a lot of these injuries don't have any warning signs. Your arm is kind of like a car tire - even brand new tires can pop from time to time," Dr. Shaia responded as he tested the mobility of Coop's elbow.

"What do you think it is?"

"It's too early to say, but if I had to guess I would say that you likely tore a ligament on the inside of your elbow called the UCL."

"UCL? Isn't that the..." Coop stopped short of finishing his sentence.

"A torn UCL usually means Tommy John surgery," Dr. Shaia confirmed. "We won't know for sure until we get an MRI and let Dr. Mueller have a look. I'm not a surgeon, but he is, and he's the best. You'll be in great hands regardless, Cooper."

"Do you think I came back too fast, Doc? Should I have trained longer before throwing?" Coop asked.

"Coop, this could've happened during your warm-up tosses. It's not unlike when a running back plants to make a cut in football and his knee gives out. These things happen. Don't beat yourself up. Instead, focus on getting back out there."

"How long will it take? Worst case scenario?"

"Well, if you need Tommy John surgery the recovery is typically a year if not longer. The good news is that some guys are saying that they feel even stronger after the surgery."

"A year?"

"Let's not focus on that right now, Cooper. We don't know for sure that's even what you need. We're going to do an MRI tomorrow morning and then Dr. Mueller will take it from there."

"What should I do until then?" Coop asked.

"Lots of ice. I'm also going to give you some painkillers to take the edge off, but only take them if you need them. Percocet can be addictive. Also, no alcohol when you take them."

As Dr. Shaia handed Coop a prescription bottle with what appeared to be about thirty pills, Coop considered telling him he did not want them. After his dad passed away, Coop self-medicated with a combination of alcohol and "perks" during his first few weeks in Cleveland. Coop often wondered what would have happened if his best friend, Cash Sterling, had not flown up to Cleveland from Mississippi and staged an intervention.

His brain told him to decline the pills from Dr. Shaia, but the pain in his elbow kept him from doing just that. He accepted the bottle and thanked the team doctor. As soon as he was alone in the training room, Coop opened the bottle up and popped two of the narcotic pain relievers in his mouth and chewed them up before swallowing with a swig from his water bottle.

3

As Coop packed his bag in the locker room he felt the euphoric surge of the pain pills permeate throughout his body. He remembered now why they were so hard to stop using. He felt guilty for taking them, but this time he made a promise to himself.

Once this bottle is gone, I'm done with them...

Coop decided to leave the stadium before the game ended. He did not want to deal with reporters, nor did he want to feel the empathy from his new teammates. He just wanted to escape back to the sanctity of the Westcott.

A few minutes earlier, Coop had texted Cara and Clarence to meet him outside the stadium by the players' only parking lot, where Clarence would be able to drive him and Cara home.

While Cara still had her dorm room at Cleveland State's Viking Hall, she rarely ever slept there anymore. Both she and Coop wanted her to stay at the Westcott, and being Cooper Madison's girlfriend had made dorm life difficult for Cara. Ever since her introduction to the world during Shane Aspen's ESPN interview, Cara had become a celebrity of sorts at CSU. Even her professors were acting differently around her, and she couldn't wait for her senior year to be over.

After the conclusion of the current semester, in order to graduate

Cara needed to complete an internship at IMG, thanks to Coop's agent, Todd "T-Squared" Taylor. As a favor to his top client, Todd had arranged for Cara to intern at IMG's Cleveland headquarters in the Public Relations department. Cara was excited for this opportunity, especially since most of her classmates were going to be doing their internships at car rental companies, insurance agencies, and banks.

As Coop exited the stadium into the players' lot, he saw Clarence's black Cadillac Escalade waiting for him. Cara emerged from the SUV as soon as she saw Coop and ran towards him, giving him a big hug before any words were spoken.

"I'm so sorry..."

Coop did not know what to say in return, so he just stood there and held her in his arms. He felt like he had let her down, not to mention himself and everyone else that were there to support him.

"What did the doctor say?" Cara asked, her cheek pressing against his chest.

"I have an MRI tomorrow morning and then an appointment with the team surgeon," Coop replied.

"What do they think it is?"

"Doc thinks that I might've torn a ligament in my elbow..."

"Oh God, I'm so sorry, Coop. Maybe he's wrong though, right? Maybe it's just a pulled muscle or something."

"Maybe..." Coop replied, but he knew the truth. Pulled muscles don't pop and make you fall to the ground like this did. He didn't need an MRI to tell him what he already felt to be true. He was going to need Tommy John surgery.

As the couple stood in the secluded parking lot, Coop wondered if he would ever pitch again.

He wondered if he even wanted to.

4

Detective Jason Knox leaned against the kitchen counter as he sipped his morning coffee, a folded newspaper in his other hand. He was reading about the injury to Cooper Madison that he had witnessed the night before from the comfort of the Owner's VIP suite at Jacobs Field.

Up until the moment that Coop dropped to the ground in agony, every part about the night had been perfect. After all, it's not often that a police officer gets to sit in a luxury box, let alone surrounded by his family and friends.

His baby sister's boyfriend, who also happened to be the starting pitcher for Cleveland that night, had even arranged for the mascot known as "Slider" to visit his daughter, Gabby, in the suite before the game.

"I think Gabby's in heaven," said his wife, Erica, as they watched Slider goof around with their 6-year-old daughter.

"I don't think she's the only one," Jason had replied, nodding towards his wheelchair-bound father, Charlie, who was laughing at the scene unfolding between the mascot and his granddaughter.

Jason had not seen his father so happy in years, at least not since the accident that had left him a paraplegic. Charlie had spent most of the evening reminiscing with his old friends, Ed Delaney and Stuart DeSmit, better known as Stucky, the latter of which owned the restaurant that

Cara worked for. Had she not been delivering food from Stucky's Place to Cooper Madison, none of this would have been happening.

Cara and Jason's mother, Joanne, might have been the happiest of all in attendance. Aside from Charlie, she was the one who had suffered the most as a result of his accident. When he was injured, it was as if the man she married disappeared with the loss of his legs. However, on this night she was witnessing small glimpses of the man that she fell in love with decades earlier.

Jason, by far the oldest of the Knox siblings, took great pride in watching his parents laugh and truly enjoy the evening. He also loved the fact that his two younger brothers, Christopher and Johnny, were there to enjoy this momentous night.

In addition to Coop, Jason had also enjoyed a taste of being a local celebrity of sorts. A few weeks earlier, Jason and his partner Michael "Mick" McCarthy, had solved the Edgewater Park Killer case. At least that's what the public thought, thanks to his Chief Horace "HoJo" Johnston's press conference declaring just that.

Jason should have felt on top of the world, but despite Ernie Page's confession that he had killed Stoya Fedorov prior to ending his own life, Jason could not shake the fact that Ernie had also insisted that he had not killed the other two victims. He had tried to convince HoJo to hold off on declaring the case as closed until they could rule out any other scenarios, but his media-hungry chief was adamant that Ernie was the EPK.

Over the next few weeks, HoJo was all over both the local and national media. He was a true media darling, giving great sound bites to whoever would put a microphone in his face. This was the case that was going to cement his career as one of the most notable officers ever to hold the position of Cleveland's Chief of Police, and HoJo was going to milk it for all it was worth.

Jason, on the other hand, decided to stay out of the media spotlight. He still had yet to grant an interview to any of the numerous outlets that had reached out to him. He had a feeling that this case was still far from over, and he did not want to make matters worse by lying to the camera. He even was in the second week of a long-overdue vacation. During the first week, Jason took his wife and daughter on their first trip to Disneyworld. Since returning, Jason had spent every second he could trying to make up for lost time with his family.

As he placed the newspaper down on the counter, his cell phone rang. It was his commander, Mick.

"What's up, Mick? Do you miss me already?" Jason asked.

"Are you watching the news by chance?" Mick responded, his voice serious in tone.

"No, I've been trying to avoid it, to be honest."

"Well, you might want to turn it on. Another body washed ashore at Edgewater early this morning…"

"Is this a joke?"

"I wish, and I'm down here at the scene now. It's too early to tell, but I think Ernie might have been telling the truth because the Jane Doe has "EPK" carved into her torso."

"Jesus…"

"I hate to do this to you, but I'm pretty sure that you might want to cut that vacation short and come down here before the coroner takes the body."

"I'm on my way…"

5

Cara Knox felt the warm light of the morning sun on her face as she rolled over in bed. The previous night had been one of two extremes, and after such an emotional night, she had no problem falling asleep once they had returned from the ballpark.

Coop did not have the same luck, and by the time Cara was awake, he had already been up for hours sitting on his balcony at the Westcott Hotel. The medicine had helped him fall asleep relatively fast, but the pain in his elbow cut his slumber short.

Two more pills and the bag of ice on his arm allowed him to at least enjoy the sunrise in relative physical comfort, but the emotional toll that had been levied upon him had no remedy. Coop had been replaying his short stint on the mound the night before over and over again, wondering how and why this had happened.

He did not need an MRI to tell him what he already knew to be true: he was going to need Tommy John surgery, and it was going to take him at least a year to get back on the mound. He was not even sure that he wanted to pitch again.

"Good morning," Cara said as she joined him on the balcony, wearing one of Coop's old t-shirts that covered her petite frame like a thigh-length nightgown.

"Morning…"

"How long have you been up?" Cara asked as she sat on the chair next to him.

"Couple hours, I suppose…"

"How's the elbow feeling?"

"Hurts…"

"Is the ice helping?"

"Kinda…"

"Did they give you anything for the pain?"

"Listen, can we just enjoy what's left of this sunrise in peace?" Coop snapped, tossing the bag of melting ice down on the ground. His abrupt reply caught Cara by surprise.

"I'm sorry… I'm just worried about you," Cara replied sheepishly.

Coop said nothing.

Cara, knowing that Coop was hurting, took the hint and sat next to him in silence. She was hurt by his words, but also knew that it was usually best to leave a wounded animal be.

Coop felt bad for snapping at Cara. He knew that she was just trying to understand where he was at mentally and physically. After a few minutes, he broke his silence.

"Listen, I'm sorry for snapping at you. I just am having a real hard time comprehending what happened last night…"

Cara abstained from replying when he paused. Despite the relative infancy of their relationship, Cara had learned that when Coop was trying to get something off his chest, that a pause did not necessarily mean he was done saying what he needed to say.

"I mean... I just don't get it, Cara. I felt so good out there on the mound. I don't remember the last time I felt that good to be honest. And then it happened," Coop said as he lifted his elbow up. It was swollen and still red from the ice that had been on it.

"For what it's worth, I was so proud of you last night," Cara said as she sat up in her chair, trying to get Coop to make eye contact with her.

"Yeah, well what about now?" Coop asked as he finally met her gaze. His eyes had tears welling up in them.

"Even more so."

"I wish that I could feel what you do then, because I just feel like a failure..."

"Well, you shouldn't..."

"Oh yeah? Why's that?" Coop's steely-gray eyes were still locked in on Cara as he tried to fight back the tears that were beginning to travel down his cheeks.

Cara had never seen Coop this vulnerable. He had always been the epitome of strength to her, and yet seeing him like this only made her love him even more.

"Because last night you gave the city of Cleveland something to cheer about. When you struck out that first batter, the entire stadium shook, Coop. Everyone sitting by me was going bonkers. It was electric. Everyone was so proud of you..."

Coop did not respond as he averted his eyes away from Cara. He did not want her to see the tears that were streaming down his face.

Cara moved off her chair and knelt down in front of Coop.

"Look at me, Coop..."

He resisted at first, but then his eyes met hers and she could see just how much pain he was in. Cara pulled his head to her chest as he began to sob, just as he had for her so many times before.

"It's going to be okay, Coop. It's going to be okay…" Cara repeated as she held him tight. He let out all of the pain that had been building up inside him since the previous night.

After a few minutes, Coop's breathing slowed and he managed to collect himself enough to sit up and meet Cara's gaze.

"I'm sorry…" Coop whispered.

"Don't be…"

"I…I don't know what to say… I feel like…"

"Nothing…" Cara cut his words short by uttering the one word that could say so much.

He had never been so thankful for their code word, which was used when they could not find the right words to say, but wanted to say everything that they were feeling.

"Nothing…" Coop replied.

6

Commander Mick McCarthy was waiting for Jason as he approached from the parking lot at Edgewater Beach. Aside from the usual crowd of beachgoers, there was a bevy of media trucks from the local news stations on hand to report on the latest body to wash ashore from the waters of Lake Erie.

"How'd Erica take the news?" Mick asked.

"That my vacation was over? Better than I expected actually. I think she's getting tired of me being around as much as I have been," Jason quipped.

"I think that's what my ex listed as the main reason for our divorce," Mick laughed.

"How is Zoey these days, anyways?"

"Not sure. That's her new husband's concern now. Thank God…"

"And the dating scene since I've been gone?"

"Non-existent. It's weird; apparently there isn't a big market for overweight, middle-aged, balding cops who work awful hours," Mick deadpanned.

"Shocker…" Jason laughed.

"C'mon, I'll show you what we're dealing with."

Mick led Jason over to the pop-up tent that was in place to shield the body from the curious onlookers. As they walked, Jason hoped there was a chance that maybe this was the work of a copycat killer. The thought of the public coming to the realization that the Edgewater Park Killer was still roaming the streets of Cleveland made his entire body shudder.

Under the tent was the naked body of a woman, who appeared to be in her late teens to early twenties at most. She was a petite Asian with dark hair. Strangulation marks were present around her throat, and visible signs of trauma dotted her face. The only difference between her and the prior Jane Does that had washed ashore were that the letters "EPK" had been carved across her chest.

"What are the odds that her prints will come up in the database?" Jason asked.

"If I had to guess, about the same odds I have of dating the lovely Miss Hannah LaMarca over there," Mick responded, nodding towards the striking young reporter for Cleveland's Channel One News.

"Well, if she only knew what a charmer you were, I'd say the odds are great…"

"Funny…"

"Have you heard from HoJo, yet?"

"Ironically, no. My guess is that right now he's trying to figure out how he's going to spin this so he doesn't look like a fool."

"We tried to tell him…" Jason sighed. "Was there anything else with the body?"

"Just the plastic sheet it was wrapped in."

"Plastic? Well, that's different than the others. Maybe we'll be able to pull some prints off it," Jason said, referencing the fact that the previous victims had all been wrapped in bed sheets.

"I wouldn't hold your breath. My guess is that he chose plastic this time so that it would expedite the time it took to wash ashore. CSI thinks that the body has only been in the water for a matter of days," Mick asserted.

"Makes sense. He obviously wanted us to find this body – quickly, at that. The plastic sheet probably acted like a pool float," Jason agreed.

"As much as I'd love to say that the plastic will be dotted with clean prints to lift off, my guess is that this guy is a little too smart to be so careless. He's taunting us."

"This is going to be a goddamn mess, isn't it?" Jason asked looking at Mick.

"You mean when the public learns that Ernie Banks wasn't the EPK and a serial killer is still walking the streets?" Mick replied sarcastically.

"Well, if this is the EPK, he's had a few weeks of anonymity. I guess he's ready to re-introduce himself to the masses though," Jason paused. "I just hope that this is the only victim."

7

"Hello, I'm Doctor Craig Mueller." The Cleveland team surgeon introduced himself to his newest patient, who was seated at one of two chairs facing a desk in the offices of Mueller and Associates Orthopedics.

Seated next to Coop was Cara, whom he had asked to join him during the MRI appointment earlier that morning. The couple had been waiting for the past fifteen minutes for the surgeon to deliver the verdict on the results.

"Pleasure to meet you, Doc," Coop said, standing up.

"Please, no need to get up. However, I do appreciate you politely lying about your excitement to meet me. I know that I'm the last guy on the team's payroll that any player wants to meet," Dr. Mueller said as he took a seat. That response caused Coop to crack a smile for the first time since the injury had occurred.

"And who might you be?" Dr. Mueller asked Cara.

"I'm Cara, nice to meet you."

"She's my girlfriend," Coop asserted, causing Cara to smile. Even though he had introduced her in that way a number of times, she still could not help but smile like it was the first time when he did.

26

"Well, it's a pleasure to meet both of you. I just finished looking over the results of the MRI."

Coop took a deep breath as he braced himself to hear the words that he already knew were coming. Cara reached over and squeezed his hand.

"Coop, I wish that I had better news for you, but unfortunately the MRI shows a pretty substantial tear to the UCL." Dr. Mueller let his words hang for a moment so that Coop could digest them.

"Tommy John?" Coop asked.

"I'm afraid so, Cooper. I'm not going to sugarcoat it either. This is going to be a long recovery. You're going to be out of action for at least a year, maybe more," Dr. Mueller stated as Cara reached across with her other hand and placed it on top of their already-interlocked grasp. She could feel Coop's hand trembling.

"How soon?" Coop questioned.

"Until surgery? Well, we need to let the swelling go down a bit first, so the earliest we are looking at is in a week or so," Dr. Mueller replied.

"So, next season is pretty much out of the question?"

"I'm afraid so. Sometimes position players can come back earlier than a year, but pitchers typically take 12 to 18 months before they are ready to compete."

"What do those months consist of?" Cara interjected.

"That's a great question, Cara. There are five phases in the recovery process: Acute, Early, Middle, Throwing, and Return to Pitching," Dr. Mueller responded.

"Acute?" Coop asked.

"Correct. That's the first week or two after surgery when you'll be placed in a brace with no movement in a 90-degree position. During that time period you'll be on some pretty strong pain meds, and it will be imperative that you focus solely on rest and recuperation. At the conclusion of that time period, we will begin to wean you off of the meds and begin the next phase."

"The 'early' phase?" Cara asked.

"That's right. During that phase of the recovery we will focus on gradually increasing your elbow mobility. You will still be in the brace for the duration of this phase, which is typically about 4 to 6 weeks; however, we will increase the amount of movement that the brace will allow. You will still be on the pain meds for most of this phase, but the goal is to have you completely off of them by the time the brace is ready to come off and you begin the next phase," Dr. Mueller stated.

"Is that when I can start throwing again?" Coop asked.

"Unfortunately, no. The 'middle' phase lasts about 6 to 18 weeks and focuses on cardiovascular fitness and strengthening the core and other muscles aside from the elbow that are imperative to throwing, which we will do in the next phase. This will consist mostly of long-toss drills, gradually building up to 250 feet. The 'throwing' phase will be another 4 to 5 months."

"Then I can pitch again?" Coop asked.

"Yes and no. While you'll be throwing off a mound, it is actually the longest phase: the final 'return to pitching' phase. This will take about 8 to 10 months, beginning with short bullpens and gradually building them up until you're back to full strength," Dr. Mueller replied.

"Jesus…" was all Coop said as he digested everything that had just been laid out for him.

"The good news is that you have three important factors to consider," Dr. Mueller stated.

"Oh yeah? What's that?" Coop asked, intrigued.

"Well, for starters, you have this beautiful young woman here to help you get through all of this. And trust me, Cara, he's going to need your help. This won't be easy on either of you," Dr. Mueller said looking at Cara.

"Absolutely, I'll do whatever I need to," Cara affirmed as she turned and smiled at Coop.

"The next thing you have going for you is that some pitchers seem to feel even stronger after Tommy John surgery. I don't know how true that actually is, but I do know that a lot of my patients have told me just that," Dr. Mueller stated.

"I've heard that too," Coop replied.

"What's the third factor?" Cara asked.

"Well, that's the one that I can assure you I know to be true," Dr. Mueller said sitting up in his chair.

"Which is?" Coop asked.

"Just like you, Cooper, I'm the *best* at what I do."

8

Hannah LaMarca could tell by their body language that the detectives were not looking forward to answering the questions that she and her fellow reporters had for them. She had covered the EPK case from the day that Stoya Fedorov's body had washed ashore on the banks of Lake Erie. Just like some of her sources on the inside, she also was not convinced that Ernie Banks was really the EPK.

That feeling was only justified when Detective Knox and Commander McCarthy refused to answer any questions from the media after Chief Horace Johnston had posthumously declared Ernie Banks the Edgewater Park Killer. In what should have been their chance to celebrate the biggest bust of their lives, neither one of them would say a word publicly about the case.

Hannah had arrived at Cleveland's Channel One News in 2005 after a two-year stint at a small station in Knoxville, Tennessee, her first on-air job after college. The EPK case was her first big story, and she had covered every detail about the murders that had haunted Cleveland in the months leading up to Ernie Page's admission that he had murdered Stoya Fedorov.

As Jason and Mick approached the small cluster of reporters, Hannah decided to wait off to the side. She knew the detectives well enough by this point to know that they were not going to give anything away on camera.

After Jason and Mick had given their standard "No comment at this time" response to the other reporters, they made their way to their vehicles, where Hannah was waiting for them.

"Miss LaMarca, how are you doing on this fine day?" Mick asked the beautiful young reporter.

"I'd be doing a lot better if I thought you'd actually give me some details on the body you just examined, Commander," she replied.

"I told you before, Hannah, you'll have a much better chance of getting information out of me over dinner," Mick said, never one to miss an opportunity to swing for the fence with a gorgeous woman.

"And as I tell you every single time, Mick, that will *never* happen," Hannah sighed.

"I guess all you're going to get is 'no comment' then," Mick chuckled.

"You two are really good at saying that line, aren't you? Must be hiding something," she pressed.

"What's that supposed to mean?" Jason asked.

"I think you know exactly what it means, Detective, and as soon as my sources at the coroner's office confirm what I think is going on here, the public will too. Why don't you guys save everybody a lot of time and just let me know once and for all that the EPK is still alive and well?"

"The EPK? C'mon, Miss LaMarca, Chief Johnston already told you guys over and over that the EPK case is closed," Mick said with a hint of sarcasm, which earned a sideways glance from Jason.

"Oh, I know all about what HoJo said, Commander. It's what you two *haven't* said that makes me think that the EPK case is *far* from closed."

"That's a big conclusion to jump to," Jason asserted.

"Isn't that what each of our jobs are all about, Detective? Jumping to conclusions and then trying to prove them?" she replied.

"No comment," Jason said with a smirk as he walked away, leaving Hannah LaMarca empty-handed once again.

9

"Well, what's the verdict?" Clarence Walters asked as Coop and Cara entered the back of his SUV, which was parked outside Dr. Mueller's office.

"Death Row, with little chance of parole..." Coop responded.

"Oh, stop that right now," Cara admonished.

"Tommy John?" Clarence asked.

"Yessir," Coop replied.

"I'm sorry to hear that, Coop."

"Thanks..."

"The doctor said that he might even come back stronger after the surgery," Cara said, trying to lighten the mood.

"Well, that's good news," Clarence responded.

"Can we just not talk about it right now?" Coop asked.

"You're right, let's take it one step at a time. No need to talk about playing again, yet," Cara agreed.

"No, I mean talking about any of it. In fact, I don't want to talk about a damn thing right now," Coop snapped back.

Nobody said a word the rest of the ride back to the Westcott. The uncomfortable silence was finally broken when Clarence pulled Coop aside as he and Cara exited the SUV.

"Hey man, I know you're hurting right now, but she's just trying to keep your spirits up," Clarence whispered.

"I know…" Coop responded as he shook Clarence's hand.

Cara was waiting for Coop just inside the lobby as he entered the Westcott. She gave Coop a smile as he approached, but was afraid to say anything else. She knew that he was hurting and did not want to make anything worse than it already was.

"Listen… back in the car… I didn't…"

"Nothing…" Cara interrupted.

"No, I need to apologize," Coop insisted.

"Nothing…" Cara replied putting her finger to his lips.

"Nothing…" Coop gave in.

"Now, let's go upstairs and I'll make you my famous grilled cheese sandwich," Cara said, as she took him by the hand and led him towards the antique birdcage elevator that graced the lobby of the Westcott Hotel.

"Grilled cheese? Wow, I haven't had one of those in years," Coop chuckled.

"Well, I promise it will have been worth the wait."

"A grilled cheese sandwich actually sounds perfect right now. When I was a little kid I used to love them."

"Nothing like some all-natural processed cheese to make you feel better," Cara said knowing that her use of an oxymoron would not go unnoticed.

"All-natural processed cheese?" Coop laughed.

"Says the guy who hails from the land of jumbo shrimp."

"Touché…"

10

Hannah LaMarca arrived back at her one bedroom apartment located on East 4th street in downtown Cleveland after wrapping up her shift in the newsroom. She loved that her apartment, which was located in one of the many newly converted industrial buildings, was walking distance to the station.

Growing up in the rural town of Lodi, Ohio, Hannah had always dreamed of living in the city. When she landed the job at Cleveland's Channel One News it was a dream come true. Even though she could have saved a lot of money living outside the city, she chose instead to be near the action in the city closest to where she grew up.

After attending Otterbein University, a small liberal arts school near Columbus where she majored in broadcast journalism, she took her first job as a Production Assistant with Knoxville News 43. After six months of running the teleprompter, labeling tapes, and even getting coffee, Hannah finally had her chance to cover a story in front of the camera.

Ironically, Hannah's first on-air story would never have happened had she not been off work that day. There was a small apartment fire at one of the buildings in the complex in which she lived and while the station had dispatched a news van to cover it, their closest reporter was at least 30 minutes away. The News Director knew that she lived close by, so he called Hannah and told her to be ready to go live in 15 minutes.

Within 10 hectic minutes, Hannah LaMarca was outside going over the shot with her cameraman and checking her hair and make-up one last time. When she heard the producer count her down via the earpiece she had just been given, Hannah found herself more excited than nervous. After all, she had been in front of the camera hundreds of times at Otterbein and had been preparing for this moment every single day while she toiled away completing menial tasks as a PA.

Hannah's delivery was flawless. Soon after her story aired, the station began receiving calls asking for more of the cute young reporter with the strawberry blonde hair and petite frame. Her days of fetching coffee and slapping labels on tapes were over, and she spent the next 18 months covering every story she could in the Knoxville area.

When she heard that Channel One News, the station she grew up watching in Lodi, was looking for a new reporter she immediately applied and called every connection that she had in Cleveland to help her get an interview. Two weeks and three interviews later, Hannah was offered the job at Channel One.

In the two years since arriving back in Cleveland, Hannah saw her role at Channel One grow from covering county fairs to that of lead reporter on the EPK murders. She even received a local Emmy for her work on the EPK story, and when the network's national morning show featured the EPK case on the air, with it came Hannah's first national exposure.

The brass at Channel One knew then that if Hannah was ever going to try and jump ship to go to a bigger market, it was right after her national spot on the EPK. So, they offered her a new contract with higher pay to lock her up for at least two more years.

What the station did not know was that Hannah had no intention of leaving Channel One, at least not yet, when they made her the offer. She loved being in Cleveland and fancied the idea of being a big fish in a smaller pond.

By 25 years of age, Hannah had already achieved more in her career than she thought she would by age 30, so she was going to ride her current gig out at Channel One as long as possible. The station had even alluded to the fact that they planned on putting her behind the anchor desk sometime before her contract was up. Being an anchor at Channel One was her dream job, and she was close to making that dream a reality.

The one regret that she did have though, was the fact that besides the attention that the EPK case had given her, she still felt that the story was far from over. Hannah LaMarca was certain that the EPK was still on the loose, and she was going to do everything in her power to be in front of the camera when the EPK was finally caught.

As she sat down to eat her takeout dinner from Stucky's Place, the restaurant that Cara Knox had worked for when she met Cooper Madison, Hannah decided that the only way she would get the information she wanted was to convince Detective Jason Knox that he should trust her with what he knew. She knew that if she took Commander McCarthy up on his dinner offer that she likely could get what she wanted, but she also did not want to feel like she was whoring herself out for a story. Jason was the safer play. He was happily married, or so it seemed, and she knew that whatever information she could get from him would be a lot more genuine than whatever Mick would try to appease her with in hopes of getting her into bed.

The thought of that alone made her shiver. She knew of some young female colleagues who likely would have taken Mick up on his pay-for-play offers, but Hannah would never be able to look at herself in the mirror if she did.

She was going to sink or swim the old-fashioned way on the EPK story, and she already had a plan in place for how she would try and convince Jason to keep her in the loop.

11

Detective Jason Knox slowly approached the woman sitting at the bar located inside the Riviera Cantina, which was located near Cleveland's theater district. She had not seen him arrive, but he definitely saw her.

She was in her thirties and had long brunette hair and a subtle tan. Her dress was a unique shade of orange and showed just enough leg to catch the attention of any red-blooded heterosexual man who witnessed it. She was drinking a margarita with a salted rim, which she almost spilled when Jason wrapped his arms around her from behind.

"Oh my God, babe! You almost made me spill my drink!" she giggled as she turned to give him a small kiss on the lips.

"I hope I didn't keep you waiting long," Jason said as he sat down next to her at the bar.

"I just got here a few minutes ago actually. Gabby's sitter was running behind so I didn't make it out of the house until after six."

"How is our gorgeous daughter?" Jason asked his wife, Erica, who told him that he had to meet her after work for dinner to make up for cutting his vacation short.

"She's wonderful, as always, but she's not too happy that her daddy isn't going to be home all day like he has been the past two weeks," Erica replied.

"And what about her mommy? Is she upset too?"

"Not as long as you keep these margaritas coming," Erica smiled as she raised the salted rim to her lips.

"I can certainly do that, especially since it's still Happy Hour," Jason chuckled as he gestured to the bartender for another round.

"So, tell me. What's up with the body at Edgewater? The news said that there are rumors that it might be the work of the EPK, or at least a copycat."

"Too early to tell, on both accounts, unfortunately," Jason replied.

"I can't believe I'm saying this, but I hope that you're wrong about the EPK still being alive, Babe."

"Yeah, me too…"

"Is this one like the others?" Erica asked about the victim.

"Well, she was definitely a younger girl, but this one was actually Asian. The others were all Russian or some sort of Eastern European," Jason said softly so that only Erica could hear his words.

"Asian? Wow. Any leads?" Erica asked, also lowering her voice to a whisper.

"Not yet, but the lab is running the standard tests, and the precinct is checking all the possible missing person cases that could potentially be a match."

"Well, hopefully they get a match. Could you imagine being that girl's parents?"

"I couldn't fathom it. I guess that's what keeps me going though. I just keep thinking that God forbid something like this ever happened to

Gabby that the detectives on the case would do everything in their power to solve it," Jason said before taking a sip of his drink.

"Oh my God, the thought of that makes me want to put Gabby in a convent. This world is a scary place," Erica stated as she finished off her margarita.

"You're telling me. Do you want another before we're seated?" Jason asked, nodding at her empty glass.

"Do you really need to ask? We don't get out like this very often, Babe. Keep them coming!"

"Good thing we still have about ten minutes left of Happy Hour," Jason laughed.

"Very funny. Just for that, you have to order me one with the top-shelf tequila now," Erica replied with a smile before giving her husband a soft kiss.

"Top-shelf, huh? Hope you're ready to work that bar tab off later when we get home," Jason said as he leaned in for a longer kiss.

"Oh, it's like that, huh?"

"You better believe it. It's your own fault though."

"My fault? How's that?"

"You just look too damn hot in that dress for me not to want you."

"Well, when you put it that way, I might just have to give you your wish…"

12

Cooper Madison had just finished off his eighth beer of the evening as a sleepy Cara Knox opened up the door to the balcony of his penthouse suite to check on him. It was past midnight and Coop had moved his pity party outside a few hours earlier when Cara fell asleep on the couch.

The evening had been one of silence following a brief respite of normalcy earlier in the day when Cara prepared a few delicious grilled cheese sandwiches for lunch. After eating, the couple spent the rest of the afternoon watching TV while Coop alternated between icing his elbow and drinking beer. Despite the doctor's warnings not to combine them with alcohol, he had also snuck off twice to pop pain pills while hoping to escape what had permeated both his elbow and his psyche.

While the shame he felt from hiding his use of the Percocet from Cara was strong, the need to escape the pain he was feeling was even greater. Despite sitting through countless shows, Coop could not even remember what they had watched. Everything at this point was simply background noise to the drama playing inside his head.

Cara knew that she did not like to see this side of Coop, but she also did not want to seem overbearing at this point. After all, Coop's world had seemingly become unraveled in the past 24 hours, and Cara knew him well enough to give him the space he needed.

She decided to let him wallow in his self-pity for the day, but if it continued, she knew that she would have to intervene. She had been down this road before after the accident that left her father paralyzed from the waist down.

While a torn elbow ligament was nowhere near the extent of paralysis, to a world-class athlete like Cooper Madison, it may as well have been. People like Coop, whose entire identity relied solely on the use of their supremely talented bodies, were more likely to slip into a deep depression when their bodies betrayed them.

"Are you coming to bed?" Cara asked, yawning.

"Eventually…"

Cara made her way over to Coop and sat on his lap.

"You're leaking," Cara said, nodding toward the bag of ice on his elbow that had become more liquid than solid.

"Yeah, but the numbness it brings outweighs the mess."

"Maybe I could help you take your mind off of your elbow in a different way?" Cara whispered suggestively.

For the entirety of their still-new relationship, Coop could not keep his hands off of Cara, and likewise her with him. That fact alone made his next comment sting that much more.

"I'm good…"

"Well then," Cara responded, trying to hide the hurt that those words had just caused.

What made it worse was that Coop, usually quick to apologize during the few times he stuck his foot in his mouth with Cara, said nothing in return. Instead, he reached into the small cooler he had with him on the balcony and grabbed another beer.

Cara glanced at the small table next to Coop's chair, which was lined up with empty beer bottles and sighed.

"What? Are you going to tell me I can't have a few beers now?" he asked.

"I didn't say that. I didn't say anything," she replied, regretting her inability to hold in her sigh. While it definitely did bother her, she also did not want to appear as if she was judging.

"You didn't have to… your sigh said it all."

"I'm sorry. I'm just really tired and I know you've had a rough day. I don't want to make things worse; I just want to make everything better."

"Well, you can't," Coop asserted, taking a swig of his fresh beer.

"It doesn't mean that I can't try though. I feel helpless," Cara quipped as she stood up.

"Welcome to the club." Coop raised his beer, as if to toast.

Cara, realizing that she was in a lose-lose situation, decided to leave him be. Before she exited the balcony, she paused, hoping that when she looked back that the steely eyes that she fell in love with would be looking back at her.

However, this time they were not.

"Goodnight," she said as she re-entered the penthouse suite and closed the door behind her. She did not wait to see if he responded. She did not need to.

13

Hannah LaMarca stood outside the entrance to the 1st District precinct on Cleveland's west side, hoping to catch Detective Jason Knox upon his arrival at work that morning. Her source at the coroner's office had informed her the previous night of a startling discovery that involved the body that had washed ashore just a day earlier.

Trustworthy inside sources are crucial to a reporter, and Hannah had spent just as much time building those relationships since arriving back in Cleveland as she had in front of the camera. In this case, her source at the coroner's office was the sister-in-law of a Channel One News cameraman that Hannah worked with for most of her spots.

The woman, Keri Urban, had delivered crucial inside information from the coroner's office to Hannah a number of times and had proven to be an invaluable asset to the young reporter. Like all sources of this nature, Keri's help was strictly off the record, and she trusted that Hannah would never break that bond. Doing so would likely cost Keri her job and possibly more.

"The body had 'EPK' carved across its torso," Keri had told Hannah the night before via a gas station payphone. By 2006, there were fewer and fewer payphones in operation, but the ones that remained played a vital role in keeping Keri's identity a secret.

"Wow. Well, that's definitely something new. I heard that she's

Asian, right? Anything else you can give me?" Hannah asked.

"Yeah, she is, and this Jane Doe has a name…"

"You're kidding, right?" Hannah said shocked. Aside from the first victim, Stoya Fedorov, neither of the other bodies was ever identified.

"Nope. We were able to ID her via her fingerprints. Her name is Vivian Tong. She had a prior arrest for solicitation. Misdemeanor charge, I guess, but her prints were in the system."

"Tong… That's probably Chinese, right?" Hannah asked.

"Likely, but I don't know anything past what I told you. I'm sure you'll be able to take it from here," Keri replied.

"Absolutely. Thank you so much. This is great stuff!" Hannah exclaimed, her heart racing. She could not wait to find out more about Vivian Tong.

"Just be discreet, please. This is a big one, and it can't come back to bite me," Keri warned.

"It won't. You have my word."

Hannah spent the rest of the evening trying to research the Internet for anything she could find on Vivian Tong. Unfortunately, she was not able to come up with anything solid. Tong is a very common Chinese surname, and if Vivian had immigrated to the country, as Hannah felt she likely had, there probably would not be much of a digital footprint.

Before turning in for the night, Hannah had come to the realization that she was going to have to exhaust her chances of getting Jason to talk with her. She knew that it was not going to be an easy task, as Jason had proven to be a tough nut to crack. Still, she had to give it a try, which is what had brought her to the 1st District precinct on that seasonal October morning.

14

Detective Jason Knox saw her standing on the steps outside of Cleveland's 1st District precinct as he arrived to work on a day when he still should have been relaxing at home; however, being the lead detective on the city's highest profile murder case meant that his vacation was over when yet another body washed ashore the day prior.

He knew that it was no coincidence that the striking young reporter from Channel One News was standing on the steps, a coffee in each hand. In his various interactions with Hannah LaMarca, he had quickly realized that she was more than just a pretty face in front of the camera. She was as smart and tenacious as she was beautiful, if not more.

"Good morning, Detective. I brought you a coffee - figured you might need it today," Hannah said with a smile as she greeted him on the steps.

"Well, I'm not going to disagree with you on that one, Miss LaMarca," Jason laughed as he accepted the warm gift.

"Can we talk before you go in? Off the record…"

"I guess I can spare a few minutes. Let's take a walk though," Jason said, nodding towards the sidewalk that led to Worthington Park. Located behind the station, Worthington Park boasted an oval walking path that would serve as a perfect setting to talk in private.

"I know that I don't need to tell you what I think about the EPK again, Detective," Hannah announced, referencing their discussion at Edgewater Park the day before.

"No, you made that abundantly clear yesterday, Miss LaMarca," Jason chuckled, thinking back to the reporter's claim that she believed that the EPK was still alive and well.

"You can call me Hannah, you know," she said, hoping to make the conversation less formal.

"I know, but I'd rather not, Miss LaMarca."

"Fair enough. What can you tell me about the body that washed ashore yesterday?"

"Well, my guess is you already know just about as much as I do, so why don't you tell me what you know first," Jason said with a laugh.

"How would I know anything, Detective? The department hasn't released any details about the body yet," Hannah replied, calling his bluff.

"C'mon, Miss LaMarca. You and I both know that you have sources all over this city, and I'm sure that you do at the coroner's office too."

Hannah said nothing.

"And, since we are off the record, let's cut to the chase and stop pretending that you're here for any other reason than to see if I will corroborate what you've already been told," Jason stated, looking Hannah straight in the eyes.

Hannah had always thought that Jason was attractive, at least for a cop who was approaching forty, but she had never felt the power that his eyes had just emitted in that moment. Despite having talked to him on numerous occasions, this was the first time that she had ever been alone with him, and it threw her off for a second before she was able to recover and respond.

"Well… I understand that the victim had 'EPK' carved into her torso. Can you confirm that?" she asked.

"Off the record?"

"Completely. I would never report anything you say until you give me the okay first. All I ask in return is that I'm the first one you give that permission to," she replied.

"Okay, then I'd say your source is giving you valid information."

"My source also said that she's likely Chinese and that she was able to be identified using her fingerprints. Her name is Vivian Tong, and she had a misdemeanor arrest on her record."

"Again, I would say that your source is a good one," Jason confirmed.

"That's good to know, but that's all I have. Can you give me anything else?" Hannah pressed.

"Well, I can tell you that later this morning I'm going to be checking out a few known addresses where the victim may have lived. I also have been told that she was in the country legally and had actually become a US citizen a few years ago, which is why she wasn't deported after her arrest. Aside from that, you know as much as I do," Jason responded.

"That certainly is a departure from the previous victims, isn't it?"

"Sure is, which raises all sorts of questions."

"Like what?"

"Well, for starters, if this truly is the work of the EPK, he's moved on to a new type of victim. That, and he's becoming more violent. He obviously wanted the body to be found, and he wanted everyone to know who did it."

"Does that mean that you are finally admitting to me that you think Ernie Page was *not* the EPK?" Hannah asked with a grin.

"I think you already know the answer to that, Miss LaMarca," Jason said, his eyes piercing hers as if to emphasize his words.

"If this is the real EPK's work, what do you think the department will tell the public? I mean, your chief has spent the past month doing a victory lap on the fact that the EPK case was closed."

"That's HoJo's problem, not mine. Which is why I never did any interviews on the case after Ernie took his own life."

"Do you think Chief Johnston will actually consider admitting he was wrong? Or will he just say that this is a copycat killer seeking attention?" Hannah asked.

"Well, if I know HoJo, he won't admit anything until it's obvious to everyone else. Even then, he might not," Jason chuckled.

"Jesus, this city is going to be a mess once they realize that the EPK is still out there. I have a feeling that yesterday's victim won't be the last one, especially if the department continues to deny the EPK's existence. He obviously wants the notoriety, and he will keep killing until he gets it," Hannah asserted.

"Sadly, I couldn't agree more, Miss LaMarca. Which is why I need to politely excuse myself so that I can get back to work on catching this guy before that happens. Thanks again for the coffee," Jason replied as he raised his cup and began walking away.

"Detective?" Hannah asked.

"Yes, Miss LaMarca?"

"Thank you… I truly appreciate you speaking with me today, and I promise that I won't go public with anything unless you give me the okay."

"You're welcome, and I appreciate your discretion."

"Will you let me know if you find anything out when you visit those addresses today?" Hannah asked.

Jason paused for a moment and stared at the young reporter standing in front of him. He could not believe that he had just divulged as much information as he did, but there was something about her that made him feel safe in doing so. It did not hurt that she was absolutely gorgeous, but so were a lot of the reporters who had tried to get him to talk over the years. While Jason was physically attracted to her, he was also a happily married man who just had a wonderful evening the night before with his beautiful wife. This had nothing to do with her appearance.

Jason felt that Hannah LaMarca was a kindred spirit trying to get the job done the right way, as opposed to getting it done the fastest. He thought that she might even be a help to him as he tried to track down the monster responsible for the deaths that had put his city on edge.

"I'll tell you what, meet me tomorrow morning at Edgewater Park. Seven o'clock. Look for my cruiser," Jason instructed.

"Absolutely. I'll be there," she replied, a tinge of excitement in her voice.

"Oh, and one more thing, Miss LaMarca…"

"Yes, Detective?"

"Bring more of that good coffee…"

15

"How are we doing on this beautiful morning, young lady?"
Clarence asked Cara as he drove his SUV away from the Westcott Hotel.
As usual, Clarence would be driving Cara to and from her classes at
Cleveland State University.

"Well, I'm okay, I suppose. I wish I could say the same thing for
Coop though," she replied from the rear passenger side of the vehicle.

"He's probably going to be that way for a while, you know,"
Clarence uttered as he glanced at his passenger in the rearview mirror.

"I know, I just wish there was something I could do besides
walking around on eggshells all day. I feel like I can't say anything right,
and I'm not even saying everything that I want to."

"Is he still in a lot of pain?"

"Big time. He drank himself to sleep last night too. It's the most
I've ever actually seen him drink," Cara replied with a sigh.

"Well, I'd probably be doing the same thing if I was in his shoes.
I know it's probably not what you want to hear, but as long as it doesn't
become a habit, it might be good for him to just sulk for a bit. Sometimes
we need to just throw ourselves a big old pity party before we are

mentally ready to get better," Clarence pointed out.

"I sure hope you're right, Clarence. It's the first time in our relationship where he's made me feel unwanted."

"You know that's not his intention though, right?"

"I suppose, but I still hate it. I feel like he just wants me to leave him alone."

"That's how we are, Cara."

"We?"

"Men. That's how we are. We've been groomed our entire lives to be the strong ones in a relationship. The older I get, the more I realize that it's the women that are truly the strongest though. They might be more willing to express their emotions, but they also deal with them. Men lock it away. True strength is dealing with what's going on, regardless of how you choose to do it."

Cara let his words sink in for a moment. She truly appreciated Clarence's advice during their daily rides to and from her classes. He filled a void in her life that disappeared after her father's accident, and she thought that Clarence was one of the wisest people she had ever met.

"Clarence?" Cara asked.

"Yes?"

"Have you always been this wise?"

"Oh, stop that, now…"

"I'm serious. You really are!"

"Can you tell my wife that? She would likely tell a completely different story."

"I highly doubt that…"

"In all seriousness though, I'm far from perfect. It's always easier to give advice than to heed it."

"I'll agree with you on that."

"Besides, I've had a couple decades of extra experience too. The twenty-something version of me would not have had very much worthwhile advice to give," Clarence chuckled.

"So, what does present-day Clarence think that I should do in regards to Coop?" Cara asked.

"I guess I would say to keep allowing him the space he needs to work through this for a few days. Let him feel sorry for himself a little bit. My guess is that he will come to the realization on his own sooner or later that he needs to move forward and start healing, both emotionally and physically."

"And what if he doesn't come to that conclusion on his own? When do I step in?" Cara pressed.

"I'm afraid that only you'll know when that is, Cara. However, I do think if it comes to that, you won't need me or anyone else to tell you that it's time..."

16

Cooper Madison awoke feeling as if he had been in a car accident the night before. His head was pounding from the empty 12 pack of beer still sitting on his balcony, and his elbow was throbbing.

"Cara? What time is it?" Coop asked as he rolled over in bed, completely unaware that Cara had left for class almost two hours earlier.

He rolled over again towards where he thought he would find Cara. It was not until he felt the empty spot with his hand that he realized she was not there. Coop fought through the pain in his head and mustered the strength to open his eyes and read the alarm clock on his nightstand.

"Jesus, it's already eleven?" he asked the empty bedroom.

Coop barely remembered making it into his bed the night before, let alone what time it was when he did. Between drinking more beer than he had in a long time and the four pain pills he mixed with them, the night had pretty much been a blur after Cara had visited him on the balcony.

After giving himself an internal pep talk, Coop managed to get out of bed and stagger towards the bathroom. When he caught a glimpse of himself in the mirror still wearing the same clothes he had the day before, he could not help but laugh. Unfortunately, the laughter made his head hurt even more.

When Coop raised his arm to see if it would release some of the stiffness in his elbow, the smell of alcohol coming from his pores almost made him gag. He immediately turned the shower on in hopes that a nice long soak would cure more than just the odor coming off his body.

He wanted to wash away the regret of the night before too. He remembered his conversation with Cara and how he had been short with her. He felt bad.

She was only trying to help...

The ten-minute shower did its job and Coop was happy that he no longer smelled like a brewery. Unfortunately, the headache and feeling of remorse had not rinsed off as he had hoped.

After throwing on a t-shirt and shorts, Coop made his way into the kitchen where he was pleasantly surprised to see that a pot of coffee had been made. Next to it was a note, along with two tablets of ibuprofen.

Dear Coop, I hope this helps. I'll be home after my class and will bring lunch. I hope that you have a great day! I can't wait to see you! Love, Cara

Coop smiled as he put the note down and then poured himself a cup of coffee. Since the coffee was too hot to drink, he opened a bottle of water that he retrieved from the refrigerator and washed the ibuprofen down.

He leaned on the counter in the kitchen for a few minutes with his eyes closed, hoping that the ibuprofen would kick in quickly. His head felt as if a vice grip had been squeezing on it while he slept, and his elbow was still on fire.

That combination of pain caused Coop to rummage through the

duffel bag that was sitting on his kitchen table. When he felt the cylindrical plastic container, he felt a tingle make its way through his body in anticipation of the narcotic pain relief he would soon feel. He had hoped that he would not need to take any of the twenty or so remaining Percocet until later in the day, but the pain in his body said otherwise as he took one of the pills out and immediately chewed it up.

The thought of eating anything besides the pills made Coop's stomach nauseous, but he also knew that he had to get something in his system. He forced a granola bar down before taking his coffee and a bag of ice to the balcony.

October weather in Cleveland, as he was learning, was a lesson in contradictions. In the last week alone, temperatures had dropped as low as the 40's and reached as high as the 80's.

On this morning, the clear skies and sun overhead had created a picture-perfect day. It was a comfortable 70 degrees with a gentle breeze off of Lake Erie, and Coop felt that perhaps the weather would help him get out of his funk as he wrapped the bag of ice around his still-throbbing elbow.

Within minutes, Coop could feel the euphoric surge that always accompanied the first dose of Percocet begin to do its magic. Unfortunately, he also knew that to duplicate that feeling later, he would likely need to take a heavier dose and again for every subsequent dose until the next day. It was a vicious cycle, but Coop felt that it was also a necessary one at this point, at least until after the surgery.

Coop took a long swig of his coffee as he gazed out towards the lake. While the weather was beyond pleasant, the waves he could see crashing in the distance were anything but.

17

Detective Jason Knox and Commander Mick McCarthy approached the entrance of a small apartment building on Cleveland's west side a little past noon. Located in the Clark-Fulton neighborhood, the 1920's era four-unit dwelling was once considered prime real estate during Cleveland's Golden Age.

Like so many of the buildings within the city's limits, it was now just another rundown tenement building with a revolving door of occupants. According to the information obtained by the police department, it was Vivian Tong's last known address.

"They don't build them like this anymore," Mick said, referencing the once-proud craftsmanship of the structure, which was solid brick with detailed wooden accents. The view from the street disguised just how deep the over 4,000 square foot structure was.

"Hard to believe that this was once somebody's dream house," Jason replied as the pair entered the small lobby.

"Looks like Unit D is upstairs. Think anyone's home?" Mick asked.

"Besides the bed bugs?" Jason laughed as they ascended the

narrow staircase that led to the top two units.

"Cleveland Police! Open up!" Mick bellowed as he pounded firmly on the door to Unit D, with the newly obtained search warrant in hand.

Nobody answered.

"Cleveland Police Department! Open up! We have a search warrant to enter the premises!" Mick tried again.

Still, there was no answer from within.

"Time to let ourselves in, I guess," Jason affirmed.

Mick had called the landlord earlier to see if he would meet them at the scene to open the apartment in the event nobody was home. Unfortunately, like so many of the real estate properties in Cleveland's low-income neighborhoods, the building was actually owned by out-of-state investors.

For the past decade, real estate investors from all over the country had been buying up cheap multi-family properties in Cleveland and renting them out far below market value while still turning a decent profit. It was a quantity-over-quality operation, and it was not uncommon for one investor to own as many as fifty such properties. Even if they put no additional money into the property, which many did not, there was never a shortage of renters willing to take advantage of the low cost living.

Even at half-occupancy, each of the properties would turn a modest profit each month. Multiply that by fifty, and it was a lucrative investment for the landlords, many of whom had never set foot in Cleveland. The downside for the city was that the property owners had no vested interest in anything other than making a profit, and the steady decline in the value of the properties was the result. With no watchful eyes on the buildings, crime rates in and around such properties had risen as sharply as the values had diminished.

Since there was no landlord present to let them in, Mick had informed the owner of the property that he had the legal right to enter the apartment by any means necessary. He did not seem to mind and only asked that he keep the damage to the door at a minimum.

Luckily for the landlord, when Mick tried the door handle it was unlocked. "Damn, I was looking forward to kicking it in, to be honest," Mick growled.

"Save your strength, old man. You're not a kid anymore," Jason chuckled as they slowly entered the unit, hands on their guns in the event of any surprises.

The front of the apartment was empty, with the exception of a tattered sofa and makeshift coffee table that was actually just an old packing crate. The air was stuffy inside, as all the windows were closed. A small kitchenette was located in the far corner and a door, presumably to a bedroom, was in the other.

Mick approached the door and nodded to Jason, who positioned himself so that he could cover his partner as he opened it. Inside was a queen-sized mattress sitting directly on the floor, no bed frame underneath. Next to it was a battered dresser, which must not have been used much because there were women's clothes strewn all over the floor.

A small bathroom was located in the far corner of the room. The bathroom counter had the usual toiletries and cosmetics on it that you might expect from a female occupant, but inside the medicine cabinet above the sink were a number of prescription pill bottles. Most of the bottles were empty, and none of them had labels on them.

"Looks like somebody liked her pills," Mick said.

"Nobody here!" a loud voice speaking broken English came from the entrance to the unit. The voice had startled Jason, and he drew his firearm and pointed it at the intruder, who turned out to be an elderly Asian woman. Despite having a gun pointed at her, the woman seemed unphased.

"I said nobody here. She not here. What you want?" the woman shouted at the men standing before her.

"Jesus, lady! You can't just sneak up on us like that. You could've got shot," Jason said as he holstered his weapon.

"She not here for weeks. What you want?"

"Did you know the woman who lives here, ma'am?" Mick asked the old woman.

"I know Vivian. But, she not here. Not for weeks," the woman replied.

"But, you did know her, right? Vivian Tong?" Jason asked.

"Yes. She live here. I live there," the woman gestured across the hall to Unit C.

"What can you tell us about Vivian?" Mick questioned.

"Vivian bad girl. She dancer," the woman said judgingly.

"Dancer? Like a stripper? Do you know where?" Jason pressed.

"She work at club down street. Vivian bad girl. She whore too," the woman replied.

"She's a prostitute too?" Mick asked looking at Jason.

"She hooker. Lots of men. Always here late at night. She bring them back from club. Bad girl, Vivian," the woman answered.

"The only strip club near here is Buddy's Speakeasy. That must be where she worked," Mick stated to Jason.

"Buddy's?" Jason replied.

"Yes. Buddy's. That where she dancer. Bad place," the woman interjected.

"When was the last time you saw Vivian?" Mick asked the

woman.

"I said not for weeks," the woman replied, annoyed.

"How many weeks?" Mick countered.

"Two weeks. Not for two weeks."

"Was she with anyone the last time that you saw her?" Jason asked.

"Vivian always with someone. Bring men back here. Lots of men. I tell her this not whorehouse."

"Can you describe the man she was with the last time you saw her? What did he look like?" Jason asked.

The old woman paused for a moment before responding.

"He look like him," she said pointing at Mick.

"Like him? So he was white?" Jason replied.

"Yes. White. He fat, too. Just like him."

Jason tried not to laugh as the old woman held her hands out as if to show a robust midsection before pointing at Mick, who was shaking his head in disbelief.

"Are you enjoying this?" Mick said to Jason.

"You have no idea, my man," Jason replied.

"He bald like him too," the woman interjected.

"Did he have any hair? Or was he completely bald?" Jason asked.

"No hair. But big belly. Like him," the woman reiterated as she pointed at Mick again.

Mick walked away, shaking his head.

"Would you come back to the station with us, ma'am? We'd like you to speak with our sketch artist and answer a few more questions," Jason asked.

"Why don't you just save some time and give them a picture of me?" Mick said with a chuckle.

"Oh, c'mon, big guy. He can't possibly be as ugly as you," Jason deadpanned.

"You do remember that I'm your superior, right?" Mick replied.

"How could I forget? You remind me every chance you get," Jason chuckled.

"Okay. I go," the woman said, bringing Jason and Mick back to the issue at hand.

"Fantastic! We really appreciate it, ma'am," Jason responded.

"You two funny. I like funny guys, so I go with you."

"See, Mick, you still got it," Jason whispered as they walked the old woman out to their cruiser.

"Let's just hope that what she has is worth my pain," Mick replied.

"Hey, it's something at least."

"After we drop her off, let's pay a visit to Buddy's Speakeasy. Maybe we'll get lucky twice in one day..."

18

Cara Knox stepped off of the elevator on the 11th floor of the Westcott Hotel after finishing her classes for the day. As she approached the door to suite 1100, she noticed that a box containing a dozen long-stemmed roses had been placed in front of the entryway.

Taped to the box was an envelope with Cara's name written on the front. She smiled when she read the enclosed card.

Cara, I'm sorry for the way I acted last night. Come inside and let me make it up to you…" –Coop

Cara had spent the entire day dreading that she would come back and find Coop picking up where he had left off the night before. Seeing the man that she had fallen in love with in so much pain was hard enough, but the helplessness that went along with it had completely drained her emotionally to the point that she had a hard time staying awake during her classes.

Seeing the roses and the card that accompanied them triggered an emotional response that apparently had been lying dormant inside her. Tears of happiness began streaming down her cheeks, and she felt butterflies of anticipation for what Coop had in store for the remainder of the evening.

As Cara entered the penthouse suite, she was greeted by the familiar smell of the shrimp boil that Coop had prepared for her on the night of their first date. From the living room she could hear Billy Joel's "She's Always a Woman" playing softly, which brought even more tears. Cara had told Coop early in their relationship that she felt it was the perfect love song, performed by the perfect musician.

Cara followed the trail of rose petals that had been placed on the ground to the kitchen as she tried to wipe away the tears that would not seem to stop. Upon entering the kitchen, Cara noticed that the table had been covered in the same beige newsprint-like paper that Coop had introduced her to on their first date. Two frosted mugs were also on the table, as were two glass bottles of Barq's Root Beer and a pair of plastic lobster bibs.

"I hope you're hungry," said Coop, who was standing next to stove. On it was a steaming pot of shrimp, Andouille sausage, and corn.

Cara tried to respond, but no words came out. Instead, she walked over towards Coop and wrapped her arms around him, crying.

"Why are you crying?" Coop asked as he squeezed her tight, her face buried in his broad chest.

This only made her cry more, so Coop just continued to hold her. Eventually, Cara managed to verbalize what her tears were trying to say.

"I'm sorry… I just really did not expect this, at all. I wasn't sure what to expect, actually…"

"I know that I was not myself yesterday, and I feel awful. I just wanted to make it up to you…"

"It's perfect. The flowers. The music. The food. All of it," Cara said before kissing Coop.

"You're perfect," he responded after the kiss, pressing her head against his chest.

"No, I'm not. But, you make me feel like I am…"

"Cara?" Coop asked.

"Yes?"

"I just want you to know that I'm really sorry. I know that you were just trying to help yesterday, and I was a real jerk. I promise that it was just a bad day, and I'm done feeling sorry for myself. I guess I just needed a day to wallow in my own misery."

"I know you did, and I accept your apology. I just wish I could do something to make it all go away."

Coop leaned in and kissed her in a way that was both firm and tender. "I promise that I'm going to try real hard to never make you feel that way again, Cara," Coop said. He started to say more, but Cara pressed her finger to his lips.

"Nothing," she whispered.

"Nothing," he replied with a smile before kissing her again.

19

"Can I get you guys something to drink?" asked Vance Gold, owner of Buddy's Speakeasy, a rundown gentleman's club located at the corner of Clark Avenue and West 56th street. Calling it a gentleman's club was a bit of a misnomer, as very few of the male customers ever acted as such.

"No thanks, Mr. Gold. We are only going to take up a little bit of your time," Jason answered.

"Please, call me Vance. If this is about the incident last week with the brawl, I can assure you that I fired that bouncer immediately after the cops left. I'm really trying to clean things up," Vance replied.

This was not the first time Vance Gold had been visited by the Cleveland Police Department during the three years his club had been in business, so he did not think much of Jason and Mick stopping by. In fact, the club averaged at least one call a week, usually for fighting or disorderly conduct. It had even reached a point where Vance was warned that he would lose his liquor license if things did not improve.

"This isn't about the brawl or your liquor license," Mick stated, leading Vance to let out a sigh of relief.

"We need to ask you a few questions about a girl that we understand works for you. Her name is Vivian Tong," Jason said.

"*Worked* for me, you mean. She hasn't shown up here in weeks, so as far as I'm concerned, she's fired. I can walk down Clark Avenue and get a dozen girls willing to get up on stage. I don't put up with no-shows," Vance asserted.

"Well, that's good to know, Vance. Glad to know that you run such a tight ship," Mick said sarcastically to Vance, who rolled his eyes.

"Vance, I think what Commander McCarthy is trying to say is that we don't give a shit about your attendance policy. Just tell us about Vivian Tong," Jason instructed.

"Vivian? She started working here about six months ago. Cute girl. Really knew how to play up the Chinese schoolgirl routine. Her English was pretty good and I even saw her papers. She was a legal citizen. I don't hire illegals here…"

"How righteous of you," Mick added.

"How'd you meet her?" Jason inquired.

"She worked at a Chinese takeout place I go to. Let's just say she had the intangibles that I was looking for, but it took some time to convince her to ditch that job and come here. I ate Chinese takeout for two weeks straight just so I could work on her."

"So you groomed her?" Mick asked.

"Molesters *groom* girls, Commander. I'm an honest businessman. I just made her realize that she could make ten times as much money as she did selling egg rolls."

"What made her change her mind and come dance here?" Jason pressed.

"Turns out she had paid a lot of money to an official in Hong Kong to get over here and wanted to do the same for her cousin. It was going to take her years to get that kind of dough, so I told her how much faster she could make that kind of scratch working for me. Before you knew it, she was shaking her ass up there. She used the stage name Butterfly," Vance said, nodding to the small stage behind him.

"Did you also teach her how to make even more money on the side as a hooker?" Mick asked accusingly.

"Whoa, whoa, whoa. I'm no pimp. Anything she did after her shift is on her, man. I'm not their babysitter when they leave here each night."

"But you knew she was taking guys home from your club, right?" Jason countered.

"Listen, I see a lot of things. For all I know, if she went home with a customer it was because of a mutual attraction," Vance replied coyly.

"I've seen your customers, pal. I highly doubt that's ever the case, so let's stop the bullshit," Mick snapped.

"As I keep saying, whatever the girls do on their own is their business. Not mine," Mick answered.

"So, you're telling us that you don't get a cut of any of that action, Vance? I find that hard to believe. I mean, they're *using* you as a meet and greet to make money. You should at least get something for providing that," Mick said.

"I'm doing just fine, Commander. I got enough heat on me just owning this place. I don't need to worry about getting popped for prostitution too."

"Did Vivian have any regular customers that you would see her leave with at the end of a shift?" Jason asked.

"Vivian had a lot of admirers. She looked like a petite teenager and she knew how to work those guys," Vance replied.

"What about the last night she was here? Did she leave with a guy that night?" Jason continued to press.

Vance looked around to make sure nobody could hear what he was about to say. "I can tell you that she left that night with one of our regulars. Weird guy, too. I saw him leave with her a few times."

"Do you have a name? You're supposed to be checking ID's at the door, so I'm sure you have a name for the guy," Mick asked.

"What's this all about, anyways? What do you guys care about Vivian for?" Vance inquired.

"Leave the questions to us, Vance. Just give us the name," Jason replied.

"Fine. The guy's name is Gene. Eugene Lankford."

"When was the last time you saw him here?"

"That's the thing… Gene hasn't been here since the last time I saw Vivian…"

20

Grace Brooks stood next to her SUV, which was parked near the entrance to the Westcott Hotel, as the sun began to set nearby on Lake Erie. It had been a few days since her services as a bodyguard for Cara Knox and Cooper Madison were needed, but that changed earlier in the afternoon when she received a call from her boss at CW Security Solutions, Clarence Walters.

Since she began working a regular second shift for Coop and Cara, she had been asked to do everything from driving to scaring off paparazzi for her clients on an almost daily basis. Most nights involved shuttling the couple to and from dinner at a local restaurant, but tonight she was being asked to take them to the Coe Lake gazebo in Berea where Coop and Cara had visited on the night of their first date.

Grace had received specific instructions not to tell Cara where they were going, no matter how much Cara asked. Coop wanted their destination to be a surprise, and Grace was just part of the plan he had in place.

When she was not working for Cleveland's newest power couple, Grace spent the majority of her free time training to be an MMA fighter. If things worked out the way she had hoped they would, she would get a shot at her first professional bout sometime in the next year.

In the meantime, she had fully dedicated herself to the sport, going as far as following a strict diet and workout regimen that often included two workouts a day. Having a steady shift for the first time since resigning from her job as a police officer had given her the necessary stability that was required to commit to a fighter's lifestyle.

Grace was blessed with an athletic body, similar to that of an Olympic swimmer. Her triangular shoulders dominated her tall frame, and her core was toned from years as a long distance runner, which also gave her an advantage in regards to stamina in the octagon.

As Coop and Cara exited the Westcott, hand in hand, Grace noticed that Coop's usual smile had returned to his face. Clarence had informed her of Coop's struggles since the injury, so Grace was not sure what to expect from him before the evening began.

"How are you on this fine evening?" Coop asked Grace as she opened the rear passenger door for him and Cara to enter.

"Living the dream, Mr. Madison," Grace answered with a smile.

"We've been over this, Grace. Call me Coop."

"I'm sorry, force of habit," Grace replied.

"Hi, Grace! So, where are we going?" Cara asked, hoping that Grace would fill her in.

"Hello, Cara…" Grace smiled, purposely ignoring the question.

"Not gonna budge, are you?" Cara relented.

"He pays my salary," Grace laughed, nodding at Coop.

"Touché," Cara replied.

"You'll find out, soon enough," Coop said with a grin as he gestured for Cara to climb in the back seat. "Are we all set?" Coop whispered to Grace after Cara had entered the vehicle.

"Yessir."

"Atta girl," he said with a wink before climbing in the back of the SUV next to Cara.

21

Charlie Knox sat in his wheelchair and looked out at the still waters of Coe Lake, a small inland reservoir located in Berea, Ohio. Once a sandstone quarry, Coe Lake had been transformed over the past decade into a recreational oasis for nature, recreation, and fishing enthusiasts.

"They should be here soon," Joanne Knox said to her husband from her seat on one of the many benches that had been installed for visitors to the lake.

Earlier that day, Joanne had received a call from Coop asking that she and Charlie meet him at Coe Lake that evening. He informed her that Cara would not know that he would be taking her there and had asked Joanne not to say anything to her about it.

"We can be there. What time?" Joanne had asked.

"We will be leaving the Westcott at six, so I would say by quarter after to be safe. Should be a beautiful night!" Coop replied, a tinge of excitement in his voice.

"So, what's the surprise?" Joanne asked, hoping that this was not going to be an impulsive marriage proposal. They had only been dating for a little more than a month, and Joanne still had her reservations about the rapid pace of the relationship to begin with.

"Don't worry, I'm not popping the question, Miz Knox," Coop said, sensing that she was worried.

"Oh, that didn't even cross my mind, Coop," Joanne lied.

"I figured," Coop laughed.

"Should we bring anything?" Joanne asked.

"Just yourselves. I promise that it'll be worth the trip. We'll meet you by the gazebo."

"Okay, Sweetie. We'll see you then."

Joanne had spent the rest of the day trying to figure out what exactly Coop had planned. She assumed it had something to do with the fact that Cara had brought Coop to Coe Lake on their first date, but beyond that she was stumped.

"Are you still trying to figure out what this is all about?" Charlie asked his wife. He was taking some pleasure in the fact that it bothered her so much.

It was a microcosm of their relationship. Joanne had always been the worrisome one, especially since his accident. Charlie had always been the laid back one, and the accident only made him realize more that there was so little in life that he had control over.

"Not anymore. I gave up," Joanne sighed.

"You always did hate surprises."

"Almost as much as I hate you reminding me that I do."

"I can think of a few times where you actually enjoyed the surprise, you know. Remember when I blindfolded you and drove you to Blossom to see Michael Stanley?" Charlie asked.

The Michael Stanley Band was once the most popular band in Cleveland in the late 70's and early 80's; however, they had never obtained that same level of success nationwide. In 1982, the band set a record for attendance at Blossom Music Center, an outdoor pavilion in Richfield, Ohio. Over four nights in late August that year, more than 74,000 people witnessed their act, including Charlie and Joanne.

"How could I forget? I remember being so mad at you in the car. It seemed like I had that stupid blindfold on for hours. You wouldn't even talk to me!" Joanne recalled.

"But, it was worth it, wasn't it?" Charlie asked, reaching his hand out towards Joanne.

"Yes, it certainly was," Joanne replied, taking his hand in hers.

Joanne and Charlie, after years of marital discord following his accident, were in the midst of a renaissance. Coincidence or not, their marriage had taken a turn for the better around the same time that their daughter began dating Cooper Madison. They even began sleeping in the same bedroom for the first time since his accident, and Joanne had been silently praying that this change would be a permanent one. She was not sure if her heart could take it otherwise.

A few minutes later, Grace Brook's black SUV pulled into the parking lot next to the Coe Lake gazebo. It did not take Cara long to figure out where they were headed once Grace exited the freeway onto Route 237 and headed south towards Berea.

"Are you taking me to Coe Lake?" Cara had asked, squeezing Coop's hand in the back seat.

"Yes, ma'am, but I have a few more surprises in store for you," Coop replied coyly.

"Oh my God, this is the sweetest thing ever!" Cara said as she planted a big kiss on Coop's cheek.

Grace Brooks smiled as she looked at the happy couple in her rearview mirror. She hoped that some day she would find someone who would treat her just as well. Unfortunately, most of the men she had dated were too insecure about her professions, both as a bodyguard and fighter. The ones who were okay with it typically were over-the-top Alpha males, a trait that she despised.

"Oh. My. God. You brought my parents here too?" Cara said as she exited the SUV and saw Charlie and Joanne near the gazebo.

"Yes, ma'am," Coop said with a smile as he then watched Cara excitedly run over to her parents.

"I'll open the back so you can get the rods," Grace told Coop, who had asked her to pick up his fishing rods and tackle box from a storage unit.

"Good deal. Thanks a lot for making that stop for me. Did you get the bait too?" Coop asked.

"Two dozen extremely gross Canadian night crawlers, just like you asked," Grace chuckled, referring to the worms that Coop had also instructed her to get.

"Gross? I figured a trained killer like yourself wasn't afraid of anything, let alone a few worms," Coop chided.

"I'd rather fight Mike Tyson than touch those things!"

"Well, hopefully we will never need you to protect us from a gang of earthworms," Coop teased.

"Yeah, you'd be on your own there," Grace laughed. "I'll be waiting here if you need me."

Coop retrieved the rods, tackle box, and bait from the back of the SUV before carrying them over to Cara and her parents.

"Hope y'all are ready to catch some fish!" Coop said to the three faces that were staring back at him with a puzzled look.

"You brought us here to go *fishing*, Coop?" Joanne asked her daughter's strapping boyfriend as he approached.

"Not you, Miz Knox. The rods are for Cara and her dad," he proclaimed, nodding to Charlie.

Early on in their relationship, Cara had told Coop that one of her favorite things to do was go fishing with her father, but he had not taken her since the accident. Tonight Coop was going to remedy that.

"I figure that you guys can fish from the gazebo, maybe you'll even get some catfish since it's getting late," Coop said as he handed Cara the rods. In addition to being a prime spot to catch fish, the gazebo offered a safe area for Charlie to fish from while sitting in his wheelchair.

"You are seriously going to make me cry, Cooper Madison! Well, Dad, what do you say? Want to go fish with your little girl?" Cara asked her father, who was trying to fight back the tears that had started to well up in his eyes.

Charlie Knox knew that he had stopped doing a lot of the things he used to prior to his injury, and not taking his baby girl fishing was the one he regretted the most. He had thought about it a few times, but his insecurity about being in a wheelchair always made him squash the idea. Charlie realized Coop knew that this was the one way he would be able to fish with his daughter again, and his admiration for the young man standing before him grew.

"I'd love that," Charlie managed to say.

"What about you and Mom? What are you guys going to do while we're fishing?" Cara asked.

"Well, that too, is a surprise. Charlie, do you mind if I steal your wife for a bit while you and your daughter fish?" Coop asked with a smile.

"Not at all," Charlie replied.

"Good deal. Y'all go ahead and get started without me and I'll be back soon. Grace will be over there if you need her. I better hear about all the fish you caught when I get back," Coop said as he held out his arm for Joanne to take.

"Oh my, this is making me a bit nervous," Joanne said as she took his arm.

"Mom hates surprises," Cara stated.

"Have faith, Miz Knox…"

22

The Serenity Day Spa, located in Berea's historic shopping district, was just steps away from Coe Lake. Cooper Madison had taken Joanne by the arm and walked her to the spa's entrance after making sure that Cara and Charlie were ready to fish.

"I figured that you'd rather be in here than fishin' at the gazebo," Coop stated as he opened the door for Joanne.

"Oh my, I've always wanted to come here. You really shouldn't have, Cooper," Joanne replied.

"Well, I did. These ladies are going to take good care of you for the next hour or so while we try to land us some fish."

A young woman approached them after they stepped inside. "Hello, Mrs. Knox. Welcome to the Serenity Day Spa. We're going to start you off with a facial, followed by a manicure, pedicure, and blowout," the young woman said as she gestured for Joanne to follow her to the back of the spa.

"I don't know what to say, Cooper. This is such a sweet surprise. Thank you so much," Joanne said.

"See, not all surprises are bad, right?" Coop asked.

"I'm beginning to realize that now," Joanne replied.

"Enjoy yourself, Miz Knox. You deserve it. We'll be by to get you after you're done," Coop said before walking out.

A few minutes later, Coop paused as he came upon Charlie and Cara. Charlie was seated in his wheelchair on the gazebo and was slowly reeling in his line. Cara stood a few feet next to him, rod in hand, smiling.

Coop was proud of himself. He had really wanted to make this night special for Cara and her parents, and everything was going perfectly.

"Y'all catch any fish yet?" Coop asked as he ascended the steps of the gazebo, which had been built in the 90's as the first phase of the beautification process of Coe Lake.

"We've had some nibbles, but no fish just yet. I think it's only a matter of time before we get one," Charlie replied as he threw his line over the small fence rail and into the dark waters below.

"Oh, we're gonna get more than one, Baby!" Cara said, reeling slowly, a determined look on her face.

"Where's Joanne?" Charlie asked, keeping his eyes focused on the task at hand. While the sun was barely visible by this point, the lights from the gazebo illuminated the water just enough to bring visibility to his fluorescent green and orange bobber in the distance.

"She's enjoying an evening of relaxation at the spa over there," Coop said, nodding to the nearby buildings.

Known as the "Berea Triangle" due to the triangular intersection of roads that were lined with a mixture of historic and contemporary buildings, the Triangle had long been home to small businesses, including the Serenity Day Spa.

"You planned a spa trip for my mom?" Cara asked, impressed.

"Yes, ma'am…"

"You certainly are full of surprises tonight, aren't you?" Cara asked smiling.

"That's very nice of you, son. It's been a long time since… hold on now. I think I got one!" Charlie exclaimed as he began to try and set the hook on his prey.

Coop ran over to the rail and searched for the bobber, but it was nowhere to be seen. "I think you're right, Charlie! Set that hook!" Coop instructed, excitement in his voice.

"I hope I still remember how! It's been a long time," Charlie replied, his fishing rod bending toward the water below.

"Like riding a bike," Coop replied, unaware of the irony in his choice of simile.

"Been even longer since I've done that," Charlie laughed, reeling.

"Oh man, I'm an idiot. I'm so sorry," Coop said embarrassed.

"Don't be, Cooper. I'm faster in this thing anyways," Charlie replied.

"Get him, Dad!" Cara encouraged. She had reeled her line in and set her rod down so she that could get a better look at the battle that was taking place.

"Oh, I got him!" Charlie grunted, reeling faster.

"There he is! I see him!" Cara yelled, pointing to a spot in the water about ten feet from the gazebo.

"Oh yeah! I see him too! Looks like a catfish!" Coop concurred, pointing to the dark silhouette that was fighting for its life near the surface of the water. At one point, the fish's tail splashed above the surface.

"C'mon, you bastard!" Charlie exclaimed, his voice straining with each crank of the reel.

"Just a little bit closer and I'll grab the tip of your rod so it doesn't snap. He's a big one, Charlie!" Coop declared, leaning over the rail even farther.

"You got this, Dad! Reel!" Cara cheered.

"Get ready, Coop!" Charlie instructed as Coop grabbed the tip of the fishing rod with his right hand and the line with his left, helping to ease the strain on the rod.

"Lift up, Charlie!"

"Oh my God, he's a MONSTER, Dad!" Cara yelled as Coop pulled the catfish out of the water, guiding the line as the large bottom feeder tried to shake itself off of the hook. With a cautious hand over hand approach, Coop slowly inched the fish up and over the rail of the gazebo and onto the wooden planks below, trying his best to hide the pain coming from his elbow.

It was a blue catfish, a species known for the blueish grey coloring of their scales, which were now glimmering in the overhead lighting of the gazebo. Blue catfish, native to many of the inland lakes in Ohio, could reach weights of over a hundred pounds. This one, while nowhere near record weight, was still a giant of a fish for Coe Lake.

"You got yourself a 'blue cat', Charlie!" Coop declared.

"I'll be damned! That has to be at least a ten pounder!" Charlie stated, his breathing hard and fast. It had taken nearly all of his energy just to reel in the catch.

"Is he croaking?" Cara asked, referring to the repetitive frog-like sounds coming from the catfish.

"Yes, ma'am, blue cats are noisy suckers!" Coop concurred.

"Look at his whiskers!" Cara said, pointing at the long whiskerlike appendages near the mouth of the catfish.

Coop picked the noisy fish up and removed the hook from its mouth before offering it to Charlie to hold.

"Wanna give him a kiss before we throw him back?" Coop asked, knowing that Cara had told him that her father used to make her kiss every fish she caught prior to releasing it back to the water.

Cara, realizing Coop's intent, felt tears of happiness welling up in her eyes. Charlie believed that if his daughter gave the fish a smooch that she would not be afraid to hold them as she got older. He wanted his only daughter to be able to take her own fish off the hook so that she never had to rely on a man to do it for her. It was not just a lesson in fishing, but rather a metaphor for how he wanted her to live her life. Independently.

Charlie looked up at Coop and smiled. He was beginning to learn that everything Coop did seemed to have a purpose, and he came to the realization that Coop must have known about his daughter's fish-kissing routine. Like most fathers, Charlie felt that nobody was ever going to be "good enough" for his daughter, but Coop was certainly making a case to prove him wrong.

"Bring that sucker here and I'll plant one right on his ugly mug," Charlie instructed.

"Watch his whiskers, Dad. They sting, don't they?" Cara asked.

"Nah, that's an old wives' tale. They're harmless," Coop responded, referring to the common misconception regarding catfish, as he handed the fish over to Charlie.

"Pucker up, big boy!" Charlie said as he planted a kiss on the mouth of the croaking catfish.

"I think he likes you, Charlie! Listen to him purr," Coop joked.

"Don't tell Joanne; she might get jealous," Charlie chuckled, before handing the fish back to Coop, who then offered Cara the same opportunity for a kiss.

"I'll pass, thank you. I only kiss the ones that I catch," Cara laughed, shaking her head as she backed away a few steps.

"Your loss," Coop replied as he planted a big smooch on the catfish, which was still croaking loudly, before tossing it back into the dark waters below.

"That was so exciting!" Cara exclaimed.

"It sure was! It's been so long since I've felt the joy of pulling in a big ol' fish. Thank you, Cooper. This was truly a nice surprise," Charlie said, a thankful tone in his voice.

"My pleasure, Charlie. Let's see if we can get another now," Coop said as he put another worm on the hook.

Cara walked over to Coop and gave him a kiss on the cheek as he worked on Charlie's rig.

"You're amazing," she whispered in his ear.

"Just trying to keep up with you," Coop whispered back.

"Nothing…" Cara replied.

"Nothing…"

23

Detective Jason Knox sat in his unmarked cruiser in the second row of the Edgewater Park Marina lot awaiting the arrival of Hannah LaMarca. The day prior, he had asked the tenacious young reporter from Cleveland's Channel One News to meet him there in the morning.

Jason still was not sure if he was making a mistake by trusting Hannah with information about his investigation of the EPK case, but sensing that a public relations nightmare was on the horizon, he figured that he was going to need all of the allies he could gather from the local media.

It was only a matter of time before the public found out that the Edgewater Park Killer was not the late Ernie Page, despite Chief Horace Johnston's many declarations to the contrary. Once the citizens of Cleveland realized that the EPK was still roaming the streets killing innocent victims, the fear and mistrust that would accompany it would likely lead to public outcry.

Jason had tried to warn his chief about this possibility coming to fruition, but HoJo was intent on declaring the case as being solved. In his defense, Ernie Page had admitted to killing Stoya Fedorov before taking his own life just steps away from where Jason's cruiser was parked on this chilly October morning. However, Ernie had also insisted that he had nothing to do with the other two deaths attributed to the EPK. Nonetheless, HoJo chose to ignore that and seize the opportunity to gain national attention as the chief who oversaw the capture of a serial killer.

The discovery of the latest victim, Vivian Tong, had only reaffirmed Jason's biggest fear that he was right, after all. Faith in the department was at an all-time high following HoJo's announcement that the city no longer had to live in fear of the EPK, but that faith was about to be put to the test.

Jason knew that the only way to repair the damage that was certain to come was to catch the real EPK, and fast. With any luck, he would be able to do just that before the public ever knew otherwise.

Jason's cell phone sprang to life from inside his jacket pocket. He pulled the phone out and looked at the number. It was his commander.

"Good morning, Mick," Jason answered.

"Knox, where are you?" Mick asked, his tone urgent.

"Waiting to meet with someone before I come in. Why?"

"It's HoJo. I just got done meeting with him. I filled him in on the newest victim and told him about our visit to Buddy's."

"How'd that go?" Jason asked, knowing that the answer would not be anything positive.

"Awful. He about broke his goddamn desk…"

"I've personally seen that move myself," Jason said, referring to the time his chief ripped him for a lack of progress early on in the EPK case. In front of the camera, HoJo was a beacon of calmness, but in private he was known for emotional outbursts that often involved screaming and the pounding of his desk.

"He doesn't want us to release anything to the press. Not the victim's name, not the fact that she had EPK carved in her torso, nothing."

Jason's heart sank. He felt awful not telling his commander about the discussion he had with Hannah LaMarca the day before, not to mention that he was about to meet with her again in a few minutes.

"How is he certain that the press doesn't already know? I mean, there's a lot of people who were at the crime scene, not to mention the people working at the coroner's office. Does he really think that he's going to be able to keep all of them from talking?"

"Well, let's pray that they don't. HoJo just informed me, in no uncertain terms, that it was going to be *my* ass on the line if anything gets out," Mick stated.

"He can't hold you responsible for what other people might say!" Jason exclaimed.

"Knox, don't be naïve. He can… and he will."

24

"Good morning," Cara Knox whispered in Cooper Madison's ear as she stretched her arms out from her place next to him in bed.

"It's about time you woke up, girl," Coop chuckled. He had been awake for over an hour. The pain in his arm would not let him sleep in regardless of how late he was up the night before.

After returning home from their evening at Coe Lake, Cara wasted no time showing Coop her appreciation for his efforts to make the date a special one. Passion was never a problem for the couple, but the events of the past week had definitely quieted the flames down for the first time in their young relationship.

Last night, however, they made up for lost time. Cara, usually the more submissive of the two, set the tone early that she would be calling the shots.

"Whoa, girl!" Coop laughed when the petite Cara shoved him up against the door to his apartment.

"Shhhhhh…." Cara said as she pressed her index finger to his lips. She then grabbed his shirt, pulled his face close to hers, and whispered in his ear exactly what she was going to do to him.

"Oh my…" Coop managed to respond.

What followed was the most intoxicating evening of lovemaking that either had ever experienced. By the time they were through, nearly every room in Coop's penthouse had been used as their own personal playground. The exhausted, yet completely satisfied, couple fell asleep in each other's arms just past three in the morning.

"Have you been up long?" Cara asked.

"Only for a bit," Coop lied, as he had already fetched two pain pills to help qualm the throbbing in his elbow. While Coop had cut back his alcohol consumption, at least in the massive amounts that he had consumed the other day, he still felt the need to take the Percocet. He felt ashamed for hiding it from Cara, but he also felt that she would think he was being weak if she knew just how much he was relying on them.

"You were on fire last night," Cara said as she kissed his bare chest.

"I was just trying to keep up with you, girl," he replied as he ran his broad fingers through her hair.

"I don't know what got into me," Cara laughed, slightly embarrassed of her aggressive behavior during their romp.

"Me either, but it was hot as hell…"

"I honestly don't think I've ever been as attracted to you as I was last night. What you did, not just for me but also for my parents, was so amazing. It was a perfect evening."

"Your dad seemed to have a blast catching that big ol' catfish, didn't he?" Coop asked, smiling at the thought of Charlie reeling in his big catch.

"Not as much as I did watching him do it. I haven't seen him that happy in a long time, Coop. Thank you," Cara said, her head on Coop's chest.

"It was the least I could do. I owed you for the way I was acting."

"Well, it was worth it, and my mom absolutely loved her spa treatment."

"She deserved a little pampering, I think. She's so selfless in the way she cares for your dad."

"Yeah, she's a saint. I'm pretty sure that they both like you more than me now though," Cara chuckled.

"Well, that's my plan, you know," Coop laughed.

"Mission accomplished, Agent Madison."

"Speaking of agents, I'm supposed to call T-Squared today. He wants an update on my arm," Coop said, referring to his agent, Todd Taylor.

"How's your elbow feeling today?" Cara asked.

"Oh, it hurts like hell…"

"Well, hopefully you'll get that surgery soon and you can begin to heal. When's your next appointment with Dr. Mueller?"

"Tomorrow morning. He's going to check the swelling, and if it's not too bad we will set a date."

"Do you need me to go with you? I have class, but can probably skip it."

"I always want you there, and anywhere else for that matter, but this will be a quick one. You should probably just go to class. Besides, I'm gonna need you big time after he cuts me open."

"Good, because you're stuck with me," she replied as she climbed on top of him, her legs straddling his hips.

"Well, hello there, beautiful," Coop said, cupping her face with his hands.

"You know, as exhausting and enjoyable as last night was, I still think that I have a little left in the tank this morning," Cara whispered as she leaned forward and began to kiss his neck.

"Well, then, I think we need to do something about that..."

25

"Here you go, as promised," Hannah LaMarca said as she handed Jason a hot cup of coffee from the passenger seat of his cruiser. Moments earlier, the vivacious young reporter had knocked on his car window and startled the detective, who was deep in thought as he recalled his conversation with Mick.

"Thank you," Jason replied, failing to make eye contact with Hannah.

"Is something wrong?" Hannah asked, sensing that his demeanor was off.

"Oh, sorry… My mind is just wandering…"

"Can't blame you, Detective. You've had a pretty interesting 48 hours," Hannah laughed.

"More than you know," Jason sighed.

"Care to tell me? Off the record, of course," Hannah reassured him.

"Let's just say that if anyone at the station knew that I was sitting here talking to you that I'd have a lot of explaining to do…"

"Gotcha. Just to reiterate what I told you yesterday, and to put your mind at ease, whatever we discuss will stay between us until you give me the green light to move forward with the story. I just want your word in return that I'll be the first to get that green light," Hanna replied.

"I know, and I believe you," Jason said as he looked Hannah in the eyes for the first time since she entered his vehicle.

"Good. So, did you learn anything new about Vivian Tong since we last spoke?" Hannah asked.

"We sure did, but we still have a lot of questions that need to be answered."

"Like what?"

"Well, it turns out that Miss Tong was a dancer at Buddy's Speakeasy," Jason said, deliberately pausing after he spoke to gauge what Hannah already might know. Despite the fact he trusted her, it was still a delicate waltz.

"You mean that dump over on Clark? We've run a few stories on that place. It's a punch palace masquerading as a strip club," Hannah chuckled.

"That's the one, but the bigger story there is that a lot of the dancers apparently subsidize their income by taking clients home after their shifts are over, including our victim."

"Whoa, that's a story in itself. Is the owner like a pimp too?" Hannah pressed.

"He claims he isn't, but he did admit to being well aware of the practice. He insisted that while he knows it's going on, he doesn't have anything to do with it."

"Do you believe him?" Hannah asked.

"I don't think you can ever trust guys like Vance Gold…"

"Vance Gold? Is that a stage name?"

"Sadly, no, but with a name like that I'm pretty sure he was destined to own a strip club," Jason laughed.

"What did he have to say about Vivian?"

"Oh, he was very proud to tell us that he 'rescued' her from her job at a Chinese takeout place, so that she could make enough money to bring her cousin over to the States from Hong Kong."

"What a saint," Hannah sighed sarcastically.

"He sure sees himself as one…"

"Did he say when he saw her last?"

"He told us that Vivian stopped showing up a couple weeks ago and that he hasn't seen her since she left her last shift."

"Did she leave with a guy that night?" Hannah asked.

"According to Vance, she left with a guy almost every night at the end of her shift. The lady that we encountered back at her apartment confirmed his story too," Jason said, referring to the old woman who had informed him.

"You went to her apartment too?" Hannah asked, leaning forward at this revelation.

"Yup, before we went to Buddy's Speakeasy. That's actually how we knew that she worked there. If her nosy neighbor hadn't told us, we may never have known. I doubt those girls are getting any W-2's from Vance…"

"This old lady, did she say anything else?"

"Oh yeah, she was a trip! She's this old Chinese woman who speaks broken English, and she was not a fan of Vivian's choice of occupation. I guess Vivian would bring the men she met at the club back to her apartment, which didn't sit well with the woman. She kept saying,

'Vivian bad girl... She whore..' Over and over," Jason replied, mimicking the old woman.

"Okay, in all seriousness, that's pretty funny," Hannah laughed.

"It was hard to keep a straight face," Jason agreed.

"Did either of them have a description of the last guy they saw her with?"

"The old woman said he looked like Mick, actually," Jason chuckled.

"Oh my God, that must've gone over real well with him..."

"You know it..."

"What about Vance Gold? Did he give a description too?"

"Better yet, he gave us a name. Eugene Lankford."

"What do you have on him?" Hannah asked, hoping that Jason would keep giving her more.

"Nothing yet, but that's what we'll be working on today. Vance said he's a regular at Buddy's. But, get this, he hasn't seen him since the last night when he left with Vivian."

"Holy... Shit. Do you think this guy's the EPK?" Hannah asked, excitement in her voice.

"I'd say that he's certainly the leading candidate, but who knows. We have to find him first. Speaking of, I really have to get back to the station. This stays between us, right?" Jason asked for reassurance.

"Of course. Just keep me in the loop. See you here again tomorrow? I'll bring more coffee," Hannah promised as she began to exit his cruiser.

"I'll be here."

26

"So, how's the old wing doing, my man?" asked Todd "T-Squared" Taylor over the phone.

"Are you running or something, T? You sound out of breath," Coop said, as he could tell that his longtime agent and friend seemed to be breathing heavily as he was talking.

"I'm at LAX... Running through the damn terminal... Trying to make my damn flight!" Todd replied, the sounds of the busy airport accompanying his bated breath as he tried his best to subdue it.

"You didn't have to answer my call, brother! You could've waited," Coop chuckled.

"Hey, T-Squared is *never* too busy... To take a call... From his top client!" Todd asserted in his typical third-person fashion, albeit between breaths.

"Yeah, well since your top client is going to be on the shelf for at least a year, I sure hope you have more eggs in that basket of yours..."

"You know that I have dozens... But, you're the Golden Egg... Besides, they've come a long way with Tommy John... You'll probably come back stronger!"

"That's what everyone keeps telling me…" Coop answered, amazed that his agent could still sound like an agent, even while sprinting through a busy airport.

"Because it's the truth! I just read an article the other day on it. Some guys are coming back in *less* than a year, and those guys don't have half of your ability or work ethic."

Coop grinned when he heard Todd's words, which seemed to be less strained than they were at the onset of the conversation. "You must have made it to your gate; you don't sound like you're trying to stretch a single into a double anymore," Coop asserted.

"Damn straight I did, baby! Hey, I have to let you go. I'm about to board. I'll hit you up tomorrow after your appointment."

"Where are you going anyways?" Coop asked, always curious about his agent's whirlwind lifestyle.

"Meh-hee-kho, Señor!" Todd replied, doing his best to pronounce Mexico like a true Latino.

"Mexico?"

"Going to check out a 17-year-old shortstop. He's supposed to be the real deal. If he is, I'm going to try and sign him."

"Can I give you a bit of advice?" Coop asked.

"Always…"

"Don't try and speak Spanish anymore while you're down there," Coop laughed.

"What? Come on, man! That was spot-on!"

"You're a trip, T…"

"You know you love me, Coop! I'll call you tomorrow. Say hi to Cara for me."

"Will do. Be safe down there, and remember, no more Spanish!"

"Buenos Dias!" Todd said as he ended the call.

Coop smiled as he walked back into his suite from the balcony. Cara was sitting on the couch, sipping on a cup of coffee.

"Todd said to tell you hi," Coop informed Cara as he sat next to her.

"What's he up to?" Cara asked.

"On his way to Mexico to try and sign a young shortstop."

"I don't know how he does it. He always seems like he's on his way somewhere. Is he ever home with his family?"

"It comes with the territory, I suppose."

"His wife must be a saint," Cara chuckled.

"Joy? Yeah, she certainly is. You'd love her," Coop replied.

"Hopefully, I'll get to meet her soon."

"You will. We usually try and get together around Christmas."

"I'd like that."

"Hey, it's Wednesday. Aren't you going to class today?" Coop asked, changing the subject.

"Nope. I'm all yours today. I only was supposed to have stats today, but he gave us off. I guess he wanted a day off," Cara replied.

"Well then, what should we do with this blessing that has been bestowed upon us?"

"I'm glad you asked. I actually called Clarence when you were on the phone and told him to pick us up in an hour," Cara said coyly.

"Oh yeah? Where are we going?" Coop asked.

"It's a surprise…"

"Really? Not even a hint?"

"Well, after the masterful job you did last night with my parents, I felt it necessary to try and repay the favor," Cara responded, grinning.

"You know you don't always have to match me, right? I mean, I just don't want you to always think that you have to, is all."

"I know, but guess what?"

"What?"

"I want to…"

27

"Where the hell have you been? HoJo's so far up my ass that I can't even sit down," Mick said to Jason as he arrived at the 1st District precinct.

"I told you, I was waiting to meet someone," Jason replied.

"Yeah, about that. Who exactly *were* you meeting?" Mick asked.

"Just a friend. Not work-related," Jason responded. He felt awful that he was lying to his commander and friend, but he knew that he could not tell Mick about Hannah. Especially not after Mick's earlier warning not to talk about the case with anyone, let alone a reporter.

"I see," Mick said. He was not buying it, but he also trusted Jason as much as anyone in the entire department, so he let it go.

"So, any news on Eugene Lankford?" Jason asked, hoping to change the subject.

"Yes and no. Turns out that there is no record of a Eugene Lankford living anywhere in Cleveland, let alone Ohio."

"Do you think Vance was jerking us around?"

"That, or the guy was using a fake ID when he went to the club," Mick answered.

"What's your gut saying?"

"I was going to ask you the same thing," Mick chuckled.

"It'd be a lot easier if Vance was lying. We could lean on him and get the truth. If Vance was actually being honest, which I still find highly unlikely, we aren't going to have much to go on."

"What about the camera? I noticed that there was a security camera near the entrance at Buddy's Speakeasy. Maybe we'll be able to see our man Gene on the tape?"

"Can't hurt to ask, I suppose. If he refuses, we'll get a warrant. I'm sure that Vance would love to see us again," Jason said sarcastically.

"Listen, Knox, I have a bad feeling about what HoJo's going to do once the public figures out that the EPK is alive and well. He'd push his own mother under the bus if it meant that it would save his ass. It's only a matter of time before all this gets out, and when it does, I have a hunch that I'm going to be facing that Greyhound head on while he stands and watches," Mick retorted in a nervous tone.

"You mean *us*, Mick. He'll throw both of us to the wolves. You're not in this alone," Jason reassured his commander.

"I won't let that happen to you, Knox. No sense in both of us taking the fall for that bastard."

"Then let's not. Screw him. We'll go to the union," Jason replied.

"HoJo's a very powerful man, Knox. It'll be an uphill battle even with the union on our side. They'll be able to help us keep our jobs, but HoJo will be able to reassign us and in the court of public opinion, we'll be as guilty as the EPK."

"Well, I guess there's only one thing for us to do then," Jason stated, grinning.

"I'm all ears, partner."

"Let's go catch this asshole before HoJo has a chance to do any of that."

"Sounds good to me. Let's go pay Mr. Gold a visit at his fine establishment," Mick said with a smile and a nod.

"I'll drive."

28

"How's my favorite couple doing on this fine day?" Clarence Walters asked as he pulled away from the Westcott Hotel with Coop and Cara in the rear seat of his Cadillac Escalade.

"Excellent, Clarence. How about you?" Coop replied.

"Can't complain. How's the elbow feeling?"

"So sore I can't touch it with a powder puff," Coop responded, using one of his many Southern expressions.

"I bet. How about you, Cara?"

"Any day that the professor cancels class is a great day, Clarence. Are you good to go with the plan for today?" Cara asked.

"Yes, ma'am, we are good to go," Clarence confirmed.

"So, when exactly do I get to find out where y'all are taking me?" Coop inquired, knowing that Cara was thoroughly enjoying putting him on the other side of a mystery trip.

"Soon enough, but it's going to take about an hour to get there, so just sit back and relax," Cara replied as she squeezed his hand.

"It'll be worth the wait, Coop. I promise," Clarence asserted as the SUV made its way onto Interstate 90 Westbound.

"So, you've been where we're going?" Coop pressed.

"Yessir, many times. But, it's been a few years," Clarence responded.

"You're going to love it," Cara said with a smile before giving Coop a soft kiss on his cheek.

Cara leaned next to Coop and placed her head on his broad chest as he wrapped his left arm around her petite frame and held her close to his heart. They remained that way for the remainder of their time on the road, which changed from the interstate to State Route 2.

It was not until the SUV exited Route 2 that Coop started to figure out where it was they were headed. Sandusky, Ohio, located midway between Cleveland and Toledo, was known across the country for one thing in particular.

"Are y'all taking me to Cedar Point?" Coop asked as he leaned forward.

"Yup, I hope you like roller coasters," Cara replied, excitement in her voice.

Cedar Point, the nation's second oldest operating amusement park, is also known as "America's Roller Coast". Boasting a world-record number of rides, Cedar Point had become a must-see destination for thrill seekers from all over the world.

Recent coaster additions such as the Millennium Force and the Top Thrill Dragster joined park favorites like the Magnum XL-200, Corkscrew, and Gemini to provide patrons with endless options to feed their needs.

"Like them? Hell, I *love* them!" Coop affirmed.

"Well, you'll really be happy then, Coop. This place is unreal,"

Clarence said, grinning as he peeked in the rearview mirror at the couple in the back seat.

"That's what I've heard, man. This is going to be awesome! Thanks, baby," Coop said as he gave Cara a kiss.

"I thought you'd like it, and I can't wait to hear you scream like a little girl on the Millennium Force," Cara laughed as Clarence drove the SUV into the park's entrance.

29

"I'm guessing that you fellas ain't here to check out our amazing lunch buffet," Vance Gold said to Jason and Mick as he took a seat across from them in his office at Buddy's Speakeasy.

"I can't even begin to imagine how many violations the Board of Health would find in that dumpster fire you call a kitchen, Vance," Mick replied.

"I'll have you know that not only is our food top notch, but so is the cleanliness of our kitchen," Vance asserted, miffed by Mick's comments.

"That's great, Vance, but we aren't here to eat," Jason chimed in.

"Then why are you here? I told you everything I know. I'm telling you, Eugene Lankford is who you should be looking for," Vance responded, pointing his finger at the detectives.

"Yeah, we know, Vance. Thanks a lot for wasting our time with that bullshit story," Mick countered.

"Bullshit story? How so?" Vance replied incredulously.

"There is no Eugene Lankford, Vance," Jason informed.

"Like hell there isn't! We always check ID's and even keep a written log of every guy that comes through this door," Vance barked emphatically.

"This might come as a shock to you, Vance, but you and your staff must not be very good at spotting a bogus ID," Mick said.

"What exactly do you write in that log, Vance?" Jason asked.

"Just their names and if it is an Ohio license or not," Vance replied.

"Just curious if you had an address or date of birth, is all," Jason said.

"Nope, just the name and state. Most joints don't even do that, you know," Vance rebuked.

"Was it even an Ohio license, Vance?" Mick asked.

"Actually, it wasn't. I think it was from West Virginia. It was the old laminated kind, not the new digital ones like we have here," Vance confessed, referencing the initiative brought on by the Real ID Act of 2005 that required stricter guidelines for state issued identification cards.

"The laminated ones are a lot easier to forge," Mick stated.

"I wish I had more information to give you guys, but that's all I got," Vance reiterated.

"Is it, Vance? What about that security camera by the entrance?" Jason countered.

Vance paused, then let out a laugh.

"What's so funny?" Mick asked, not amused by Vance's response.

"That thing ain't real, fellas! Cost me twenty bucks at Radio Shack. It's just for show," Vance declared.

"You're telling me that you don't have a working security camera anywhere in this joint?" Mick pressed.

"Hell no, too much money. That thing runs on a 9-volt battery to give off the illusion. It has a blinking red light and everything!" Vance responded. He was seemingly proud that his pseudo-security camera had even fooled the cops.

"Jesus Christ, Vance, you're killing me," Mick stated, shaking his head in disbelief.

"Sorry, fellas," Vance laughed, holding his hands up in the air.

"Hope you're still laughing when you're at the station," Mick responded.

"Station? What for?" Vance asked, the laughter gone from his voice.

"Well, since you don't have any tape for us to see, you're going to have to give a statement and meet with our sketch artist," Jason informed.

"You do know what he looks like, right?" Mick added.

"Yeah, I suppose I do. To be honest, he kinda looks like you," Vance said, nodding at Mick.

This revelation caused Jason to shoot a humorous look at Mick as he took great pleasure in the fact that two people had now given the same description.

Mick was less enthused. "You're really enjoying this, aren't you?" Mick asked his partner.

"You better believe it," Jason chuckled.

"He's a little older than you, though, and taller," Vance added.

"Besides the fact he was devastatingly handsome, like my partner here, are there any other distinguishing features you can recall?

Scars or tattoos?" Jason asked, trying his best to maintain a professional tone. Mick just shook his head and sighed.

"Not that I can recall, but we keep the lights down in the club. Nobody wants a bright strip club," Vance answered.

"What about his clothing?" Mick countered.

"Nothing that stands out," Vance responded.

"Did he ever use a credit card here?" Jason asked, hoping that maybe there would be a digital footprint left behind.

"I'm cash only, fellas, for obvious reasons," Vance replied.

"Of course you are," Mick sighed.

"We're going to have you ride with us back to the precinct so we can get your official statement and you can meet with the sketch artist," Jason informed as he stood up.

"Right now? We're just about to get busy," Vance replied.

"Yes, right now. Let's go," Mick confirmed as he stood up and gestured towards the door of Vance's office.

"You guys are killing me," Vance replied as he reluctantly stood up and followed the detectives out of his office and into the main area of the club.

30

"Are you scared?" Cara asked Coop, who was seated next to her in the front car of the Millennium Force roller coaster.

"Scared? Me? No ma'am," Coop replied, trying not to show the fear that was creeping in.

"Is that why you're squeezing the handles so hard that your knuckles are white?" Cara laughed.

"Is it that obvious?" Coop relented.

"Do you want to hold my hand?" Cara asked, using a tone not unlike a mother asking her child.

"Very funny," Coop replied rolling his eyes.

The Millennium Force broke six world records when it was built in 2000, and standing at over 300 feet, was one of the tallest rollercoasters in the world. Not only was the Millennium Force tall, it was also extremely fast, reaching speeds close to 100 miles per hour.

"Hope you're ready, big man," Clarence chimed in from his spot one row behind the couple. Cara had insisted earlier that Clarence accompany them in the park, not only to do his job as a bodyguard, but also to enjoy the day with them.

"Lord willing and the creek don't rise," Coop replied, using another Southern colloquialism.

"I'm assuming that means yes," Cara chuckled.

"Yes ma'am," Coop confirmed.

"Here we go!" Clarence announced as the coaster began moving slowly up the 45-degree lift hill that ran parallel to the Lake Erie shoreline.

"I'm so glad that we waited for the front car! You're going to feel like you're flying when we go down the hill!" Cara exclaimed, holding her hands up in the air.

"You're assuming that my eyes are going to be open," Coop responded.

"They better be! Here we go!" Cara yelled as the coaster reached the top of the 310-foot hill.

"Yeah baby!" Clarence shouted.

"Dear Baby Jesus!" Coop gasped as the coaster plummeted.

For the next two minutes, Coop screamed and gasped his way through all of the twists and turns that made the Millennium Force one of the top steel rollercoasters in the world year in and year out. He had been on a lot of coasters in his lifetime, but nothing quite like the Millennium Force.

"So, what'd you think?" Cara asked as the ride came to an end.

"That. Was. AMAZING!" Coop yelled.

"Hell yeah, Coop!" Clarence said as he gave Coop a high five on the platform after they exited the ride.

"C'mon, let's go see our picture!" Cara said as she led Coop by the hand.

"Picture?" Coop asked.

"There's a camera in one of the tunnels that snaps photos of the riders," Cara replied.

"Oh yeah, I can't wait to see your face, Coop," Clarence added.

"Lovely…" Coop replied, worried about just how terrified he was going to look in the photo.

"There we are!" Cara said as she pointed to one of the many television monitors that displayed the ride photos from each passenger car.

"Oh my Lord, Coop, look at your face," Clarence laughed.

Coop dropped his head in embarrassment after seeing the picture on the screen. On it, a smiling Cara could be seen with her arms raised in the air. Behind her, Clarence was doing the same. Coop, on the other hand, was grasping the handles of his shoulder harness and his eyes were squeezed shut in fear.

"Oh yeah, we are definitely getting a keychain made," Cara announced, referring to one of the many options that riders could immortalize their experience on the Millennium Force.

"Do we really have to do that?" Coop asked.

"Hell yes we do. I'll even pay for them!" Clarence responded.

"Them?" Coop asked.

"One for you and one for me, brother!" Clarence said in return, giving Coop a playful smack on the back.

After receiving their keepsakes, the trio made their way to the Frontiertown portion of the park. Clarence had insisted that they went there next for lunch.

"Man, I haven't had one of these in years. I forgot how much I loved them," Clarence declared as he bit into one of Cedar Point's famous smoked turkey legs.

"I wasn't so sure what the big deal was when y'all were talking about these turkey legs, but I'm a believer now," Coop replied as he held up the giant piece of turkey, which was a staple for park goers and only available in Frontiertown.

Clarence and Cara had been talking about the grilled turkey legs nearly the entire time they waited in line for the Millennium Force. Cara, the only one of the three willing to risk getting wet on the nearby Snake River Falls ride, passed on the turkey and instead got in line to ride solo down the popular water ride.

"This ain't your typical amusement park food, that's for sure," Clarence stated as he took a giant bite.

"I bet you wish you could eat one of these bad boys for lunch every day, Clarence," Coop replied.

"Nah, man. Then I wouldn't love them as much as I do."

"I suppose you're right. You know, I used to love pears as a kid. I would ask my momma for one in my lunch every day during first grade. Every. Single. Day. Loved them so much that I ended up getting sick of them. Haven't had a pear in years because of it," Coop laughed.

"I feel you, man. I was the same way with bologna as a kid. Fried bologna for breakfast, bologna sandwich at lunch, and sometimes even for dinner. Now, I won't touch it. Good thing the people we love aren't like that," Clarence said.

"People? Did you just compare human beings to bologna?" Coop chuckled.

"It's like this. In life, our favorite things are usually not something we let ourselves become too familiar with - favorite foods, vacation spots, clothes. If we did, they would lose their appeal. But, people? That's a whole different story, Coop. If someone is truly one of our favorites, we can't get familiar enough. They're like water. We can't survive without them. In fact, we become terrified of losing them. That's when you know you truly love someone."

"I'll be damned, Clarence. Someday, I'll learn not to doubt you, brother. That just made a whole lot of sense. For real…"

"What about Cara?" Clarence asked.

"Cara?"

"Yeah. Is she a pear to you? Or is she water?"

"She's more than water," Coop replied.

"More than water?" Clarence asked.

"Yup," Coop replied, thoroughly enjoying the rare reversal of roles.

"How so?"

"Before I met Cara, I didn't realize just how different the taste of water could be. It's like I had been drinking well water my whole life. Then, one day, I took a big sip of the purest spring water you could imagine. After that, I realized that I could never settle for well water ever again."

"Look at you, man. I love it," Clarence responded.

"You're not the only one with analogies, you know," Coop laughed.

"No, I guess I'm not. In fact, I couldn't have stated it any better myself."

31

By the time they had dropped Vance Gold off at the precinct to describe the mysterious Eugene Lankford to the department's sketch artist, Mick and Jason had already made a call to the county jail to meet with one of the inmates who was currently in the midst of a plea deal that would save him from going to prison.

Timothy "Tick" Braun was well acquainted with the two detectives. He had been the middleman for Vladimir Popov's prostitution ring that the late Ernie Page had used when Jason had first spotted the latter's odd meeting with Tick at Edgewater Park, where he witnessed their clandestine communication using a Styrofoam ice cream cup to set-up a date with one of Vlad's girls.

It was through Vlad's service that Ernie had met Stoya Fedorov, whom he quickly became obsessed with. His infatuation with the young Russian prostitute ultimately led to her demise, and Ernie's admission of the murder left many to assume that he was the EPK, despite his insistence to the contrary.

Facing a laundry list of charges after Ernie's death, Tick decided to do what he always did best – save his own skin. He gave the police everything he knew about Vlad and his prostitution ring, including the phone numbers of every client that visited him at Edgewater Park. That list produced a number of men from every walk of life, including a few police officers and even a local television evangelist.

In return for his cooperation, Tick was going to be spared a long prison sentence, as long as his information would help lead to a conviction for Vlad. That case was months away from going to trial, so in the meantime, Tick was being kept in protective custody at the county jail for precautionary measures. Vladimir Popov was not the type of man who would let a snitch survive very long in general population, especially one who was going to testify against him in court.

Jason and Mick figured that Tick might have something to offer regarding Vance Gold, or possibly even Vivian Tong. Despite being in custody, Tick was allowed visitors as part of his deal, and the officers at the jail had confirmed to the detectives that he had already been visited twice in the past two days by the same woman.

"Why you guys always harrassin' me?" Timothy "Tick" Braun asked Jason and Mick, who were seated across from him in a private visitation room at the county jail.

"Don't flatter yourself, Eminem. We aren't here to charge you with anything new. At least not yet," Mick replied.

"Eminem? Oh, cause I'm white, huh? Funny one, flatfoot, but I've been hearin' that lame ass joke since those whack ass shoes you wearin' were in style. You guys are always trippin' on me, man. I'm takin' care of my business, though, so I ain't even sweatin' you," Tick asserted in his usual rapid-fire cadence.

Tick was used to the Eminem comparison, and to an outsider, his dialect could easily have been misjudged as being a front. In reality, it was as authentic as his credibility was on some of the roughest streets in Cleveland.

"Nobody's harassing you, Tick," Jason chimed in.

"Then, why *are* you here?" Tick asked.

"We thought maybe you could help us out," Jason replied.

"Yo, haven't I already helped you enough?" Tick answered, referring to his cooperation in the prostitution case.

"Hey, don't forget that we helped you just as much, Dipshit. That's why you're facing probation and not the prospect of becoming somebody's wife in prison right now," Mick fired back.

"Yo, I ain't nobody's bitch," Tick responded angrily.

"That's not what I heard. What'd they call you in juvie? Wasn't it Tina?" Mick teased.

"That's not what yo wife called me," Tick countered.

"Alright, let's stop the pissing contest for now. What can you tell us about this guy? Do you know him?" Jason asked as he slid a picture of Vance Gold across the table to Tick.

Tick looked at the picture for a moment, which was a standard headshot from the Bureau of Motor Vehicles, before passing it back across the table.

"That depends. What you wanna know?" Tick asked as he looked up. He was not going to tip his hand one way or the other until he knew what was in it for him.

"I guess that depends on whether or not you know him," Mick replied.

"Man, I ain't sayin' another word until you offer me something good," Tick stated, holding his ground.

"How about you tell us what you want first?" Jason asked.

"A crib… You know, like for a baby."

Tick's words had caught the detectives off guard. They figured that he'd ask for time off his pending probation or maybe even better food while he was in jail, but definitely not a baby crib.

"A baby crib? For you? You're kidding, right?" Mick said in response.

"Not for me, Tubby. For my girl," Tick corrected.

"Your girlfriend? Or one you pay for?" Mick asked, never missing a chance to get a shot in at Tick.

"Kiss my ass, fat boy," Tick hissed.

"Why does your girlfriend need a crib, Tick?" Jason asked.

"She's pregnant…"

"Is the baby yours?" Jason asked.

"Yeah…"

"Is that who has been visiting you?" Jason asked.

"Yup," Tick replied.

"Can you just do us a favor and promise *not* to be a part of that child's life?" Mick asked shaking his head at the thought of Tick being a father.

"Keep crackin' jokes, Detective Donut, and you won't get a damn thing from me," Tick hissed.

"Ok, relax, Tick. Let me get this straight though. You want us to get your girlfriend a baby crib in exchange for the information you have on this man," Jason said, pointing at the photograph of Vance Gold.

"Yup, and a good one. Brand new. No Goodwill bullshit," Tick replied.

"Tick, if you have something on this guy that will help me out, I promise that I will buy you a brand new crib myself. But, it has to be credible and worth the time it's gonna take us to follow it up. That's the best I can do," Jason said, his voice firm, yet sincere.

"I'm down with that, and what I know about your boy Vance Gold is going to blow your mind," Tick said with a smile.

Jason looked at Mick, whose facial expression could not hide the fact that he was surprised that Tick knew Vance Gold's name. As a test, the detectives had made sure not to mention Vance's name when they gave Tick the photograph.

Mick was so confident that he had made a wager with Jason earlier that there was no way Tick would even know Vance Gold's name, let alone any credible information.

Jason had a feeling that the confident look on Tick's face was just the first sign that he had made the right decision in visiting the county jail.

"One more thing though," Tick said.

"What's that?" Jason replied.

"He needs to go. I ain't talking to him," Tick said, directing his gaze at Mick.

Jason looked at Mick to gauge his reaction, which appeared to be a strange combination of anger and joy.

"I'll gladly leave. I can't stand being in the same room as this little shit," Mick announced as he abruptly stood up and left the room.

Jason knew that Mick's reaction was just for show, as he would be able to watch from the other room anyways, but he used it as an opportunity to build a rapport with Tick.

"Wow, you must really have gotten under his skin," Jason said, shaking his head in disbelief.

"Yo, that guy sucks ass," Tick replied.

"Try working for him," Jason laughed, hoping to gain Tick's trust, but knowing that he would catch hell for it later.

After a moment, Jason leaned forward in his chair, confident that he had laid the groundwork for a beneficial conversation.

"Okay, Tick. Convince me to go buy that crib…"

32

"So, how'd I do? Was it a great surprise date?" Cara asked Coop as they plopped down on his living room couch.

The couple had just returned from a long day at Cedar Point, where they hit almost every roller coaster in the park, ate lots of delicious park food, and even convinced Clarence to get up on stage during one of the park's shows.

Aside from a few people asking for autographs, Coop managed to enjoy the day in relative anonymity, which was an added bonus. One of Cara's fears when she planned the trip was that people would recognize Coop and constantly pester him for autographs and pictures.

"It was, by far, the coolest date any girl has ever planned for me. Y'all know how to build an amusement park up here, for sure. Thank you," Coop replied before giving her a soft kiss.

"How's your elbow feeling?"

"Not gonna lie; it's been better."

"Can I get you a bag of ice?" Cara asked.

"That'd be amazing. Thank you kindly," Coop replied.

"I'll be right back," she said before giving him a peck on the cheek.

"Hey, can you get me something to drink too?" Coop called out as she walked away.

"You read my mind. I was going to grab us a couple beers!"

"Now we're talking!"

After Cara had exited into the kitchen, Coop pulled out the small container that he had been sneaking pain pills from throughout the day and popped one in his mouth. He was almost completely out of his original prescription and hoped that he would be able to get a refill at his appointment the next day.

He still felt ashamed hiding the pills from her, as his injury more than called for such strong pain relievers, but he was also still afraid that she would think he was being weak. Even though it seemed at times like they had been together forever, they were still only a month into their relationship, and he was still trying to put forth the best image of himself.

"Here you go, ice and an ice-cold beer," Cara announced as she placed the large bag of crushed ice under his elbow.

"You're the best," Coop said before swallowing his pill down with a swig of beer.

"Back atcha," she replied as she sat next to him, a beer in her hand as well.

"So, what was your favorite ride today?" Coop asked.

"Definitely this one," Cara said as she pulled out the photo keychain they had purchased after their ride on the Millennium Force.

"That was mine too, despite the fact there's photographic evidence of my terrified face," Coop laughed.

"If you're ever mean to me, that's the first thing I'm selling to

CMZ," Cara teased.

"Damn, girl, are you blackmailing me?"

"Just stating facts…"

"I suppose I better never hurt you then. Good thing for me is that I wasn't planning on it," Coop whispered in her ear before kissing her softly.

"You know what my other favorite part was?" Cara asked.

"How could it be anything other than Clarence getting pulled up on that stage to hula hoop?"

"Oh. My. God. Yes! He was so mad at you for volunteering him!" Cara recalled, trying to hold in her laughter.

"He sure was having a blood rush, wasn't he?" Coop laughed.

"Having a blood rush? You really need to get me a Southern slang translation dictionary, Coop," Cara chuckled.

"Like I've said before, it's not my fault you Yankees don't know how to talk right," Coop countered.

"I will say, though, I find your Southern accent extremely sexy, despite all the weird expressions." Cara locked eyes with Coop.

"Well, ma'am, that's just how I was raised," Coop replied, playing up his accent.

"Keep talking…"

"Ashes to ashes and dust to dust, if it wasn't for women like you our hearts would rust," Coop responded, really laying it on thick for effect.

"Oh my…" Cara whispered, biting her lip as she straddled Coop.

"Give me some sugar, girl," Coop whispered softly in her ear, his lips gently making contact, causing Cara to let out a hushed moan.

"Keep doing that and I'll give you whatever you want," she whispered.

"I should probably move this bag," Coop said, referring to the ice under his elbow.

"You're not going to move anything..."

"Oh yeah?"

"Nope. You're going to stay right where you are and ice that elbow, but here's what I'm going to do," Cara replied before whispering in his ear exactly what she intended to do to him.

"Oh my..."

33

"Hello?" said Hannah LaMarca as she answered her cell phone. It was early in the morning on Thursday and she was about to leave her apartment to pick up coffee and meet Jason at Edgewater Park, just as they had the day before.

"Hey, it's Jason. Listen, I can't meet up this morning. I hope that you haven't left yet."

"No, I haven't left yet. Is everything okay?"

"Yeah, absolutely. I just didn't want to waste your time today. Unfortunately, I don't really have anything new to discuss," Jason responded. It was a lie, of course. He could have told her about his meeting with Tick, but Mick's insistence that he not talk to anyone about the case was weighing heavily on his mind.

"Oh, I understand. I don't have anything new either, unfortunately," Hannah said in return. She was also guilty of not being completely honest, as she had made a discovery of her own not long after she left Jason at the marina.

"Listen, I'll call you if anything big changes. Until then, I don't see any reason to meet up. I hope you understand," Jason said, hoping that she would.

"Yes, of course. I'll do the same on my end. Take care, Detective Knox," Hannah responded.

After the two ended their call, Hannah sat down at her kitchen table and looked at the notes she had compiled the day before. She wondered if Jason had come across the same information that she was able to get from a few of her most trusted sources.

"Vance Gold" was written across the top of the page on the legal pad in front of her. After learning about Vivian's employment as a dancer for Vance, Hannah made a call to a person that she was certain would be able to give her some background on the owner of Buddy's Speakeasy.

Hannah had met Cliff Scriven, a longtime private investigator in the Cleveland area, when a colleague at Channel One News gave her his business card. At the time, Hannah was close to breaking a big story on a city councilman, who had allegedly been stealing money from a fundraising campaign intended to fix up the very neighborhood he was supposed to be representing.

She had hit a roadblock in her investigation and was not getting any help from the police who were running an investigation of their own and did not want the story leaked until they had concluded their work. That is when she was given Cliff Scriven's business card by a fellow reporter who insisted that the private investigator was a relentless bulldog, willing to do whatever it took to complete the job.

"Scriv", as he preferred to be addressed, was a former detective who had grown tired of the politics associated with his former career. After 10 years on the force, he turned in his badge and went into business for himself. He found it liberating to be able to do the same type of investigative work that he loved, but without all of the restrictions that he had to adhere to as a member of the police department.

Within a week of meeting with Hannah, Scriv managed to provide her with a bevy of evidence that enabled her to break the story before the police had even finished their investigation. Thanks to Hannah's bombshell story, aided by Scriv's outstanding investigative work, the councilman resigned. Ironically, the police ended up using the evidence that Hannah and Scriv had provided in her story to charge him with theft, and he was sentenced to a short prison term in return.

From that point on, Hannah would hire Scriv to help her dig up information when investigating a big story. The television station, knowing that it was worth every penny, would even pay for his work on Hannah's behalf.

It did not take Scriv long after receiving a phone call from Hannah that morning to dig up some preliminary background information on Vance Gold. As a private investigator, he had access to databases that Hannah did not, so he was able to provide her far more information than a Google search would.

"Based on the information I was able to find, it appears that Mr. Gold did not have very many financial records on file with the state prior to opening up Buddy's Speakeasy," Scriv had informed Hannah over the phone on Wednesday afternoon.

"That's odd. Makes you wonder how he got the money to open up the club then," she replied, knowing that her trusted PI likely already had the answer.

"My thoughts exactly, which is why I ran him through the criminal database. While he didn't have much of a record, he did have a drug arrest in 1994, but charges were never filed. Sadly, that's not uncommon though. I could write a book on why so many drug arrests never make it to trial," he informed her.

"I bet you could. Sounds like Vance likely used drug money to open up Buddy's, but he had to have had someone else backing him. There's no way that the city would allow someone to open up a strip club without more of a documented background, right?" Hannah questioned.

"Bingo. That's why I did a little more digging on the permit that was filed with the city for the club. It appears that Vance has a silent partner, a guy by the name of Salvatore Furio," Scriv replied.

"What's his claim to fame?"

"Turns out that Mr. Furio is the owner of a local construction business, mostly commercial projects and stuff like that. Seems to be a pretty successful business too."

"Why would he want to be a partner in a strip club then?"

"That I'm not so sure of yet. My guess is he's either an old pal of Vance Gold or he's looking for a place to launder some of his construction money. Maybe both even. A lot of construction owners like this Furio guy are always looking for ways to increase their profits, so they hire illegal aliens to work for pennies and launder the excess," Scriv said in return.

"What better place to funnel money through than a cash business like a strip club, I suppose," Hannah said.

"It's certainly a plausible theory, but also very hard to prove. That's why you'll often come across construction company owners who also own places like car washes and bars. As long as they have a loyal bookkeeper willing to sign off on their quarterly statements and help them cook their books, they tend to get away with it too. Most of the time when these guys get busted for money laundering, it's because of a disgruntled bookkeeper who blows the whistle on them in exchange for immunity," Scriv chuckled.

"What a world we live in, right? The bookkeeper gets paid handsomely for breaking the law, then avoids jail time by being a snitch and biting the hand that feeds him," Hannah sighed.

"That right there is why I left the force, Hannah. I got tired of watching guilty people walk free after playing the game," he replied.

"Well, I for one am extremely grateful that you did. You're the best, Scriv."

"I aim to please. I will make it a priority to look into both Vance

Gold and this Furio guy some more over the next few days. I'll be in touch."

As Hannah perused the notes in front of her, she wondered what Scriv would be able to dig up. Whatever it was, she was certain that it would help her get that much closer to what happened to Vivian Tong.

34

"Hey, you know it's almost seven, right?" Erica Knox asked her husband, who had just finished a set of curls in the makeshift workout room located in the basement of their modest West Park home. In reality, their home gym only consisted of an old treadmill, a flat bench, and an assortment of dumbbells. The only time Jason even used it was when something heavy was weighing on his mind, and on this morning he had already been at it for an hour.

"Yeah, I'm heading in a little later today. I have a feeling I won't be home until later," Jason replied, his grey t-shirt wet around the collar with sweat.

"Is everything okay?" Erica asked, knowing the answer but hoping he would let her inside whatever battle was brewing in his head.

"I wish I could say yes, but I can't…"

"Anything you want to talk about?" she asked.

"In time, but I need to wrap my own brain around it first," he answered, which was actually far more of a response than he would typically give his wife.

Erica recognized this as well and fought the urge to press him any further as he began another set of curls.

"Well, I'm making breakfast and Gabby will be up soon. Hopefully, you can join us when you're done in here," she said before leaving.

Jason nodded and smiled as he carried out the rest of his set, alternating arms with each repetition. He had been replaying the conversation that he had the day prior with Tick ever since he left him at the county jail, and he could not shake the sick feeling that had accompanied him after his visit.

"Alright, Tick, you have me to yourself. What can you tell me about Vance Gold?" Jason had asked.

"Yo, that dude is a cockroach," Tick replied.

"How so?"

"You ever tried to kill a cockroach, detective?"

"Yes, they're hard to kill, for sure. They say that they can survive a nuclear blast too. I know that I've stomped on a lot of roaches, only to watch them scurry away as if I never touched them," Jason chuckled.

"Exactly. Yo, I've lived in a lot of dumps. Roaches everywhere, man. Did you know that if a cockroach loses its freakin' leg it can grow a new one? That's twisted, man."

"Okay, but I hope you have more than that for me. Saying a guy like Vance is like a cockroach isn't exactly a revelation," Jason stated.

"Yo, relax... I'm gettin' there," Tick laughed.

"I hope so, if you want that crib for your baby mama."

"There's been lots of dudes that wanted that guy dead," Tick said as he pointed at the picture.

"Were you one of them?"

"Yo, I ain't tryin' to catch a rap, so let's just say I wouldn't send no flowers to the funeral if someone capped his ass."

"Fair enough. He doesn't seem like a very tough guy. If so many people wanted this guy dead, then why's he still alive?

"Cuz he's protected."

"Protected? Like by the mafia?"

"Nope…"

"Then by who?"

"Information…"

"Information?"

"Yup…"

"Okay, you have to elaborate, Tick. I'm done with the guessing game."

"Listen, that dude right there used to be a drug dealer. One of the biggest slingers in the state."

"Used to be?"

"Yup. He got out the game after…"

Tick paused before continuing his sentence, looked around as if to make sure that nobody would be able to hear the next words that came out of his mouth, and then gestured for Jason to come in closer.

When Detective Jason Knox heard the words that Tick whispered into his ear, he recoiled and immediately felt dizzy.

Tick, obviously proud of himself for causing such a strong reaction, leaned back in his chair and chuckled. Jason looked back at Tick and gave him a look of disbelief.

"Yo… You still glad you came to see me, Detective?"

35

"Well, Coop, it looks like the swelling has reduced significantly. You must be icing properly, which is a good thing," Dr. Craig Mueller said to his most famous patient who was seated on an examination table.

"One thing a pitcher is good at is icing the old wing, Doc," Coop replied.

"You'd be surprised at how many aren't though. The good news for you is that it looks like we will be able to schedule a date for the surgery. How's your pain level these days?"

"I'm not gonna lie, Doc, it's been pretty brutal…"

"Are you taking the pain meds from Dr. Shaia?" Dr. Mueller asked.

"Yessir, in fact I only have a couple left. I was hoping you could give me some more, to be honest," Coop replied.

"I see. It says here in his notes that he gave you thirty of the

Percocet on Sunday, which means that you've been popping those at a pretty good rate the past four days, five counting today," Dr. Mueller stated, looking up at Coop, who was visibly embarrassed.

"Yessir, I know, but I really feel like I need them," Coop insisted.

"Well, that's normal, Coop. The reason being is that while effective, they are also extremely addictive. My only concern is that you will become too dependent on them," Dr. Mueller said in return.

"I understand, Doc, but you don't have to worry about that. I've been on them before over the years, and it was never a problem," Coop said, hoping that Dr. Mueller would not see through his lie.

In reality, Coop had used every pain pill he could get his hands on not long after moving to Cleveland. Being a professional athlete had a lot of perks, one of which was being able to walk into a doctor's office and obtain a script for pain meds without any questions being asked.

One doctor, in particular, had even asked for his autograph after writing him a script for 180 pain pills. Coop had lied to him that the real reason he retired early was due to shoulder, elbow, and back pain; but he did not want that information to be made public in the event he ever wanted to make a comeback.

In reality, his body was healthy back then. It was his mind and his heart that were in constant pain, and the pills had helped him cope with both. Between the sudden loss of his father during Hurricane Katrina and the void that retiring early from baseball had created, Coop wanted nothing more than to spend his days holed up in his penthouse, numb to the world around him.

For the first week that he started combining pain pills and alcohol, he managed to keep it relatively under control. In the weeks that followed, he began taking more pills each day and washing them down with even more alcohol.

If his best friend from childhood, Cash Sterling, hadn't flown up to Cleveland and staged an intervention, Coop was pretty certain that he would have ended up dead.

Cash not only stayed with him for an entire week, disposing of all of the remaining pills and helping Coop get through the horrendous side effects that accompanied his withdrawal from the narcotics, but he also managed to do so without anyone else finding out.

For that, Coop was eternally grateful and promised his oldest friend that he would not have a relapse. He kept that promise too, until suffering the elbow injury on Sunday.

This time it was different, Coop had convinced himself. Besides, he had Cara in his life now, and her presence was reason enough to keep it under control. Aside from that awful display on the balcony Monday night, Coop had only taken the pills when he needed them.

The only issue was that he had built up a strong tolerance to the pills before Cash intervened, and one pill was often not enough. Coop hoped that Dr. Mueller would somehow understand that, even though he had not given him any specific reason to do so.

"Here's what I can do, Coop. I would like to do this surgery as soon as possible, likely this Monday. In the meantime, I'm going to give you a script for 20 more pills, but only to be taken as directed, which means no more than four per day. How does that sound?" Dr. Mueller asked.

"Yessir, that sounds perfect, Doc. I truly appreciate it. So, Monday's the day?" Coop replied.

"Assuming that you don't suffer any more setbacks, we will go in there on Monday and begin the process of getting you back on that mound," Dr. Mueller confirmed as he handed Coop the prescription he had just written.

"Sounds like a plan, Doc. Thanks again."

"The ladies in the front will give you the instructions that you'll need to follow before Monday, when to stop eating and stuff like that. Standard pre-op stuff. I'm assuming you'll have someone to help look after you after the surgery?"

"Yessir, Cara will be around to help. I already teased her that I was going to get a bell and ring it whenever I needed something," Coop laughed.

"Ah, yes, that was the young lady who was in here with you the other day. Seems like a sweet girl. You better hang on to that one," Dr. Mueller said with a wink.

"Yessir, she certainly is a keeper. Thanks again, Doc. I'll see you on Monday, I suppose," Coop replied as he exited the office.

As he watched Cooper Madison exit his office, Dr. Mueller hoped that he had made the right decision by giving him more pain meds, but he also knew that someone of Coop's size would require more of any medication for it to be effective. Regardless, Coop just needed to get through until Monday, after which he was about to experience a whole new level of pain as he began his recovery from the surgery.

36

"Carebear!" Lucy Eckert shrieked as Cara emerged from her last class of the day at Cleveland State University's tallest building, Rhodes Tower, located in the heart of the campus.

"Lulu!" Cara shouted in return as the two best friends embraced each other.

"So, how's Coop's arm?" Lucy asked. She had not spoken with Cara since the night of the game, aside from the text messages they exchanged to set up their lunch date.

"Not good, but he just texted me a little bit ago to tell me that they are going to operate on Monday, which is a lot sooner than they expected. So, that's a good thing, I guess."

"How long until he can play again?"

"Probably not until the end of next season, if he's lucky. He could miss an entire year though."

"How's he doing with that?"

"Well, at first, it was awful. But, the past few days he seems to be doing better. Listen, Clarence is waiting for us over there; we can talk more over lunch," Cara said as she nodded to the Escalade that was parked along Chester Avenue.

Clarence was assuming his usual post near the rear passenger door, vigilant as always. Coop had already been dropped off back at the Westcott Hotel after his appointment and a quick stop at the drug store to fill his prescription when Clarence received a call from Cara regarding her lunch date with Lucy.

"I wish I had Clarence to drive me around in an Escalade and protect me," Lucy chuckled as they made their way to the oversized SUV.

"Well, you do today," Cara replied with a laugh as Clarence opened the rear passenger door for them.

"Hi Clarence, I'm Lucy. We never got to formally meet at the game on Sunday," she introduced herself. The last time that Cara and Lucy met up for dinner, it was Grace Brooks who had escorted them.

"Pleasure to meet you, Lucy," Clarence replied, shaking her hand.

"Hi, Clarence. Thanks for adding a stop to our itinerary today," Cara said as she gave him a hug.

"Hey, I work for you, remember," Clarence chuckled before he closed the rear door and made his way to the driver's seat. "Alpha, this is Baker. Departing CSU now, over... Correct. I will confirm our arrival. Baker out..." Clarence stated after pressing the button on his earpiece. On the other end of his communication was his wife, Evelynn, who was the daytime dispatcher for CW Security Solutions.

"This is so cool," Lucy whispered into Cara's ear after witnessing Clarence's military-style exchange.

Cara just smiled, remembering how she felt the same way the first time she rode with Clarence.

"Coop had Simon arrange for the two of you to eat lunch at Pier W today," Clarence informed his passengers as the SUV pulled onto Chester Avenue, referring to the concierge at the Westcott, Simon Craig.

"No. Way. Pier W? I've always wanted to eat there!" Lucy declared.

"Me too! I've only heard about how amazing it is," Cara added, smiling at Lucy.

Located in nearby Lakewood, Pier W had become one of the top restaurants in Cleveland, year in and year out, since opening its doors in 1965. The building itself had received as much praise as the fine dining menu that was offered inside over the years. Perched high above Lake Erie on a cliff, the restaurant was designed to resemble the hull of an ocean liner overlooking the lake and providing a magnificent view of the Cleveland skyline.

"First Lola, and now Pier W? I hope you realize how lucky you are," Lucy said to Cara.

"I definitely do," Cara replied, smiling back at her friend as the SUV rolled along.

37

"Absolutely, send him on up. Thanks, Simon," Coop said before hanging up his phone.

Simon Craig, the Westcott's concierge, had just informed Coop that he had a visitor asking to come up to see him. After hearing the name, Coop made Simon repeat himself just to make sure that he had heard the name correctly.

Coop stood outside the entrance of his suite so that he could greet his agent, Todd "T-Squared" Taylor, when he exited the vintage Otis Birdcage elevator that had just stopped on the 11th floor. He chuckled upon hearing Todd's loud voice before the elevator had even opened all the way.

"Thanks, Manny! Best elevator operator in the C-L-E right there!" Todd exclaimed, giving Manny a fist bump on his way out. It always amused Coop how Todd would "talk-up" every person he interacted with from professional athletes to elevator operators.

"Be careful, Manny, he might try and take a cut of your next paycheck!" Coop laughed as the elevator doors closed.

"Hey, that's not a bad idea," Todd mused as he dramatically dropped his shoulder bag and held his hands up in the air, as if to announce his presence.

"You could've called first, you know, T! What if I wouldn't have been home?" Coop greeted his agent and friend.

"You kiddin' me? You're always home. You're like a damn recluse!" Todd teased his top client before giving him a big hug.

"I will have you know, sir, that I went to Cedar Point yesterday *and* to the doctor today," Coop informed in a sarcastically prideful tone.

"Look at you, Coop! What's on tap tomorrow? Grocery store? Trip to the zoo?"

"Ah, I see you've still got jokes. Now, get your loud ass in here before we get a noise complaint from the floor below," Coop replied, gesturing for Todd to enter.

"You know, if every place in Cleveland looked like this, I might consider moving here," Todd announced as he entered Coop's luxurious penthouse suite.

"T, you and I both know that this city is not big enough for that ego of yours. Pop a squat on the couch. Can I get you a beer or something?"

"Yessir, I'll take a cold one," Todd replied as he sat down. Coop, after taking another pain pill, reemerged from the kitchen and handed his agent and friend an ice-cold mug of beer.

"Frosted glass and everything? Now we're talkin'! Much obliged," Todd said as he took a swig.

"So, what brings you to Cleveland?"

"Are you kidding me? To see my number one client!"

"Long layover, huh?" Coop chuckled in return.

"Well, that too. I have a bit until I have to be back at the airport though," Todd smiled and raised his glass for a toast.

"Regardless of the reason, it's great to see you, brother," Coop replied as he raised his mug in return.

"So, what'd the doc say this morning?" Todd asked.

"Well, he said that things are progressing better than expected, so Monday is the day."

"Wow, that was fast! Hey, that means you'll be back on the bump that much quicker too."

"It's gonna be a long time, regardless. Not lookin' forward to the rehab, that's for sure," Coop said, shaking his head at the thought.

"True, but your boy T-Squared already has a surprise for you to help out during your recovery," Todd hinted.

"Please don't tell me you're gonna dress up like a nurse and take care of me," Coop joked.

"Well, I would, but you know I hate the way I look in white…"

"So, what is it?"

"If I told you, then it wouldn't be a surprise, Coop. Trust me, you'll love it!"

"Why is it that every time you tell me that, I get a feeling that I won't?" Coop laughed.

"Because you have no faith in your boy, that's why. So, where's Cara?" Todd asked.

"She's out to eat with her friend, Lucy. You met her at the game on Sunday."

"Oh yeah, petite girl with strawberry blonde hair. One of Cara's brothers was trying to hit on her all night, but she didn't seem to notice.

Poor kid," Todd replied, shaking his head.

"That's the one, and you must be referring to Christopher. He's the one in the Navy. Cara said that he always seemed to have a thing for Lucy, but never would admit it. Probably for the best; he already shipped off back to Japan."

"Speaking of shipping off, I have to let you know what your surprise is. I can't hold it in anymore," Todd said, sitting forward as he prepared to deliver the news.

"Man, you made it an entire minute. Good job," Coop joked.

"So, here's the deal. You... Me... Cara... Joy... Nokomis, baby!" Todd said, dramatically.

"Nokomis?" Coop replied, puzzled.

"Florida, baby! You remember that beach house near Sarasota that I've been telling you about? Well, I bought it! As soon as you get past the first few days of your surgery, I'm going to fly you and Cara down for as long as you'd like. Private jet, of course. What better way to recover than on the beach?"

"Wow, I really appreciate that, T. But, I'm not sure that I am gonna be much of a houseguest after surgery..."

"Nonsense! It's the perfect place for you to relax. The house is on Casey Key Road and has its own private stretch of beach. You know who else lives there?" Todd did not wait for Coop to answer. "Stephen King and Martina Navratilova. It's going to be my own little piece of paradise when I need to get away."

"Well, it does sound nice, and I'm sure that Cara can talk to her professors about missing some classes," Coop relented.

"Atta boy! It'll be great, plus Joy will love to meet Cara. I think they'll hit it off," Todd said.

"Sounds like a plan then. Listen, I really appreciate you doing all this."

"Hey, you know you're more than just a client. You're family. I want to make sure that you get this recovery off to a great start," Todd said, his voice sincere.

Coop smiled and nodded in return.

"Listen, I gotta run. Flight leaves in about an hour," Todd said as he stood up.

"Always on the move," Coop laughed as he stood and gave Todd a typical "Bro Hug" - a handshake coupled with a one-armed hug.

"On my way to Boston. Gotta meet with my newest shortstop to discuss his upcoming free agency. I think I can get Cincy to quadruple what Boston was paying him."

"That's why you're the best, T!" Coop said as he escorted Todd to the elevator.

"T-Squared always wins, baby!"

38

Commander Mick McCarthy sat nervously inside the office of Chief Horace "HoJo" Johnston at Cleveland's downtown police headquarters. Earlier in the day, HoJo phoned Mick and invited him to come to his office and provide an update on the Vivian Tong case.

As Mick waited for the Chief to arrive, he sat in silence, fully aware that his upcoming conversation would not be a pleasant one. HoJo was not a patient man, and the lack of progress in the case was certain to test the little bit of patience that he did possess.

"Commander, welcome," HoJo announced as he entered his spacious office and immediately took a seat behind his massive oak desk.

Mick stood up when HoJo entered and greeted his boss, who did not even make eye contact in return. Instead, he opened up the manila file folder that sat on his desk and began perusing the notes that Mick had provided.

"Is this it?" the Chief asked, finally looking up at Mick.

"Yes, Chief, but we are still following up on some of those items listed. We have a feeling that Mr. Gold has not been as forthcoming as he could be, so we are still looking into him as a possible suspect," Mick responded.

HoJo said nothing in return, as if he was waiting for more.

"Sir, we have reason to believe that Mr. Gold may be withholding information about the man who allegedly left the club with Vivian that night," Mick continued, hoping that he was not doing himself more harm than good.

"Ah, yes. The mysterious Eugene Lankford, who apparently does not exist," HoJo replied sarcastically.

"Yes, that is correct, sir. We'd really like to be able to lean on Vance Gold, if possible, but if we aren't charging him with anything then he will just stay quiet," Mick added.

"So, Commander, what is it that you're asking of me?" HoJo asked.

"Well, sir, we were hoping that we could get a warrant to search Buddy's Speakeasy," Mick stated.

"A warrant? On what grounds? Believe it or not, Mr. Gold has kept himself clean, aside from the occasional bar fight. How could I possibly get a judge to issue a warrant?" HoJo asked in return.

"What if I said that we could get enough evidence to convince the judge that illegal prostitution is occurring at the club?" Mick asked, which seemed to catch the chief's attention.

"Go on…" HoJo replied.

"We want to send in an undercover officer and see if he can't get one of the girls to offer sex in exchange for money. We were thinking that one of the guys from our department would be a perfect choice. He's middle-aged, a little overweight, and balding," Mick added.

"Is he your twin brother?" HoJo asked, chuckling at his own joke.

"No sir, he's nowhere near as handsome as me, but he does fit the bill of a typical John," Mick replied with a wry smile.

"This officer, has he ever worked in that area of town? Is there any chance that someone might recognize him?" HoJo asked.

"No sir, in fact, he was just transferred to our precinct from the airport office to work in the evidence room. He hasn't been on the streets for years," Mick responded.

"I'm assuming that he will be wearing a wire?"

"Correct. He will have one of our pagers on his belt that will transmit to our van outside. In the event he is successful, we will enter the premises and make an arrest," Mick asserted.

"And what if he doesn't get a girl to offer sex in exchange for money? I have to assume that Vance Gold is smart enough to know that he's under our microscope right now. He probably has instructed his girls to be cautious, assuming he is guilty of it in the first place," HoJo countered.

"Well, sir, we feel that it's our best bet."

"When do you plan on making this sting happen?" HoJo asked.

"Tomorrow night. It's a Friday and also pay day for most people. He'll have his full roster on stage, which means that there will be more girls for our guy to talk to," Mick responded.

"What about the alcohol factor? Don't you think that if this guy is in the club and not having any alcohol that it will raise suspicions?" HoJo pressed.

"I agree, and that's why he's going to tell his server that he's a recovering alcoholic."

"Fair enough. Here's what I will do. I'm going to go ahead and approve this operation, but only for three hours, max. I'll approve $300 cash for your guy to take inside, but if he can't get something in the amount of time I have allotted, then he leaves. Understand?" HoJo instructed.

"Loud and clear, sir. Thank you, Chief," Mick replied, a sense of relief in his voice.

"Don't thank me yet, Commander. If this little operation falls through, I'm going to seriously reconsider assigning the Vivian Tong case to someone else. We need to put this case to bed before the public finds out that somebody is out there falsely claiming to be the EPK," HoJo warned.

"I understand, sir," Mick replied.

39

"So, how was lunch with Lucy?" Coop asked Cara as she joined him on his balcony. It was early in the afternoon and Coop had been icing his arm off and on outside ever since Todd had left. The ice, along with two more pills, helped ease the pain.

"It was amazing, and I have a new favorite restaurant now, thanks to you." Cara leaned over and gave Coop a soft kiss.

"I've only heard good things about Pier W," Coop replied.

"You mean you've never been there?"

"Nope..."

"How'd you know how to choose it for us then?"

"I asked Simon..."

"Of course," Cara laughed.

"So, what's new with Lucy?" Coop asked.

"Well, she started dating a guy that she goes to college with at

Oberlin. His name is Colton."

"Colton?"

"Yup, Colton Finn. I guess his family owns a chain of furniture stores in upstate New York."

"Colton Finn? Did his parents not like him?" Coop chuckled.

"I can't speak for his parents, but I sure know that Lucy does. She couldn't stop talking about him. I guess he's a Cinema Studies major and hopes to be a filmmaker someday."

"Cinema Studies major? So, basically he watches movies for four years and gets a degree?" Coop asked, a look of disbelief on his face.

"Well, I think it's a little more complicated than that. You know Oberlin is one of the hardest schools to get into, right?" Cara responded.

"I find that hard to believe if they give out degrees for watching movies," Coop replied, shaking his head.

"Give him a chance, Mister Judgey McJudgerton," Cara said as she playfully hit Coop on the shoulder.

"I'll try…"

"Good, because she really seems happy, and that makes me happy."

"You know what makes me happy?" Coop asked.

"What?"

"You."

"You're sweet."

"Just speaking the truth…"

"That's one of my favorite parts of you, I think," Cara smiled.

"That I'm sweet?"

"I guess it's more that you're not afraid to be sweet."

"You make it easy to be that way," Coop said in return.

"Can I ask you a question?"

"Always."

"What's your favorite part about me?" Cara asked, reluctant to make eye contact with Coop.

"Well, that's just it, I can't pick just one," Coop replied.

"That's such a copout, Madison."

"No, ma'am, it sure is not," Coop said in response, using his best Southern charm for effect. "Will you let me explain?"

"Only if it's good…"

"It's like this, Miz Cara Knox… Each day I'm with you I find a new favorite part of you…"

"Go on…" Cara said, warming to the notion that his response was going to be a suitable one.

"Take yesterday, for example, when you planned the Cedar Point trip. I did *not* see that coming, and if you would've asked me yesterday what my favorite part about you was, I would've said your spontaneity."

"What about today?"

"Not gonna lie. Seeing how happy you were for your best friend made you even more attractive to me, even though she's dating a guy with a weird name," Coop replied sincerely, despite the humorous jab at Colton Finn.

"It is kind of an odd name, isn't it?" Cara laughed.

"Good thing his mommy and daddy have money, I suppose,"

Coop said, shaking his head.

"From what Lucy told me, Finn Furniture is quite the profitable business."

"Well, that's good. At least he has a fallback in the rare instance his film career doesn't take off."

"He could always make his own Finn Furniture commercials too."

"Best of both worlds!" Coop laughed.

"Must be nice to know that you could inherit a successful business from your parents as a fallback plan."

"Yeah…" Coop said as he directed his gaze towards the lake. Cara could tell that he was likely thinking of his own parents. Whenever the topic of parents came up she would often notice that it triggered this response.

"Thinking about your parents?" she asked, causing Coop to snap out of his trance.

"Yeah," he replied.

"What do you miss the most about them?"

"Besides everything?"

"Including everything," Cara replied, reaching her hand across and placing it on his.

"It's crazy, you know, my momma's been gone for so long now, but it doesn't seem like it at times. I suppose I miss her strength the most, even before the cancer. She was a tough cookie."

"Was she strict?" Cara asked.

"She was definitely the enforcer, for sure, and she knew how to swing a wooden spoon when I got out of line. My daddy was the big softie," Coop chuckled.

"Wooden spoon, huh? My mom's weapon of choice was a rubber spatula. Christopher and Johnny got that the most though."

"Isn't it funny how sometimes it's the moms that tend to be the disciplinarians?" Coop asked.

"I think it's because they tend to be around the kids more, at least for our parents generation."

"Yeah, boy, she ran a tight ship, my momma. But, she was also the first to hug me and tell me that she loved me when I needed it." Coop paused before asking, "You know what else I miss?"

"What's that?" Cara asked.

"How much she loved the holidays, especially Christmas. My momma loved Christmas. She'd start decorating the day after Thanksgiving. Our house would look like something out of a catalogue by the time she was done."

"I bet it was beautiful."

"It was…"

"What about your dad? What do you miss most about him?" Cara asked, her thumb gently caressing the top of Coop's hand.

"Talking…"

"About what?"

"Everything. Anything. Even after I left home we spoke on the phone at least once or twice a day. He was the best listener. He knew when to let me just vent and when I needed advice, whether I wanted it or not. I suppose I miss that the most. I would give anything to call him again," Coop said, his eyes misty.

"I'm sorry…"

"Don't be. He would've loved you, you know. They both would've," Coop said as he reached across his body and covered her hand.

"I wish that I could have met them."

"Me too…"

"Aren't you going to ask me?" Cara asked.

"Ask you what?" Coop replied, puzzled.

"What I miss most about my parents."

"Uh, Cara, your parents are still alive, girl."

"True, but the people you know as Charlie and Joanne Knox are definitely not the same parents I knew growing up," Cara said, her eyes now beginning to well up.

"Tell me," Coop said, squeezing her hand.

"My dad used to be the best hugger in the world. Even when most of my friends were going through the phase where they never wanted to be around their parents, I always looked forward to getting a hug from him. He would always scoop me up and spin me around, even when I was a teenager. I guess I miss that the most."

"I'm sure he does too. Being in that chair has probably robbed him of a lot of things like that. What about your momma?"

"My mom, well, she's a whole different story. Before my dad's accident she used to always sing. I mean all the time, and she has an amazing voice. She'd sing songs to us at bedtime, while she was doing the dishes, and even when we'd be driving somewhere in the car. I guess I miss hearing her sing the most. I don't think I've heard her sing a song since the accident," Cara replied, a tear travelling down her cheek.

"Really? I never would've guessed that Joanne could sing. What kind of songs did she belt out?" Coop asked.

"All sorts, but my favorite was when she would sing Joni Mitchell. She would sing 'River' all the time, so much that for a while I hated that song. Now I would give anything just to hear her sing it one more time like she used to..."

"That's a beautiful song. My momma would actually play that when she was decorating the house at Christmas," Coop said smiling.

In that moment Cara realized that she had been afraid to say the words she wanted to, but something about the moment gave her the courage to lay it all on the line.

"I love you," she said, the tears still present on her cheeks, her eyes locked in on Coop's.

As soon as the words left her mouth the apprehension that had been keeping her from saying them up until this point came back over her like a wave crashing on the shores of the lake that they were enjoying in the distance.

Cara fully expected Coop's reaction to be one of trepidation and shock. They had not been together long enough by most anyone's standards to make such a declaration, which is why his response was that much more surprising.

"I love you too," he replied, his steely eyes locked in on hers. "I've been wanting to say those words to you for weeks, but I was afraid that I'd scare you off."

"You'd have to do way more than that to get rid of me," she laughed, more out of relief than humor. Cara felt as if a weight had been lifted off her.

"Well then, now that we got that out of the way, I should warn you of something," Coop said, his voice serious.

"Oh no... What? You're making me nervous."

"It's just that now that I've said it once, I'm going to say it over and over again. I'm going to say it every chance I get, so that you'll never, ever have to wonder again."

Coop's declaration made Cara smile through the tears that were now streaming down her face, and as she placed her other hand on top of his, she spoke the only word that could adequately sum up what she was feeling in that moment.

"Nothing…"

40

Detective Jason Knox waited in his unmarked cruiser at Edgewater Park Marina in the same spot that he used to meet with Hannah LaMarca.

"So, exactly why the hell are we meeting here?" Mick said as he opened the passenger door and took a seat next to Jason.

"You'll understand in a minute. Here, I splurged and got you a coffee," Jason said as he handed his commander a paper cup of decaffeinated coffee with artificial sweetener.

"This isn't decaf, is it?" Mick asked. His doctor had made him cut back his caffeine intake recently, much to his chagrin.

"Doctor's orders," Jason smiled.

"I swear, I have the ugliest 'work wife' on the force," Mick sneered.

"Just take a sip and pretend it's the good stuff, big guy."

"I'm not telling you what my doctor says anymore. I can't live like this," Mick stated as he took a reluctant sip.

"So... I brought you here because I have a bit of a confession to make, and I didn't want to do it where somebody might overhear," Jason said, his tone serious.

"Are *you* the EPK? I mean, I had my suspicions, but..." Mick asked, feigning shock.

"Very funny. Actually... It's about what I told you after I met with Tick yesterday," Jason replied, his tone hesitant.

"You mean when you said that what he whispered in your ear was nothing of substance? Yeah, I knew you were lying," Mick said matter-of-factly.

"You did? Why didn't you say something then?"

"Well, first of all, you're an awful liar. Secondly, I saw your face on the monitor when you heard whatever it was he told you. You can't fake that kind of reaction, so I knew whatever he said was something big," Mick announced proudly.

"If you knew it was something big, why didn't you ask me later then?"

"Well, I wanted to. Trust me, it's been killing me to know, but I also trust you more than anyone in this department. I figured if you weren't ready to tell me yesterday, then it meant you needed some time to process it. That's why I gave you the morning off. When you called and asked to meet with me here, I knew you were ready to talk," Mick replied.

"Wow, I'm truly impressed. I don't think that I could have waited like that."

"That's why they pay me the millions of dollars that they do," Mick chuckled.

"That doesn't even include your endorsement money, does it?"

Jason played along.

"No, but those guys pay me in donuts…"

"Alright, I've stalled long enough. Are you ready to hear what your pal, Tick, had to say?" Jason asked as he sat upright, ready to deliver the goods.

"I'm ready…"

Jason proceeded to inform Mick what Tick had told him about Vance Gold, that he was a former drug dealer who was protected over the years from ever facing any of the usual consequences that accompanied slinging dope.

"Protected? Is he connected to the mob or something?" Mick asked.

"Yeah, he sure is connected, but not to the mob," Jason replied, stringing Mick along.

"Then to who?"

"HoJo…"

Jason let his words hang for a moment and studied Mick's reaction, which started off as a look of shock, but quickly turned to one of amusement.

"HoJo? Chief Horace Johnston? Our Chief? Get the hell outta here!" Mick laughed, obviously not buying it.

"Hear me out now," Jason said as he produced a folded up piece of paper and began to open it.

"What's that?" Mick asked, nodding to the paper.

"When Tick pulled me in close, he said that the reason Vance Gold had always been untouchable was because of his relationship with HoJo. He slipped this paper into my hand and told me that everything I needed to know was on this paper," Jason said as he waved the paper, now fully opened.

"Well, what's it say?" Mick asked, his smile gone.

"Aside from all the spelling and grammar errors, it reads like something out of a movie," Jason chuckled before continuing. "Apparently, when HoJo was a young detective he collared Vance for selling dope. That's when Vance somehow convinced HoJo that he'd be more valuable to him if he were on the street and working as a C.I. instead of sitting in a prison cell. Apparently, HoJo bought what he was selling and spent the next two decades building his career off of the collars he made thanks to Vance's tips."

"Okay, now I'm intrigued. So, if this is true, Vance got to continue slinging dope on the same streets that HoJo was supposedly cleaning up. Only, he was really only getting rid of Vance's competition, in exchange for the information. While that sounds like a match made in heaven, what about all the other cops and detectives working the same beat?" Mick asked, hoping that what he was hearing was not true.

"According to this letter, HoJo had a few cops in on it too. They made sure to not only protect Vance, but also all of his grunts working out in the streets, including a young Timothy Braun."

"Tick? No shit... Really?"

"Yup..."

"So, I'm assuming Tick had a falling-out with Vance. Otherwise, why would he be talking?" Mick asked.

"That's the thing, Tick's letter doesn't mention anything like that. If revenge is the motive, he's not saying it," Jason replied.

"We need to find out what that motive is. Maybe we can persuade Tick some more?"

"I hope so. I was thinking that we get back over to see him sooner rather than later."

"There's another thing that's bothering me about this whole situation though. When I met with HoJo earlier today, he actually green-lighted our operation on Vance Gold's club for tomorrow night."

"The one with the guy from the airport station?" Jason asked.

"Yup. I was shocked he approved it, but even more so now. If he really is connected to Vance, why would he be okay with us setting up a sting?"

Jason pondered Mick's question for a moment before a smile formed across his face as he shook his head in disbelief.

"What?" Mick asked.

"Think about it – what better way for HoJo to eliminate Vance Gold as a suspect than to conduct a sting?" Jason replied.

"Jesus Christ, you're right. He's gonna tip Vance off so that everyone at the club will be on their best behavior, and it'll all be caught on surveillance tape," Mick added.

"Which will be all that he needs to get us to remove Vance as a person of interest; therefore, taking the heat off of both of them," Jason confirmed.

"HoJo's no dummy, that's for sure. He's testing us too. If we call the sting off he'll know that we discovered some new information, which we obviously couldn't tell him about, and then he'll suspect that we know about his relationship with Vance."

"Not to mention, we don't know who else in the department might be on Team HoJo, so we have to play along during the sting. Part of me wants to go straight to Internal Affairs and spill the beans, but we don't have anything other than Tick's word," Jason said, shaking his head.

"It'd be career suicide, for both of us. We need to go along with the sting tomorrow and act as upset as everyone when we get nothing on tape. Knowing HoJo, he's probably got people listening around the precinct, so we need to be aware of that," Mick replied.

"We just need to assume that someone's always listening or watching. Phone calls, emails, text messages. All of it."

"Agreed, now let's get going before we raise any red flags. Thanks again for the fake coffee, Knox," Mick said as he exited the car, purposely leaving the coffee cup on Jason's dashboard.

"You'll thank me later, after your next doctor visit!" Jason called out, chuckling. He was thankful for Mick, now more than ever.

41

"I hope I didn't keep you waiting too long," Hannah LaMarca said to the man who had just stood up and greeted her with a friendly hug.

"Not at all. Have a seat," Cliff Scriven said as he gestured to the corner table he had reserved for them at Guarino's Restaurant in Cleveland's Little Italy neighborhood.

Built in 1918, Guarino's was one of the city's oldest restaurants, and it also happened to be Scriv's favorite. The traditional Italian food and ability to hold a private conversation while tucked away in the corner of the Cleveland institution made the former prohibition era speakeasy a great choice for meetings like the one he was about to have with Hannah.

"I'm assuming you have good news for me. You always pick Guarino's when you have something juicy," Hannah said, her tone discreet so that only Scriv could hear her.

"You know me too well, Hannah. Here, take a look," he replied as he handed her a manila envelope.

Inside were a stack of color photographs and a single sheet of paper, with the one on top showing a middle-aged man exiting a construction site. Hannah recognized that the man was Salvatore Furio, as she had searched his name online after talking with Scriv.

"You can look through those later, obviously," Scriv said in reference to the photographs.

"Of course," Hannah replied, knowing that despite the intimate setting of the restaurant, discretion was a must.

"The write-up is more of what you're after anyways," he said as he nodded to the single sheet of typed paper.

Hannah tucked the photographs back into the envelope and began to read what Scriv had compiled for her. After she had finished, she looked up at the veteran investigator, a look of disbelief on her face.

"Not what you expected?" Scriv asked with a wry smile.

"No... I'm a little in shock here, and that's saying a lot..."

"Well, I still have a long way to go before I can actually prove my theory, but I wanted to share what I had thus far. I know that it's just a few photos, but I don't think that it was a coincidence that they met with each other," he asserted.

"Those pictures were taken today, right?" Hannah asked.

"Yup, just this afternoon. Barely had time to print them."

"How'd you know that they were going to be there?" Hannah whispered.

"I didn't. To be honest, it was dumb luck. I was only there to get a couple shots of the number of workers he had at the job site when the meeting took place," Scriv replied.

"Talk about being in the right place at the right time. What is he building there anyway?" Hannah asked.

"Apparently, they're converting all the land by the old steelyard into a big retail shopping area, and he managed to get one of the bids. Big money project too."

"By the looks of what you have here, its even bigger money than what's being reported, at least for him," Hannah mused.

"That I'm fairly certain of. I counted more than thirty workers, but the financial records show that less than half of that number is getting a weekly paycheck."

"So, just to make sure I understand how this all works," Hannah said, her voice barely above a whisper, "If most of the guys working for him are undocumented, how is he making money if he has to pay them under the table?"

"It's pretty simple, actually. He has a dozen guys on his payroll, all of which are legal citizens, so it's all above the board. However, within that group of legal workers, you'll likely find a handful of guys who are making five or six times what everyone else is. Those guys have two responsibilities with that extra income after they cash those fat checks each week. One is to take a small portion of it and pay the undocumented workers in cash – usually for far less than minimum wage. The next is to take the rest of the excess cash and, for the lack of a better term, invest it back into their boss's cash business," Scriv explained, using the packets from the sugar caddie located on their table to provide a visual.

"It's so simple that it's genius. He's getting almost twice the work force for pennies on the dollar, and Uncle Sam gets his cut, eliminating the red flags. What keeps his rivals from turning him in though?" Hannah asked.

"Let's just say that our guy isn't the only construction company owner partaking in this practice. In fact, in the grand scheme of things that go on in that world, it's really not even that big of a deal. Those guys all have dirt on each other, and they also know that if they say something that they'll be the next to fall."

"It's so crazy to think that this stuff goes on, not to mention that it's so prevalent. What's even crazier is who met him there," Hannah said, still trying to grasp everything that had been thrown at her.

"I wish that I could say it was just a coincidence, but I don't want to insult your intelligence. Proving that there's something more to it will be the tough part," Scriv replied.

"Do I have your permission to share this information with someone else who's helping me?" Hannah asked.

"Hey, I work for you. My job is just to gather the information. Who you share it with is up to you. I would just be very careful and make sure that it's someone you can trust. If this shakes out the way I think it's going to, things could get dicey. There's a lot of money and egos at stake," Scriv answered, his tone serious.

42

It was a crisp fall evening and Cara had suggested that they take advantage of the limited time they had left before Coop's surgery by visiting Crocker Park, the west side of Cleveland's newest shopping attraction. Upscale outdoor shopping malls like Crocker Park, located in the suburb of Westlake, had begun to gain popularity across the country since the late 1990's in comparison to traditional malls.

The couple walked hand in hand down one of Crocker's pedestrian walkways, which resembled that of a small town center. Grace Brooks followed the pair closely enough to intervene, if needed, but kept enough distance so that they could feel as if they were there alone. Even though Coop was one of the most recognizable professional athletes during his time in Chicago, he still had been able to keep somewhat of a low profile in Cleveland, aside from the occasional fan or paparazzo.

"Do you want to go in Barnes and Noble?" Cara asked, referring to the bookstore chain's two-story building located at the corner of Crocker's main intersection.

"Fine by me. I've been meaning to get a couple books for after my surgery. I'm thinking I'll get that new *Da Vinci Code* book everyone is talking about," Coop replied.

"Oh, you'll love it!"

"You read it?"

"Yup, and all of Dan Brown's other books. You should get *Angels and Demons* too. That's his first Robert Langdon book."

"So, I should read that one first?"

"Not necessarily. Even though Robert Langdon is the main character in both books, they're really stand-alone stories. I personally liked *The Da Vinci Code* better, so I'd read that one first, but you should get both."

"Are there any pictures in them? I don't read so good unless there's pictures. Remember, I didn't go to college," Coop said with a smile.

"You're such a dork," Cara said as Coop opened the door for her to enter the massive bookstore.

Despite the fact that it had been out since January of that year, *The Da Vinci Code* had a huge display that greeted the pair as soon as they entered the store. Along with multiple copies of the New York Times bestseller were copies of the author's other three books, including *Angels and Demons*.

"Well, that didn't take long," Coop said as he picked up a hardcover of *The Da Vinci Code*. "Damn, girl, this book is enormous. I don't know if I've ever read anything this long before."

"Trust me, you won't want to put it down. Here, take this one too," Cara said as she handed him a paperback of *Angels and Demons*.

"Good Lord, does he get paid by how many pages he writes?" Coop chuckled as he held up both books, each of which surpassed 600 pages in length.

"You'll thank me later. Come on, I want to head over to the biography section," Cara said as she gestured for him to follow.

"Anything in particular?" Coop asked.

"Yeah, there's this book called *Marley and Me* that I've been dying to read."

"Is that the sequel to *A Christmas Carol*?" Coop deadpanned, feigning ignorance in his usual self-deprecating way.

"No, goofball. It was actually written by a journalist about the dog that he and his family raised. It's supposed to be amazing, but everyone keeps telling me that I'll cry a lot during it too."

"Hope Marley had a different fate than Old Yeller did…"

Cara rolled her eyes at Coop's quip.

"What? Hey, that book scarred me as a child," he chuckled.

"Oh. My. God."

"What?" Coop asked as he tried to see what had caused such a reaction from Cara, who had stopped dead in her tracks right next to the "Sports" section. When he directed his gaze upon the end cap shelves and discovered what book she was reaching for, his heart sank.

"How did I *not* know about this?" Cara asked as she grabbed a copy of *Cooper Madison: Life of a Pitcher*. On the cover was a picture of a very young Coop delivering a pitch in his Chicago Cubs uniform.

"Probably because it was not exactly on the bestsellers list," Coop sighed.

"Who is Angela Colabianchi?" Cara asked, referring to the author's name.

"She was my high school English teacher. When Todd convinced me to have a book written about me, I told him only if Miz C was the author. She was my favorite teacher, and I knew that she had always talked about wanting to get a book published," Coop replied.

"Oh my God, that is too sweet! Did you help her write it?" Cara asked.

"If by help you mean I answered questions that she asked me, then yeah. She did all the actual typing. I was only 21 when it was written, so I kinda felt weird about the whole process of having a book written about me."

"Well, I'm totally buying this too. In fact, I'm even going to read this one before *Marley and Me*," Cara declared as she grabbed a copy of the latter from an end cap display that featured a picture of the now-famous yellow Labrador retriever.

"What would the chances be that I could talk you out of that decision? I'm willing to resort to bribery," Coop asked, his face strained.

"Oh stop, it can't be that bad."

"The book itself is actually fine. Miz C did a great job. It's more about some of the things in there…"

"Well, now I want to read it even more," Cara laughed.

"Only if you promise that you won't hold anything I may have said in there against me," Coop said, telling more than asking. It was very apparent that his pained expression was not an act.

"Holy crap! You're seriously stressed out over this, aren't you?" Cara said, putting her hand on the side of Coop's cheek.

"It's just… Well, I was young and dumb when it was written. I was a much different person then… I just don't want you to think any less of me or get weirded out."

"I think you're being ridiculous, but I promise I won't," Cara reassured him. "C'mon, let's go pay for these. I told Grace that we'd probably get ice cream on the way home."

43

"You better answer that," Erica Knox whispered to her husband, whose phone had been buzzing on the nightstand intermittently for the past five minutes.

"It's probably just Mick... He can wait," Jason said as he resumed kissing Erica's neck, reluctant to let a phone call interrupt his chance at a rare morning of lovemaking.

"Babe... As much as I don't want you to stop... Whoever is trying to call you must think it's pretty important..." she replied through bated breath.

"Fine..." Jason groaned in surrender as he grabbed his phone off of the bedside table.

Erica studied her husband as the screen of the department-issued cell phone illuminated his chest in the otherwise dark bedroom. Even though she had seen every inch of his body during their life together, she still loved to look. Jason had always taken tremendous care of his body, even more so since his father's accident, and he looked ten years younger than he was.

As she watched him exit the room to take the call, Erica knew that any chance of continuing what had been a steamy start to the day just followed her husband into the hallway. This was not the first, nor would it be the last time that Jason's job had interrupted an intimate moment. It had also ripped him away from family dinners, parties, holidays, and even her cousin's wedding.

While she always tried her best to make Jason feel supported, there were times that she failed to grin and bear it. To his credit, Jason would always let her vent at him, and he would never take it personally. He knew that being the wife of a cop was hard enough, and the erratic schedule that came with his promotion to detective made it that much tougher on her.

Despite it all, Erica and Jason always worked through it, and they never went to bed angry at each other. Jason knew better than most, thanks to some of the tragic things he had seen on the job, that he should never take a day with his family for granted.

Jason would go out of his way on his days off to make up for the time he was away, and he never missed a chance to tell his wife and daughter that he loved them. That, and the fact that Jason was an amazing father to Gabby, made the tough times bearable for Erica. He had exceeded her expectations as a father, and she loved that Gabby worshipped her daddy.

When Jason returned to the bedroom he looked defeated. After quietly closing the door behind him, he placed his phone back on the nightstand and sat on the edge of the bed.

"What's the matter, Babe?" Erica asked as she sat up.

"Nothing good, that's for sure," he replied.

"Is there another body?"

"Yeah..."

"Oh no... Like the last one?" she asked, referring to Vivian Tong.

"No... Actually, it's not even a woman this time," Jason replied, the tone of his voice indicating that he was having a hard time believing what he was saying.

"Well, that's a good thing, in a way. Isn't it? I mean, that means it wasn't the EPK, at least. Right?"

Jason looked at his wife and in that moment wished that he could confirm her hopes. Unfortunately, he knew that was not going to be possible.

When he had finally taken the phone call from Mick, Jason had no idea what his commander had in store for him. In fact, he made Mick repeat himself three different times just to make sure that he had heard him correctly.

"Where's the body at?" Jason had asked after finally accepting that what Mick had said was, in fact, reality.

"In his car... Outside of Buddy's Speakeasy," Mick had replied.

"You're kidding, right? Has anyone located Vance Gold for questioning?"

"Didn't need to. He's the one who called it in. He's at the precinct now."

"In custody? Do you think he was involved?" Jason asked, trying to make sense of the situation.

"Not in custody. More for his protection... And, for questioning. He was pretty shaken up. Get down to the station as quick as you can and I'll fill you in some more," Mick replied.

Jason had stood in the hallway for a few minutes before

returning to his wife in the bedroom. Now, as he sat next to her on the bed, he found himself struggling to respond.

"The body... Mick said that it had 'EPK' carved into the torso." His tone was a defeated one.

"Oh my God... Did they identify the victim yet?" she asked, her voice trembling.

"No, not yet," Jason lied.

"This victim... Was he found at Edgewater too, like the others?"

"No, the body was found in the victim's car outside a strip club. Apparently, there was a note left at the scene too."

"A note? What did it say?"

"I don't know yet. Mick said he would show it to me at the station," Jason replied, which was the truth. However, in addition to the identity of the victim, he also decided to leave out the one detail about the note that Mick had divulged.

He just was not ready to tell his wife that Chief Horace "HoJo" Johnston had been strangled to death as he sat in the driver's seat of his own car, and he certainly was not ready to tell her that the note left at the scene had been addressed to Detective Jason Knox.

44

Coop studied Cara's face from her spot on the couch as she read the biography of his life that she had insisted on purchasing the night before. She appeared to be about halfway through the book, which she had started reading after they had returned from their trip to Crocker Park and subsequently resumed as soon as she awoke.

As Coop pretended to read his copy of *The Da Vinci Code* from the other end of the couch, he tried to get a read on what she was thinking as she digested everything about his life that he had yet to tell her himself. It was not a fear of her discovering some sort of salacious details that he was purposely keeping from her, but rather that she would learn that the Cooper Madison that she had come to know was actually a version of himself that he had worked hard to leave in the pages of that very book.

It was not until he read the book himself, and some of the subsequent reviews that followed its publication, that he realized just how out of touch with reality he had become.

"Cooper Madison, while arguably the best pitcher in baseball at the tender age of 21, reveals nothing in this book to disprove the notion

that he is just another narcissistic, arrogant athlete," was how one reviewer had started his scathing critique of the book at the time.

For Coop, the hardest part about reading that reviewer's harsh words was realizing that they were mostly true. Like most other professional athletes, Coop carried himself with an air of arrogance, but being called a narcissist was tough for him to swallow.

His father, Jeffrey Madison, and his late mother, Kelsey, had raised him from an early age to be humble. Staying humble proved to be a challenge, especially as he grew older. As a teenager, it was not uncommon for opponents from other teams, and sometimes even their parents, to ask him for an autograph after a game. One time, an umpire even asked him to sign a game ball.

Beginning in Coop's sophomore year of high school, Jeffrey started to provide his son with opportunities that would help counteract those types of experiences. One of those opportunities became a monthly ritual when they would drive three hours north to Jackson, Mississippi, and volunteer at the Ronald McDonald House.

Coop would play games with the children who stayed there, most of which had a serious illness, while Jeffrey would cook breakfast for their families. It was a practice that Coop continued throughout his years in Chicago, and he would even hold an annual benefit for the charity. Those monthly interactions would always leave Coop feeling a little guilty that God had given him so much, yet had stripped so many other kids of their health. One patient, in particular, had a major impact on Coop's life.

Lane Bixby was not the skinny teenager staying at the Ronald McDonald House during treatments when he first came to know Cooper Madison. Before leukemia had ravaged his body, Lane had been Coop's teammate on a big time high school summer league baseball team.

The team, the Mississippi Crawdads, was a collection of all of the top baseball talent in the state who spent the summer of 1994 travelling all over the country and playing in baseball tournaments. The manager of the team had made his fortune in the trucking industry and wanted his son, who was a very good outfielder from Hattiesburg, to experience baseball at the highest level.

Everything about the Crawdads was first class. They had a custom charter bus, complete with the Crawdads logo, to shuttle them all over the country. They stayed at four-star hotels, were outfitted with multiple uniforms, and experienced what travelling like a pro felt like. They even had a support team consisting of a nutritionist, an athletic trainer, a strength coach, and a sports psychologist that travelled with them. To avoid any infractions that may affect their amateur status, every player on the team was required to pay a small fee, but it was not even close to covering the cost of that summer's activities.

The team backed up their big time reputations with big time play on the diamond, winning nearly every tournament they entered that summer. Seven of the players from that team would go on to be drafted out of high school, including three future major leaguers, with three more being drafted after college.

Coop was shocked and saddened that December when the Crawdads manager, Brent Bixby, informed him that the summer of 1994 would be the first and last season that the Mississippi Crawdads would field a team. Brent's son, the talented outfielder who had helped them win so many games that summer, had been diagnosed with an aggressive form of Acute Lymphoblastic Leukemia.

Coop was shocked and saddened by the news because Lane Bixby had probably been in the best shape out of anyone on that team. He had a lean, muscular build and was by far the fastest player on the team. He had received interest as an outfielder from both college and pro scouts and seemed to be destined for baseball greatness.

Since keeping in touch with friends from across the state was much more difficult in 1994, Coop did not hear much about Lane after the initial phone call. However, he knew that it was not good.

It was not until March of 1995 that he realized just how serious Lane's battle had become. Jeffrey and Coop had just arrived for their monthly visit to the Ronald McDonald House and were preparing breakfast when a frail-looking young man was wheeled into the kitchen area. Coop immediately recognized the man pushing the wheelchair as Brent Bixby, but the weakened form sitting in the chair looked nothing like his son, the speedy outfielder that could track down any fly ball hit in his direction.

"Cuppah?" asked the surprised Brent Bixby with his thick Mississippi-born accent.

"Yessir, Coach Bixby. Hello, Lane. How y'all been?" Coop could not stop those last words before they had escaped from his mouth.

He felt ashamed and ridiculous for asking a question where the answer was so plainly obvious, which is why Lane Bixby's response caught him off-guard.

"Livin' the dream, Coop! Doc's got me on this diet plan though. Only problem is that I think it's working a little too well," Lane said with a smile.

Though he was never a big kid, Lane was now at least fifty pounds lighter than the last time Coop saw him that summer. His eyes had dark circles around them, and his head was covered in a Mississippi State stocking cap.

Brent Bixby smiled down at his son, who tried his best to make everyone else feel at ease, despite his weakened condition. Coop did not know how to respond to Lane's joke, so he had just stood there, tongue-tied. Thankfully, Lane rescued him.

"Hey, Pops, would you mind if I had Coop push me around a bit?" Lane asked his father.

"I suppose I can do that. That'll give Jeffrey and I a chance to catch up," Bruce replied as he patted Coop on the shoulder before making his way over to join Jeffrey in the kitchen.

"You wanna go outside?" Coop asked his old teammate.

"Hell yeah, I do…"

Coop, who during his time as a volunteer had pushed numerous wheelchair-bound guests around the Ronald McDonald House, had a surreal feeling as he wheeled Lane outside. It was a beautiful early spring morning, the kind of day when only a few stray clouds would occasionally cross paths with the Mississippi sunshine.

"You know I'm dying, right?" Lane asked after a minute of walking.

Coop stopped pushing. The question had caught him off guard.

"Jesus Christ, Coop, don't stop pushing me! This is the closest I get to feeling fast anymore," Lane demanded, the humor in his voice contradicting the actual words.

"I… I'm sorry, Lane…" was all that Coop had managed to reply as he resumed pushing the wheelchair.

"Don't be, Coop. It's not every day that somebody just blurts out to you that they're dying."

"Isn't there anything they can do? I mean, how do they know for sure?" Coop asked.

"Well, it's in my blood, so there's nothing they can remove to get rid of it. I guess being fast was always my thing, you know, so I figured I might as well die fast too," Lane replied, finishing his sentence with a chuckle.

"How are you laughing at that? Aren't you pissed off?"

"Of course I'm pissed off, Coop. Shit, I'm furious! I guess it's just my way of dealing…"

"How'd you know you were sick? I mean, you were fine this summer. What happened?" Coop asked.

"Around the start of school I was tired. I'm talking like all the time. I thought maybe I had mono or something. Then I started to get these bruises all over my body. I looked like I got beat up. That's when my parents took me to the hospital. They ran some tests and told me it was an aggressive form of Leukemia," Lane replied.

"Did you go through chemo?"

"Yessir, and all sorts of other drugs and treatments. The chemo made my hair fall out, but I think I make bald look good," Lane said as he removed his hat, revealing his bare head.

"Damn straight, you do," Coop agreed, trying to match his friend's upbeat demeanor.

Lane laughed at Coop's sudden change in tone, but that laughter soon changed to a wheezing coughing attack that made him begin to gasp for air.

"I hate… When that… Happens…" Lane managed to say.

"Do you need anything? I can get you some water."

"I think… We should probably… Head back in…"

Coop nodded and pushed Lane back inside to the kitchen of the Ronald McDonald House, where their fathers were busy making enough pancakes for everyone in the house.

"He didn't try to talk you into taking him to the bar, did he?" Brent asked jokingly.

"We tried, but I guess the bar is closed on Sunday," Coop replied with a smile.

When it came time for Coop and Jeffrey to leave, they made the rounds and said goodbye to everyone that was still in the kitchen. When Coop approached Lane he gave his former teammate a hug as he tried to hold back the tears that were welling up in his eyes.

Coop knew that there was a good chance that he would never see Lane again, and he was not doing a good job of hiding his emotions. Lane, who also had tears in his eyes, squeezed Coop as he whispered something that Coop would never forget.

"You're going to change the game someday, Coop. When you do, promise me that you won't forget me…"

"I promise, Lane…" Coop managed to reply as he squeezed his friend.

"Good, cause I'll be watching…"

Before starting the long drive back to Pass Christian, as Coop buckled himself into the passenger seat, he broke down sobbing. Jeffrey, with tears in his eyes, reached over and hugged his son. He told him that he loved him and that it was okay to cry.

Lane Bixby passed away two weeks later with his parents by his side. That season, Coop began drawing Lane's initials in the dirt on the mound with his finger before each game he pitched.

It was a practice that he continued in every single game he pitched from that point forward, keeping the promise that he had made to his friend that morning at the Ronald McDonald House.

45

Detective Jason Knox entered the 1st District precinct, which was typically bursting at the seams with conversation, only to find the mood of the entire headquarters quiet and somber. The news of Chief Horace "HoJo" Johnston's death had obviously made its way through the station, and despite however those under his command felt about the chief, losing one of their own was always devastating to a police department.

Upon seeing Jason's arrival, Mick signaled for him to enter his office, where he was already meeting with a few of the other detectives.

"Alright, why don't you guys get started on what you need to do while I fill Knox in on what we have so far," Mick instructed the detectives, all of whom looked as if they were still in shock.

"Jesus, Mick. What the hell happened?" Jason asked as he closed the door.

"Well, here's what we know so far. Apparently, according to Vance, HoJo met with him last night at Buddy's Speakeasy just after they were closed."

"Did he say why?" Jason asked.

"Actually, he did. He even said that HoJo had warned him about the sting too," Mick replied, shaking his head in disbelief.

"Holy shit. Tick was right after all. Who else knows this?"

"Just me, and now, you. He told me in the car on our way back from the scene, and I instructed him not to talk to anyone else except you and me."

"That's good. Did he see who did it?" Jason asked.

"No. According to Vance, HoJo left the club after their meeting. Vance said he locked the place up and when he went out to his car about fifteen minutes later, he noticed that HoJo's vehicle was still in the lot. He thought that maybe the chief was waiting to tell him something else, so he approached the vehicle. That's when he found his body," Mick responded.

"You said he was apparently strangled to death?"

"Whoever did this was a pro, Knox. It appears that the killer was likely hiding in the back seat of HoJo's car, and when the chief got in, the guy put one of those heavy duty zip ties over his head and pulled it tight enough to cut off his air supply."

"Jesus... A zip tie?"

"Yup. It's likely that he already had it connected in a loop before placing it over his head. Then, he just had to pull it tight. The kind he used are the ones that are used on jobsites to hold bundles of heavy materials in place, so there was no way that HoJo would've been able to break it," Mick confirmed.

"That's just... Awful."

"We're checking for prints and fibers, but I can already tell you that they won't find anything. This guy obviously knew what he was doing."

"What about the note? You said it was addressed to me?" Jason asked.

"It's at the lab for testing too, but I took a picture of it for you," Mick answered as he produced a letter-sized photograph from the manila folder on his desk and handed it to Jason.

The photograph revealed a one-sided, handwritten note on unlined white paper. The words were written neatly in red ink, and Jason felt chills down his spine as he read what they said.

Detective Knox,

You can thank me later for helping you purge the department of your arrogant and corrupt chief. You don't know me, but I know you.

I've been watching your progress on the EPK case very closely. I'm sure that you know now, more than ever, that Ernie Page was NOT the EPK.

You may not agree with my tactics, but everything I've done so far has been to expose the hypocrisy of our justice system. I'm viewed as a criminal and a monster, while the real criminals like Chief Johnston continued to walk the streets of our once fine city.

If you and your fellow officers fail to uphold your obligation to rid the city of the evil that has consumed it, your hands will be stained with the same blood as Chief Johnston's, and I will have no choice but to ensure that you meet the same fate as my other victims.

I will NOT stop until justice has been served. There will be more victims, but I can promise you that none of them will be innocent.

DO YOUR JOB, DETECTIVE KNOX!!

-EPK

After he finished reading, Jason looked at Mick and exhaled the deep breath that he had been holding in the entire time it had taken him to digest what the note said.

"As soon as I read the note I sent a patrol car to keep an eye on your house, just in case," Mick informed his top detective.

"Yeah, I saw him when I left. I figured that it wasn't a good sign. Erica called me when she saw the car too. I told her it was just a precaution because of my role in the EPK case," Jason replied.

"Did you tell her it was HoJo?"

"No... Not yet. I wanted to see you first. Besides, she'll freak when she finds out."

"I guess that's one of the benefits of being divorced. Hell, Zoey's probably going to be disappointed when she finds out that I wasn't the victim," Mick chuckled.

"I'm assuming Nancy has been informed?" Jason asked, referring to Chief Johnston's wife of nearly 30 years.

"Yeah, Captain Petro is with her now. We will have round-the-clock eyes on her house as well. I don't know if the fact that they never had any kids makes it easier or harder on Nancy. As big of a prick as HoJo was, Nancy was always a saint, and now she's all alone."

46

"So, I'm more than halfway done with your book," Cara declared as she joined Coop on the balcony.

"Oh, lovely... That's just... Great..." Coop replied, his words drenched in sarcasm.

"Oh stop it, its way better than you made it out to be. I really enjoyed learning more about your childhood, and especially about your mom. You could tell how much you really loved her. Oh, and the story about your friend, Lane? Oh my gosh, I was practically sobbing!" Cara effused.

"Yeah, well, the book kinda goes downhill from there. Don't say I didn't warn you," Coop replied.

"For the sake of fairness, I will say that you were definitely a very confident young man, especially in the chapters about your first year in the minors. But, who could blame you, Coop? You were a millionaire at 18 whose high school teachers used to ask you for an autograph. How could anyone possibly experience things like that and not get a big head?" Cara said, her voice sincere.

"You're sweet, but you're also just being nice. I can't even read those words without feeling sick. Like when I said that I should've been able to skip the minor leagues and go straight to the Bigs because I was wasting my talent with a bunch of has-beens and never-will-be's? God, it makes me want to puke."

"I agree, that part was definitely difficult to read, but-"

"Or when I said that if the team was smart, they would stop spending money on free agents and start investing it into research on how to *clone* me? Or, better yet, when I guaranteed at least five championships by the time I was 25? Take your pick, Cara, it's all just the words of a complete and utter asshole!" Coop was now standing with both hands squeezing the concrete wall of the balcony.

Cara moved closer to Coop and wrapped her arms around him from behind, placing her cheek against his strong back. She could feel his heart pounding, and he was breathing heavily.

"Listen, I'll stop reading the book, okay? I honestly didn't think that it would bother you this much," she whispered, hoping to calm him down.

"No, you can finish it. I'm sorry... I just have worked really hard to bury that version of me forever. I even tried once to buy every copy left for sale, but they just kept making more."

"Well, I've already finished the part that I really wanted to know more about, anyway," Cara said. "Besides, shouldn't it tell you something that I would have never guessed in a million years that you were such..."

"An asshole?" Coop laughed. "Go ahead, you can say it."

"Actually, I was going to say such a great example of someone who realized that he needed to change."

"Oh..."

"I didn't fall in love with the 21-year-old boy in that book," Cara said as she squeezed him even tighter. "I fell in love with the man who my arms are wrapped around at this very moment."

Coop slowly turned around so that he could face her. He pulled her in closely and kissed the top of her head.

The moment did not last long, however, as his cell phone began to vibrate on top of the outdoor table it was resting on. Cara turned around and picked up the phone.

"I wonder why my brother's calling you?" she said before she answered the phone. "Hello, Detective Jason Knox, you've reached Coop's phone, this is your favorite sister speaking."

Cara's humorous way of answering the phone made Coop smile, but the face she made once she heard whatever it was that her oldest brother had to say gave him pause.

"Absolutely, yes... No, I don't think it's a problem, at all... He's standing right here with me out on the balcony. We'll be here all day, too... Okay, yup... Hey, Jason? Be careful, okay?" Cara ended the call and set Coop's phone back down on the table.

"Is everything okay?" Coop asked.

"To be honest, I'm not sure, but I need to apologize ahead of time in case you have a problem with it. And, it's totally okay if you do, because it's your place, but I just didn't know what to say when he asked..."

"Cara, relax, okay? Just tell me what you need, girl!" Coop laughed as he placed his hands on her shoulders.

"Jason said that somebody killed a cop," Cara replied.

"A cop? Oh my God, that's awful."

"Then he asked if there was any way that Erica and Gabby could stay here with us tonight. Maybe even for a few days. He said that he's worried that someone may be targeting cops and that you live in the safest place in the city, and he just wants to make sure that they're safe. He said that he'd sleep at his house, but he wants them somewhere else, so I told him they could. I'm sorry, I know that I should have asked you first, but I immediately thought about someone possibly hurting Gabby and I just..." Cara replied, her words fast and filled with emotion.

"Whoa, slow down, now... Of course they can stay here, and Jason can too."

"Are you sure? I feel bad for not asking first..."

"Hell yes, I'm sure. We have plenty of room and they can stay as long as they'd like. I'll have Clarence pick them up and drive them over here. Will you call Erica from your phone and let her know to expect him?"

Before he could pick up his phone to call Clarence, Cara grabbed Coop, and then hugged and kissed him. "Thank you. This means so much to me," she said.

"It's really not a big deal. Besides, I think it'll be fun to have Gabby around. I'll call Simon and have him order some groceries to be delivered too."

"How did I get so lucky? You're amazing."

"Nonsense. I'm the lucky one..."

47

"I can't believe that we just left the precinct in the middle of the murder investigation of our own police chief to come *here*. Why the hell do I listen to you? This is nuts," Mick said in disbelief as he exited the passenger seat of Jason's unmarked cruiser.

Jason did not respond. He knew that his boss was trying to convince himself that this was a good idea more than anything else as they made their way into the apartment building that was located on East 4th Street in downtown Cleveland.

Just minutes after their meeting in Mick's office, Jason had received a call from Hannah LaMarca and excused himself to the hallway.

"So, is it true? HoJo was murdered?" Hannah had immediately asked.

"You know that I can't answer that yet," Jason replied. The department had yet to release an official statement, but like in many other cases, news of HoJo's death had obviously been leaked.

"Well, that wasn't exactly a denial."

Jason said nothing in return.

"Listen, I came across some information that I think you need to see. I wasn't going to show you it until I had some time to vet it, but if what I'm hearing about HoJo is true, you're going to want to see this," Hannah said.

"When can we meet?" Jason replied.

"Meet me at my apartment as soon as you can get here. I'll text you the address."

"We'll leave right now."

"*We'll*?" Hannah asked, puzzled.

"I'm bringing Mick."

"Does he know that you've been talking to me? I thought you were trying to avoid that?"

"No, but he's about to find out. It's for the best. I'll tell you more in person," Jason said.

"Fine by me, see you soon."

Jason returned to Mick's office after the phone call and told him everything in regards to his secretive meetings with Hannah LaMarca. While Mick was not thrilled about being kept in the dark, he also told Jason that he understood why.

As they stood outside Hannah's apartment door, Mick reiterated his disbelief at the current situation. "Tell me again why the *hell* it is that I listen to you?"

"Because you love me," Jason replied with a smirk.

Just then the door opened and Hannah LaMarca, who was dressed down in a pair of sweatpants and a fleece jacket, greeted the detectives. Her hair was up in a ponytail, and even though she looked as if she had been up all night, she still was stunning.

"Come on in, fellas. I have a pot of coffee on if you want any," she said as she invited her guests to have a seat at her kitchen table.

"I'm good, thanks," Jason politely declined.

Mick was not so gracious.

"Listen, let's just see what you got so we can get back to the station. I hope whatever you have is good, because we shouldn't even be here right now," he said impatiently.

"Did you *really* have to bring him?" Hannah asked Jason.

"Alright, you two play nice," Jason chuckled.

"Well, here's what I have," Hannah said as she handed over the envelope of photographs that Scriv had given her the night before.

"Who's this guy?" Jason asked as he and Mick looked at the first photograph of a man exiting a construction site.

"That would be Salvatore Furio, owner of SFI Construction," Hannah replied.

"Why the hell would we care about this guy?" Mick asked, growing more impatient.

"Well, Commander McCarthy, because he also owns many other small businesses in the area. Mostly cash businesses like a few Laundromats. Oh, and a little place called Buddy's Speakeasy," Hannah responded.

Mick and Jason's facial expressions did little to hide their shock at this news.

"Oh, Vance never mentioned that he had a partner?" Hannah

asked, obviously enjoying the moment.

"No, he didn't," Jason replied.

"So what? I mean, I hope you have more than this," Mick interjected.

"Keep looking through the pictures, boys. These were taken the other day at the site of the shopping center that is going in by the old steelyards. SFI Construction was able to get one of the bids, but they're also cooking the books and paying illegal workers far less than prevailing wages to work there."

Hannah continued talking as the detectives continued to peruse the photographs, most of which showing the various workers at the jobsite.

"I'm fairly certain that Salvatore Furio is using Buddy's Speakeasy and his other small businesses to launder the excess money from his construction jobs. I had a private investigator there to document the number of workers so we could prove our theory, but fate stepped in when the person you will see in the final photograph happened to join Mr. Furio for a meeting that day."

"Holy shit, that's HoJo!" Mick declared as he looked up at Jason, who was equally as shocked.

"See, now aren't you glad you came over, Commander McCarthy?" Hannah chuckled.

"Yes and no, Miss LaMarca," Mick replied.

"Come again? I just gave you a photograph of your police chief meeting with the co-owner of Buddy's Speakeasy on the day he was killed, well, *allegedly* killed," Hannah fired back, the last part in reference to the fact that Mick and Jason had still not confirmed that HoJo was dead.

"You were right. HoJo was killed last night. They found him strangled to death outside Buddy's Speakeasy," Jason informed Hannah, who was expecting a much warmer reception to the information she had provided.

"Then what's the problem?" she pressed.

"The *problem* is that we were already investigating HoJo's relationship with Vance Gold. We are pretty certain that he and Vance have been helping each other out during the course of their careers," Mick replied.

"Jesus, really? Well, that's an odd couple," Hannah said.

"Not if what we believe is true," Jason chimed in.

"How so?" Hannah asked.

"We have good reason to believe that HoJo used information he obtained from Vance over the years to make arrests and build his reputation as Cleveland's top drug enforcement officer. In exchange for his tips, Vance would get HoJo's protection so he could continue to run his drug game without having to worry about the cops," Jason replied.

"That protection only got better and better over time as HoJo climbed the police department ladder. The best part for Vance was that the chief was also locking up all of his competition along the way," Mick added.

"Okay, wow..." Hannah said, shocked. "I wonder if one of those guys that HoJo put away is trying to get revenge."

"Could be, but there was something else that makes us think otherwise," Jason answered.

"What's that?" Hannah asked.

"There was a note left at the scene," Mick replied, producing the photograph of the note.

Hannah looked over the image of the note, her eyes narrowing at first, but then widening in disbelief as she digested what was written.

"Oh my God! This is crazy! Who else knows about all of this?" Hannah asked.

"About the note? Just us and a few of the cops at the scene," Mick replied.

"What about the other stuff? About HoJo and Vance Gold?" Hannah pressed.

"As far as we know, just the three of us. Well, us and obviously the person who wrote the note," Mick replied.

"And Tick too," Jason added.

"Tick? Isn't that the punk you guys arrested in the Ernie Page case?" Hannah asked.

"The one and only. He's the one who gave us the info on Vance and HoJo," Jason answered.

"Why would he do that?" Hannah questioned.

"Everyone has a price. In this case, it was the cost of a baby crib," Mick replied.

Hannah gave the detectives a puzzled look.

"Don't ask," Jason chuckled.

"Apparently, Tick used to work for Vance selling drugs. They must've had some sort of falling out though, based on what he told us," Mick added.

"How credible do you think Tick's info is?" Hannah asked.

"Well, typically, credibility and Timothy "Tick" Braun don't go hand-in-hand. That being said, he doesn't seem to have anything to gain from providing us with this information, so we're banking on that," Jason responded.

"So, what's the next move?" Hannah questioned.

"That's the tough part. Whatever we decide to do next has to be done very carefully. We don't know who we can trust in the department anymore. HoJo was a very powerful man, but not powerful enough to do all of this on his own. He had to have help from within the department," Jason replied.

"So, it should go without saying, that we are trusting you will keep a lid on all of this until we know who we can trust. If anyone who was helping HoJo gets wind that we are on to them, we might as well enter Witness Protection," Mick added.

"Of course, absolutely. Just promise me that when you are ready, that I get to break the story," Hannah replied.

"Absolutely, especially with the information that you and your investigator have given us. I hope you know how much we appreciate it," Jason confirmed.

"Speaking of my investigator," Hannah said, "I really think that he could be a huge help to what you guys are trying to accomplish. He's a former cop and will be able to fly under the radar of those in the department that might be watching closely."

Jason looked at Mick, who shrugged as if to say he was fine with the idea. "We'll take all the help we can get," Jason replied.

"You won't be sorry. His name is Cliff Scriven, but everyone calls him Scriv. Here's his contact info," Hannah said as she handed Jason his business card.

"Let him know we'll be in touch," Jason said with a smile.

"We should get going though. We need to have another visit with Vance Gold. Thanks, Miss LaMarca, for everything," Mick said as he stood up to leave.

"Yes, thank you very much, Hannah," Jason added as he and Mick made their way to the door.

"My pleasure, Detectives. Be careful…"

48

"Aunty Carebear!" Gabby Knox shrieked as she sprinted into Cooper Madison's penthouse suite at the Westcott Hotel and hugged Cara, who was waiting for her inside.

"How's my Gabby doing? Are you excited for our sleepover?" Cara asked as she squeezed her niece.

"Thank you so much for letting us stay here, Coop," Erica Knox said to Coop, who was holding the door open as she and Clarence Walters followed Gabby inside.

"Y'all don't need to thank me, and you can stay as long as you want," Coop replied.

"Here's their bags, and I already gave Erica my number if she needs me to take her back to the house at all to get anything she might've forgotten," Clarence said as he placed Erica's duffel bag and Gabby's Disney Princess suitcase on the floor.

"Thank you again, Clarence. I can't tell you how much I appreciate your help. All of you, for that matter," Erica said, her tone a mixture of gratitude and exhaustion.

Coop, sensing this, felt that Erica wanted to say more, but not in front of Gabby.

"Hey Gabby, I'm so glad that you and your mom are staying here with us. Can I show you where you're going to be sleeping tonight?" Coop asked Gabby, who was still holding on to Cara.

"Do I have to go to bed already? It's not even dark outside," Gabby asked.

"Bed? No way, kiddo. This is a sleepover, girl! We still have a lot of movies to watch and ice cream to eat. I just want to show you the place first," Coop replied, doing his best to put her mind at ease.

"Ice cream? Yes!" Gabby said as she grabbed Coop by the hand before the two of them left the others.

As soon as her daughter was out of the room, Erica put her head in her hands and exhaled. She had been trying not to show any of the anxiety she was feeling ever since she received the phone call from Jason earlier telling her why he wanted her to stay with Coop and Cara.

"Are you doing okay?" Cara asked as she walked over and comforted Erica.

"I'm trying. I swear, I've never heard Jason sound as spooked as he was. He always tries to make everything seem okay, so he must really be worried," Erica answered.

"Well, the good news is that you couldn't be in a safer location, Mrs. Knox. I've already informed the staff here that nobody is allowed up, under any circumstances, unless Grace Brooks or I approve it. One of us will be downstairs in the lobby at all times until further notice. Nobody will be able to harm you or your daughter here. I promise," Clarence said, his voice both authoritative and sincere.

"That makes me feel so much better, Clarence. Please make sure that you tell Grace the same," Erica responded.

"Absolutely. I'm going to go brief the hotel staff again. You have both Grace's and my number on the card I gave you if you need anything at all. Try to get some rest, now. Goodnight ladies, and tell Coop I hope that his arm is feeling better," Clarence said as he started to make his way out of the suite.

"We will, Clarence. Thanks again for everything," Cara said as Clarence gave them both a nod and closed the door behind him.

"Oh Cara, I'm really freaking out," Erica whispered as she buried her face in Cara's shoulder and began to weep.

"I know, sweetie. But, like Clarence said, you're safe here. We won't let anything bad happen. Besides, I think Coop might be more excited than Gabby that you guys are going to be staying with us."

Cara's last words made Erica laugh as she wiped away the tears that had trickled down her cheeks.

"He's a good man, Cara. I'm so happy for you."

"Yeah, I think I'll keep this one around," Cara chuckled.

"If you don't, I may have you institutionalized, girl!" Erica teased.

Just then, Gabby came running in, dragging Coop by the hand.

"Mommy! Mommy! Wait until you see our bed! It's huge! And we have our own bathroom!" Gabby shrieked.

"She may never want to leave," Erica mused.

"Mommy, Coop showed me his Man Cave too. Wait until you see the TV! He said that we are going to watch movies and eat sundaes!"

"I had Simon pick up a few DVD's that she might like. I hope you don't mind that I also had him get the ice cream," Coop said.

"Are you kidding? Coop, I could use a night of ice cream and movies myself," Erica laughed.

"Well then, let's go make some sundaes. I told Gabby that she can pick the first movie," Coop said as he gave Gabby a high-five.

"Will Jason be coming here later?" Cara asked Erica as Gabby dragged Coop towards the kitchen.

"He said he'd call and let me know. He and Mick were on their way to talk to a witness or something. I have a feeling he has a long night ahead of him. He might even just sleep at the precinct. Wouldn't be the first time that's happened since he started this damn EPK case."

49

"You guys gotta protect me. If this guy can get to HoJo, I'm as good as dead," Vance Gold stammered from his seat inside the 1st District interrogation room.

Across from the owner of Buddy's Speakeasy sat Jason and Mick, who had returned from their visit with Hannah LaMarca determined to figure out just how truthful Vance would be with them. They had turned the recorder and microphones in the room off before they began.

Vance had not been charged with anything, so there was no need for anyone to record or listen in to the conversation. Besides, Jason and Mick had no idea who they could trust.

"Well, Vance, the good news is that if the killer wanted you dead, he probably would've already done it last night when you walked outside the club," Mick stated.

"That is, assuming what you've told is true," Jason added.

"Of course it's true! I told you about HoJo tipping me off about the sting, didn't I? Why would I tell you that if I wasn't being honest? I'd have nothing to gain from it," Vance exclaimed, his voice hushed.

"Forgive us for our skepticism, Vance... It's just that based on our prior interactions, we think that you're a scumbag who would do anything to save himself," Mick replied matter-of-factly.

"How are you going to gain our trust, Vance? I can promise you that we will be a lot more likely to help keep you safe if we feel like we can trust you," Jason implored.

"Listen fellas, I will tell you everything I know, but you have to promise me that it won't be recorded. Some of this stuff is incriminating, to say the least, but I'm willing to tell you off the record. I want this EPK off the streets as much as you do, even if it means being a snitch."

"Fair enough, Vance. We're the only ones in the room, and we are the only ones who can hear what you tell us. Why don't you start by telling us if HoJo had mentioned any concerns that someone may have been out to get him," Jason said, his voice firm, yet sincere.

"HoJo wasn't afraid of anybody. At least, that's what he wanted me to think. If he was worried, he never told me. HoJo was all about being the most dominant person in the room, but you guys probably know that as well as anyone," Vance chuckled.

"No argument from us," Jason replied.

"What about any other partners of his? Maybe some cops in the department who were aware of your relationship with HoJo?" Mick asked.

"HoJo would only ever meet with me alone. I know he had help from within the department, but he would've never told me who. That would've given me too much power that I could possibly use against him later," Vance replied.

"What about any of his associates who aren't cops?" Jason

asked.

"You guys know as well as I do that HoJo was connected to every important person in Cleveland. This city is riddled with people who owe him favors," Vance answered.

"Like your partner, Salvatore Furio?" Jason quipped.

Vance shot the detectives a look of shock and disbelief, obviously stunned that they knew anything about Furio, as he began to shift uneasily in his chair.

"Yeah, Vance. We know all about your 'silent' partner. I thought you were ready to be honest with us, but yet again you prove that you can't be trusted," Mick admonished.

"I... Listen... Sal is just my business partner. What's he got to do with HoJo?" Vance replied.

"We were hoping you'd tell us, Vance. Otherwise, we are all just wasting our time here. If that's the case, you can just walk out the door. I'd be careful, though," Mick taunted.

"It's like this, okay? I wanted to open a club, but let's just say that while I had the cash to do it, there was no way in hell that I'd get a liquor license on my own. In my previous career I didn't exactly fill out a W-2, you know? I needed a legitimate business partner to get my foot in the door."

"Let me guess... You went to HoJo and he set you up with Salvatore Furio?" Jason pressed.

"HoJo said that Sal was looking for another business to, you know, diversify his portfolio. He said that Furio would be able to get all the permits, and would only take a thirty percent cut off the top in exchange."

"Wow, that sounds like a pretty good deal. Forgive me if I don't buy it," Mick said accusingly.

"Yeah, Mick, I think he's leaving out the part where Furio launders his construction money through the club," Jason added.

"You know what, Vance? We're done here. Get your ass out of here. I'm done playing games," Mick seethed as he stood up and pointed towards the door.

"I'm the one playing games? You guys obviously think you have all the answers, so why the hell do you keep asking me questions about shit you already know? So what if a couple of Sal's employees come in to the club periodically and drop some cash? You go to any bar, takeout joint, or dry cleaner in the area, and I guarantee that they have two different cash registers - one that Uncle Sam knows about and one that he don't. The tax man ain't never had an issue with my club, and trust me, they're looking," Vance fired back.

"Fair enough, Vance. We know it's tough being a small business owner, and guess what? We don't give a *shit* about the cash that Furio is laundering through your club. That's the IRS's problem. Our concern is HoJo's relationship with Furio, and if there's any people that they might've pissed off through their business dealings," Jason explained.

"Guys like Furio have a Christmas list of people that would want to see them dead. The construction business is as cutthroat as it comes. As far as HoJo is concerned, well, just look up the records of any drug dealer or pimp that he locked up over the years," Vance replied.

"Can you tell us why HoJo was seen meeting with Furio the day he was killed?" Mick asked as he sat back down in his chair.

"HoJo did mention that he and Sal had a meeting. He basically told him the same thing he told me, that we needed to be careful because people were watching. He said that we just needed to lay low for a bit until it blew over. He told Sal not to make any more deposits at the club until further notice," Vance admitted.

"Let's not forget that he also tipped you off about the sting too," Mick added.

"Yeah, he did, and I told you that he did. But, you know what? He didn't need to because you guys wouldn't have found anything anyways. I told you before that if any of my girls were conducting business on the side, that I had nothing to do with it. Those days are over for me. If they're making a few extra bucks after hours, that's their business. I ain't getting no cut of that action. I told HoJo that too, but I don't think he believed me either."

"Shocker…" Mick replied.

"Why do you think HoJo didn't believe you?" Jason asked.

"Because HoJo knows that I used to associate with pimps and he probably figured that I still was. Hell, I'm crazy for *not* doing it. Think about it; I have a stable of young women already working for me. It'd be easy money, but I'm telling you I ain't in that game anymore."

"Let's say that's true, Vance. However, here's a theory you might not want to hear. What if HoJo didn't just come in to warn you about the sting? Maybe he finally got tired of protecting your ass and realized that whatever kind of cut you were giving him from the club in exchange for his help wasn't worth it anymore, and he was going to cut you out of the picture all together?" Mick asked.

"If that theory is true you'd have one hell of a motive to kill HoJo, wouldn't you, Vance?" Jason concurred.

Vance Gold leaned back in the uncomfortable metal chair that so many criminals had occupied before him and let out a sigh, which was followed by a smile, and then almost uncontrollable laughter after that.

"You guys really don't have any idea, do you?" Vance asked once he was finally able to compose himself.

"Enlighten us," Mick sneered.

"HoJo wasn't going to cut *me* out of the picture, fellas," Vance stated, his eyes narrowed.

"If not you, then who? Salvatore Furio?" Mick asked.

"Nope," Vance replied.

"Then who?" Mick demanded.

"Us…" Jason's response caused Mick to do a double take. "HoJo was going to get rid of us, Mick."

50

Hannah LaMarca stood outside the entrance to the police department headquarters in downtown Cleveland. In just a few moments she would be going live on the air to confirm that the rumors of Chief Horace Johnston's death were, in fact, true.

"Going live in five, four, three, two, one..." the voice of her producer back at Channel One News counted down in her earpiece as she took a deep breath.

"Good afternoon. This is Hannah LaMarca reporting to you live outside of the Cleveland Police Department's downtown headquarters, where a spokesperson from the department has just released a statement regarding the loss of one of their own," Hannah reported as she heard the video segment that she had pre-recorded begin to play in her ear.

The thirty second clip informed viewers that HoJo had been found dead in his car outside of Buddy's Speakeasy. It did not mention the details of how he had been killed, or even that he had been killed at all, as the department had not yet publicly released that information.

"You're back live in five, four, three, two, one…" the producer's voice announced in Hannah's ear as she prepared to close the segment.

"As you can see, many questions still remain regarding Chief Horace Johnston's death. The department said that we can expect more information to be released in the coming days, but at this time they are simply asking for everyone's thoughts and prayers as they remember one of their own," Hannah said, doing her best to sound sincere despite what she had recently discovered about the late chief.

"And… We're clear…"

After getting the all-clear from her producer, Hannah thanked her cameraman for meeting her there on short notice, and then stepped away to make a phone call to Cliff Scriven.

"Hey Scriv, did you hear from the detectives yet?" she asked.

"Nope, not yet."

"Well, I hope that they get in touch with you soon."

"I'm sure they will, Hannah. Those guys are probably so swamped right now that they haven't even had a chance to eat dinner. I've been there before. I remember what it was like to be in their shoes," Scriv replied.

"You're probably right. Listen, I have to follow up with a source, so I have to let you go."

"No worries and be careful," Scriv answered before ending the call.

Hannah said goodbye to her cameraman, who was packing up his gear, and began walking toward Tower City Center. Located just a short walk from the police station, Tower City had evolved a great deal from its early days as the Cleveland Union Terminal station, which officially opened in 1930.

The crown jewel of the complex, the Terminal Tower, is a 52-

story skyscraper that held the distinction of being the tallest building in North America outside of New York City until 1964. In addition to serving as a major hub for Cleveland's Rapid Transit Authority railway system, Tower City also is home to a shopping mall, a movie theater, and a number of office buildings.

On this day, Hannah was on her way to meet up with Keri Urban, her contact from the coroner's office. Due to the consequences that Keri would face if anyone found out about her relationship with Hannah, they had planned to meet at the Tower City railway station and board RTA's Red Line together so that they could talk in relative anonymity from a secluded spot on the train.

As Hannah approached the train's boarding zone, she spotted a very tired-looking Keri waiting for her. She was still dressed in her scrubs and was clutching a cup of coffee when she recognized that Hannah was approaching.

"You look tired," Hannah said discreetly as she stood next to her on the platform.

"It's been a long day," Keri replied, not making eye contact to maintain the facade that the two were just casually waiting for their train to arrive.

"I bet," Hannah agreed as the RTA "Rapid" came to a stop in front of them and the doors opened.

The pair boarded the train, which was practically empty since it was late enough in the day on a Friday, and the majority of the regular riders had already left the city. They took a seat in the rear of the car so that their backs were facing each other.

"What can you tell me about HoJo that I don't already know?" Hannah whispered behind her as the train pulled away.

"Besides the fact that he was strangled to death by a zip tie?" Keri responded in a hushed tone.

"Yes, besides that. What an awful way to go."

"I've seen a lot of strangulations, but this one was especially violent. Whoever did this wanted him to feel every last breath leave his body. The ligature marks that were left from the zip tie showed that he must've put up a pretty desperate fight as it was happening," Keri informed.

"Well, from what I've learned, he certainly had enough people who were motivated and capable of doing such a thing," Hannah replied.

"Do you know if the police have any leads on who did this?" Keri asked.

"Not yet, unfortunately."

"This is crazy," Keri said, shaking her head in disbelief.

"Was there anything you saw on HoJo that could possibly be linked to any of the other victims?" Hannah questioned.

"Other victims?"

"Yes, like Vivian Tong, or even Stoya Fedorov."

"Whoa, so you think this might be the actual EPK? Not just a copycat?"

"I do, and so do my sources in the department," Hannah confirmed.

"That makes a lot of sense now," Keri replied.

"How do you mean?"

"Well, typically nobody from the department watches me work on a body, even when it's a cop. They usually just want the report. However, today the Deputy Chief was watching over me the entire time."

"Anthony Lawson was there?" Hannah asked, referring to the

second-highest ranking member of the department.

"He sure was."

"Did he say why?"

"Nope, nor did he ask any questions. He just observed. Honestly, it was really uncomfortable," Keri answered.

"That is odd…"

"My only guess is that because it was Chief Johnston that he wanted to make sure that everything was done properly."

"Was anyone else with him?"

"Nope, just him. As soon as I was done, he told me that he wanted the report immediately, and then he waited outside my office while I typed it up. He left as soon as I handed it to him," Keri informed Hannah, who was trying to piece together why the Deputy Chief would have been there.

"Was there anything in the report that was out of the ordinary?" Hannah asked.

"Well, it was just an initial report, so it basically was confirming the cause of death by strangulation. The lab results will show if anyone else's DNA was found anywhere on the victim's body, like under his fingernails or on the zip tie, but that won't be available for weeks, if not months," Keri replied.

"Do you think they'll find anything?"

"My guess is no. Whoever did this was a pro. I didn't see anything out of the ordinary under his nails and the zip tie appeared to be free of any prints, but you never know. Well, this is my stop. Make sure that you pick up the plastic bag I'm leaving on my seat," Keri whispered as the train came to a stop at the Puritas Station on Cleveland's west side.

"I will, and thanks Keri. I owe you," Hannah replied with a smile as Keri stood up.

"No you don't," Keri said with a wink as she exited the train.

Hannah waited until after the Rapid's doors closed behind Keri to glance around and make sure that nobody was looking before she reached behind her and discreetly picked up the small plastic grocery bag that her trusted source had purposely left on her seat. Hannah did not need to look inside to know that Keri had placed a folded copy of the initial coroner's report inside the bag for her.

While the report itself likely did not hold any secrets that would help solve the case, Hannah was confident that Keri Urban's revelation about Anthony Lawson's odd visit to the coroner's office was certainly something that Detective Jason Knox needed to be aware of.

Hannah sat on the train as it traveled to its final stop at the airport, where it would then retrace its route and take her all the way back to Tower City, and she reflected with gratitude that Keri was willing to risk everything to provide her with the information that she had so many times before.

As the buildings and trees passed by her in a blur outside the window of the train, Hannah felt more determined than ever before to make sure that Keri's efforts to help would not have been made in vain.

51

"Good morning, Detective Knox," Coop greeted Jason in the kitchen as he poured his guest a cup of coffee. "What time did you get in last night?"

"What time is it now?" Jason asked as he rubbed his tired eyes.

"Just past seven on this gorgeous Saturday in Cleveland, Ohio," Coop replied as he handed Jason the mug of hot coffee.

"Well then, about four hours ago," Jason laughed as he raised the mug in appreciation and took a sip.

"No wonder I didn't hear you come in," Coop chuckled.

"I'm just glad that I didn't wake anybody up. Wonder Woman had the front desk let me in," Jason said, referring to Grace Brooks, who had taken over for Clarence at midnight and kept vigil in the lobby of the Westcott Hotel.

"Not gonna lie, I'm pretty sure that Grace could kick my ass," Coop said with a laugh.

"Brother, she could kick both of our asses at the same time," Jason replied.

"Rough day yesterday, huh?" Coop asked.

"I've had better, that's for sure. How'd everything go here?"

"Oh, we had a blast! Cara and I entertained Gabby with movies and sugar until she crashed so that Erica could get a good night's sleep. She seemed pretty exhausted herself," Coop replied.

"Yeah, I know this has been just as hard on her as anyone. I feel awful that any of you even have to worry about this stuff, but I'm truly grateful that you are letting us crash at your place, Coop. It means a lot," Jason said sincerely.

"No thanks necessary. It's my pleasure. Besides, I really loved hanging with Gabby last night. That is one smart girl you and Erica have there."

"Good thing she takes after her mother," Jason laughed.

"Can I get you something to eat? I'm about to make my famous chocolate chip pancakes for everyone."

"Man, that sounds delicious, but unfortunately, I have to hop in the shower and then meet with Mick and a couple others about this case. I have a feeling I'm going to be late again tonight too."

"I don't know how you do it, Jason, but I'm glad to know that someone like you is on the case."

"I appreciate that. I just wish I could say that everyone in my department felt the same way," Jason replied.

"Come on now, you're the best detective in the city! Why would you say something like that?" Coop asked.

"Let's just say that I'm not so sure everyone in the department is playing for the same team on this case."

"Damn, really?"

"Really…"

"Well, for once then, I hope that your super-sleuth instincts are wrong."

"Me too, Coop."

"Are you sure there isn't something I could get you to eat before you go?" Coop asked.

"Positive. Just keep my girls happy and safe like you're already doing," Jason replied.

"Roger that, Detective."

"Hey, do you mind if I use your shower so that I don't wake up Erica and Gabby?"

"Too late for that," Erica said as she entered the kitchen, holding Gabby's hand.

"Daddy!" Gabby shrieked as she ran to Jason and hugged him.

"Hey there, Princess Gabby! Did you have fun at your sleepover last night?" Jason asked as he squeezed his daughter.

"Yes! We watched movies and ate ice cream. Aunty Cara even let me stay up as late as I wanted!" Gabby replied, still holding onto her father.

"She made it longer than I did, that's for sure," Erica laughed as she joined the hug.

"Hey there, beautiful," Jason said as he gave his wife a kiss.

"Do you really have to leave so soon?" Erica asked.

"Unfortunately, yes. I'm probably going to be late again. I'm sorry, girls," Jason replied as he squeezed them tight.

"Awe, do you have to, Daddy? Can't you stay? Pleeeeease?" Gabby begged as she began to cry.

"Trust me, baby girl, I wish I could. But, Daddy has to go catch some bad guys, okay?" Jason responded, hoping that she would understand, but knowing that she would not.

"Hey Gabby, you know what?" Coop interjected, hoping to help. "I'm about to make my famous chocolate chip pancakes, but I can't do it without a helper. Man, I sure wish that there was someone here who could help me…"

"I can! I can!" Gabby replied, wiping the tears from her cheeks.

"You can? Oh, thank God! I was worried that we weren't going to be able to have breakfast. Come on over here, girl, so we can wash our hands and get to work," Coop said as he winked at Jason, who silently thanked him.

"When do you think you'll be home?" Erica asked Jason as they snuck out of the kitchen, where Coop was lifting Gabby up so that she could wash her hands in the sink.

"Not sure. This whole situation blows," Jason replied.

"I know…" Erica said, tears beginning to well up in her eyes.

"I'm so sorry, Babe. I wish I could make this all go away."

"You will. You always do," Erica said as she wiped away her tears.

"At least I know you and Gabby are safe here, and quite frankly, that's all I care about."

"Have you talked to your parents? Should they be worried?"

"I told them what I could, and I made sure that a patrol car is routinely checking up on them. Besides, my dad might be in a wheelchair, but he also knows how to use his shotgun. I think he was actually kind of excited when I told him to keep it close by," Jason chuckled.

"Oh Lord, help us all," Erica managed to laugh in return.

52

"It's about time, Molasses," Mick teased Jason as he pretended to look at his watch.

"Sorry, everyone. The struggle is real this morning," Jason replied as he joined Mick, Hannah, and Scriv at the table that they were occupying inside The Place to Be diner in Lakewood, Ohio.

"Detective Knox, this is Cliff Scriven," Hannah said as she introduced the pair.

"Pleasure to meet you in person, Cliff. Thanks again for agreeing to help us out with this mess," Jason said as he shook Scriv's hand.

"Please, call me Scriv, and you should thank Hannah. She spoke very highly of you and that's all I needed to know before agreeing to it," Scriv replied.

"What'd she say about me, Scriv?" Mick asked.

"Well, she didn't actually say anything about you, Commander," Scriv answered, which made both Hannah and Jason laugh.

"Give me time, Miss LaMarca. I'm like a fungus; I'll grow on you," Mick said with a wink.

"Okay, moving on, fellas. I hope this was a good spot for us to meet. I figured it was best that we met somewhere outside of the city limits," Hannah said, changing topics.

"Are you kiddin' me? I love this place. Haven't been here for years, but for my money, there's no better breakfast spot on the west side," Jason affirmed.

"Good. Well, I have some news to share. Off the record, of course, as with everything else we discuss here," Hannah stated.

"Of course," Jason answered.

"I met with my source at the coroner's office yesterday, and she told me something pretty interesting," Hannah began.

"Did she perform the autopsy on HoJo?" Mick asked.

"Yes, but that's not the interesting part," Hannah continued. "Apparently, Deputy Chief Anthony Lawson paid her a visit yesterday at the coroner's office-"

"And?" Mick interrupted. "He probably was just getting the initial report from her in person because of who the victim was."

"Well, Commander, if you'd let me finish you would know that he didn't just go there to pick up the report. He actually watched her perform the entire examination," Hannah fired back.

"Really? That's definitely not standard practice," Jason said in return.

"Exactly," Hannah agreed. "So, my question to you gentleman is why?"

"You got me. That's pretty twisted," Mick replied.

"Scriv, have you ever heard of anything like this before?" Hannah asked.

"This is definitely a first for me too," he answered, shaking his head.

"Did he tell her why he was there?" Jason questioned.

"Nope. In fact, he didn't even say a word the entire time she was working, and when she was finished he demanded that she give him the report immediately and waited for her to type it up," Hannah informed the group.

"Maybe he was just making sure that everything was done properly since it was the chief?" Mick guessed.

"That's what I was thinking too," Jason agreed. "That, and now that HoJo's gone he's the acting chief, so maybe he is just being extra cautious?"

"That's definitely a plausible theory, but I still think that something isn't right here. So, my thought was that we could have you do what you do best in regards to Mr. Lawson and see if there's anything going on that we should know about," Hannah said to Scriv.

"Absolutely, I can get right on that today. I'll do a little digging and also some surveillance on him today," Scriv confirmed.

"Fine by us," Mick said, nodding at Jason.

"Yeah, that'd be great. In the meantime, we will just continue to investigate some of the leads that we are following," Jason concurred.

"Anything you can share?" Hannah asked.

Jason looked at Mick, who gave him the green light with a nod.

"Well, we spoke at length with Vance Gold yesterday, and he seems to think that HoJo was going to try and get rid of us," Jason stated.

"Like, take you off the case?" Hannah asked.

"*Like*, take us off the planet," Mick replied, mocking her use of the slang interjection.

"Holy shit. Do you think he was being serious?" Hannah pressed, ignoring Mick's slight.

"He sure wants us to think he is. In fact, he refused to leave the station last night unless we put a patrol car at his place," Jason replied.

"Who else knows about his claim?" Hannah asked.

"Just us, and now you guys. Our meeting with him was completely off the record," Jason answered.

"So, it goes without saying, that Knox and I are pretty much on an island at the precinct. At least, until we know who we can trust," Mick added.

"What about you, Miss LaMarca? Do you have anything else you can share with us?" Jason asked.

"I wish I did, Detective. It took everything in my power to hide my feelings about HoJo on the air yesterday, and I guess I'll have to just keep that act up until we get something more," Hannah said in return.

"Well, guys, it was a pleasure to meet you both. I'm going to head out so I can get started on my to-do list. Keep an eye on your six out there," Scriv warned the detectives as he stood up to leave.

"You too, Scriv," Jason replied as the two shook hands.

"Thanks again, Scriv," Hannah said as she stood up to give him a hug.

"Why don't I ever get a hug like that?" Mick asked Hannah.

"Don't answer that," Jason laughed.

"Yeah, yeah, yeah. Whatever. I guess we all should get going, anyways," Mick announced as he too stood up to leave.

"Be careful, Detectives. Even you, Mick," Hannah said as they exited the diner.

"See! I'm growing on you already…"

53

"Enjoying the view?" Coop asked Erica, who was seated on his balcony.

"Oh my God, yes. Almost as much as I enjoyed your famous chocolate chip pancakes at breakfast," she replied.

"I can't take all the credit now. Gabby helped me make them."

"That is true, and thank you for distracting her when Jason left. She's having a hard time with him being gone so much, especially since it started right after he was on vacation."

"I'm sure it is; that girl sure loves her daddy," Jason said as he took a seat next to Erica.

"She sure does. She's definitely Daddy's little girl. I'm chopped liver when he's around," Erica laughed.

"Ain't that the way it usually is?"

"I know it is for her, but I don't mind. Life could be a lot worse than having your daughter love her father so much."

"Yes, ma'am, you're right as rain."

"What are Gabby and Cara up to?" Erica asked.

"Well, Miss Gabby is currently in phase one of the makeover that she insisted on giving Cara. All I know is that Gabby told me that I wasn't allowed to see Cara until she was done making her beautiful," Coop replied.

"Oh Lord, poor Cara. I've been on the receiving end of Gabby's makeovers enough to know that this could take hours," Erica laughed.

"Well, I do believe that Cara is enjoying every second of it. She probably didn't get to do a whole lot of makeovers with three older brothers."

"Yeah, I would have to agree with you on that one, although Jason has also been one of Gabby's salon clients. He's even let her paint his toenails before."

"That's a good daddy, right there. Jason is a good man," Coop said.

"He is, but I'm also starting to really worry about him. This EPK case just won't go away, and now it's just downright scary, Coop."

"I know. However, I also know that I can't think of anyone else that I would want trying to solve that case. That guy really messed up when he threatened y'all. Jason's not gonna stop until he locks that psychopath up."

"That's kind of what is worrying me so much. I'm more afraid that Jason is going to work himself to death than I am of the EPK coming after us. I mean, what if he never catches him? He can't keep burning the candle at both ends forever," Erica sighed.

"How'd y'all meet, anyway?" Coop asked, changing the topic.

"Well, it's kind of a funny story," Erica chuckled.

"How so?"

"Jason actually pulled me over for speeding when he was a rookie patrolman."

"Well, shut my mouth," Coop replied in classic southern fashion.

"I'm serious! I was 21 and had this little red Mazda Miata convertible, which I'm not gonna lie, I loved driving faster than I should. He clocked me going 55 in a 25 miles-per-hour stretch of road," Erica giggled.

"Damn, girl! Let me guess, he let you off with a warning and then asked you out?"

"Oh no, not Jason, especially when he was a rookie. Not only did he not let me off, it was the fifth ticket that I had received in a short amount of time. I even had to go to court for the damn thing or risk having my license suspended."

"You must be pullin' my leg now!" Coop declared in disbelief.

"I'm being dead honest, Coop! Thankfully, the judge showed some mercy on me and didn't give me any points, so I kept my license. I only had to pay the fine."

"That's good, at least. So, how'd Jason parlay that debacle into a date?"

"Well, he had to be present in court that day, since he wrote the ticket. He waited for me outside the courthouse and apologized for giving me the ticket. He told me that as a new cop that he was afraid that he'd get in trouble if he had let me off with a warning. Then he asked if he could make it up to me by taking me out to dinner." Erica smiled.

"My boy Jason was smooth as silk!" Coop laughed.

"Not so fast, Coop. I turned him down," Erica said proudly.

"You didn't."

"I most certainly did! Even though I did think he looked cute as hell in that uniform, I was still so mad at him that I shot his ass down," Erica asserted.

"So what happened next?"

"Well, the next morning I went out to my car to go to class – I was a senior at CSU – and he was out there writing a ticket because I had parked too close to a fire hydrant by my apartment building. Can you believe that?" Erica asked.

"Okay, I think I gotta take back my smooth as silk comment," Coop replied.

"Actually, he was pretty smooth, because it turns out that he was just pretending to write the ticket. When he handed me the piece of paper from his pad, it was just his name and phone number on it. He told me to call him or he'd come back the next day and really write the ticket."

"He was blackmailing you for a date?"

"Gotta give him credit; he was as persistent then as he is now. I called him that night, and the rest is history," Erica laughed.

"Wow, that is one helluva story y'all have. I'm impressed," Coop said smiling.

"Well, you certainly can relate, can't you? I mean, look at how you and Cara met. Maybe someday you'll be able to tell that story just like I told mine after you and Cara get married," Erica said, confident that the last part would certainly make him nervous, but his response came without hesitation.

"I certainly hope so…"

54

"Well, folks, I sure hope that you had a great time out on the water today. It's always a good thing to catch your limit. You folks are gonna have one heck of a fish fry this weekend!" the man said to the trio of amateur anglers that had just completed a fishing trip on his boat, *Jane's Justice.*

"You're the man, Captain! Thanks again!" one of the three confirmed as they walked off.

"My pleasure, fellas. Tell your friends!" the captain replied.

Captain Phillip Worthington was not only good at putting his boat in the perfect spot to catch walleye, but he was also very personable and patient with his customers, many of whom had never cast a line in the water before chartering a trip.

Jane's Fishing Charters was in its third year of existence and made routine trips for walleye on the waters of Lake Erie. Despite the fact that it was one of the smallest charter boats at Edgewater, Jane's

Fishing Charters always had steady business. All of the advertising was done by word of mouth, and Phil took great pride in the fact that his customers always came back happy.

It was shortly after his retirement as a trucker that he knew he needed something to occupy his time. It was a vast departure from his years as a long-haul truck driver, when he often went days without any face-to-face human interaction, save from a gas station attendant or rest stop employee, and Captain Phil loved it. Besides the added income, it helped fill the void that awaited him every night when he returned to his empty house in Cleveland's West Park neighborhood.

West Park, located inside Cleveland's city limits, had become one of the most desirable places to live over the past two decades. In November of 1982, in an effort to stabilize neighborhoods, Cleveland city council members voted in favor of a residency requirement that prevented city employees from migrating to the suburbs.

The controversial ruling meant that all city employees, especially police officers and firefighters, were forced to live within the city or face termination. While the intent was to have those safety force employees living throughout the city they protected, what eventually occurred was that the majority of them moved to the West Park neighborhood, making it one of the safest places to live in Cleveland. If you lived in West Park, the joke was that you were either a cop, a firefighter, or each of your neighbors was.

When Phil moved his family into their modest bungalow, not long after the ruling came down, he loved the fact that he had landed in such a safe and desirable neighborhood. While he was on the road too often to really form any close bonds with his neighbors, many of whom were police officers, he took comfort in the fact that they were close by in the event something bad happened when he was on the road.

However, as Phil soon learned, simply living in the safest of Cleveland's neighborhoods was not enough to shield his family from sadness and pain.

First came the loss of his wife, Irene, who had passed away from complications of pneumonia at the age of 38. Her death was a shock to everyone at the time, especially since it likely could have been treated had she sought medical help sooner than she did.

Irene knew that she had not been feeling well, but Phil was in the middle of a five-day haul and she had to look after their daughter, so she decided against going to the doctor until he returned home.

It was Jane, just entering her teen years at the time, who called the ambulance and then her father. She had returned home from school that day and found her mother, unresponsive on the couch, just hours before Phil was to return home from his trip.

By the time he made it to the hospital, Irene had been placed into a medically induced coma. He and Jane sat with her for the next two days, taking turns holding her hand and telling her how much they loved her.

Irene never recovered.

He did his best, or so he thought, raising Jane on his own in the following years. When he was home he was as present and active as any father could be. However, during his multi-day stretches on the open road, Jane was left in the care of a live-in nanny.

Calling Ethel Levine a nanny was a bit of a stretch. In reality, she was a widowed neighbor in her late seventies, and Jane had learned to manipulate her very quickly. As a teenager, Jane became more rebellious, often lying to Mrs. Levine about her whereabouts. Late night study sessions were actually parties at whatever house Jane and her friends could smoke cigarettes and drink alcohol without adult supervision. Mrs. Levine would typically be fast asleep on the couch hours before Jane would sneak back in, and Jane was an expert on covering her tracks.

Mrs. Levine was not the only one oblivious to her extracurricular activities, as Jane would make sure that she only partied when her father was on the road. Whenever he returned home, she would revert back to being his baby girl. It was as if she was living two separate lives, and she found some sort of distorted comfort in that. She would escape the pain she felt from the death of her mother while he was gone, and heal in the comfort that her father provided when he was home.

It was an exhausting high-wire act, and the cigarettes soon were replaced by marijuana and alcohol. By the time she was 17, Jane had graduated to acid, cocaine, and whatever pills she could get her hands on.

Jane was so good at hiding her growing addiction that her father may never have known just how much damage that her double life was causing. It was not that he thought that she was perfect. Her grades were barely average, and she had even been suspended from school her junior year for cheating on a test. Still, he credited that to typical teenage antics and felt that she would soon find her purpose in life.

Like many young girls who were lured into the drug scene, Jane had started by experimenting with marijuana, but soon graduated to acid. That was followed by cocaine and whatever pills she could get her hands on. When her growing addiction surpassed the monetary resources that she had to pay the dealers for the drugs that her body desired, one of their pimp associates stepped into the picture.

His name was Timothy "Tick" Braun, and Jane soon became his number one girl. She was young, pretty, and petite. Besides that, her father was rarely ever home and the old lady who was supposed to look after her was clueless, so Tick had no trouble making boatloads of money off of her. She would routinely pull in an average of four hundred dollars per night, which meant that Tick would get three hundred of that, and Jane would spend her cut on the drugs that had consumed her life by that point.

That vicious cycle paired with the grooming of a young girl to truly believe that he had her best interests at heart was what Tick prided himself on. His small stature and youthful appearance made him seem less intimidating to the girls he turned out, and by the time any of them came to the realization that he did not actually care about them, they were far too dependent on his services to break away.

A few girls over the years did try to sever their ties to Tick, for various reasons, and that was when he would make an example of them so that the others would not dare to try the same. Tick once beat a girl who had informed him that she would no longer work for him, within an inch of her life in front of all the other girls with the butt of his pistol.

"All you bitches take a look at her! Look at her! She wants out? Fine, but ain't nobody gonna want her now!" Tick declared in front of the other girls, one of which was Jane.

The sad irony was that the very girl he beat in front of them was back working for Tick a few days later, albeit for even less of a cut than she had originally given him, and that fact did not go unnoticed by the other girls. They were his prisoners, and he relished his role as their warden.

Jane continued to work for Tick, going by the name Britney, on the nights her father was away over the next six months. On the nights he was home, she would sneak bumps of cocaine so that she could put on the best performance of being the typical teenage girl that he expected her to be.

Her father knew that she had been smoking cigarettes from the time she started high school, but being an early smoker himself and the fact he harbored so much guilt over not being home when her mother died, made him turn a blind eye.

Unfortunately, that's where Phil Worthington thought his daughter's rebellious ways began and ended, and he had been punishing himself for being so naïve ever since.

55

Timothy "Tick" Braun had been pacing all morning in his county jail cell. He was still having a hard time coming to grips with the fact that he once again had found himself locked-up. However, with a baby on the way, he knew that he had to get out.

By the time he had met Vladimir Popov for the first time, Tick had fallen quite far down the ladder as far as being a pimp was concerned. A few years earlier, Vlad and his group of Russian mobsters had moved into Tick's territory and soon started running their own prostitution ring. Not wanting to lose any more business, let alone his "street cred", Tick confronted the head of the Russians that had already pilfered the majority of what used to be his territory.

Vladimir Popov, as Tick soon discovered, was not a man that was to be messed with. Within minutes of their meeting, Popov's men had beaten Tick to a bloody pulp and shoved the barrel of a 9mm pistol into his mouth.

That is when Tick did what he did best – he talked his way out of it. He convinced Vlad to let him work for him, citing his knowledge of the city and his connections. He would no longer be a pimp, instead becoming nothing more than a dispatcher of sorts for Vlad's growing business.

He soon proved his worth to the Russians, and it was even his idea to use numbers written on Styrofoam cups and burner phones to book clients to visit Vlad's motel on Brookpark Road. Tick had convinced Vlad that this was a foolproof system that removed the process of actually speaking to another human being about paying for sex.

While Tick did not like losing the power he had as a pimp, not to mention the income that came with it, he realized that it was better than the alternative. Vlad, for his part, treated Tick well and even grew to like the scrawny young man that he had almost killed.

All of that goodwill disappeared though when Tick flipped on him after the raid on the motel to save his own skin. Tick knew that Popov wanted him dead, but he also knew that as long as Vlad was in prison, the police would protect him. They had warned the Russian that his very own deal to avoid a much longer prison sentence would be in jeopardy if anything happened to Tick while he was behind bars. Vlad, knowing that his desire to get out of prison outweighed his need to exact revenge on Tick, decided that he would gladly wait until he was out in a few years to do just that.

In the meantime, Tick knew that he had to do whatever it would take to get out of jail. It was not until he learned that he was going to be a father that he finally felt that he was ready to leave his criminal past behind him.

When Tick was arrested during the Ernie Page bust, he had already made plans to flee with his girlfriend to start a new life in Florida. He had been saving almost every dollar that he had made working for Vlad, and he only needed a couple more weeks to achieve his goal. The day he was busted at Edgewater Park Marina changed all of that in an instant; however, he knew that by helping the police put Vlad away, he would still have a chance to make good on his exit strategy.

Like the rest of Cleveland's population, Tick had assumed that the EPK case was solved when Ernie Page took his own life. In a warped way, Tick felt proud that he had led the police to the alleged serial killer.

While Tick had spent his adult life as a pimp, drug dealer, and thief, he viewed those who were rapists and serial killers as members of the criminal world that he did not care to be associated with. To guys like Tick, they were truly the scum of the planet, and he was as happy as anyone when Ernie Page had been caught.

That pride proved to be short-lived. Tick had seen the news of Vivian Tong's body being found at Edgewater Beach on the jailhouse television during one of his supervised recreational periods. While nothing was said on the news about whom the victim was, let alone any of the grisly details, one of the guards present in the room with Tick commented on what he had heard.

"You know they're saying that the EPK is still out there. One of my buddies was at the scene, and he said this chick even had his initials carved into her. I guess maybe that loser Ernie Page wasn't the EPK after all," the guard said, seemingly proud to be able to break the news to the inmate.

While Tick did not know if Vance Gold was involved with the victim, he certainly suspected that he would need more leverage to get himself out of jail if the EPK was still at large. Knowing that his value as an informant would be diminished if the killer were still on the streets, he wrote down everything he knew about Vance's relationship with Chief Horace Johnston, just in case any detectives came by to question him.

Even if Vance had nothing to do with the EPK, Tick knew that his relationship with HoJo would possibly be even more valuable in the long run to those that held the power to set him free. That proved to be wise when Mick and Jason paid him a visit in jail. While they were there to ask about Vance Gold, Tick knew that they were really after whoever had killed that girl, so he gave them everything he had on Vance and HoJo.

As the news of Chief Johnston's death made its way through the county jail, Tick was even more convinced that he had done the right thing by providing Detective Knox the information, and now he just needed the cards to fall in his favor. It had been a bit of a gamble, but it was one that he was willing to take to increase his chances of becoming a free man once again.

56

"Is that your daddy?" Gabby asked Coop as she pointed at a photograph on the wall taken the day Coop was drafted with the first pick of the 1996 draft.

"Yes, ma'am, it sure is," he replied.

It was one of many pictures that adorned the wall of his man cave, but also one of his most cherished. Jeffrey Madison was so proud of his son that day, as were the dozens of people from Pass Christian, Mississippi, who had congregated at their house to celebrate one of their own.

"The Pass", like many towns across America, had its fair share of local celebrities. Television journalist Robin Roberts headlined that list, but Cooper Madison was by far the most talented athlete to ever come out of the coastal town.

In addition to baseball, he had excelled at football, basketball, and for one year, even wrestling. By the time he was a junior in high school he had become a household name throughout the state, and by the time the 1996 draft rolled around, everyone in the country who followed baseball knew the name Cooper Madison.

While it was no secret that Chicago would select Coop number one overall, the excitement and anticipation that was felt in the Madison household that day was palpable. As the time drew near for the announcement of the first pick, all of the conversations in the room seemed to cease, aside from the children in attendance who likely had no idea that they were about to witness something historic.

It was not until after Chicago's manager, Donald "Skip" Parsons, finally telephoned to confirm the pick that Coop finally was able to enjoy the moment. He could still remember the way that Jeffrey's stubbly cheek felt against his as the two embraced and how his father had told him how proud his mother would have been.

Kelsey Madison, who had succumbed to cancer when Coop was only 12, was always Coop's biggest fan. While Jeffrey could always be found coaching Coop's teams, it was Kelsey that cheered her heart out after every pitch, catch, and swing of the bat.

Coop still could remember how quiet the ballpark felt in his first game back after Kelsey's death. He struggled those first few games, unable to find the strike zone on the mound and failing to make contact at the plate.

It was not until Jeffrey did something that nobody, especially Coop, ever would have imagined him doing. He announced to the team that he would step down as their coach for the remainder of the season. Jeffrey knew that his son did not need him as a coach that summer as much as he needed him to just be his biggest fan.

For the remaining games on the schedule, Jeffrey could be found sitting in the stands in the same spot that his late wife always did, cheering his heart out just as she would have been.

It worked.

In his very first at-bat, with his father looking on from the bleachers, Coop launched the first pitch he saw clear over the centerfield fence. In his second trip to the plate, he did it again, this time to right field. Coop added a double and a single to go 4-for-4 on the day, and even pitched three hitless innings in relief, striking out all nine batters that he faced.

For Jeffrey, it was the proudest he had ever been of his son's performance on the field. For Coop, it was a reminder that despite the loss of his mother that he was not alone.

Coop continued to excel during the remainder of that season, and before the following summer, Jeffrey sat down with his only child and had a heart-to-heart talk.

"Cuppah, I'm going to ask you something, and I need you to be honest with me, okay?" Jeffrey had said.

"Yessir," Coop affirmed.

"I want to know if you'd like me to coach your team again next season, or if you'd rather have me in the stands like I was to end the year. There is no wrong answer, son, and I promise that I will honor whatever decision you make."

"I want you to coach, Daddy," Coop said without hesitation.

"Are you sure?"

"Yessir. I mean, I like having you in the stands and all, but I love having you as my coach. I'll be okay."

Jeffrey did not say anything in return. Instead, he hugged his son tight, thankful that he too was not alone.

57

Phil Worthington stared at the framed photograph that he held in his hands, the same hands that bore the wear and tear of a man who had spent the past few years battling walleye on Lake Erie. He had his fair share of fishing hooks embedded in his hands during his countless trips out on the water, not to mention the many times those same hands were sliced open by fishing line.

The young girl in the photograph was missing her two front teeth and was smiling in front of a Christmas tree that was in the background. It was Phil's favorite photograph of his daughter, Jane, taken at a time when everyone she knew referred her to as "Janey".

Phil often wished that he could go back in time to that very day, when his baby girl was 8 years old and had yet to experience the traumatic loss of her mother, let alone the dark journey that awaited her in the years following.

He wished that he could hold her one more time and tell her that he loved her. If he could, he would go back in time and do so many things differently. He would protect her from the evils that awaited his only child.

It was just ten years after that picture was taken that Phil received yet another phone call while on the road that would shatter his world forever. He was less than an hour from home after a four-day haul when his cell phone rang. When he saw his home phone number on the caller ID he smiled. He assumed that Jane was calling to see when he would be home. After all, it was Christmas Eve morning and he had promised her that he would be home for his favorite holiday of the year.

Even after the death of his wife, Irene, Phil made sure to give Jane the best Christmas that he could each year. He would spend the entire weekend following Thanksgiving every year stringing lights on the house, and he and Jane would always go and cut down a live Christmas tree, which they would spend the evening decorating as they listened to holiday music.

Like many kids, and even some adults, Christmas represented a magical time for Jane. She loved everything about the holiday, but especially the time she spent with her father. As Jane got older, she would still get as excited as a little girl for Christmas, even though she had started doing drugs and partying in her teenage years. The holidays always provided a brief respite from the darkness that had consumed her reality.

"Hey Janey, I'm almost home, baby girl," Phil said as he answered the call.

"Phil, it's Ethel. Something's wrong with Jane," Mrs. Levine said in a frantic tone, which caused Phil's heart to drop.

"Janey? What's wrong?" Phil asked, hoping she was just battling a case of the flu or maybe a cold.

"I don't know! I tried to wake her up this morning and I can't!" Mrs. Levine answered, her voice wrought with panic.

"Can't wake her up? Is she breathing?" Phil asked, his voice now matching her frantic tone.

"Yes, she's breathing, but I think she is really sick! She has vomit in her mouth and all over her pillow. I don't know what's wrong with her, Phil!"

"Vomit? Was she feeling sick last night?"

"I... I don't think so, but I was asleep by the time she got home. I don't even remember her coming in the house!"

"But, she's breathing, right? Ethel, tell me she's breathing!" Phil demanded.

"She is, but I can't wake her up! Jane, wake up! Jane!"

"Ethel, listen to me. You need to hang up and call 9-1-1. Tell them you need an ambulance immediately and then call me back as soon as possible. Do you understand?" Phil asked his daughter's elderly caretaker.

"Yes, of course," Ethel replied before hanging up and calling for an ambulance.

Phil was not sure what was happening to his daughter. As crazy as it sounds, he was actually hoping that maybe she had been drinking with her friends and had too much alcohol for her petite frame. She was 18, after all, and that would not be out of the realm of possibility.

It was not until he arrived at the hospital, still driving his semi-truck, that he learned the truth about how little he knew his own daughter.

"Heroin? But, that can't be possible," Phil said to the doctor who had just informed him that Jane had suffered a heroin overdose.

"I'm sorry, Mr. Worthington, but preliminary toxicology reports show that Jane tested positive not only for heroin, but also a combination of other opioids and even trace amounts of cocaine. We currently have her in a medically induced coma," the doctor informed Phil, who was in a total state of shock.

"Coma...?"

"Correct. It is very likely that she may have suffered anoxic brain damage due to the lack of oxygen as a result of her overdose, so it's standard procedure in these types of situations to put her in a medically induced coma so that we can try and help her recover."

"Brain damage...? But, I don't understand... How did this happen?" Phil responded, trying to make sense of things.

"Unfortunately, Jane likely had a period of multiple hours where her brain was not receiving enough oxygen, which would likely have caused brain damage on some level. We can't be sure just yet, but by placing her in the coma we can do our best to stabilize and monitor her while her body begins the detoxification process."

"How long will she be like that? When can I see my daughter?" Phil asked.

"It's too early to tell at this time, but in most cases it can be anywhere from a few days to a few weeks before we attempt to bring her out of the coma. As far as seeing your daughter, I apologize, but we can't bring you back there just yet. You should be able to see her in a few hours though."

"But... You will be able to bring her out of it, right?" Phil asked desperately hoping for any reassurance from the doctor.

"Mr. Worthington, we are going to do everything we can to make sure that your daughter recovers, but I also want you to be aware of the obstacles she is facing in the upcoming days. Her body is likely going to suffer major withdrawal symptoms as the drugs that she has been taking leave her system. We will do our best to control those symptoms using various medicines that will help her body deal with the withdrawal. Unfortunately, it is not uncommon for the body to suffer additional setbacks, namely in the form of strokes."

"Strokes? But, she's just a kid. She's barely 18 years old…"

"I know that this is all very hard to take all at once, but your daughter has likely been using drugs for quite some time. Were you aware that she had been using?" the doctor asked.

"Aware? No… I mean, I knew she smoked cigarettes, but nothing like this. I am on the road a lot, though… I drive a truck and am gone a lot… How did this happen?"

"I'm afraid that only Jane knows the answer to that, Mr. Worthington. To be honest, that's not what's important right now, anyway. What is important is that we give her the best care we can and hope that in the next few days she doesn't sustain any further trauma to her brain."

"Will her brain be okay? I mean, when she comes out of the coma?" Phil asked.

"I wish I could give you an answer, but in cases like these, we often won't be able to gauge just how much damage has been caused until she is out of the coma. In the event she suffers any strokes while she is induced, she could have some lasting side effects to deal with," the doctor replied.

"What kind of side effects?" Phil pressed.

"Let's cross that bridge when we get there, Mr. Worthington. In the meantime, I'm going to have you speak with one of the hospital's drug counselors, Elizabeth Iannicca. She will be able to walk you through what the next steps are going to be, not only for Jane, but also for you as her father. I'm going to head back in and continue to monitor your daughter. Why don't you have a seat and try to get some rest? Beth will be out shortly," the doctor responded.

Phil just nodded and walked back to his seat in the waiting room, wondering how all of this could have happened. He blamed himself, of course. All those years on the road, especially after the death of his wife, had made him an absentee father to his daughter.

The sound of his kitchen timer going off snapped Phil out of his recollection of that fateful night, her framed photograph still in his hands. He carefully placed the picture back on his mantle and retrieved his frozen dinner from the oven.

As he picked at the mediocre Salisbury steak dinner in front of him, he felt the rage return. It was that rage that ignited his quest to bring justice for his daughter, and to bring suffering to all of those who had caused her harm.

58

Salvatore Furio ignored the "Closed Until Further Notice" sign on the front door of Buddy's Speakeasy as he unlocked and entered through the door of the club of which he was part owner. Due to the fact that the club's parking lot was still an active crime scene, the police had informed Vance that he could not open back up until they gave him the green light.

Outside the club, two patrolmen sat in their cruiser. They had been ordered to keep an eye on not only the taped-off crime scene, but also the owner of the establishment where their chief had been killed just two nights earlier.

Vance had told the officers assigned to protect him earlier in the day that he would be expecting a visit from his partner that evening, and that he would have a key to let himself in. Anyone else, he said, should be considered an uninvited guest.

Furio, after locking the door behind him, looked around the dimly lit club for a moment and sighed. As someone who had always prided himself on overseeing a business that had built so many of Cleveland's newest industrial buildings, becoming the co-owner of a strip club was not something that he had embraced.

If it were not for his old friend, Chief Horace Johnston, and his insistence that the club would be a perfect way for him to funnel his construction money, Furio never would have agreed to help finance the club. However, HoJo had helped him out so many times over the years, and he felt obligated to return the favor.

"Come on back to the office, Sal! Grab a drink from the bar if you want," the voice of Vance Gold echoed off the walls of the empty club.

"Asshole," Furio muttered under his breath in response as he made his way toward the beer cooler and grabbed a bottle.

Furio had despised Vance Gold from the moment that the two had met. While he knew that some of his business dealings were not exactly legal, Furio never saw himself as being a criminal like Vance. Knowing that his partner used to deal drugs made their union even more difficult, as Furio's own son, Giovanni had died of a heroin overdose three years earlier.

In fact, one of the stipulations that Furio had insisted upon when brokering the deal was that HoJo had to assure him that Vance was no longer in the drug game. HoJo had promised him that Vance was no longer dealing, but despite that promise, Furio had suspected that his new business partner could never be fully trusted.

One time, about a month after Buddy's opened, Furio even sent one of his workers to the club to try and score some dope from Vance. Surprisingly, the worker was not only informed by Vance that he did not sell drugs, but was also barred from ever returning to the club again.

After passing that test, Furio felt a little more comfortable about his working relationship with Vance. In fact, the club proved to be an excellent way for him to launder his money, and the two maintained a cordial partnership.

"Have a seat," Vance said as he gestured to the two chairs across from his desk.

"What's up with the cops outside, Vance?" Furio asked as he took a seat.

"Protection," Vance said as he poured himself a glass of whiskey.

"Protection? From who? Disgruntled strippers?" Furio teased.

"Very funny, Sal."

"Really, though. You worried that whoever killed HoJo is coming for you next?" Furio asked.

"Maybe. Or maybe he'll come after you," Vance replied as he raised his glass and took a sip.

"Well, first off, coming after me would be a mistake on his part. I have two knuckle-draggers that he'd have to get through. Secondly, and don't take this the wrong way, but don't you think he would've killed you the same night he killed HoJo?"

"Perhaps... But if this guy really is the EPK, then maybe he wants to drag this out as long as he can," Vance replied.

"Oh yeah? Why is that, Vance?"

"Think about it, Sal. What do serial killers want the most, besides notoriety?"

"I wouldn't know," Sal responded.

"Fear. They want to strike fear into the hearts of an entire city, and let me tell you, I'm scared shitless," Vance declared as he finished his drink and began to pour another.

"So, what, you gonna have cops like those two dipshits out there follow you around the rest of your life? You really think that they'll actually want to protect you when the time comes?"

"Hey, not all of us can afford to have bodyguards like you, Sal. Right now, I'm doing what I gotta do to survive," Vance said as he took a swig.

"Alright, then, what's the rest of the plan?" Furio asked.

"You mean for the club? I don't know, I guess whenever we can we reopen it," Vance replied.

"That's all you got? Jesus Christ, Vance, this is more than just a shitty strip joint. I need this place; at least until the steelyard job is complete."

"So, what's the problem? I just told you we'd open back up. It'll probably be sometime this week," Vance ensured.

"Yeah? Well, what if you never get the green light to open back up? In case you forgot, our biggest ally in the city is in a damn cooler at the morgue," Furio seethed.

"What are you saying? You think that they won't let us open back up?" Vance questioned.

"All I know is that the one guy who could've made sure of that is dead. I don't trust anyone else in that department, and neither should you. Speaking of, what'd you tell the cops?" Furio demanded.

"Tell the cops about what?" Vance replied incredulously.

"Jesus, Vance, what do you think? About us? About HoJo? About Arliss? You and I both know that this is about way more than our arrangement at this crappy joint," Furio pressed.

"Nothing, Sal. What do you think I am, an idiot? I didn't say shit!"

"I sure hope not, Vance," Furio warned. "Because if I find out that you're lying, the EPK won't be the only one you'll have to fear."

59

"So, are you nervous for tomorrow?" Cara asked Coop as the pair stretched just outside the lobby of the Westcott Hotel. They had decided the night before to partake in a Sunday morning jog, as Coop's surgery was scheduled for early the next day, and he knew that it would be awhile before he'd be able to do much of anything physical in the weeks that followed.

Clarence, when informed of their plans, was not thrilled that they would be running through the streets of Cleveland by themselves. He had relieved Grace Brooks earlier that morning to keep an eye on the lobby of the Westcott, which meant that he could not accompany the couple on their jog. Coop had assured him that they would be just fine, and he had also promised to take his cell phone with him just in case.

"For the surgery itself? Nah. It's the recovery that has me as nervous as a cat in a room full of rockers," he replied with a chuckle.

"Speaking of, are you sure you're okay with my family still staying at your place while you recover?"

"Yes, ma'am. Why wouldn't I be?"

"Well, I just want to make sure. I mean, I know that those first few days are going to be rough, and I just don't want to make it any harder on you by having them there."

"I'd be more worried about them dealing with me, especially if I'm whining like a baby," Coop laughed.

"I won't let that happen because I'm going to take great care of you."

"What about your classes? I don't want you getting off track with your studies on account of me."

"I already took care of that. I spoke to all of my professors and they're letting me do the work from home."

"So, you're gonna be my nurse?" Coop asked.

"Like Florence Nightingale," Cara confirmed.

"Darn, I was hoping you'd be more like a sexy nurse in one of those little white outfits," Coop said with a smile.

"Oh yeah? Well, maybe I'll pick one of those up for when you're feeling better and we don't have a 6 year-old running around the place."

"Now we're talking…"

"Listen, I just want you to know how much I appreciate how awesome you've been with Gabby. She thinks you walk on water, you know," Cara said sincerely.

"No need to thank me; Gabby's my little buddy. That girl is so smart, you know? She was reading one of her little books to me last night, and I swear that I couldn't read that well even when I was ten!"

"She's a pistol too. That girl is going to give my brother a run for his money when she gets older," Cara agreed.

"How come they don't have more kids? I mean, they're great parents. They should have a baker's dozen of little Knoxes."

"Well, they tried to. Erica actually was pregnant two more times after Gabby, but ended up losing both. That was really tough on both of them, and I think they just decided that they couldn't go through that again," Cara replied.

"Oh man, I didn't know. My momma had a miscarriage a few years after I was born too."

"I'm sorry to hear that."

"She lost the baby in the third trimester, so it was really hard on all of us. I was young, but I remember we even had a nursery done up in the house and everything. Took them years to finally paint the walls and turn it back into a guest room," Coop recalled solemnly.

"Oh my God, the third trimester? That's terrible! I can't even imagine going through something like that."

"Well, hopefully, we won't have to," Coop replied, not even realizing that he had used the plural pronoun.

"We?" Cara asked surprised.

"Oh, umm, I'm sorry… It just came out that way," Coop replied flustered.

"Don't be. Really, it's okay," Cara assured.

"You sure?"

"Positive. To be honest, I kinda like that you said it. Don't get me wrong, I know it's way too early for us to even think about our future together like that, but I'd be lying if I said that I didn't imagine us like that someday," Cara admitted.

"Well, that's good, because every time I think about the future, you're in it," Coop said smiling.

"So, does that mean you want kids someday?" Cara asked.

"Yes, ma'am. I'm thinking at least seven or eight," Coop deadpanned, knowing that it would get a reaction from Cara.

"Seven or eight, huh? Well then, it's been nice knowing you, Cooper Madison," Cara replied calling his bluff.

"Oh, so that's it, huh?" he laughed.

"Only if you want it to be," she replied, playing along.

"Never," Coop said, his tone serious.

"Good," Cara smiled. "Because I'm not going anywhere."

"Promise?"

"Promise."

The two kissed, followed by a long embrace. It was a crisp autumn morning and the streets outside the Westcott Hotel were quiet.

"So, are you ready to get one last run in before you're out of commission for awhile?" Cara asked.

"That depends. Are you going to be able to keep up with me?" Coop replied.

"Umm, you must be forgetting that I ran track at Berea High, Mister. Be careful what you wish for," Cara warned.

"Well then, the gauntlet has been thrown."

"Don't worry, I'll take it easy on you."

"Oh, it's on!" Coop said as he took off running without warning.

"Cheater!" Cara exclaimed, as she chased after him, her laughter echoing off the tall buildings that lined the downtown street.

60

"Daddy's making omelets, Mommy!" Gabby said excitedly as she greeted Erica inside the kitchen of Coop's penthouse.

"Is he? Well, that sure sounds delicious, doesn't it?" Erica replied as she gave her daughter, who was seated at the kitchen table, a kiss.

"You're just in time to see the master at work," Jason claimed as he executed a perfect flip of the omelet.

"Not gonna lie, that was kinda hot," Erica whispered in her husband's ear as she wrapped her arms around him from behind.

"Wait til you see me fold in the cheese," Jason whispered back, giving Erica a kiss.

"Where's Coop and Cara?" Erica asked.

"They should be back soon. They decided to go for a run," he replied.

"Better them than me," Erica laughed.

"I think Coop has some nervous energy to get rid of before his surgery tomorrow," Jason added.

"That, and we're probably driving him nuts by now," Erica mused.

"Oh, I'm sure that factored into the equation," Jason agreed.

"What time did you get home last night?" Erica asked as she poured herself a cup of coffee.

"It was around eleven. I wish I could say that we made a lot of progress on the case, but I'd be lying. You and Gabby were out cold, so I didn't want to wake you," Jason answered.

"Please tell me that you don't have to go in today? I'm worried about you," Erica said as she took a sip from her mug.

"Well, the plan is that I'm not. Mick insisted that I stayed home with you today. But if something big comes up, I'm going to have to. He and I are supposed to touch base this afternoon over the phone."

"How's Mick holding up? I feel bad for him, especially since the divorce. He has to be lonely," Erica lamented.

"You know Mick – if he is, he's not showing it. That being said, he never misses an opportunity to badmouth Zoey," Jason chuckled.

"Well, she did run off on him with her personal trainer, so I don't blame him," Erica recounted.

"Agreed, which is why you're never allowed to have a personal trainer," Jason teased.

"I thought that was only because you convinced me that this body didn't need to work out," Erica countered.

"Oh, yeah. Well, that's the *obvious* reason, but I thought that went without saying. I was just saying that I know a personal trainer would never be able to resist you, so it's more for his protection," Jason retreated.

"You should quit while you're ahead, Detective," Erica chided as she took a seat at the table with Gabby, who was in the process of finishing up a page in her princess coloring book.

"You know, I was thinking that we should see if Coop and Cara would be okay with my parents coming over for lunch. We could watch the football game and catch up. I feel like I haven't seen them in ages," Jason suggested as he served his wife and daughter each an omelet.

"I want Grandma Jo and Grandpa Charlie to come over!" Gabby exclaimed upon hearing the plan.

"I think that would be nice, and I'm sure Coop and Cara would agree. We could also see if Johnny could come over. It would be nice to have everyone together. We could certainly use some normalcy for a change," Erica sighed.

"I think Johnny usually works at the gym on Sunday, but we could definitely ask," Jason replied, as he sat down at the table with an omelet of his own.

"Well, hopefully Johnny isn't dating any of his clients, especially the ones that are already spoken for," Erica mused.

"Let's hope not. That's a slippery slope," Jason replied, shaking his head in amusement.

"This omelet is absolutely delicious, Babe," Erica gushed before taking another bite.

"Well, thank you very much. How about you, Gabby? Did Daddy do a good job on the omelet?"

"Uh-huh," Gabby replied, her mouth full of food.

"Good. After we're done, you guys can thank me by doing the dishes then," Jason stated as he gestured toward the kitchen counter.

"You know, normally I'd argue with you, but this is so good that I'll gladly clean up your mess," Erica replied.

"Must be my lucky day," Jason laughed. "You know, if Cleveland actually pulls out a win today, I'll have to go play the lottery."

"If that happens, we all will," Erica agreed.

"Do we *have* to watch football? It's so boring," Gabby pleaded.

"Yes, we do, young lady. It's our duty as Cleveland fans to subject our brains to a minimum of three hours of bad football each week," Jason replied, his words dripping with sarcasm.

"What does subject mean?" Gabby asked.

"It means that your daddy is right, Baby. It's what we do here in Cleveland," Erica insisted.

"Just another reason why I love you," Jason said to his wife smiling.

"You know it, Babe," Erica replied. "Now let's finish enjoying this meal so we can plan our big day."

61

"I didn't wake you up, did I?" Cliff Scriven asked Hannah after she answered his phone call.

"I wish I could say you did, but I didn't sleep well last night," Hannah replied.

"Well, I don't have anything on Deputy Chief Lawson yet, but I have some updates on our guy, Salvatore Furio."

"Awesome! What do you have for me?"

"Well, after I left the diner, I went back to my office and tried to see if I could make any more connections between Furio and Chief Johnston."

"Any luck?" Hannah asked.

"Nothing concrete, but I do think I see a pattern based on all of the bids that Furio's company won over the past decade that were within

Cleveland's city-limits," Scriv replied.

"What kind of patterns?" Hannah questioned as she grabbed her notepad and pen, ready to jot down any notes that her trusted PI could give her.

"Well, it seems that on every winning bid that SFI Construction obtained during the timeframe that I was looking at, came in just under another company's offer. In fact, SFI and this company would always come in far below all of the other bids. Every single one was like that."

"That is odd," Hannah agreed. "What's the other company?"

"Erie Shores Construction. They're about the same size as SFI, and they've won plenty of other bids over the years, mainly municipal projects."

"So, they're a legitimate company?"

"ESC? Oh yes, a pretty profitable one from what I gather too," Scriv confirmed.

"So, why do you think they were just missing out on all the bids that SFI won?" Hannah asked, trying to see where Scriv was going.

"How about I tell you who the owner of Erie Shores Construction is, and you see if you can guess where I'm going?" Scriv countered.

"You know I love a challenge. Go for it."

"The owner of ESC is a guy by the name of Arliss Gold," Scriv replied, letting his words hang for effect.

"Arliss *Gold*? You're joking, right? He can't possibly be related to Vance, can he?" Hannah asked, astonished at the possibility.

"It appears that Arliss is Vance's older, far more successful, brother."

"Wow. Okay, while I don't know much about the bidding

process for construction jobs, my guess is that it wasn't a coincidence that Furio's company would know just how much they had to bid in order to beat out ESC for a job."

"Bingo. While it would be hard to prove without an admission from either side, my theory is that Erie Shores would purposely make low bids for these jobs, and then would provide Furio with the number that he had to beat to win them," Scriv stated.

"I'm assuming that you believe HoJo was the common denominator in these deals then?" Hannah guessed.

"It certainly seems plausible, especially when you factor in that Vance and HoJo were in the business of doing favors for each other. The only thing I don't know for certain, is how Salvatore Furio figures into the equation."

"Well, he certainly has benefitted from it. Maybe HoJo was getting a cut of the action for every job that Furio won?"

"That would make sense, for sure," Scriv agreed.

"And what about Vance's brother? He had to be getting something out of this as well."

"While I haven't had time to go through all the bids that Arliss Gold's company has won over the years, my guess is that we will likely see the same pattern in reverse."

"This is nuts. Any chance you can look today and see if Erie Shores magically outbid SFI on any jobs during the same period of time?" Hannah asked.

"Planning on it, but I also wanted to tell you what I witnessed last night," Scriv replied.

"Let me have it," Hannah encouraged.

"I was doing some surveillance on Salvatore Furio, just to see if he would give us anything, and he didn't disappoint."

"Go on…"

"At about 10 pm, Furio was driven by his two bodyguards to Buddy's Speakeasy. I'm assuming Vance was holed-up in his office there, because there was a patrol car watching over the place."

"That was probably the security detail that the detectives told us about," Hannah added.

"Agreed."

"How long was he inside?" Hannah asked.

"Not too long, maybe a half hour, but I'm guessing that he and Vance were coming up with a game plan on how to deal with their business arrangement going forward, now that HoJo is no longer in the picture," Scriv responded.

"Did Furio go anywhere else after he left Buddy's?"

"He just went home, and that's when I called it a night."

"Have you talked to the detectives about any of this yet?" Hannah asked.

"Not yet. In fact, I'd like to do some more digging today before we tell them. I will have some eyes on Arliss Gold and Anthony Lawson today too. I have a couple guys that do surveillance for me when needed. They're pros and they won't ask any questions as to why they're watching them, which is exactly the type of discretion that we need."

"I trust your judgment, Scriv. This could get sticky," Hannah stated.

"It's already sticky, Hannah. This is could get dangerous."

62

Phil Worthington watched his target from the front seat of his 1992 Chevrolet 1500 pick-up truck. He could have sold the old truck years ago, as the money from his fishing charters alone would have easily enabled him to buy a newer model. However, this was last the truck he had owned when Jane was still alive and he could not bear to let it go.

When Jane was younger, she used to love staring up at the clouds from the bed of the truck, her father at her side, as they would call out whatever shapes they thought the clouds resembled. Despite the fact that Phil was often away from home for days at a time, he always made sure to maximize the time he spent with Jane when he was present.

On the dashboard of the truck was a wallet-sized photograph of Jane - her fourth grade school picture. Most people despise being stuck at red lights, but not Phil. He would use those moments to admire the smiling girl staring back at him from the dash and reminisce about happier times – sometimes even talking to his daughter as if she were in the passenger seat.

"There he is, Janey. Don't worry, baby girl... Justice will be served," Phil declared as his gaze narrowed upon his prey. By that point, his only child had been gone for nearly four years, but the pain of her death was as prevalent as ever.

In the days following her overdose, Jane suffered multiple strokes while in the medically induced coma, leaving her brain dead beyond any chance of recovery. Even if they had been able to pull her from the coma, the doctors insisted that she would never again be able to live without the assistance of machines to keep her alive.

That was when Phil made the hardest decision a parent could ever make, and he allowed the doctors to remove her from life support. A few hours later, with her father at her side, Jane Worthington died peacefully in her sleep.

Phil had tried to make sense of it all shortly after her death by reaching out to the other teenagers from school that she used to hang out with. Unfortunately, Jane had lost contact with pretty much anyone who was not working the streets with her at the time of her death, as she had convinced her father to let her drop out of school and get her GED before the start of her senior year.

Phil was less than thrilled that his only child had insisted on dropping out, but she had promised him that she would go to cosmetology school once she earned her GED. That at least gave him some hope.

As fate would have it, Jane had been scheduled to complete the high school equivalency program just weeks after her overdose. It would be the first of many missed milestones in a life cut far too short.

It was a few weeks following her death, after he received a visit from Jane's best friend from childhood, when Phil finally learned just how his daughter was able to afford her drug habit. Despite the fact that the two had grown estranged during their teenage years, Mia Santiago admitted to Phil that she had been keeping a secret about his daughter – a secret that she felt she could not keep from him any longer.

Mia confided in him that it was common knowledge amongst their classmates that Jane had become a prostitute in order to feed her growing habit.

Incredulous, Phil refused to believe it.

"A hooker? Janey? That's a lie, Mia," Phil had replied.

"I wish it was," Mia lamented.

The thought of his daughter selling her body for drug money was both absurd and haunting to digest for Phil. However, as he witnessed his daughter's childhood friend sobbing as she conveyed the news, he could not deny that it was plausible.

Since her fatal overdose, Phil had not been able to figure out how Jane had paid for the drugs that killed her. She did not have a job, and she never even asked him for any money outside of the cash he would leave for her and Mrs. Levine to get food with while he was on the road. It was as if Mia's words were the missing lines to the dots that he had been trying to connect.

"If she really was, you know," Phil began to ask, unable to speak the actual word, "Then who did she work for?"

He had been around enough rest stops during his time as a truck driver to know that almost every prostitute had a pimp waiting in the wings to get his cut of the profits.

"I don't know. Jane and I stopped hanging out a long time ago. The last time I went to a party that Jane was at, she was so wasted and hanging out with these people I didn't even know. When I said something to her about it she got angry and started calling me names, saying that I wasn't her friend anymore. I ended up leaving the party, and… Well, that was really the last time I talked to her. It was as if she was a totally different person," Mia replied.

Before she left, Mia apologized to Phil for not telling him

sooner. She begged for his forgiveness, adding that she knew that she would never be able to forgive herself.

Phil, finally coming to terms that Mia's revelation might be true, reassured her that she was not to blame. He felt bad for the girl standing in front of him, the same girl that used to sleep over at his house almost every weekend, as she wiped away tears of sadness and regret.

He forgave her.

Phil knew that she was hurting too, and that she would spend the rest of her life wondering if she could have done more to prevent Jane's death.

He, too, would carry that life sentence of regret.

63

"Thank you again for having us over, Cooper. I can't get over how beautiful your apartment is," Joanne Knox said as she took a seat on one of the two leather couches located in Coop's den.

"Apartment? This is no apartment, Joanne. That little studio we had in Lakewood after we got married was an apartment," Charlie Knox chided his wife.

Cara's parents had joined them for pizza and football earlier that afternoon, and now they were all unwinding after yet another Cleveland loss.

"I'm just happy we could have y'all over, even though the football game was a bit of a letdown," Coop deflected.

"It always is, but yet, we still watch them every Sunday for some reason," Jason interjected as he entered the room.

"Welcome to Cleveland football," Charlie said to Coop.

"Well, at least since '99," Jason added, referencing the Cleveland's lack of football success since rejoining the league during the 1999 season.

"Isn't that the definition of insanity?" Erica asked to the group. "Doing the same thing over and over again, yet expecting a different result?"

"I know. I feel like I should have my head examined every Sunday after watching this garbage they call a team," Charlie replied.

"At least y'all have a pro team to watch lose on Sundays. Mizzippy doesn't even have one," Coop pointed out.

"Be thankful for that!" Jason replied before being interrupted by the familiar ring of his cell phone.

Jason had been expecting the call from Mick, but had also thoroughly enjoyed not thinking about the case throughout the course of the day. He had learned early on in his career the importance of turning his brain off in regards to a case from time to time, especially when he was with his family. Despite the gravity of the EPK case, he had done an admirable job living in the moment during the game.

"Talk to me, Mick," Jason said as he walked out of the room and made his way to the balcony.

"Did you enjoy the game?" Mick asked.

"I don't know if it's possible to enjoy watching a team that bad, but I certainly enjoyed the company and the break. I really appreciate you giving me the time off today," Jason replied.

"No worries. You got a family and all that crap," Mick, who was never very good at conversations with Jason that did not involve insults, said in return.

"So, anything new?" Jason asked.

"Actually, no. I'm still waiting to hear from that Scriv guy though. As far as I'm concerned, just take the rest of the day off. If something changes, I'll call you."

"I won't argue with that. Hopefully, this guy is as good as Hannah says he is. We could use the help."

"I won't hold my breath, but hopefully I'm wrong."

"Has that ever happened before?" Jason asked jokingly.

"What? Me being wrong? Just once," Mick replied, playing along.

"Once? When was that?"

"When I got married," Mick laughed. "I have the alimony payments to prove it too!"

64

Phil Worthington tried his best not to grow impatient as he waited on his target to leave the safe confines of his place of business. As he sat in his truck waiting, he reflected on the series of events that led to him being there.

It was not long after Mia's revelation that Phil retired from his job as a truck driver and started his fishing charter business to fill the void that had relentlessly consumed him. He found his time on the boat to be both cathartic and enjoyable.

After years of working in solitude, Phil welcomed the socialization that accompanied being a charter captain. He truly enjoyed helping people from all walks of life pull in walleye from Lake Erie, and he was confident that none of his customers ever would have known the darkness that surrounded him when they walked off his boat.

Sure, almost every group that paid for his services asked why he named his boat "Jane's Justice", but he would always lie and tell them that it was the name that came with the boat when he bought it.

As healing as it was for his soul to be on the boat during those first few years after his daughter's death, it was the complete opposite when he would return home from a trip. Like many parents who lose a child, Phil left Jane's bedroom practically untouched following her death. Some nights he would even sit on the edge of her bed in hopes that he would feel closer to her spirit.

It was not until he finally mustered up the courage to begin the process of cleaning out some of her belongings, on the third anniversary of her passing, that he discovered a journal she had apparently hidden in the attic crawlspace above her closet.

Through tears in his eyes, Phil read about Jane's first experience with marijuana, the night she lost her virginity, and her eventual introduction to prostitution in order to pay for the drugs that she so desperately needed. It was in those same pages that Phil discovered the names, and even some of the phone numbers, of those responsible for his daughter's journey into the world of drugs and prostitution. Over the next few weeks, Phil began to put faces to the names listed in Jane's journal. Some of the names had to be crossed off though, as he learned that they had suffered the same fate as his beloved daughter.

For those that he had contact information, Phil would call them individually and ask if they had known his daughter. Since there were only a few male names listed, he started by contacting just the female names in her book. Phil figured that they were likely living the same life that his daughter had and would be more likely to try and help.

It proved to be a challenging task. Most of the girls, weary that he might be a cop denied ever knowing her and hung up within seconds after telling him as much. It was not until he contacted a young woman who went by the name of Sadie, that he was able to arrange a face-to-face meeting with someone from Jane's list.

It was Sadie who helped Phil understand the hierarchy of people that acted like puppet masters in Jane's life. She told him about the two Russian girls that would befriend attractive young females that they discovered at local parties around the city and how they would supply them with drugs.

At first, the drugs would be free, otherwise known as a "taste". Once the girls became hooked, the Russians would explain that the drugs were no longer on the house. For most of the girls, like Jane, their need to catch the next high would make them vulnerable. That's when they would be introduced to a young man who would tell them everything that they wanted to hear.

Tick, as he was known on the streets, would shower the girls with compliments and sell them on the premise that they could soon be making more than enough money to buy the things that they desired: clothes, jewelry, and especially drugs.

All they had to do, he would assure them, was go on "dates" with lonely men. He even promised them that they would be safe because nobody messed with "his girls". All they had to do, he explained, was go out for a few hours each night and do the things that a lot of them were already doing for free.

When Phil asked whom it was that Tick worked for, Sadie talked about a man who was in charge of the biggest drug ring in Cleveland. She explained that the man had a reputation for being untouchable, even to the police. She even spoke of the man's rumored relationship with none other than the Chief of Police himself.

She told Phil about a man named Vance Gold.

65

"So, I know I already asked you this morning, but now are you getting nervous for tomorrow?" Cara asked Coop, as the two enjoyed some time alone, holding hands on the balcony of his penthouse suite at the Westcott Hotel.

Cara's parents had just left and Jason and his family were watching a movie in the den, so the couple decided to enjoy the crisp autumn evening outside.

"Wait… What's happening tomorrow? I mean, I know it's a Monday, but I'm drawing a blank. Remind me again?" Coop asked, acting oblivious.

"Very funny," Cara replied, not taking the bait.

"Oh! You meant am I nervous about that pesky Tommy John surgery I have tomorrow morning… I didn't put two and two together…"

"It's okay if you are, you know," Cara reassured him, while ignoring his attempt at deflection.

Coop, realizing that she was not going to let him slide, decided that he would finally respond to Cara in a serious manner. "Same as I was this morning, I suppose. Not really worried about the surgery, but the rehab is another story."

"Well, I'll be there every step of the way to help you get through that," Cara reminded him.

"I know, and I appreciate that. I'm just worried how you're gonna keep up with your classes if you're tryin' to look after me."

"Well, that's not an issue, so don't even worry about it," Cara replied.

"How so? You didn't drop out, did you?" Coop asked.

"Oh my God, no, you dork! The college and my professors are letting me finish the semester from home. They know this is it before my internship, so they're fine with it."

"Well, that's good, as long as you don't slack off," Coop teased.

"Oh no, I can see the finish line, so I'm going to check every box I need to. I can't wait to be done."

"I bet…"

Coop let his words hang for a moment before changing the subject. "So, I have been meaning to talk to you about something since Thursday. Todd invited us down to his new place in Florida to recover after the surgery. I didn't say anything earlier because of your classes and all, but now that you're able to work from home, I figured I'd see what you think."

"Florida?" Cara replied. "Wow… When?"

"He said as soon as I was allowed to fly. I figure I can ask Dr.

Mueller tomorrow. My guess is a few days after the surgery."

"Well, I don't see why we couldn't. I mean, assuming you want to go?" Cara asked.

"To be honest, it sounds like it would be a nice getaway, and I can think of worse places to recover from a surgery. I guess his house is right on the beach and it's in a real quiet spot called Casey Key. He said he's neighbors with some celebrities, so it must be nice."

"Casey Key? Never heard of it, but maybe that's why it's such a quiet spot," Cara said in return.

"He said it's near Sarasota. The town it's in is called Nokomis, or something like that. He said he'd fly us there on a private jet even, and we just need to say the word when we want to come down. He and Joy will be there until after the holidays since this is his only real downtime."

"Private jet? Wow, I've never even flown coach before," Cara replied.

"Really?"

"True story. All of our vacations involved brutally long trips in the family station wagon," Cara laughed.

"Well then, sounds like you'll get to fly the first time in style."

"This might be good for my brother and his family too. I mean, if they're going to be staying here while we're gone," Cara said.

"Of course they're going to be staying here. I said they'd be welcome to stay as long as they want, and you're right, it would be good for them to have the place to themselves," Coop agreed.

"You're amazing. I really can't thank you enough. How'd I get so lucky?" Cara asked.

"Come on now, I'm the lucky one," Coop dismissed.

"Well, if you play your cards right, you will be later," Cara whispered.

"See, I told you I'm the lucky one," Coop replied. "I think this trip is gonna be good for us. Besides, I can't wait to see you in a bikini…"

"Well, I do own a couple, you know… But, I might need a drink before the flight. Not gonna lie, flying in a plane seems kinda scary to me," Cara admitted.

"Oh, you'll be fine. It's safer than driving," Coop responded.

"That's what they say, but still…"

"Well, I'll be there next to you. You can hold on to me if the plane goes down," Coop chuckled.

"Don't even joke like that!" Cara playfully admonished Coop.

"I'm just getting' your goat. So, should we go tell Jason and Erica that they'll have the place to themselves for awhile?" Coop asked.

"Do you mind if we wait a bit?" Cara asked. "I'm just really enjoying this time with you out here."

"Hey, it's your world, girl. I'm just livin' in it," Coop replied.

"You're such a dork."

"You have the sweetest nicknames for me," Coop chuckled.

"Well, you are a dork… But you're the cutest dork I know," Cara said with a smile as she squeezed his hand.

"I love you," Coop said as his steely eyes locked in on Cara.

"I love you more…"

66

Phil Worthington decided to call it quits just before midnight. His target had yet to leave the building he had been holed-up in all day and showed no signs of changing. Phil knew that he would resume the hunt in the morning. His prey was not going to escape. Besides, he was starving, so he drove towards the late-night diner that he had become a regular at since Jane's death. It was the same diner where Phil met Sadie when she had informed him about those responsible for his daughter's fall from grace.

"So, let me get this straight… This Vance Gold fella… He's the boss of this whole operation?" Phil had asked Sadie as the two sat across from each other in the corner booth of the diner.

"Was…" Sadie replied.

"What do you mean, *was*?"

"I mean he was the boss, but he got out when the Russians moved in."

"I thought you said the Russian girls worked for him?" Phil asked, confused.

"Not *those* Russians. The Russian mob," Sadie sighed, getting annoyed.

"Please," Phil said as he slid two $100 bills across the table, "Help me understand."

Sadie glanced down at the crisp notes and took a deep breath. "Fine, but only if you promise never to contact me again after tonight," Sadie said as she discreetly pocketed the cash.

"Deal."

"Okay, so before the Russian mob took over, Vance Gold ran the show. If you spent a dime on drugs or girls in Cleveland, he was getting at least some of that paper."

"Paper?" Phil asked.

"Yeah, paper. You know, money?" Sadie asked, almost laughing at Phil's naiveté.

"Gotcha."

"The point is, Vance was like the CEO of all the drugs and prostitutes in the city. He wasn't out there slingin' dope on the streets, but all the dealers who worked for him were. Same with the girls," Sadie explained.

"What about the chief? You said he helped this Vance guy?" Phil asked.

"That's what they say, but I never saw the guy. All I know is that Vance never got popped by the cops. Not once. And when one of his dealers or girls did, they'd usually be released without charges the next day. Well, except for Tick..."

"Tick? I thought he was a pimp, not a dealer?" Phil asked.

"Tick *was* a pimp, but he also would deal on the side. That dude would do just about anything to make money," Sadie replied.

"So, if Tick was one of his guys, why didn't Vance or the chief bail him out?" Phil pressed.

"It's a long story, but right around the time Vance was getting out of the game, Tick got popped for slingin' rock. He tried to run, but some badass chick cop tackled him and broke his damn arm. Before they could book him, they had to take him to the hospital. I guess his arm was legit hanging like a noodle. Somebody at the hospital leaked it to the press that a female cop had broken some drug dealer's arm, so next thing you know it's all over the news. Vance told Tick he was on his own because he had too much heat on him and the chief couldn't make it disappear."

"I bet that didn't make Tick happy," Phil replied.

"Not at all, but you know what? That dude beat the rap anyway. They said the chick cop used excessive force, so a couple months later, he walked. By the time he was out, Vance was already out of the game. We all were..." Sadie recalled.

"Because of the Russian mob?" Phil asked.

"Yup. It didn't take them long to move in either. Those dudes are ruthless. They started by poaching all of Tick's girls while he was locked up."

"Including you?" Phil interjected.

"No, but they tried. Scared the shit outta me though. I decided to go straight. Went to rehab, moved back in with my folks. I'm done with the game. Been clean for six months, " Sadie asserted.

"Good for you," Phil replied approvingly.

"Thanks. I'm just tryin' to get through one day at a time..."

"So what happened to Vance?"

"He laid low for a while I guess. After I got out of rehab I ran into a girl I used to work the streets with. She said the Russians had threatened to put a hit out on Vance if he didn't get out, so I guess that's all it took. Like I said, Vance was more of a CEO than anything. He wasn't built to take on the Russians. She told me he was going to open a strip club, which I guess he did."

"A strip club? What's it called?" Phil asked.

"Buddy's Speakeasy. It's over on Clark Avenue. Hard to believe Vance Gold is a legit businessman," Sadie chuckled.

"I'd hardly call running a strip club a legit occupation," Phil countered, which caused Sadie to roll her eyes.

"I gotta get goin'. I've already told you more than I should have…"

"What about the two Russian girls? The ones that would lure the girls into being prostitutes? What happened to them?" Phil pressed.

"Far as I know, they're doing the same thing for the Russians that they did for Tick and Vance."

"Can you tell me their names? Or where I could find them?" Phil asked.

"They go by Svetlana and Nina, but I don't know where you'd find them. Like I said, I'm done with that life," Sadie replied.

"Okay, well, where'd they used to hang out? Can you at least tell me that? I'm begging you," Phil pleaded.

"I guess you could try this dance club over on Triskett called The Study Hall. That's where they used to hang, at least."

"The *Study* Hall? Well, isn't that cute…" Phil said, obviously not amused by the club's attempt at irony.

"It's supposed to be an underage dance club for teenagers. They can't sell alcohol, but you'd be lucky to find a single kid in there who wasn't drunk or high," Sadie said as she stood up to leave.

"Sounds like the perfect place to prey on girls," Phil replied.

"Yo, thanks for the cash, but I gotta go. Remember, I'm done with that life, and I plan on staying that way for good," Sadie reminded Phil before she walked away.

As Phil Worthington took a seat in the exact same booth that he had shared with Sadie on that fateful night, he recalled the decision that he made after she left. It was a decision that would change not only his life, but also the lives of so many others as a result.

It was in that booth, on that night, that Phil Worthington decided to kill.

67

"Okay, Mr. Madison, I'm going to have you count backwards from ten. We'll take great care of you, and when you wake up it'll be all over," the anesthesiologist said in a soothing tone.

Cooper Madison, who was trying not to look directly at the extremely bright LED light fixtures that hung above the operating table he was occupying, nodded. He had already received an IV containing benzodiazepines, so he was feeling more than relaxed prior to the anesthesiologist administering the drug that would knock him out for the procedure.

"Ten… Nine… Eight…" was all Coop was able to say before succumbing to the anesthesia.

One floor down in the VIP waiting room of the hospital sat Cara Knox and Clarence Walters. Cara was nervously staring at the TV that was mounted near the ceiling of the beautifully appointed room, which was reserved for high-profile patients and their families to use during their stay, while Clarence leafed through the pages of a boating magazine.

"Why do hospitals and doctors' offices always have boating magazines? I mean, how many people actually own a boat, let alone the yachts that they feature in these things?" Clarence asked, hoping to help take Cara's mind off of the surgery.

"I'm sorry, what?" Cara asked in return.

"Never mind, it was a dumb question," Clarence chuckled.

"I'm sorry… I'm just nervous. I'm in my own world right now…"

"I understand, and I've been there before, so I'm not judging."

"You have?"

"Yes, ma'am, just about a year ago when Evelynn had surgery," Clarence replied, referencing his wife.

"Was it anything serious?"

"Well, I think that any time you go under the knife, it's serious; but her surgery was actually for an emergency gall bladder removal."

"Oh my God! What happened?"

"She had been having a lot of abdominal pain, and it wasn't until the second day that I made her go into the ER. She kept insisting it was nothing, but it's a good thing she listened because within a few hours of being at the hospital, they had her in the OR and removed her gall bladder," Clarence recalled.

"Holy crap! Were you freaking out?"

"Not on the outside, but on the inside I was a mess. I did my best to stay strong for her because she was definitely scared, but as soon as she went back for surgery I lost it. The hospital even sent a grief counselor out to talk to me because I was so visibly upset."

"I don't blame you, Clarence. I'm assuming everything went okay though, right?" Cara asked.

"Yes, ma'am. I did a lot of praying while she was in surgery, and I truly believe that God heard me."

"Do you pray a lot?" Cara asked before quickly following it up with an apology. "I'm sorry; that was a really personal thing to ask."

"Well, first of all, don't apologize. Secondly, I do pray a lot. Always have..." Clarence replied, his voice sincere. "What about you? Are you a religious person?"

"Me? Not really, to be honest. I mean, I do believe in God. Growing up we always went to church too. We're Catholic, but after my dad's accident we kind of stopped going. My mom still goes from time to time, but my dad wants nothing to with it. He's pretty much mad at the world, including God," Cara responded.

"That's understandable, but I also know that even though he's given up on God, God will never give up on him. Or you, Cara. There were so many times that I questioned God's plan when I was a cop. I saw a lot of awful things on the job, but every time I started to question Him, God would do something in my life that would only reaffirm my faith."

"I appreciate that, Clarence," Cara said with a smile.

"Do you want to know when I really knew that God existed?" Clarence asked.

"Sure, I'm all ears..."

"Well, I was 16 years old, and my folks let me take the family car down to Akron to visit my grandparents for the weekend. It was my first time driving anywhere outside of the city, and even though I had ridden in the back of that very car a hundred times to their house, I ended up getting lost on the outskirts of Akron. I was almost out of gas because I had been driving around for so long thinking that I'd eventually find my way there," Clarence recalled, laughing and shaking his head at the thought.

"Let me guess, you didn't stop and ask for directions? Typical man!" Cara teased.

"No, I certainly did not. I was too proud, and I also was broke as a joke, except for the change my folks kept in the ashtray. I finally pulled into a gas station and decided that I'd call my grandma from the payphone and beg for her or my gramps to come get me, because there was no way I was going to make it much farther on that empty tank," Clarence said, still shaking his head in disbelief that he had let it come to that.

"Did they come get you?" Cara asked.

"That's actually where God came into the picture," Clarence replied. "Before I got out of the car, I prayed to God that he would help me get out of the jam that my pride had put me in. I asked for His forgiveness and promised him that I would never let my pride get in the way like that again. As I was about to call my grandma, I looked over at a man standing at the gas pump, and it was my gramps. He was at the end of his shift as a runner for the bank, and he was filling up his company car."

"No. Way. What are the odds?" Cara exclaimed as she leaned forward in her chair, hanging on every word.

"Well, I don't know about the odds, but I can tell you that I had never been so happy to see my gramps. Man, I ran over to him, screaming his name. I almost gave him a heart attack! He was as surprised to see me, as I was to see him, especially since we were about twenty miles from his house. In fact, he told me that he almost didn't stop at that gas station because there was another one closer to the bank he worked for, but for whatever reason, he decided to pull in there," Clarence replied, his voice beginning to crack with emotion as tears started to well up in his eyes.

"Clarence… You're gonna make me cry!"

"That was God, Cara. He was really looking after me that day. Gramps gave me ten bucks to put some gas in my tank and drew me a map back to his house. You know what? I still carry that map he drew with me everywhere I go as a reminder," Clarence stated as he produced a small, folded piece of yellowed paper encased in plastic from his wallet and handed it to Cara. "I laminated it when it started to get too worn, so that I could keep it safe forever."

"Clarence, that had to be the most beautiful story I've ever heard," Cara said as she examined the handmade map. "Maybe someday I'll have a moment like that to remind me that God is here too."

"Oh, he's here, Cara," Clarence insisted. "He's always here…"

68

Vance Gold tried to scream, but the sudden onset of cerebral anoxia he was experiencing from the painful tightening around his throat would not let him.

He did not know the man who was standing over him and ignoring his outstretched hand that, in lieu of his absent voice, was desperately begging for mercy. In fact, up until the moment he realized what was happening, Vance had assumed that he was alone in the confines of his office inside Buddy's Speakeasy.

Just minutes earlier one of the two police officers that had been assigned to keep an eye on Vance had pounded on the door of the club.

"What's going on?" Vance, bewildered, had asked the officer upon opening the door.

In the three days since he had been given a police detail for his own safety, they had barely even spoken to him, let alone pounded on the front door.

"We just got a call for an 11-99 in progress not far from here, so lock up and stay put until we get back!" the officer barked.

"What the hell is an 11-99?" Vance asked.

"It means an officer needs immediate assistance from any cops nearby, including us, so just lock the damn door and stay put!" the officer commanded once more as he quickly returned to the cruiser, which was already waiting for him with its lights on.

"Okay, okay! I'm locking the door!" Vance declared as he complied with the officer's wishes and locked the entrance to the club.

It was early in the day, but anyone inside of Buddy's Speakeasy would have had no idea that the Monday morning sun was shining brightly outside. Gentlemen's clubs as a rule don't typically have many, if any, windows and Buddy's was no exception.

Normally, that darkness worked to Vance's advantage, as he never wanted his paying customers to ever know what time of day it was. It was the same reason that he refused to hang any clocks on the walls and why his workers were instructed to change the subject if a patron asked for the time.

On this day, however, the darkness betrayed Vance Gold. The last thing he had heard before feeling the searing pain that simultaneously took his breath away was a familiar zipping sound.

Vance frantically tried to pull the thick plastic band away from his throat, but the industrial strength zip-tie was pulled so tight that he could not even get a finger between the plastic and his skin. Within seconds Vance found himself feeling disoriented and he fell to the ground, still trying to pull the plastic noose from his neck. That's when he first saw the man.

"The more you move, the faster you'll die, Vance. Just ask your pal, HoJo, when you see him in Hell," the man said, his voice calm and calculated, as he produced a photograph from his jacket pocket.

Vance stopped pulling on the plastic with his right hand and instead thrust it towards the stranger standing over him, hoping that the man would show him mercy. He felt a moment of hope when the man kneeled down next to him, but no mercy was offered.

Instead, the man held a photograph of a pretty teenage girl just a few inches from Vance's face, which was beginning to change in color from the lack of oxygen and blood circulating above the neck.

Vance Gold tried to focus long enough on the girl in the photograph to see who she was, but the darkness began to cloud his vision. He had stopped struggling by this point, mostly because his body was not responding to what his brain was trying to order it to do.

As he felt his life slip away into the darkness, Vance Gold's final thoughts were accompanied by the words of his killer.

"This was my daughter Jane," the man said. "And your drugs killed her…"

69

Cooper Madison struggled to open his eyelids, which felt extremely heavy due to the anesthesia that was gradually making its way out of his system. He could hear the voice of a woman, who sounded so close that it seemed as though she was talking directly into his ear.

"Open your eyes slowly, but only when you're ready to, Mr. Madison," the voice said in a reassuring and soothing tone.

Coop tried to respond but his throat would not allow that to happen. He tried to swallow, but that effort was also denied.

"Easy now, no need to talk just yet. Remember, you just had a tube down your throat during surgery, so you're probably feeling a little sore when you try and swallow. As soon as you open your eyes I'll give you a sip of water or some ice chips to help with the dryness," the woman reassured.

Coop, wanting water more than anything he could imagine in that very moment, forced his eyes to open just enough to see the woman seated next to his hospital bed. She was the anesthesiologist who had asked him to count backwards from ten just prior to his surgery, but Coop could not remember her name at the moment.

"There you go. Just so you know, everything went very smoothly during the procedure. Are you ready for a sip of water?" she asked.

Coop nodded yes.

"Alright, here you go. Just a small sip to start. Remember, if you're feeling nauseous that's not uncommon," she said as she held the Styrofoam cup close to his mouth.

Coop took a sip from the flexible straw and felt immediate relief as the ice-cold water traveled down his parched esophagus.

"Thank you," Coop managed to whisper.

"Did that help?"

"Yes, ma'am."

"How are you feeling?"

"Plum tuckered…"

"That's to be expected, but it will get better as the meds leave your system," she reassured.

"Where's Cara?" Coop asked.

"She's in the waiting room. Dr. Mueller just went out to talk to her a little bit ago. Would you like me to have someone get her?"

"Yes, ma'am."

The woman pressed a button on the wireless hospital pager that was attached to her lanyard and instructed the voice on the other end to bring Cara back to the recovery room.

"Well, Cooper, I think that went as well as it could have," Dr.

Craig Mueller said as he entered the room. "Is Dr. Sislowski taking good care of you? You know, in addition to being our best anesthesiologist, Michelle is also a huge baseball fan."

Coop glanced over at the anesthesiologist, thankful that Dr. Mueller had said her name. She nodded in agreement and smiled at Coop.

"Tribe fan?" Coop asked her.

"Actually, I'm a Cubs fan. Born and raised on the north side of Chicago," she replied.

"Oh boy, I should be lucky that you didn't put me to sleep forever," Coop jokingly groaned.

"Well, you did break my heart when you left the Cubs, but I *am* a professional," she chuckled.

"Don't worry, Cooper, I kept an eye on her just in case," Dr. Mueller said with a wink. "Now, let's talk about the next week or so. Cara informed me in the waiting room that you are planning to travel to Florida later this week, which is fine, just not until Wednesday. We are going to keep you here until tomorrow, which is when we are going to show you some of the range of motion exercises that you will need to do while you're away. Other than when you're doing those, you will need to keep your arm in the immobilizer that you'll be receiving later. I'm also going to give you another script for pain meds, but I'll want you off of those by the time you are back here in about 10 days. Sound good?"

"Yessir, thank you, Doc," Coop replied.

"We will go into further detail later, but for now the most important thing is that you get some rest. We'll continue to monitor you during your stay and will answer any questions as they arise. In the meantime, I think you have someone who is dying to see you," Dr. Mueller said as he turned to welcome the visitor.

Cara Knox wore a weary smile as she made her way into the

recovery room. Her eyes could not hide the emotions that they had endured throughout the day as she waited for the surgery to end.

"Well, now, there's the girl I've been dying to see," Coop said, his voice still a bit gravelly from the anesthesia.

"How are you feeling?" Cara said, fighting the urge to throw herself on the bed next to him and kiss him and tell him how much she loved him.

In fact, she was caught off-guard by how deeply worried she was as she sat in the waiting room. It was as if the hours Coop was back in surgery had triggered something inside her that made her realize just how much she cared for him.

"Better now that I see your beautiful face," Coop replied with a smile.

"Well, I'll leave you two alone. I'll be up to see you once you are settled in your room, Cooper. Until then, Dr. Sislowski will be monitoring you and will get you anything you need," Dr. Mueller said as he began to exit the room.

"Thank you, Doc," Coop replied.

"I'm going to go get you some more water. I'll be back soon," Dr. Sislowski said, giving the young couple some privacy, to which both Coop and Cara thanked her.

"Come here so I can kiss those lips that drive me crazy," Coop said as he raised his left hand, his good arm, inviting her to come closer.

Cara obliged and carefully leaned in, kissing Coop.

"I'm afraid I'm going to hurt you," Cara said after the kiss.

"It's my arm that's hurt, not my lips, girl," Coop mused as he guided her closer for another kiss.

Cara, though she tried, could not control the emotions that were inside her and tears began streaming down her cheeks.

"Hey now, why the tears?" Coop asked.

"I'm sorry, I just am so happy to see you…"

"Well, the feeling is mutual," Coop replied, kissing her on the forehead as she pressed her cheek to his chest.

"I was so worried…"

"Worried? Why on Earth, girl? It's not like I was having open-heart surgery or something…"

"I know, it's silly… I'm sorry. I'm being ridiculous…"

"No, you're not… To be honest, I'm kinda flattered..."

"You don't have to say that…"

"Hey, look at me," Coop said, cocking his head so that he could see her face.

"What?" Cara asked, looking up embarrassed.

"I love you."

"I love you too."

"Good. Then you need to know that if the roles were reversed, and you were the one in surgery - for anything – even a splinter removal – I'd be a freaking disaster. They'd have to medicate me."

His words seemed to work, and Cara kissed him again, with even more passion than before, so much so that the two did not even notice Dr. Sislowski reenter the room with a fresh cup of ice water.

The veteran anesthesiologist paused, smiled, and quietly exited the room.

70

Detective Jason Knox gazed down upon Vance Gold's lifeless body trying to figure out how he felt about the whole situation. On one hand, he was happy that a scumbag like Vance finally got what he deserved. On the other, he was mad that the police officers had abandoned their post to chase after a bogus 9-1-1 call, though he was pretty sure he would have done the same if he would have been in their shoes.

This time there was no threatening letter attached to the body, nor were there letters carved into the victim, but there was a photograph of a teenage girl lying next to Vance's body. On the back of the photo was a handwritten inscription: *Jane – Age 13*.

"So, who do you think the girl is?" an out-of-breath Mick McCarthy asked Jason as he returned to the murder scene. A few minutes earlier, one of the uniformed cops on the scene summoned the commander to check out something on the roof.

"No clue… You all right, Mick? I don't think you should be

climbing up any more ladders," Jason chided.

"Very funny, asshole," Mick fired back. "Looks like our suspect came in through the roof's access door. You know what never ceases to amaze me?"

"What's that?" Jason replied, holding back the slew of witty insults that he wanted to say for the sake of the case.

"Just that so many places spend all this money on security systems, locks, cameras… You name it… But then all they put on a rooftop access door is a freaking padlock," Mick said, amused at the absurdity.

"Think the perp went out the same way he came in?" Jason asked.

"Both doors were still locked from the inside when the officers came back, so it looks like it," Mick confirmed.

"And how long were you guys gone on the bogus 11-99?" Jason asked the two officers who, after returning to their post at Buddy's, discovered Vance's body.

"The call came in this morning around nine," the taller and younger of the two embarrassed officers replied. "Once we realized it was a false alarm, we came straight back here. We were only gone for about fifteen minutes, tops."

"How long after you dumbasses returned did you find the body?" Mick asked, disgusted that they would have abandoned their post.

"I knocked on the door as soon as we got back, but nobody answered," the older and shorter of the two replied. "We figured he was taking a shit or something, so we waited about five minutes before using the key to go inside."

"How polite of you," Mick snapped back.

"Twenty minutes is more than enough time to do the job and get out," Jason stated as he knelt down and placed the photograph into an evidence bag.

"We're sorry, sir," the younger cop said to Mick. "When we heard the 11-99 come across we thought we were doing the right thing."

"You mean the bogus 11-99? You guys had one goddamn job to do and that was to stay put. Get the hell back to the station. I'll deal with your sorry asses later," Mick seethed, dismissing the officers.

"You know you would've done the same thing, Mick. We both would've," Jason said to his commander after the two officers had left the club.

"Yeah, I know," Mick relented. "I just needed to yell at somebody."

"We need to find out who this Jane girl is," Jason said as he examined the photograph through the plastic bag.

"Think she's a stripper here? It's an old photo, she's got to be old enough by now to work the main stage," Mick said.

"Perhaps, but I'm guessing that the EPK left this as a gift for us. He's messing with us now."

"Maybe he left it to throw us off. He might not even know this Jane girl, but he knows that we are going to follow up on it, and that will give him more time to go after his next victim."

"Who do you think the next victim is?" Jason asked.

"Well, after HoJo, Vance was the obvious mark. I'd say Tick, but with him in jail I don't see how he'd get that done. Maybe his partner, the construction guy, Furio?"

"Could be, and he was here the other night according to our guys, but from the sounds of it he has an entire security detail watching over him like a hawk."

"So did Vance," Mick chuckled.

"Touché... We should pay him a visit anyways."

"Have you heard anything else from Scriv or Hannah?" Mick asked, his voice hushed so that none of the others at the scene would hear.

"Nothing new, but I'll give them a call," Jason replied quietly.

"Well, hopefully we will get something from forensics on the photograph. A picture that old has to have some prints on it, right?"

"Unless he wiped it clean before he came here. Sure wish Vance had a real security camera right about now. Think any of the other properties around here have cameras?" Jason asked.

"We have officers checking on that right now, but most of the nearby buildings are residential," Mick replied.

"Hey, maybe Furio had this done to get rid of Vance so he would be the sole owner of the club?" Jason guessed.

"It's definitely a possibility. Furio might have been worried about what Vance had told us and decided to get rid of him."

"What better way than to make it look like it was the EPK, too," Jason added.

"Let's go see if we can track him down and have a chat then," Mick stated.

71

Three miles away from Buddy's Speakeasy, Phil Worthington had just untethered his boat from the dock at Edgewater Park Marina and began his journey to one of the deepest parts of Lake Erie. He knew it would be the best place for him to get rid of the burner phone and bolt cutters that had just assisted him in his most satisfying kill yet.

He had travelled there before. The first time was when he disposed of the two Russian girls, Svetlana and Nina, who had lured his sweet Jane into a void that she never escaped. They were his first kills, and it surprised him how good it felt to watch each of them take their last breaths. It was on that night that the EPK was born.

Shortly after his meeting with Sadie, who had told him about how the two Russian girls would hang out at The Study Hall teen club, that the news of a young woman's body washing ashore at Edgewater Park had given him the idea.

At first, nobody knew who the young woman was, only that she had been choked to death. Eventually the body had a name, Stoya

Fedorov, a young Russian woman who was in the country illegally and believed to have been working as a prostitute.

Phil could not believe his good fortune. He believed that it had to be Jane looking over him, giving him a sign.

He knew that once he was able to find and kill the two Russian girls, he would throw their bodies into Lake Erie, just as Stoya's had been. Phil figured that they'd eventually wash ashore too, especially since he only dumped them about a half mile out in the water.

Capturing Svetlana and Nina was much easier than he had thought it would be. A few days after Stoya's body was identified, Phil parked his truck outside The Study Hall and waited. He had hoped that if he went there every night that the duo would eventually show up looking to corrupt more innocent girls.

Jane came through again, he thought, on the first night as he watched two very inebriated young women exit the club. They were at least five years older than the majority of the teenagers who he had witnessed going in and out of the club that night.

He watched as the taller one, a leggy brunette wearing a short skirt and halter-top, fumbled with her keys as she tried to open the door to her BMW two-door coupe. It had to be them, Phil figured, because most of the teenagers that were old enough to drive to the club did so in the type of beat-up used cars that new drivers can afford to own.

Before the brunette could get her car door open, the other girl with her shuffled quickly away from the passenger side of the car and vomited against the building. She was shorter and curvy, with dark red hair and was wearing skintight leather pants and a tank top, which was now splashed with the remnants of an apparent night of binge drinking.

When the brunette saw her friend violently throwing up, she dropped her keys, leaving them abandoned on the asphalt, as she rushed over to hold the other's hair. The smell must have gotten to the brunette, because within seconds she too was puking alongside her friend. That's when Phil made his move.

He looked around after exiting his pick-up to see if anyone else was in the parking lot, but it was empty, save for a few cars. Phil casually walked over to the BMW and picked up the keys from the pavement. The girls, who apparently had jettisoned the last of the poison from their stomachs, were on their knees with their hands pressed firmly against the cinder block building, groaning. They did not even realize that they had company until Phil spoke.

"You ladies okay?" Phil asked in a concerned, yet soothing, manner.

The brunette, startled, turned around quickly to see who the voice belonged to. A look of relief came across her face when she realized that it was not a cop, but rather a friendly-looking middle-aged man in jeans and a flannel shirt.

"We are fine. We just need minute to rest. Too much vodka tonight," she said in broken English.

Phil smiled when he heard her thick Russian accent.

Thank you Janey...

"Oh, I don't think you're fine, ladies. There's no way I can let you two try to drive either. I wouldn't be able to sleep tonight if I did," Phil replied, doing his best to sound as genuine and non-threatening as possible.

"We can drive. It's no worry. Just need rest first," the redhead replied, wiping vomit from her chin. Like the brunette, she too spoke with a Russian accent, albeit a less pronounced one.

"I'm sorry, ladies, but I just can't let that happen. I'd never forgive myself if I let you two drive home and something happened, God forbid," Phil answered in his best fatherly tone. "Why don't you ladies hop in my truck and I'll drive you home. You can come back tomorrow and get your car."

"Nyet... No. We drive," the brunette declared as she awkwardly stood up, only to turn right back around and vomit on the building once more.

"See, now, this is why I can't let you two drive home," Phil insisted.

It was then that the redhead said something to the brunette in Russian. While he did not know what she was saying, Phil could make out that she called the brunette Nina and she seemed to be pleading with her.

Nina, her tone exhausted, seemed to agree with whatever it was that the redhead had said to her in Russian. Then she looked at Phil before speaking.

"Svetlana say you can drive us home. I just need my keys," Nina relented.

"Got them right here. Saw them on the ground over there and picked them up. Don't worry; I'll take good care of you girls. You know, I have a daughter around your age inside the club. I was actually just dropping her off when I saw you two needed some help. I'll be sure to treat you the same way you would treat her," Phil said with a reassuring smile, the irony not lost on him.

"Ok, we go…" Svetlana said as she stood up and took Nina by the hand.

"My truck is just over here; there's plenty of room. I'll drop you two off at home and then come back here to get my daughter," Phil said as he led them to his pick-up.

He opened the passenger side door so the inebriated duo could climb in. Svetlana sat in the middle seat and Nina followed in the passenger side before Phil closed the door, discreetly locking it first. He then walked around the front of the truck and entered. Nina had her head resting against the window and appeared to be passed out already; Svetlana had her head slumped forward, moaning something in Russian.

Phil started the truck and pulled out of the parking lot, amused that both girls were so drunk that neither one of them seemed to realize that they never gave him an address to drive them to. For the next twenty minutes, Phil drove the truck on Interstate 90 westbound as far away from the city as he could, hoping that he could get them to an area where there would be no witnesses to what he was about to do.

Always the planner, Phil was mad at himself for not already having a location picked out. Then again, he thought that he was only going to observe that night.

After years on the road as a truck driver, Phil knew every exit off of every highway and interstate in Ohio, and he had already decided on what he felt would be a perfect location.

Both of the girls were completely passed out as his truck exited the interstate twenty minutes later at an exit in Lorain County, west of Cleveland. Colorado Avenue, which is the name given to the road known as State Route 611, connects the cities of Avon and Lorain. It also runs through a smaller town called Sheffield Lake, which is exactly the reason that Phil decided to head in that direction after exiting.

Sheffield Lake, while a rapidly growing community, still was predominantly filled with rural farmland and wooded areas, including French Creek Reservation in the Metroparks. Phil turned off of Colorado Avenue onto East River Road and followed the dark road as it wound its way through the dense woods that the park is known for.

As long as he did not encounter a nosy park ranger, Phil assumed French Creek would be a perfect place to begin his journey towards justice. It was late in the evening, so the park felt empty and peaceful as the moonlight beamed from above.

Phil made a left-hand turn onto French Creek Road and followed it to one of the park's main entrances, where he pulled his truck in and continued to follow the parkway until it came to an end in a secluded pavilion area near a playground. As he came to a stop and put the truck in park, Nina opened her eyes.

"Where we are?" she asked, confused.

Phil did not answer.

"Where we are?" Nina asked again as her growing state of alarm began to show in her tone.

Nina's words brought Svetlana out of her stupor, but before she could say anything Phil smashed the back of his hand across her jaw, sending her back to sleep.

Nina immediately screamed and tried to open the passenger door, but it was locked. She frantically searched for the lock, but her inebriated brain failed to allow her hands to locate it.

Phil leaned across Svetlana's limp body and wrapped his calloused hands around her throat. She tried desperately to pull his firm grip away from her throat, her artificial fingernails tearing into the tops of his hands. Phil squeezed harder as he watched her eyes begin to roll back into her head as she tried to summon the oxygen that just would not allow itself into her lungs.

Saying nothing, but thinking of Jane, his beloved Janey, Phil continued to press harder and harder against her trachea until he could feel it collapsing beneath his thumbs. Her legs, which had been violently kicking just seconds earlier, began to stiffen. A single tear began its journey down her left cheek as Phil felt the life escape her body with it.

She was dead.

Phil could feel Svetlana start to regain consciousness from underneath him. He pulled himself away and watched Svetlana stare warily at Nina, realizing that something was very wrong with her friend. As she looked back towards Phil, the last thing Svetlana saw was Phil's icy stare as he wrapped his strong hands around her neck, pressing his thumbs hard against her throat. Within minutes she was gone.

Phil collected himself and looked around the park pavilion area to make sure that there were no park rangers who happened to drive through on patrol during the altercation. They were alone. He thanked Jane, once again, for looking over him and calmly put his truck into gear before pulling back out onto the parkway.

An hour later, Phil was on his boat with the bodies of Nina and Svetlana lying in the hull, cruising towards his destination about a half-mile off shore. Getting the bodies on the boat without being noticed had proven to be a little tricky, as there were some nighttime charters heading out or coming in despite it being after midnight.

Luckily, for Phil, his boat slip happened to be located right next to the parking lot near the boat ramps – far away from the yacht club and the nighttime anglers. The boat ramps were there mainly for weekend warriors who towed their boat to and from the marina, so it was pretty empty by that time in the evening; thus, making it pretty easy for him to quickly transport the girls into his boat.

Again, he thanked Jane for looking over him.

When it came time for him to throw their bodies overboard, Phil felt an overwhelming sense of rage permeate through his body. Yes, he had killed the two women who had lured his daughter into the abyss, but their deaths were far less painful than he had imagined they would be.

They had to suffer more, he thought. So, he grabbed his sharpest filet knife and began stabbing their lifeless bodies as he cursed them, tears streaming down his face. He knew that they did not feel the sharp tip of the knife piercing their skin, yet it did not matter to him. It was as if he was killing their souls too.

Phil thought of that night as he pressed forward in his boat, skipping across the sun kissed water at a high speed, wishing that he could have given Vance Gold the same water burial. Then he reminded himself that he was lucky to have even escaped Buddy's Speakeasy earlier, as the cops had returned more quickly than he had hoped for.

He had left back through the roof of the club in such a hurry that he did not even realize that he had left the photograph of Jane behind until it was too late to go back and get it. Thankfully, Phil had wiped it down with an alcohol wipe before sticking the photograph in his pocket. Between that and the gloves that he wore to kill Vance, he was fairly confident that they would not be able to lift any of his prints off of it.

Nonetheless, Phil decided that he would lay low for a while and head out of town. Besides, Phil only had one more target left on his list, and he was sitting in the county jail.

72

"So, I'm assuming you've heard about Vance?" Jason asked Hannah over the phone.

"Funny you should ask that, Detective Knox. I'm actually on my way to Buddy's Speakeasy now to do a live shot," Hannah replied. Her tone did not match the levity of her words.

"This is a mess," Jason sighed.

"Sure is. My sources tell me it was a zip tie, just like HoJo. That true?" she asked.

"Off the record? Yes. But, you can't say that in your report, at least not yet."

"Of course," she replied.

"Thanks…"

"No need to thank me."

"I know," Jason answered. "Listen, Mick and I are on our way to speak with Mr. Furio. Has Scriv had any luck with him?"

Even though Hannah had yet to speak with Scriv since he had told her that he was going to have some of his guys watch Vance's brother, she figured that she could not keep what she did know from the detectives any longer.

"Actually, yes," she said. "It turns out that Furio met with Vance on Saturday night."

"I know," Jason replied.

"Oh, yeah, of course," Hannah said, embarrassed that she forgot that Vance had cops watching him who obviously would have told the detectives that Furio had been there.

"Is that it?" Jason asked.

"No, actually. It turns out that Vance and Furio have more in common than being partners of a strip club together."

"Really? How so?"

"Get this – Vance has an older brother named Arliss Gold who happens to own a company called Erie Shores Construction. Scriv seems to think that he and Furio are in cahoots when it comes to bidding on jobs, basically taking turns making sure that they each get the jobs they want by manipulating the bidding process."

"Wow, that's crazy!" Jason replied, shocked.

"The plot thickens," Hannah chuckled.

"You're not kidding. Maybe we should be paying Vance's brother a visit too."

Mick, who had been listening in to the conversation from the passenger seat of the cruiser, shot Jason a look of bewilderment upon hearing those words.

"Wait, there's more," Hannah said.

"Go on…"

"Scriv had a guy tail Deputy Chief Lawson the past two days, so I have an update there."

"Let's hear it," Jason sighed, expecting more bad news.

"He said he doesn't think Lawson is being anything other than a big-time micromanager. Scriv thinks the reason Lawson may have insisted on watching the autopsy was because he knows that this is his chance to become Chief and he wants to make sure that nothing derails that."

"Really? That's a relief. I don't know if I can deal with any more crooked cops."

"I guess Scriv dug deep into his bag of tricks to try and find something, anything that would raise a red flag on Lawson, but apparently he's a Boy Scout," Hannah confirmed.

"Wish I could say the same for our buddy, Furio."

"About him, do you think it's even worth going to talk to him?" Hannah asked tentatively, knowing that she was straying from her lane as a reporter.

"Why wouldn't we?"

"Well, I just think that if Scriv is right on Furio, the guy has absolutely nothing to gain by Vance's death. With the club being shut down, maybe even for good, he just lost one of his main avenues to launder his money. Maybe it would be best to just keep watching Furio and Arliss Gold to see how they react to this new development."

"You make a great point; you ever thought of wearing a badge?" Jason asked.

"Me? Heck no, but I love to second-guess people for a living,"

Hannah laughed, thankful that he did not take offense to her suggestion.

"Well, that's 80 percent of what we do, so you'd make a great detective," Jason chuckled. "I'm going to see what Mick thinks. Maybe we can meet later with you and Scriv?"

"Sounds good to me."

"I'll be in touch then," Jason said.

"Take care."

After ending the call, Jason looked at Mick and smiled. He knew that his commander was waiting on him to convey the details of his phone call, so Jason took full advantage and pretended as if he had nothing to say. He loved driving Mick crazy, and it made his extremely stressful occupation a little more bearable.

"Hellllllllooooo? Are you going to tell me what that call was all about?" Mick asked incredulously.

"Oh, you meant *that* call? The one with Hannah LaMarca?" Jason said, keeping up the act.

"No, the one with President Bush," Mick snapped back. "Yes, the one with Hannah LaMarca. You know, your secret admirer…"

"Secret admirer? Sounds like somebody's jealous…"

"Oh whatever, Knox, I've seen the way she looks at you. She wants it. *Bad*," Mick replied, figuring that he might as well get back at Jason for messing with him.

"Now I know you're full of shit…"

"I'm just glad that I have a front row seat to witness all of the sexual tension between the two of you," Mick chided, laying it on.

"Okay, okay, you win," Jason sighed, knowing that it was a losing battle.

He filled Mick in on everything that Hannah had told him. About Arliss Gold. About Furio. About Lawson. He even told him, based off of Hannah's suggestion, that he thought they should turn around and table their interrogation of Salvatore Furio.

Surprisingly, Mick agreed.

"No sense in forcing it, might as well let nature take its course," Mick had said. "Maybe she's right? Maybe if we back off, they'll hang themselves for us."

73

Coop stood there smiling, as he watched Cara dancing in the middle of what had to be about 200 strangers. The rhythmic sounds of hand drums like the Congo and the African djembe filled the air as an eclectic crowd containing people of all ages danced along.

It was Wednesday evening on the thin island known as Casey Key, located in the town of Nokomis, Florida, and that meant that the drum circle would be there, just as they are every Wednesday and Saturday, to play until the sun set on the horizon.

Coop and Cara had arrived about two hours earlier via Todd "T-Squared" Taylor's private jet, or at least the one he rented to fly them down following Coop's surgery. While Coop had flown on private jets ever since he was drafted at the age of 18, he never had forgotten how cool his first flight in one was, and he loved that he was able to share in Cara's first experience on one.

She had never even flown on a plane before, let alone a Cessna Citation Excel XLS private jet. It was a first-class experience from the moment they had arrived at the private hanger at Burke Lakefront Airport until they landed at Sarasota-Bradenton Airport.

Aside from the extremely attentive flight attendant who made sure that Coop was as comfortable as he could be post-surgery by bringing him fresh bags of ice and pillows to support his arm, the couple had the 7-passenger cabin all to themselves during the two and a half hour flight.

Thanks to the jet's interior configuration, Coop and Cara were able to sit in plush leather seats that faced each other, her feet intertwined with his. He loved that he was able to witness Cara experience her first takeoff and smiled as she reacted to how quickly the city of Cleveland seemed to shrink in the distance as the jet climbed away from the lake.

With the exception of the short nap Coop enjoyed, thanks largely in part to the pain meds he had been taking as ordered after the surgery, the couple talked for most of the flight. Cara expressed that she was worried for her brother, Jason, as he had barely come home the past two days due to yet another murder.

While Jason did not give her many details, Cara could tell that he was as worried as she had ever seen him. She even told him that she and Coop would postpone their trip so they could stay back at the Westcott and help Erica with Gabby, but Jason insisted that they go. He reassured her that Gabby and Erica were as safe as could be in Coop's penthouse, and that Clarence and Grace were going to continue to a keep around-the-clock vigil on them.

Coop did his best to echo Jason's sentiments for the remainder of the flight and managed to change the topic of conversation to how they were going to spend the next week on the beach. It seemed to work, as Cara was still chatting about how much she was looking forward to watching the sunset over the Gulf as the plane landed in Sarasota.

Todd would not be down himself until the next day, so Joy had met them at the airport and was introduced to Cara. The two really seemed to hit it off on the car ride back to the Taylor's beach house, just as Coop knew they would.

Coop had always loved Joy; she was as beautiful on the inside as she was on the outside. She was a southern belle who could assimilate herself into any group of people, whether it was with millionaires at a country club or bleacher bums at a baseball game. She was the only woman in the world, Coop imagined, who was strong enough to put up with being married to Todd.

After settling in at the stunning new beach house, which was more like a private oceanfront resort, Joy had insisted that Coop and Cara take a long walk down the beach. One of the most important things, Coop was told after his surgery, was to get as much walking in over the next few weeks as possible to help prevent any blood clots from forming.

"Nothing like a Gulf of Mexico sunset," Coop declared.

"It's beautiful," Cara replied. "It's hard to believe that it's the same sun we see in Cleveland."

"This ain't Lake Erie," Coop joked as he gazed out over the clear water that gently folded itself over and over into the white sand beach.

"You got that right," Cara agreed.

"It's almost as beautiful as you are."

"Go on..." Cara laughed.

"I will..."

"Promise?"

"For as long as you'll let me."

"Well, I'm not planning on stopping you. Ever..."

"Nothing," Coop said before pulling her a little closer and kissing the top of her head.

"Nothing," she replied, smiling.

Cara could not get over how surreal the moment felt. Just a day earlier she had helped Coop get settled in back at the Westcott after his stay in the hospital where she had spent the night there with him. The surgery went as well as it could, Dr. Mueller had said, and in return that raised Coop's spirits. Her biggest fear following the operation was that he was going to slip back into the angry state he was in immediately after the injury, but he had been anything but angry thus far.

As they had strolled their way south on the beach, Coop's right arm tight to his body in a brace and his left draped over Cara's slender shoulders, they could hear the sounds of drums being played in the distance. A few hundred feet farther they came upon a large crowd of people who had formed a human ring on the beach.

In the middle of the circle was a makeshift shrine containing flowers, letters, palm branches, and even a hula-hoop. There was a fire twirler spinning his flaming baton alongside a striking middle-aged woman with silver hair whose body effortlessly moved with the sounds of the drums. Like many of the other participants, the woman was clad only in a bikini top with a long colorful skirt that hugged her lean hips. There were children and adults alike wearing glow necklaces and many also had flowers in their hair.

Coop and Cara were immediately drawn to the ritualistic spectacle, and soon they had made their way amongst the revelers that included everyone from lifelong hippies to yuppie tourists. At one point, the silver haired woman took Cara by the hand and pulled her inside the circle. Coop laughed as the woman silently instructed Cara on how to move her hips to the sound of the music.

Coop could not get over how beautiful Cara looked as she giggled and laughed alongside her new dance instructor, who gently tucked a flower in her hair just above her ear once Cara got the hang of it. This caused Cara to look over at Coop, hoping that he had witnessed what she had felt was like a rite of passage.

He was looking, of course.

She smiled and moved slightly closer to him, making sure to maintain eye contact as she moved her athletic hips to the sound of the drums, their tempo steadily increasing as the sun began to disappear over the water behind her. Coop kept his eyes locked in on hers in return, though it was a struggle not to gaze down at her hips as they moved effortlessly in rhythm.

It was all so seductive. The music, the dancing, the beach, and the sunset all seemed to work in unison to the point that the whole world faded away around them.

Which is probably why Gary Boardman went unnoticed. The paparazzi photographer stood just ten feet away, blending in with the crowd in a Hawaiian shirt, cargo shorts, and ball cap as he snapped dozens of pictures of the couple. He made sure to get lots of shots of Coop's arm in a sling and even more of Cara's hips as she danced.

The overweight and bald photographer smiled as he thought of the fat paycheck that typically accompanied any shots of the reclusive pitcher and his new girlfriend. CMZ had paid him top dollar when he sold the very first pictures of the couple, and he could not imagine what they would pay him for the pictures that he was hoping to get in the days that followed.

"Yeah, they're here, and I already got some great shots," Gary Boardman said to his contact at CMZ as he casually walked away from the drum circle with his cell phone up to his ear.

"Send me what you have," the contact, an editor at CMZ, replied. He was the same contact who had tipped Gary off that Cooper Madison was headed to Nokomis to recover from his Tommy John surgery.

"Not yet," Gary said.

"Why not? Sounds like you have some money shots."

"Yeah, these would pay nicely. That Cara girl has a body that you could bounce a quarter off of, but I'm gonna wait it out a bit. I'm gonna follow them out of here so I know where they're staying," Gary answered.

"Wait it out for what? You don't want to get paid?" the editor asked, confused.

"Yessir, I do," Gary replied. "And if my plan works the way I think it will, you guys are gonna have to back the Brinks truck up to pay me…"

74

Phil Worthington leaned on the railing of his motel room's second floor balcony and listened to the babbling stream that ran below. Experiencing autumn in the Great Smoky Mountains had always been on his bucket list, and so far Gatlinburg, Tennessee, had lived up to his expectations.

Great Smoky Mountains National Park, the most visited National Park in the United States, serves as a beautiful backdrop to many tourist traps. The most notable of those towns is Gatlinburg, which is home to restaurants, souvenir shops, and an abundance of motels along its main drag.

After dumping his burner phone and bolt cutters in Lake Erie on Monday, Phil packed a suitcase and drove eight hours straight, arriving in Gatlinburg the next morning. He spent most of Tuesday and Wednesday in bed with the sliding glass door to the balcony open. The combination of the fresh mountain air and soothing sounds of the stream below worked as a natural sedative.

Phil was confident that the purpose of his trip was not to run from the authorities, but rather to celebrate. His plan to enact revenge upon those individuals responsible for Jane's death could not have gone any better than it did. Nina, Svetlana, HoJo, and Vance were all dead, and the police were clueless as to who the EPK was. Thanks to Phil, they even believed, at least for a while, that Ernie Page was the killer.

Only Tick remained on Phil's hit list, but as long as he was sitting in jail, that would have to wait. Phil considered paying someone to do the job from the inside, but realized that would have robbed him of the satisfaction that came with doing it himself.

Tick would have to wait to receive his punishment. In the meantime, Phil decided to thoroughly enjoy the first vacation he had been on since Jane died. After he finally dragged himself out of bed on Wednesday, he took in a dinner show in nearby Pigeon Forge called the Dixie Stampede. He enjoyed the Civil War themed show, which featured horses, music, and pyrotechnics before returning to Gatlinburg, where he walked up and down the strip.

Phil had never been much of a drinker, mostly due to the fact that he was a control freak, but as he walked along the various shops and bars, he felt the urge to tie one on. Since he could walk back to his motel room from anywhere on the strip, Phil decided to do just that at Blaine's Grill and Bar, one of Gatlinburg's most popular spots.

He found an open seat at the bar and ordered a boilermaker.

"Somebody's on a mission," chuckled a woman's voice.

Phil looked over to see a middle-aged woman smiling at him from the end of the bar, her glass raised in a toast.

"I guess you could say that," Phil replied, raising his glass in return.

"Want some company?" the woman asked, nodding towards the open stool next to him.

"Help yourself," he answered.

The woman, who Phil assumed was about the same age as he was, had frizzy blonde hair that framed her tired eyes. She was dressed in a tight pair of denim jeans and a sweatshirt that had been cut into a V-neck.

She was of average height and had a thick, curvy body, which Phil liked. However, he had not been with a woman since his wife died and could feel himself growing nervous as she sat down next to him at the bar.

"What's your name?" she asked.

"Phil. You?"

"Dolly."

"Dolly? Like Parton?"

"Yes, but not after her. Heck, we're not that far apart in age," Dolly laughed.

"I bet you get asked that all the time," Phil said.

"Especially down here. I'm pretty sure that she owns half this town," she said in reference to the famous country singer who did in fact own a lot of the commercial properties in and around Gatlinburg.

"I was thinking about going to her amusement park while I'm down here," Phil said referring to Dollywood, a theme park in nearby Pigeon Forge.

"How long are you in town?"

"Not sure. Maybe a week, maybe more."

"Michigan or Ohio?" Dolly asked.

"Ohio. Is it that obvious?" Phil chuckled.

"That and I'm from Detroit originally. It takes one to know one," she said as she raised her glass.

"What about now? You live down here?"

"Here? Heck no. I'm on a celebration vacation, but I live in Buffalo."

"What are you celebrating?" Phil asked as he signaled the bartender for another round of drinks.

"I just lost about 300 pounds," she replied.

"Really? Well, good for you. You look amazing," Phil said, which elicited a laugh from Dolly.

"Not literally, Phil. I meant that I got a divorce from my fat ass, lazy ex-husband. I'm down here celebrating my newfound freedom."

"I'm an idiot," Phil groaned, shaking his head. "I've never been good at reading between the lines."

"Are you here alone? Or am I flirting with a married man?" Dolly asked.

"Alone and single," Phil said raising his glass.

"Must be my lucky day, unless you're some sort of serial killer or something," she deadpanned before letting out a laugh.

"Oh, no. The only thing I kill are fish," Phil replied, his hands feigning surrender.

"You're a fisherman?"

"I own a small fishing charter on Lake Erie. It's my retirement gig; I used to be a long-haul truck driver."

"A real blue collar guy, huh? Let me see your hands," Dolly said as she grabbed Phil by the wrists, turning his palms upward for examination. "Oh yeah, these hands have definitely worked for a living."

"They say that every scar has a story, right?" Phil said.

"They do, but I also say that there's nothing sexier than a man who works with this hands and has the scars to prove it."

Phil leaned in and kissed Dolly on the lips, catching even himself off guard at the brashness of the move. He fully expected Dolly to recoil at the advance, maybe even slap him, but instead she pulled him tight and straddled him on the barstool.

They continued that way for the next minute, neither one wanting to pull away. Phil could feel his heart racing and the butterflies in his stomach felt like they were ready to explode. The whole thing felt surreal to him.

It's been so long...

Finally, Dolly pulled her face away, her bright red lipstick smeared.

"Where are you staying?" she asked.

"Rocky Waters Motor Inn. You?"

"Midtown Lodge."

"You're closer..."

"Let's go."

Phil threw a twenty-dollar bill down on the bar and finished off his boilermaker before they walked outside into the crisp autumn evening. As is the case with most vacation destinations, even a Wednesday can feel like a Friday, and the sidewalks were still packed with people.

Dolly led him by the hand towards her room at the Midtown Lodge, which was located near the pool. She stopped and turned around after opening the door to her room.

"Wait, I need to know your last name before we go inside. Mine is Barnes," Dolly informed a perplexed Phil. Picking up on this, Dolly explained. "I'm sorry, it's just one of those things I need to know before I sleep with someone. I guess it makes me feel less cheap."

"Well, first off, it's Worthington," Phil replied. "Secondly, I don't think you could be cheap if you tried."

"It's been a long time," she informed. "Please, be patient with me."

"I was just going to ask the same of you," Phil replied, a sense of relief in his voice.

Dolly responded with a long, passionate kiss before she pulled him inside her room and gently closed the door.

75

Detective Jason Knox sat next to his wife on the balcony outside of Cooper Madison's penthouse suite at the Westcott Hotel. It was a colder morning than normal, even for autumn in Cleveland, and the two cupped their coffee mugs with their hands to stay warm.

"What time do you have to go in?" Erica asked.

"About an hour ago," Jason chuckled.

"You better get moving then, Detective."

"Nah, I already told Mick I'd be in late today. He has an appointment with his doctor at nine, so I'm just going to meet him after he's done," Jason said, looking dejected just as he had the past few days. He was so consumed with the case that he did not even notice that his apathetic demeanor was beginning to wear on Erica.

It had been three days since Vance Gold had been found dead on the floor of his strip club. Aside from the growing buzz around

Cleveland that the EPK was still walking the streets, not much new had happened in regards to the case. As was the case with HoJo, the crime scene did not turn up any leads as to who may have killed the owner of Buddy's Speakeasy.

Mick and Jason did not need a smoking gun to tell them that this was the work of the EPK, but as obvious as it was, they were no closer to figuring out just who their killer was. They had hoped that the photograph left with Vance's body would have had identifiable fingerprints, but it had been wiped clean.

They had spent the days since Vance's murder showing the photograph of the girl around every neighborhood within two miles of the crime scene hoping that somebody would recognize her, only to come up empty. On Wednesday evening Jason and Mick decided to take advantage of Hannah's offer to help with the case and gave her the photograph to broadcast on the news, which she was set to do later that Thursday.

With any luck, somebody watching Channel One news would be able to identify the mystery girl and call the tip line that they had set up. As with any tip line situation, Jason and Mick knew that the biggest challenge would be sifting through the onslaught of bogus calls that would inevitably occur. It was the nature of the beast, but if it yielded just one legitimate lead, then it would be worth it.

Hannah had told Jason that the story would air during the midday newscast and then again during the afternoon and evening shows. With any luck, calls would start coming in shortly after noon.

"Penny for your thoughts?" Erica asked. It was one of her favorite phrases and she used it so often that sometimes she would just say, "Penny?"

"I don't think they're worth that much right now," Jason replied, his lips pursed.

"Well, I'm feeling charitable this morning, so give it up," she chuckled.

"Just feeling like I'm being tested right now, and I'm failing miserably."

"Why would you say that?"

"Look at us!" Jason replied, his smile in conflict with his tone. "My family has basically had to move into hiding because I can't catch the *one* guy that might hurt them. Hell, I couldn't even keep him from killing a guy who was under police protection!"

"Stop that!" Erica snapped back.

"Stop what?"

"I didn't marry a narcissistic asshole, so stop acting like one!"

Her words, and even more so her tone, caught Jason off guard. Nobody who knew Jason, especially his wife, would describe him as being self-centered or egotistical. In fact, he had built his reputation on being the opposite of that in a world known as a breeding ground for narcissistic people – both criminals and cops.

"Oh, you didn't like being called that?" Erica continued. "Then quit making this case all about *you*. There are dozens of people working this case, not just you, and I'll be damned if I'm going to let the man I love have a freaking pity-party!"

"Babe, I didn't think I was-"

Erica cut him off.

"Damn straight you didn't think. You want Gabby to see her father moping around like a sad puppy? Or do you want her to see you strong and confident in the face of adversity?"

"Strong and confident," Jason relented.

"Good, then start by eliminating all this negative body language you've been carrying around. Frankly, it's not a very attractive look for you," Erica demanded. "Then get your ass out there and find this EPK asshole so we can move back home. He's won a few battles, but you're gonna win the war, Babe. You have to believe that."

"Do *you* believe that?" Jason countered.

"Babe, nobody believes in you more than I do, which is why I can't let this go on any longer."

Jason wrapped his arms around her and squeezed her tight, gently kissing the top of her head. "Well, I guess I better hop in the shower so I can get my ass moving," Jason said.

"Yeah, we better."

"We?" Jason asked.

"I like to use many different forms of motivational strategies. Now that I've torn you down a bit, I need to build you back up," Erica said in a seductive tone as she led Jason back inside the penthouse.

76

"I can't believe how warm the weather still is down here!" Cara said as she dipped her foot into the sprawling pool located behind Todd "T-Squared" Taylor's mansion on Casey Key. The extravagant pool and patio area made the young couple feel as if they were in their own little paradise. Palm trees, flowers, and plants surrounded the infinity pool that overlooked the Gulf of Mexico.

A secluded path connected the house to a small slice of private beach about fifty yards away, but Coop had no intentions of getting in the Gulf. In fact, the prior evening's stroll along the beach was the closest he had been to the body of water that changed his life forever.

Joy was on her way to the airport to pick up Todd, so the young couple had decided to soak up the Florida morning sun next to the pool. "You ain't kiddin', girl. It's probably half this temperature in the C-L-E," Coop laughed as he eased himself into a chaise lounger, a bag of ice in his good hand.

Coop had on a pair of navy blue board shorts that coincidentally matched the color of his arm brace and a pair of Oakley sunglasses. His body, though still not back to where he would have preferred it to be, was no doubt that of a professional athlete. His shoulders and chest were every bit as toned as the six-pack that he sported in his abdominal region.

"C-L-E? Look at you, Coop. Better be careful; you're going to turn into a true Clevelander talking like that," Cara said as she made her way towards Coop, who had already rested his elbow on the bag of ice.

Cara was wearing an athletic cut red lifeguard bikini with a white sarong around her waist like a mini-skirt. Her body was still as firm and slender as it was when she ran track at Berea High School. Just like her mother, Joanne, Cara was blessed with a naturally fit body, and she had always been able to eat what she wanted without having to worry about it showing in her midsection.

"I don't know what you were whining about with that bathing suit. You look hot, girl," Coop said, whistling for effect. Cara had informed Coop the day before they left that the only bathing suit she could find that still fit was her old lifeguard two-piece from the last summer when she worked at the Brook Park Recreation Center's outdoor water park. Coop had insisted that she would look great in anything, and then followed that up with a playful joke about her performing resuscitation on him.

"If you say so, I just know that I'm going to hate the tan lines that come with wearing this suit. I wish the stores in Cleveland would have had more of a selection of suits left to try on," Cara said, referring to the perils of swimwear shopping in a colder climate.

"I told you we can get you one while we're down here," Coop reminded her of his offer.

"I know, it's a real 'First World Problem', right?" Cara sighed as she lowered the top of her chaise lounger so that she could lie flat.

"Well, I happen to think tan lines are sexy," Coop replied.

"Yeah, maybe when you're wearing a normal bikini. This thing is like a sports bra," she said as she gestured to the red top, which had a white lifeguard logo emblazoned on the front.

"Then just take it off," Coop joked, knowing that she would never do something like that.

"Okay," Cara said, calling his bluff.

"Really? I was just joking..."

"Why not? I mean, Todd and Joy won't be home for at least another hour. Besides, this place is totally secluded," Cara said as she stood up and removed the white sarong from around her waist.

"Very funny, Cara. You had me going for a sec-"

The sight of Cara slowly pulling the bikini top over her head made Coop stop short of finishing his sentence. Cara winked at him and tossed the forsaken top onto his lap before she returned to her chair and stretched out onto her stomach.

Cara felt an adrenaline rush as she felt the warm sun beat down on her bare back, which would now be free of any tan lines. She could not believe that she had the nerve to do it, and she was certain that Coop was even more surprised, if not shocked.

Gary Boardman also felt a sense of adrenaline from his position close to 500 feet away as the viewfinder on his Canon EOS 5D camera confirmed what he had hoped it would when he first arrived earlier that morning. He had used a 300mm telephoto lens as he hid in the sand amongst the tall grass and sea oats hoping to snap pictures of Cooper Madison and his girlfriend Cara next to the pool, but was admittedly disappointed when he saw her lifeguard swimsuit. CMZ was not going to pay very much money for pictures of a girl in a suit like that, regardless of how hot she was. He had been hoping to capture her in a thong, or at the very least, a string bikini.

All of that changed in an instant when the college girl removed her top. Gary immediately began snapping as many pictures as the D-

SLR would allow him to, hoping that he would get at least a few clear money shots.

As he quickly clicked through the captured images, many of which very clearly featured a topless Cara, he started to wonder just how much CMZ would pay him for the rights. He was not going to wait long to find out as he called his contact at CMZ from his spot right there in the sand.

"Hey, it's Boardman," he said, smiling at his good fortune. "I hope you have that Brinks truck ready…"

77

Hannah LaMarca sat up straight from her place behind the anchor desk at Cleveland's Channel One News, looked directly at the teleprompter located above camera #2, and waited for the red light to turn on.

"Going live in 5...4...3...2..." the midday news producer instructed via her earpiece just before the light kicked on.

"Good afternoon. As Cleveland Police continue to search for answers related to the murder of local businessman, Vance Gold, there is a new development that you will only see here on Channel One News," Hannah said as she began her report. "Detectives from the Cleveland Police Department's violent crime task force are hoping that you can help identify the female in this picture," she continued as the photograph of a young Jane Worthington appeared on the broadcast.

"The photograph, which is believed to have been taken at least five years ago, could be of assistance in helping the police identify persons of interest. While police are not giving any further information regarding the case or the young woman in the picture, they are asking anyone in our viewing area with information to contact them at the tip line shown here," Hannah said as the phone number appeared on the screen.

Back at the 1ˢᵗ District precinct it did not take long for the calls to start rolling in. All five of the phone lines that were manned by officers began ringing off the hook within minutes of Hannah's public plea for help on Channel One News.

Jason and Mick stood and watched as the officers logged each phone call into a spreadsheet on the laptop computers that the IT department had set up for the tip line. Each entry on the spreadsheet was automatically saved into a department folder that only Jason and Mick had access to.

"Well, let's go see what we got," Mick said after fifteen minutes of phone calls.

"Patient as always, Mick," Jason chided.

"Kiss my fat ass."

"Speaking of, what'd the doctor say at your check-up?"

"Doctor? You mean the rapist?"

"Oh, someone had the old prostate exam, I'm guessing?" Jason chuckled.

"I don't want to talk about it..."

Jason sat down at the computer in Mick's office and opened the network folder that the tip line spreadsheet was located in. Commander McCarthy detested computers, so he was always more than happy to let Jason man the keyboard.

"Twenty-seven calls have been logged so far," Jason said.

"Not bad. Can you do that thing where you move those little

boxes around so that we can see if any of the tips are saying the same thing?" Mick asked.

"You mean sort the data?" Jason laughed.

"Yeah, sort the data, smartass…"

Jason held his breath as he highlighted the columns on the spreadsheet and sorted the data by the name the caller gave for the girl in the photograph. One name appeared more than any other.

"Jane Worthington. Does that name ring a bell for you?" Jason asked.

"Nope. What does it say in the notes?" Mick replied, referring to the section on the spreadsheet where the officers typed in any other information that the callers gave.

"Looks like she's dead, at least that's what most of them said. A few said that she was a drug addict. Even more said she was also a prostitute."

"Any of them say where she lived?" Mick asked.

"Looks like West Park, at least that's what the majority of the callers said," Jason replied.

"West Park? Shit, if she was working as a prostitute on the west side a few years ago then that's-"

"Tick…" Jason finished Mick's thought.

"That little prick better talk. No more deals either. He talks or we pull everything off the table," Mick said.

"I agree…"

"First, let's find out where this girl lived. Hopefully we can talk to her parents or neighbors that can give us more on her," Mick said.

"I'm running her name now," Jason said as he scrolled through the results of his search. "Huh… Looks like she passed away in 2002."

"2002? Buddy's Speakeasy wasn't even around then," Mick responded. "What about her parents? Siblings?"

"No siblings. Mother, Irene, deceased. Father is alive. Phillip Worthington of Cleveland. No prior arrests," Jason said. "Boom, there it is. West Park address."

"Well, let's see what her dad has to say," said Mick.

"I'll drive," Jason announced as he grabbed his jacket.

78

"These tell a story," Dolly said as she held Phil's hands up for inspection as they sat across from each other at a table inside Gatlinburg's famous Log Cabin Pancake House.

"That's what we said last night at the bar," Phil chuckled.

"I know, but there's more than just years of hard work written all over these hands," she replied.

"Isn't there always?"

"I suppose, but I feel like these have seen a lot of pain."

"Well, they've had their fair share of fishing lures embedded in them, that's for sure."

"That's not what I'm talking about."

"Well, then tell me."

"Okay," she began. "I see sadness in these hands. Like you've lost someone very close to you."

"I have…"

"Was it your wife? I mean, you said you were single, but never said why."

"Irene, my wife, passed away suddenly when she was 38. From pneumonia," Phil replied.

"Oh my God, I'm so sorry!" Dolly gasped.

"Thank you. It happened while I was on the road, like I always was. She knew she was sick, but she had to take care of our daughter, Jane. If she just would've went in to the doctor…"

Phil did not finish the sentence.

"Phil, I don't even know what to say. I'm so sorry. What about your daughter, Jane? How old is she now?"

Phil looked away, his lips pursed as he tried to steel himself.

"She would be 22…"

A confused look came over Dolly's face before she realized exactly what Phil was trying to convey to her.

"Oh my God, Phil… I… I don't…"

"Drugs," Phil said as he turned his attention back to Dolly, his eyes unable to mask their pain. "She was only 18 when she passed."

"You poor thing," Dolly replied, clasping both of his hands tightly. "Nobody should ever have to go through what you have."

"I blame myself," Phil said, looking down as tears began to stream down his cheeks, his body shaking.

"No, Phil. You can't do that to yourself…"

"I was always gone. Weeks at a time driving that goddamn truck. If I just would've been around more..."

"You were doing what you had to do to provide for your family, Phil. You can't blame yourself for that."

"Yeah, well, I do," he said as he looked up.

"I suppose I would too, if I were in your shoes," she relented. "But, that doesn't make it true. I hope you know that."

"I'm not sure what I know anymore..."

"Is that why you're down here? Searching for answers?" Dolly asked.

"I don't think so. I've spent the past four years doing that."

"Then why are you here?"

"I think, at first, it was to escape reality for a bit. But, now I realize that maybe the universe brought me down here for a different reason," Phil said, a smile forming as he looked Dolly in the eyes.

"And what would that be?" she asked.

"To meet you..."

79

"I'm telling you that this will be the best seafood lunch you've ever had," Todd "T-Squared" Taylor reassured the passengers in his SUV as they pulled into a parking spot at Pop's Sunset Grill.

Located along the Intracoastal Waterway that runs between Casey Key and the mainland of Florida, Pop's had long been a favorite dining destination for both tourists and locals in Nokomis. Also known as the ICW, the Intracoastal Waterway also enabled boaters to "park" their boats alongside the docks that Pop's Sunset Grill provided.

"You know that I grew up in the shrimpin' capital of the United States, right?" Coop reminded his agent and friend as they exited the vehicle.

"There's more to life than shrimp, Coop!" Todd replied.

"You watch your mouth, T," Coop teased.

Once seated inside the quaint restaurant with a beautiful view of the ICW, Todd, Joy, Coop, and Cara enjoyed a round of drinks as they waited for their meals. Todd had insisted on ordering everyone one of Pop's famous "Steamship Pots", which were loaded with shrimp, lobster tails, oysters, and mussels.

"I'd like to make a toast," Todd said as he raised his glass. "Here's to the beginning of a great week with even greater friends. Coop and Cara, Joy and I are so glad that you could join us this week. Here's to a speedy recovery too. I need you healthy, Coop, mainly so I can continue to afford that beautiful house we are all staying at. Salute!"

The rest of the table joined in on the toast, laughing at Todd's quip, which Coop figured likely had a bit of truth to it. While Todd had made a small fortune on other clients in and out of professional baseball, Cooper Madison was still his most valuable.

"Oh, and one more thing," Todd said, raising his glass again. "You may have noticed that Joy was only drinking water, and while she may be doing that so she can drive our day-drinking vacationing asses home, there is another reason…"

Todd looked over at Joy and nodded.

"I'm expecting!" she announced as she raised her glass.

"Oh my God! Congratulations!" Cara exclaimed before reaching over and giving Joy a hug.

"Well, I'll be damned. That's great news!" Coop agreed as he shook Todd's hand with his healthy arm.

"Thanks, Brother. We've been trying for so long, but it finally happened for us," Todd replied, smiling at Joy.

"How far along are you?" Cara asked Joy.

"I just started my second trimester. The baby is due the first week of March," Joy replied.

"Are you going to find out the gender?" Cara asked.

"Nope," Todd interjected.

"Oh man, that's got to be *killing* you, T! Patience is not exactly your virtue," Coop laughed.

"Actually, it was his idea," Joy said.

"Really?" a stunned Coop replied.

"Yessir."

"I'm shocked," Coop laughed, shaking his head in disbelief.

"Now, now, hear me out," Todd said, holding court. "As I get older and wiser I have come to the realization that during adulthood there are only so many surprises left in life - and most of those surprises are bad – so this one will be worth the wait."

"Awe, I love it!" Cara said.

"Better watch out, Coop. I'm detecting some baby fever here," Todd teased, nodding at Cara.

"Todd Taylor! Don't you do that to these poor kids!" Joy admonished her husband.

"Awe, they know I'm just bustin' balls," Todd said, waving it off.

"Well then, I would like to propose a toast to the future parents," Coop said, raising his glass. "May God bless you and the baby with all the happiness in the world."

80

Mick and Jason stood on the front stoop of Phil Worthington's West Park home, but no answer came from within after numerous attempts knocking on both the front and side doors. There was at least a few days worth of mail jammed into the letter slot that was located near the front door and three newspapers, still rolled up, were sitting on the steps.

"He's been gone all week!"

The detectives turned to see an elderly woman talking to them through an open window at the house next door.

"Hello, ma'am," Jason said. "Do you happen to know where Mr. Worthington is? Or when he will be back?"

"Who's asking?" the woman countered.

"Commander McCarthy and Detective Knox, ma'am. We are with Cleveland Police," Mick answered, as they both showed their badges.

"May we ask what your name is, ma'am?" Jason added.

"Ethel. Ethel Levine," she replied. "Is Phil in some sort of trouble?"

"Not that we know of, Ms. Levine," Jason replied. "Have you known Mr. Worthington for a long time?"

"Oh yes, I've known Phil for almost twenty years," she replied. "He's a great neighbor too. He looks after me. Cuts my grass, shovels the driveway. He'll even come over to open a jar for me if I ask."

"Man, I wish I had a neighbor like that. You're one lucky lady," Mick laughed.

"Would you mind if we came over and asked you a few more questions, Ms. Levine?" Jason asked.

"I'll meet you at the front door," Ethel replied before she closed the window.

Mick and Jason walked over to Ethel's house where she greeted them at the door. She had on a floral housecoat, fuzzy slippers, and was using a walker for support.

"Did Mr. Worthington tell you that he was heading out of town, ma'am?" Mick asked.

"No, which isn't like him," Ethel replied, shaking her head. "But, he obviously went somewhere because his truck hasn't been here all week either."

"When was the last time you spoke to him?" Jason asked.

"Well, I suppose it was Saturday night. He brought some walleye for me," Ethel replied, smiling. "He's a charter captain at Edgewater, you know, and he always brings me fresh fish back."

Hearing that Phil Worthington had a boat at Edgewater Park

Marina sent a shiver down Jason's spine. Mick must have felt it too, because he shot Jason a wide-eyed look.

"What can you tell us about her?" Jason asked, holding up the picture of Jane. "Was this Mr. Worthington's daughter?"

Seeing the picture of Jane brought an immediate look of pain and grief to Ethel's face. She had blamed herself so much for what had happened to Jane under her watch as a nanny, despite Phil's insistence that it was not her fault.

"Yes, that was our Janey," Ethel replied, her tone solemn. "I used to look after her after Phil's wife, Irene, passed away. Phil used to drive a truck and he'd be gone for days at a time, so I'd watch after Jane when he was gone. I didn't do a very good job though."

"Why would you say that, ma'am?" Mick asked.

"Because, I was so blind that I didn't know what she was up to," Ethel replied.

"What was it that she was up to, Ms. Levine?" Jason pressed.

"She was always such a sweet little girl, you know, and I guess that's the only way that I would allow myself to see her… Even as she got older and started doing drugs," Ethel responded.

"Is that how she died, ma'am? From the drugs?" Mick asked, hoping to confirm the information that they had received from the tip line.

"Yes…"

"Was Jane involved in anything else before her death that we should know about?" Jason asked, already knowing the answer.

"She was involved in something else that was just awful. I'm not even supposed to know about it," Ethel answered.

"What do you mean by that?" Mick asked.

"Well, I overheard Phil talking to one of Jane's friends outside his house one night, not long after she died," Ethel replied. "I wasn't trying to eavesdrop, I swear, but I could hear them talking through my window."

"What did you hear, Ms. Levine?"

"That our sweet Jane was working as…" Ethel lowered her voice to a whisper. "A prostitute."

"I see. Well, I'm sure that all of this was very hard on her father, and you. How did Mr. Worthington deal with it?" Jason asked.

"He was heartbroken, of course. He and Jane were very close. He retired from trucking not long after her death and that's when he started his fishing charter. He even named his boat after Jane. He calls it *Jane's Justice*."

Mick and Jason looked at each other upon hearing the name of the vessel.

"Does Mr. Worthington have any place you think he might have gone to stay at? Maybe a hunting cabin or lake house?" Mick asked.

"Oh heaven's no," Ethel replied. "Phil hasn't even been on a vacation since before Jane passed. He's always around. It worries me that he's gone. Will you gentlemen promise to tell me when you find him? Maybe have him call me?"

"I think we can do that, and here, take my card. If you happen to see Mr. Worthington or hear from him, please give us a call," Jason said as he handed her the card.

"Better yet, have him call us," Mick said.

"Of course, I most certainly will," she replied.

"Thank you, Ms. Levine," Jason said. "You've been more than helpful."

81

"Have you ever seen anything so beautiful?" Dolly asked.

"Not in a long time," Phil answered.

They had just finished the half-mile hike that connected the parking lot to the observation tower located at Clingmans Dome. It had been Dolly's idea to take the 45-minute drive from Gatlinburg to the highest mountain in the Smokies, and the view from atop the uniquely designed observation tower did not disappoint.

"You probably saw all sorts of beautiful places during your time as a trucker," she said.

"That I did, but this is right up there with any of them," he replied.

"My ex never wanted to travel anywhere with me."

"His loss..."

"You're sweet," Dolly said as she rested her head on his shoulder.

"Just stating the obvious." Phil replied as he put his arm around her.

"What's the prettiest place you've ever been to?"

"That's a tough one. I've been to almost every state, but I'd have to say nothing beats Red Rock Canyon at sunset."

"I could only imagine. I'd love to go out west someday."

"What's stopping you?"

"Nothing now that I'm divorced, I suppose. I hope that I didn't bore you on the way here talking about my marriage. I guess I'm still coming to grips with the fact that it's finally over after twenty plus years."

"No need to apologize, Dolly. It's not easy letting go."

"Especially of the regrets," she agreed. "I know that I told you on the way here that I couldn't have any kids of my own, but if I could go back in time I would've tried adoption. I think I would've been a real good mom."

"I think so too."

"Tell me more about your daughter, Jane. I mean, if it's not too hard to talk about."

"It's never hard to talk about the good times, so that's what I try to focus on," Phil replied. "It's strange, but when I think about her, I always think about when she was a little girl, before Irene passed."

"I don't think that's strange at all, Phil. It's good to remember the happy times."

"When she was about five or six she used to have this stuffed animal she carried with her everywhere," Phil recalled. "It was this cheap toy giraffe that I picked up for her at a truck stop – I used to always bring her something home at the end of a trip – and for whatever reason she fell in love with that darn thing. Irene used to have to wash it at night when Jane was asleep because she wouldn't let that thing out of her sight during the day."

"Well, that's just about the most adorable thing I've ever heard, Phil."

"One day though, Irene took Jane to the park and it started to thunderstorm. Somehow, when she and Jane ran back to the car to get out of the rain, the giraffe got left behind. When they went back later that evening to find it, the giraffe was nowhere to be found. I was on my way back from Indiana when I called Irene from a truck stop pay phone and I could barely hear her over Jane's crying in the background," Phil laughed at the memory.

"Oh my, what did you do?"

"Well, I stopped at every damn truck stop from Indianapolis to Cleveland looking for another one. I had just about given up hope when I finally found one about thirty miles from home. There was only one problem though. Her giraffe was yellow and this one was pink, but I figured it was better than nothing."

"Oh, no! Did she like it?" Dolly asked.

"Surprisingly, yes. When I gave it to her I told her that another little kid must have really needed the yellow one, but that the pink one was even more special because only little girls who learned how to share could take care of a pink giraffe."

"Oh my God, Phil, you're gonna make me cry! What a good dad."

"I would've done anything for her. Anything," Phil said.

I still would...

82

Cara Knox was tired of hearing the non-stop notifications on her cell phone that had been coming through for the past hour and a half when she finally powered it off. Most of them came from friends and family who were likely just trying to check on her, but some of the numbers were either blocked or from numbers that she did not recognize.

It was not long before the first call came that a frantic-looking Todd Taylor came out to the pool area where she and Coop were doing their best to recover after their big lunch at Pop's Sunset Grill.

"I think you two should come inside. There's something you need to see," he said.

They could tell by the tone of his voice that whatever it was that needed their attention must have been serious. Once inside the house, Todd told them to sit down on the couch next to Joy, who also had a worried expression on her face.

"What's goin' on, T? I don't like this. Is everyone okay?" Coop asked.

"I think it's better if I just show you," Todd said as he placed his laptop computer on the coffee table in front of them.

"Oh my God," Cara gasped when she saw that the computer was displaying the CMZ homepage.

"Jesus," was all that Coop could say when he saw the headline *Cara Bares it All* plastered above a photo gallery showing he and Cara from their time next to the pool earlier that morning.

There were eighteen pictures in the gallery, and even though the ones of Cara topless had black boxes covering her exposed chest, there was a promise that the uncensored images would soon be available.

"How did they get these?" Cara asked. "I mean, I even looked around and made sure that nobody was around first."

"I don't know, but whoever it was had to be trespassing because I own everything up to the water. When I find out, you better believe that I'm going to press charges, not to mention sue the hell out of CMZ," Todd seethed.

"I think I'm going to be sick," Cara said as she stood up and ran towards the nearest bathroom. Coop started to get up to chase after her, but Joy stopped him.

"I'll go check on her, you stay here for now," she ordered before heading towards the sounds of Cara dry heaving in the bathroom between sobs.

"This isn't good, T," Coop said, stating the obvious.

"No, it certainly is not," Todd agreed. "We have to go after these assholes, Coop. Does it say anywhere on there who took the pictures?"

"That's what I'm looking for now," Coop said as he scrolled through the page. "It doesn't list anyone, but I bet it was that piece of shit, Gary Boardman."

"The same guy that took the pictures of you two when you went fishing?" Todd asked.

"The one and only. Man, I wish Clarence was here right now," Coop replied. "This would have never happened."

"Don't do that to yourself, Coop."

"Well, what do you suggest we do, then?"

"For starters, I'm going to get a judge to order CMZ to take the pictures down immediately. Hopefully, we'll be able to stop them from posting the uncensored ones too. I'll file an injunction if I have to," Todd replied, wielding his phone as if it were a magic wand that could make everything disappear.

"Do you really think that's gonna stop these from spreading everywhere?" Coop asked, his head in his hands.

"I can't promise you that, but it will give us the leverage to sue anyone who does."

"She doesn't deserve this, T," Coop said. "And all her family has already been through. This is such a mess."

"I blame myself," Todd countered. "I should have put better security in place here. I don't even have security cameras installed yet."

"Security cameras definitely would have been nice," Coop agreed. "At least we might've caught the bastard trespassing on film."

"Wait a minute," Todd said. "All of these properties extend from the road to the water, which means that there's only two ways that he could've gained access to our section of the beach."

"What are you saying, T?"

"I'm saying that unless he swam up, which is highly unlikely, he had to have snuck onto the property – probably through one of the other houses next door."

"You think they have cameras that might have caught him?" Coop asked, a gleam of hope in his voice.

"I know they do," Todd replied.

"Then let's go. Now."

"It's worth a shot," Todd said. "You better check on Cara first though. I'm going to make a few quick calls and see if we can't get the ball rolling on the cease and desist order."

83

Jason and Mick stood outside an interrogation room at the Cuyahoga County Jail and looked in at the scrawny young man sitting at the table. They had just arrived after a stop at Edgewater Park Marina where they had hoped to find Phil Worthington. While his boat, *Jane's Justice*, was docked in its usual spot at the harbor, he was nowhere to be found.

Timothy "Tick" Braun sat nervously as he waited on the detectives, though he tried to put up a good facade. He had not expected to hear from Jason or Mick again, at least not so soon, especially since he had already given them everything he knew about Vance Gold. He hoped that maybe they were going to offer him some good news in regard to his plea deal, but the looks on their faces as he was escorted past them minutes earlier told him otherwise.

"What are the odds he was Jane's pimp?" Mick asked.

"Better yet, if he was her pimp, what are the odds that he has any clue whatsoever that's why we're even here?" Jason replied.

"How do you want to play this?"

"Well, he already hates you," Jason said, "So, let's shake it up a bit."

"You mean I get to be the good cop for once?"

"That's gonna have to be an Oscar-worthy performance," Jason chuckled.

"Very funny, Knox. This will be easy," Mick replied. "Hell, I pretend to like you every day."

"That stings, Mick," Jason said, acting hurt as he opened the door to the room.

"Sup, detectives?" Tick asked as they took a seat across from him.

"Hey there, Tick. How's that girlfriend of yours doing? Did she like the crib we sent her?" Mick asked in as pleasant a tone as Jason had ever heard from him.

"Oh, yeah, she said it's nice," Tick replied, his expression showing just as much confusion as his tone.

"Good, that's great to hear. Listen, we really appreciated that info you gave us on Vance Gold. It was the least we could do," Mick said, keeping up the act.

"Yo, is that why y'all dragged me here? Cuz I already told you everything I got," Tick replied.

"Have you, Tick?" Jason fired back, staring straight into Tick's eyes.

"Hold on, Detective Knox," Mick said, placing his hand on Jason's shoulder. "Let's give Mr. Braun a chance to tell us what he knows first."

"Know about what, yo?" Tick said in return.

"Jane Worthington," Jason snapped back.

"Who? Yo, I don't know no *Jane Worthington*," Tick replied, incredulously.

"See, I told you this guy's been messing with us, Commander!" Jason yelled as he smacked the table with his hand. "You think you're funny, asshole? Well, we'll see how funny you are when we throw you in the same cell block as Vladimir Popov!"

"Yo, why you trippin'? What's wrong with this dude?" Tick asked Mick, looking for some sort of help.

"Oh, *now* you want his help?" Jason laughed. "What? Now you're not gonna call him all the names you usually do? Give me a goddamn break…"

"Okay, okay. Everybody relax for a second," Mick said. "Detective Knox, why don't you show him her picture first? Maybe he'll recognize her face."

Jason begrudgingly pulled the picture of Jane out and slid it across the table towards Tick, who was grinning in disbelief. That smile quickly disappeared when he saw her face.

"What's the matter, Tick? See a ghost?" Jason asked. Tick said nothing.

"Tick, do you recognize that girl?" Mick asked.

"Nah man, never seen her before," Tick replied, shaking his head.

"Bullshit!" Jason shouted as he stood up.

"Tick, now's the time to be honest with us, buddy. If we find out that you knew this girl, and you lied to us about it, my partner here will make sure that you never get that plea deal you're counting on. Think about that baby, Tick. You want to see that baby, right?" Mick pleaded.

"Listen, yo. Let's say I do know her, how do I know that y'all aren't gonna use that against me later and charge me with some bullshit?" Tick asked in return.

"We're not here to get you in any more trouble than you already are, Tick," Mick said, his tone reassuring. "We just really need to know more about what happened to this girl."

Tick looked up at Mick, and then at Jason, who was angrily pacing back and forth. He let out a deep breath.

"She used to work for me," Tick admitted.

"Keep going," Mick encouraged.

"Y'all are callin' her Jane, but to me, that right there is *Britney*," Tick said.

"Britney?" Mick asked.

"Yeah, at least that's what she went by on the streets," Tick replied.

"How'd she end up working for you?" Mick pressed.

"Same way they all did. Daddy issues and shit like that. Got hooked on drugs, needed to make that paper to pay for them. Then she came to me."

"Who brought her to you?" Mick asked.

"We always had a couple girls scoutin' the clubs for talent."

"Names, Tick. We need names," Jason demanded as he returned to his chair.

"Svetlana and Nina."

"Russians?" Mick asked.

"Yeah. They used to work for Vance, just like me, until he got out the game."

"Did they go to work for Popov too?" Jason asked.

"Yo, they didn't have a choice," Tick replied.

"You did, though. Why'd you go work for Popov?" Jason countered.

"What else was I gonna do?"

"Were they still working for Popov when we busted you at Edgewater?" Mick asked.

"Yo, I don't know. Popov ain't no Vance Gold, you feel me? I only knew what I had to do for his Russian ass. That's the truth."

"I hope for your sake it is," Jason said. "If Popov tells us otherwise, well, you can forget any more help from us."

84

"I could really use some of that patented Clarence Walters wisdom right now," Coop sighed into the phone.

"How's Cara holding up?" Clarence asked. He had seen the pictures on CMZ, just like most of the country and felt just as helpless as Coop.

"Oh, she's in bed. Been there for hours. One minute sobbing, the next angry. I just wish I could make it all go away."

"You mentioned that your agent was working on getting the pictures removed from the website. Any luck with that?"

"Not yet, but we were able to look at the neighbor's security footage. It was Gary Boardman. Caught his fat ass trespassing right there on the video," Coop replied.

"Well, that's a start. Did you report it to the local authorities?" Clarence asked.

"Yessir. T is next door talking to them right now and showing them the tape."

"Good. At the very least, they'll be able to arrest him for trespassing. Maybe that'll scare him and CMZ into taking the pictures down."

"I sure hope so. They gotta find him first though. Hopefully, he's still in town."

"It's a start," Clarence replied.

"What else should I do, Clarence? I feel awful for Cara."

"Well, the only thing you can do is continue to be there for her, Coop. Comfort her and reassure her that it'll all be okay," Clarence advised.

"How can I tell her that though?" Coop asked. "I mean, what if the uncensored pictures do get released? I can assure you that things will definitely not be okay."

"No, they won't. At least not at first," Clarence replied. "But, even if that happens, it's your job to make sure that she knows that it won't be the end of the world. Life will go on. This won't define her."

"I don't know, Clarence…"

"Listen to me, Coop. It isn't important whether or not you can prove to her that everything will be okay, because you can't. What's important is that she knows that no matter what happens, that you'll be there for her to make the best of it. Women don't always need us to fix things, even though it's in our DNA to try and do that. What they need is to know that even when we can't fix something, that we'll do everything else in our power to help them get through it."

"You're right. I just hope, at least in this case, that I can do both," Coop replied.

"And maybe you can," Clarence added. "But, if you can't, you have got to make sure that she knows you're going to take this thing on *together*. That's the only thing you can control."

"I got you," Coop replied. "How's everything going up there?"

"Well, Jason has been working like crazy. He's got his hands full with this EPK case."

"What about Erica? How's she holding up?" Coop asked.

"Erica's putting on a good front, for both Jason and Gabby, but I can tell that it's taking its toll on her," Clarence replied.

"And Gabby? How's she doing?"

"That girl is a trip," Clarence laughed. "She's a pistol, that's for sure, but such a sweetheart. And smart! She reminds me of my girls. In fact, she's already colored a bunch of pictures for me just like they used to do when they were her age."

"Man, what I wouldn't give to be a kid again. Not a care in the world," Coop sighed.

"Wouldn't we all," Clarence agreed.

"Well, I'm fixin' to check in on Cara before I go next door and see what's doin' there. I'll be in touch," Coop said.

"Sounds good," Clarence replied.

"Hey, Clarence?"

"Yes?"

"Thanks, man. For everything."

"You know I got you, Coop. Keep me posted on everything and give Cara a hug for me."

"Will do, Clarence."

85

"Tell us about Svetlana and Nina. Where can we find them?" Jason asked Vladimir Popov.

After their visit with Tick, Jason and Mick had the guards bring Popov down to the same interrogation at the Cuyahoga County Jail. The Russian, who has been awaiting trial for his involvement in the prostitution bust that was part of the Ernie Page case, was also calling the county lockup his temporary home.

"What you want to know about them for?" Popov asked, his Russian accent as pronounced as his broken English.

"We have some questions for them regarding a young woman that they are believed to have known," Jason replied.

"What young woman?" Popov asked.

"Doesn't matter, just tell us where we can find them," Mick countered.

"It does matter. It matters to me very much," Popov fired back. "Popov doesn't work for free."

"Well, Popov better work for free," Mick mocked. "Otherwise, Popov will have some of those charges that we were so kind as to withhold slapped right back onto his case before trial."

Vladimir Popov, despite owning a brothel and engaging in a shootout with Cleveland SWAT during the Ernie Page saga, had cooperated with police when they were looking for Stoya Fedorov's killer. Since he was the one who had told Jason that Ernie Page was her killer, Popov had managed to get many of his charges reduced or dropped.

"Idi na fig," Vlad seethed.

"I don't speak Russian, Vlad, but I'm guessing that what you said wasn't very nice," Jason replied.

"I say kiss my ass," Vlad clarified.

"C'mon, Vlad. Let's not do anything that would jeopardize that sweet deal you have going for you. Just tell us where we can find those two girls," Jason replied. "We know they worked for you."

"Unless Tick was lying," Mick added, knowing that even the mention of his name would get a reaction out of the Russian.

"Tick can kiss Popov's ass!" Vlad said, slamming his fist on the table.

"Well, unless you have anything else to add, we're just going to have to believe everything he's told us," Mick said.

"What did midget Tick tell to you?" Popov asked.

"He said that those two girls went to work for you after you swooped in and basically drove Vance Gold out of business. He said that they recruited girls to work for you just like they did for Vance," Jason replied.

"Listen, Popov, we're not trying to add any more charges to you here. Just tell us where we can find these two and I promise you that it won't come back to bite you. This isn't even about you," Mick added.

Popov took in a deep breath before letting it out in a long exhale.

"You can't talk to girls," Popov stated.

"C'mon, Vlad! You don't seem like the kind of guy that wouldn't know where his workers are – even from inside a jail," Mick said.

"Nyet! No… I did not say I don't know where they are," Popov hissed.

"Then what are you saying, Vlad? Clock is ticking here," Jason replied.

"I telling you that you already found girls," Popov said, his eyes narrowed.

"Obviously we didn't, Vlad, or we wouldn't be wasting our time talking to your communist ass," Mick replied.

"You did find girls," Popov reiterated. "You found them on beach."

"On the beach?" Mick laughed. "What beach?"

"Holy shit," Jason said. "Wait a minute, Vlad. Are you telling us that these are the two Jane Does?"

Vlad, upon hearing Jason, raised his eyebrows and nodded in affirmation.

"EPK…" is all Vlad said in return.

"You've known all along who those girls were? Why didn't you say something?" Mick asked incredulously.

"Why would I say?" Vlad countered. "So police could arrest

me?"

"We get that, Vlad," Jason agreed. "But, why not say something after your arrest?"

"You never ask," Vlad replied. "Besides, what good it would do now?"

"That's beside the point, Vlad!" Mick shouted, which only caused Popov to start laughing at him.

"You are joke," Vlad said to Mick.

"Oh, you're gonna think I'm real funny after I talk to the DA about your case," Mick seethed.

"Alright, hold on a minute," Jason said as he slid the photograph of Jane Worthington across the table. "Just tell us if you know who this girl is."

"Nyet," Vlad said, sliding the picture back. "She not work for me. I never seen girl before."

"Fair enough, Vlad. I actually believe you," Jason said, taking the picture back. "Just answer one last thing before we go."

"What you want now?" Popov asked.

"You said those girls were killed by the EPK," Jason replied. "Do you think that Ernie Page was the EPK? Did he kill those girls, too?"

"Nyet…"

86

"There's something about me that you should know," Dolly said to Phil as she stared at the ceiling of her room at the Midtown Lodge.

The couple had retreated back to the Gatlinburg Strip after their visit to Clingmans Dome with every intention of going to dinner after a quick stop to Dolly's motel room. Once inside, however, they opted to postpone dinner for an evening of lovemaking.

"There's a lot about you that I should know, Dolly, and I can't wait to find out all of it," Phil replied.

"That's really sweet, but this is different. I've been wanting to tell you all day, but we were having such a wonderful time that I didn't want to ruin it," she said, fighting back tears.

"Hey, don't cry," Phil said as he sat up and tried to console her. "Whatever it is, you can tell me."

"Promise me that you won't judge me?"

"Of course. I promise," Phil reassured.

"I'm broke. I barely have a hundred dollars to my name," Dolly admitted, sobbing. "I don't even have a car. The only reason I'm able to stay here is because I booked it on my ex's credit card – which I don't even have – and when they try to charge the full amount I just know it will be denied. I'm so worried I'm going to get in trouble, Phil!"

"Whoa, whoa, slow down... Relax, now," Phil said, comforting her. "You're getting yourself all worked up, Dolly."

"I'm sorry, I just am so scared..."

"Didn't you get any money in the divorce?" Phil asked.

"What money? There isn't any. The whole reason that I left Lance is because he blew through what we did have playing online poker," Dolly revealed. "My credit is shot because he took out loans in my name, all of my cards have been maxed out, and I rode down here on a bus. I figured maybe I'd find a job and a place to stay. I just had to get out of Buffalo and away from him."

"I don't even know what to say, except that I'm so sorry you've had to go through this," Phil said.

"No, I'm sorry. This is ridiculous," Dolly replied, wiping tears away. "We just met and here I am ruining your vacation by telling you my sob story."

"You're not ruining anything," Phil disagreed. "In fact, meeting you is the best thing that's happened to me in a long time."

"Why are you so sweet?" Dolly asked. "I don't deserve someone so nice."

"Now, why would you say that? It sounds like he didn't deserve you, and you definitely don't deserve to have your life ruined because of his mistakes."

"I guess because I blame myself," Dolly confessed.

"For what?"

"Because I let it happen to me. I should've known better, but he kept convincing me that he was making good money. He'd even show me the bank statements with big deposits. What he didn't tell me was that those deposits were all from personal loans that he wasn't paying back."

"How would you have known though? You can't do that to yourself, Dolly," Phil said.

"It wasn't until I got the foreclosure notice from the bank that I finally realized something was up. We lost everything; well, I should say that I did. Lance is doing just fine for himself."

"How's that? Was he hiding money?"

"Nope, he moved in with the older widow lady across the street. Sweet old Janice got tons of dough from her old man when he died, so Lance seized the opportunity to ruin her life too," Dolly replied. "I give him a year before he blows through all of her money."

"Doesn't she know about his gambling problem?" Phil asked.

"I tried to warn her, but she told me I was the reason Lance had a problem in the first place. She said that he's so happy with her that he doesn't need to play poker anymore. She was so mean to me that now I hope he loses all of her money."

"Was her late husband rich?" Phil asked.

"Nope, but he was killed by a drunk driver who was," Dolly replied. "So, she got a fat settlement check. I heard it was over half a million bucks."

"Wow," Phil said.

"Yup, so while my fat, lazy ex-husband is living on easy street, I'm broke and alone," she sighed.

"You're not alone," Phil said, placing his hand on her shoulder. "And don't worry about paying for the motel room. I'm gonna take care of it."

"Oh, Phil, I can't let you do that. That wasn't my intention at all when I started telling you all of this," she replied, shaking her head. "I was actually just trying to warn you."

"Warn me?" Phil asked, puzzled.

"That I was damaged goods. I didn't want to burden you," Dolly replied, tears in her eyes.

"You are not damaged goods, you have to know that," Phil said. "And as far as the money goes, it's okay to accept help, you know. This wasn't your fault. I'm in a position financially to help, so let me."

"I don't know, Phil..."

"C'mon," Phil insisted. "My house has been paid off for years, I collect a healthy pension, and I make good money with my charter boat. All that money, most of which I'll never spend, and I'm all alone."

Dolly rolled over to her side so that she was eyelevel with Phil and draped her arm over his shoulders. She smiled, kissed him, and then whispered in his ear.

"You're not alone anymore..."

87

Cara was staring at the ceiling of the guest bedroom, just as she had been all afternoon, when Coop came in to check on her. It was Thursday evening, and despite numerous attempts by Todd to get CMZ to take the photos down, they balked at the request.

The only saving grace, Cara felt, was that at least the uncensored pictures had not yet been leaked online. Even though she had already begun to prepare herself for the likelihood of that happening, she knew that she would still be absolutely destroyed if it did.

Coop had been doing his best all day to help her deal with the situation. She could tell that he was not quite sure how to act around her, which made her feel even worse than she already did.

"You know this wasn't your fault, right?" Cara asked him as he took a seat at the foot of the bed.

"I suppose, but I still feel responsible," Coop replied.

"Well, you shouldn't," Cara said. "You didn't do this to me."

"I know," Coop replied.

"I did this to myself," Cara stated.

"Why on Earth would you say that?" Coop asked incredulously.

"Because I was being stupid and careless. I should've known better, and now I'm going to have to face the consequences for my actions."

"Ok, hold on," Coop replied, standing up. "You were on private property, for God's sake! Not to mention that asshole Boardman was trespassing. I'm not going to let you blame yourself for this."

"He might have taken the pictures, but I should've known better," she sighed. "I guess I just keep forgetting…"

"Forgetting what?"

"That my life is different, now…"

"I hope you don't think that's a bad thing," Coop said.

"Of course I don't," Cara responded immediately before elaborating. "It's just… different. My new reality didn't come with an instruction manual."

"I know…" Coop agreed, feeling responsible.

"You know what really sucks?"

"Besides CMZ?" Coop chuckled.

"That goes without saying," Cara replied. "But, more than that is the fact that we were supposed to come down here so you could relax in a peaceful, stress-free environment. Now look at us! I haven't even asked you how your arm felt since this morning…"

"To be honest, I haven't thought much about it," Coop lied. The reality was that his arm had been throbbing all afternoon.

"You're a crappy liar, Madison," Cara smiled.

"That's a good thing, right?"

"We don't deserve this," she answered, her lip quivering, followed by a wave of tears.

"No, we don't," Coop said as he sat next to her and cradled her as best he could with his good arm. "But, we'll get through it. All of it."

"Do you promise?" Cara asked, fighting back sobs.

"With everything I got. I'm fixin' to be on the eighty year plan with you," Coop reassured her.

Todd Taylor had paused just outside the door of the guest bedroom when he heard Cara's sobbing, then became glad that he had not entered before hearing the last part of their conversation. He had spent most of the day blaming himself, and the rest of it trying to make it all go away for Cara and Coop.

Coop, in addition to being his top client, was also his best friend. He had been there from the start, and he was not about to let CMZ hurt his friends anymore.

After making multiple phone calls, composing just as many emails, and sending even more text messages, Todd was convinced that CMZ would finally cave and take the pictures down. He even figured it might happen by morning. The plan, which Todd had only thought of after getting nowhere with CMZ executives, had literally appeared before his eyes as he scrolled through their website.

CMZ had made a name for itself thanks to America's never-ending obsession with celebrity gossip, and the increasing role that social media was playing in society had only made their influence that much stronger. What had made CMZ unique was its ambush style of celebrity interviews that were splashed all over its page.

Up until CMZ had arrived on the scene, it was very rare to ever see a celebrity being interviewed in an impromptu fashion. Within two years of going live, famous people from every industry had been interviewed while leaving a restaurant, yoga studio, and even their children's school play.

The interviews were usually conducted in an amateurish style, complete with shaky filming and whacky interview questions that often caught the celebrities off guard. It did not take long for the public to realize that not every celebrity or star athlete was as nice they seemed in commercials and studio interviews.

Some stars, unhappy to be pestered by a guy with a handheld camera asking dumb questions, were quick to shout vulgarities at the camera. A few even physically attacked the CMZ crews that were following them around. In some cases, the reputation of an A-lister being interviewed was ruined beyond repair due to something he or she said candidly.

America loved it.

While CMZ had built themselves into a multi-million dollar business by posting unflattering videos and pictures of celebrities, they were ready to expand. Todd almost laughed when he saw the press release at the top of CMZ's homepage:

CMZ Sports Set to Debut in January

Upon clicking the link, Todd learned that CMZ was gearing up to release a spinoff of their website dedicated solely to professional athletes. In the press release, CMZ touted "Unprecedented Access to Athletes" and "1-on-1 Interviews with Sports Legends".

Todd went to work immediately, launching a full-on campaign contacting every major sports agent he knew, and asking them to pass the word on to the ones he did not. Like Todd, many of them had clients who had been burned by CMZ, and they were more than happy to provide some payback.

The word was out. Athletes and the agents that represented them were going on every form of social media available and announcing a boycott of the future CMZ Sports website unless CMZ took the photos of Cara Knox down.

It was not only athletes that joined the boycott. Dozens of movie stars, television actors, and musicians jumped on board, threatening to never grant another interview to CMZ unless action was taken.

All of this was unknown to Coop, and especially Cara, who had spent most of the day in the guest bedroom away from any and all electronic devices. Todd had been excited to tell them, hoping that it would give them a glimmer of hope that a resolution was near.

After hearing Coop's declaration that he was in this relationship for the long haul, Todd quietly turned away from the door and walked back down the hallway. His good news could wait, and even if the boycott failed to get the pictures taken down, Todd had a strong feeling that the young couple would be just fine.

88

"Where the hell is Gatlinburg?" Mick asked Jason as they exited the home of Phil Worthington.

A judge had issued a search warrant earlier that Friday morning for his house and boat based off of the evidence, as circumstantial as it was, that Phil might have had something to do with Vance's murder.

However, that was not the main reason that the detectives wanted to search the house. Circumstantial or not, they were pretty positive that Phil was responsible for Vance Gold's murder and possibly even HoJo's.

Without mentioning it to the judge, or anyone else for that matter, they were actually there hoping to find evidence that would connect Phil to the deaths of the two Russian girls. Thanks to Tick and Vlad those two Jane Does, the second and third victims of the EPK, now had names.

Phil's fishing boat did not yield anything even remotely

suspicious. The house was not any better as he seemed to live a relatively Spartan existence. Nonetheless, both *Jane's Justice* and the house, along with the filet knives found on the boat, would be tested for any traces of human blood that could have been left behind.

"Tennessee. I guess it's a tourist trap in the Smokies or something," Jason replied.

He had just received word that Phil Worthington had used his credit card to pay for room charges belonging to a Dolly Barnes at a place called the Midtown Lodge in Gatlinburg, Tennessee. It was the first activity on Phil's card since before Vance Gold's murder, according to the bank, and that only raised more questions.

"So, if he was purposely not using his card to avoid leaving a trail, why would he use it now to pay for someone else's room?" Mick asked.

"Maybe the fact that he wasn't using his credit card was just a coincidence?" Jason replied. "My old man tries to pay cash for everything, to this day. A lot of mom and pop motels will just take your card number down and not actually run it when you pay for a room up front because they don't want to get charged a transaction fee."

"Or he never actually booked a room under his name anywhere," Mick said. "I mean, think about it. If he's the freaking EPK, who's to say that this Dolly Barnes lady isn't in trouble? Or dead? He could've killed her and used her room."

"Yeah, but why the hell would he pay for the room then?" Jason asked. "If that was the case, there'd be no reason to that I can think of, especially since the reservation wasn't in his name."

"Maybe she's his accomplice," Mick replied. "What did they come up with on her anyway?"

"Nothing…"

"Nothing?" Mick asked, puzzled.

"No record anywhere of a Dolly Barnes. The motel staff faxed the copy of the driver's license she gave them when she checked-in, but it was bogus."

"Did she use a credit card to book her room?" Mick asked.

"That's the part that doesn't make sense," Jason replied. "She did use a card, but it belonged to a guy named Lance Barnes from Buffalo."

"Another person named Barnes?"

"Yeah, but apparently this Barnes guy is real. Or, at least his credit card is. I'll put a call into Buffalo to see if they can track him down and find out why some lady in Tennessee is using his credit card," Jason replied.

"Good. Fax them a copy of the mystery woman's license too. Maybe we'll get lucky," Mick instructed. "I'll get on the horn with the local police in Gatlinburg and have them check things out. I'll warn them of what they could be dealing with and to approach with caution."

89

Phil Worthington could not remember the last time that he had felt the mixture of excitement and nervousness that often accompanies a new romance, but they were certainly in full force as he drove away from the Rocky Waters Motor Inn. He had not slept there since Tuesday night, opting instead to stay with Dolly, but he kept the room anyways since he had prepaid for it in cash.

Just as it was for a lot of people from his generation, whose Depression-Era parents often scared their children into believing that another crash could happen at any time, Phil preferred to pay for things with cash.

Thanks to the cash-only policy used for his fishing charter, he had plenty of it with him too. While Phil still was quite confident that nobody from the Cleveland Police Department was looking for him he did not want to leave any sort of electronic trail behind unless he absolutely had to, and paying for everything in cash ensured that would not happen.

Now on his way back to the Midtown Lodge after packing up his belongings, which included the more than six thousand dollars in cash he had locked away in his motel safe, and he was absolutely giddy for the adventures that lay ahead.

Phil would have already used that cash to pay for Dolly's room charges at the Midtown Lodge before he left her there earlier that morning, but he did not have enough on him to cover it since most of it was locked away back in his motel room's safe.

"Listen," Phil had said to Dolly before he left. "After I get out of the shower, I'm gonna go and check out of my room at Rocky Waters. Call the front desk here and tell them that you're checking out today and that your bill will be paid in full, with cash."

"Cash? Phil, I don't think you understand," Dolly replied. "My bill is going to be at least two grand."

"And?" Phil chuckled.

"And… Will we still have enough money left over for our trip?" she asked, referring to Phil's plan to checkout and head for Red Rock, just as Dolly had always wanted.

"Trust me, money is not going to be an issue," Phil said as he entered the shower.

It had been a long time since he was able to play the role of provider and protector for anyone other than himself, and Phil loved the way it made him feel. Dolly seemed to like the way it made her feel as well.

"There's a problem," Dolly said to Phil after he was done with his shower.

"What's that?"

"I called the front desk and they said that they needed me to square my bill up now, before we left, and that if I didn't they would report me," she said sounding worried.

"Report you? Didn't you tell them that I was going to come back and pay it off with cash?" Phil asked.

"Of course I did, but I don't think they believed me…"

"What's the problem with these people?" Phil asked incredulously.

"Well, they probably think I'm just saying that so we can skip town without paying. I even told them I'd stay here in the room until you got back, but I guess that wasn't good enough either," Dolly replied.

"I think I need to go talk to the manager," Phil declared. "I've never heard of a motel treating a customer so harshly because of a declined credit card. That stuff happens every day, for Christ sakes!"

"Please don't do that, Phil."

"Why not?"

"Because… It really is my fault and I'm already embarrassed enough as it is."

"How so?" Phil asked.

"Well, earlier this morning, I guess they tried to put the bill on the credit card that I used when I booked the room - you know Lance's old card – and, of course, it was declined. I asked them why they ran it without my permission and they said that I had given them permission when I checked in. They said that since I was scheduled to checkout today that it was standard practice to bill the card," Dolly replied, the tone of her voice going up an octave as she spoke.

"Okay, but that still doesn't make sense, Dolly. Why would they threaten you over a declined credit card?" Phil asked, frustrated.

"Because, it was declined for a different reason than the one I told you about." Dolly admitted, her words slow and measured. "It was declined because Lance must have reported it lost or stolen. So, now the motel probably thinks I'm a thief. I tried to explain to them that it was my ex-husband's card and that my name was still on the account, but they didn't believe me..."

Dolly sat on the bed and put her head in her hands. The sight of which broke Phil's heart. He wanted to fix this situation for her. Protect her.

"Well, since you won't let me go talk to them, what *can* I do?" Phil asked.

"I'm too embarrassed to ask," she replied. "You've already done so much for me and are planning to do even more. I couldn't possibly ask you for another favor."

"That's ridiculous, Dolly," Phil said, reassuringly. "Just tell me what it is and I'll do it. All I have been able to think about since this morning was our trip. You and me on the open road... Red Rock sunsets. Hey, whatever we want!"

"I don't deserve you, Phil," Dolly said, wiping the tears from her face.

"The feeling is mutual," he replied. "Now, tell me what you need."

"Your driver's license," Dolly replied.

"That's it?" Phil answered as he pulled his wallet out to retrieve his license.

"And your credit card..."

"My credit card? But, I'm going to pay in cash," Phil replied.

"They said that's fine, and you can, but they need those as collateral until you return with the cash."

"I see," Phil said. "Well, I suppose that'd be okay, but only if they aren't going to run my card."

"They won't. I'll make sure of it," Dolly promised.

"It's just that I didn't call my bank to tell them that I'd be travelling and I know that a big charge like that would probably raise a red flag," Phil lied. "That's why I paid for my room in cash. I just don't want to deal with any of that…"

"You have my word," Dolly reassured him as she leaned in and gave him a long kiss. "Now, hurry back so we can get a jump on our trip. I'm going to spend our entire time together showing you just how much I appreciate all of this."

Back at the Midtown Lodge, Phil parked his truck and grabbed the worn leather duffel bag that held his cash before walking back to Dolly's room. She had told him that she would wait for him there so that he could help her carry her belongings out to his truck before they returned to the front desk to check out.

"It's open," Dolly said from inside her room after Phil knocked on the door.

"You ready to go?" Phil said as he entered the room.

"Almost," she replied from inside the bathroom. "Have a seat on the bed. I'll be out in a second. Just needed to freshen up a bit before we leave."

Her bags were neatly stacked on the floor at the foot of the bed and Phil could feel the butterflies in his stomach strengthen. As he took a seat on the edge of the bed he hoped that Dolly was experiencing the same level of anticipation that he was.

"Lay down," Dolly said seductively as she emerged from the bathroom.

"Lay down?" Phil asked, puzzled.

"You heard me," she replied, her voice playful, yet demanding.

"Do we really have time for this?" Phil asked, now realizing where this was heading.

"We have nothing but time," Dolly replied, her voice sultry. "Besides, I told you that I was going to show you my appreciation. Now lay down and close your eyes and let me do all the work. This won't take long…"

Phil smiled and did as he was told as she straddled him on the bed. If this type of spontaneous love was going to be his new reality, he was going to let go and enjoy every minute of it.

He felt Dolly's hand gently caress the side of his face and he turned his head to the side, only to feel her pull away. A few uneventful seconds passed before his curiosity got the best of him.

With his head still turned to the side, facing the nightstand, Phil slowly opened his eyes. A puzzled look came over his face when he saw his credit card and driver's license, which should have been waiting for him at the front desk, sitting on the table next to the bed.

Confused, Phil turned his gaze back towards Dolly to ask her why she had not taken them to the front desk, but he never had the chance.

Dolly, smiling while gripping a large buck knife with both hands above her head, violently plunged the blade deep into his chest and began to twist it. The pain was sharp and incapacitating. Every time Phil tried to raise his arms, Dolly twisted the knife even more.

"Shhhhhh," she whispered, her eyes disturbingly calm as she maintained her gaze upon his horrified face.

Phil tried to speak, ask her why, but each time he tried to open his mouth she rotated the long serrated blade to silence him. His brain fought to keep his eyes open, but it was losing the battle.

As his world began to go dark, Phil thought he could hear Jane in the distance, beckoning him to join her.

I'm coming Janey… Daddy's… Coming home, baby girl…

90

"How'd you do it, T?" Coop asked, staring at the laptop.

He was logged on to CMZ's homepage, on which any trace of Cara's pictures seemed to have disappeared. Todd, sitting across from him at the kitchen table, simply raised his hands and smiled.

"I've told you a hundred times, Coop" Todd replied, clearly proud of himself. "T-Squared always wins, baby!"

"I promise that I will never doubt that ever again," Coop replied. "But, how?"

Todd went on to explain how he had organized the boycott of CMZ and how, facing pressure from worried investors and the threat of a lawsuit, the website quickly caved and removed the story. He added that they had even faxed over a signed document promising that they would permanently delete all of the images, both censored and uncensored, from their servers.

"That's amazing, T. I can't thank you enough," Coop said. "But, what about Gary Boardman? He's still out there, and you know that he has the originals. How are we going to stop him from selling them to another website?"

"That's going to be tough for him to do, Coop," Todd replied, smiling.

"How so?"

"Because he was picked up last night by the cops in Sarasota when he tried checking into a hotel. Apparently, he didn't know that there was a warrant out for his arrest on the trespassing charges we filed against him," Todd chuckled.

"That's awesome!" Coop replied. "Were they able to get the photos or at least the memory cards or whatever he uses to store them?"

"That's the best part, and also why we don't have to worry about him getting out anytime soon."

"They won't be able to keep him locked up too long on a trespassing charge, though. He might already be bailed out by now," Coop said.

"No, they wouldn't," Todd agreed. "Trespassing would likely only be a misdemeanor, felony misdemeanor at most when you add in the voyeurism charges."

"Then how are you so confident that he won't get out?" Coop asked, confused.

"Well, because when I spoke to the detective handling the case he informed me that they found thousands of similar pictures on his computer and memory sticks," Todd replied. "Turns out, Gary is even creepier than we thought. They said the guy has apparently been using his telescopic lens to peep in on hundreds of unsuspecting women, and even some girls, as they got undressed in their bedrooms. He's going to be locked-up for a long, long time. The best part is that all of the images are now going to be locked away as evidence and the detective assured me that the pictures of Cara will never see the light of day."

"What a sick bastard!" Coop declared, shaking his head in disbelief. "I seriously can't thank you enough, T."

"You can thank me by using the rest of your time down here to enjoy yourselves and get healthy. I need my star client back on the mound mowing down batters as soon as possible," Todd replied, smiling. "Speaking of, how's the arm feeling?"

"To be honest, it's hard to feel much of anything with this brace on it," Coop replied, nodding towards the immobilizer. "But, it does throb occasionally."

"I can only imagine, but if I know my guy, you're going to be back stronger than ever after this is all said and done," Todd said.

"I hope you're right, but first, I better go tell Cara the good news," Coop said, standing up. "She was just waking up when I came out here."

"Good deal. Joy and I are planning on going for a long walk on the beach. We'll be back in about an hour, so start thinking about where you guys want to go for lunch," Todd said as he too stood up. The pair, who had been through so much together over the past decade, gave each other a hug.

"Alright, enough of this. Go tell your girl the good news," Todd laughed.

When he entered the guest bedroom, Coop found Cara sitting up in the bed. Her eyes were puffy and looked tired, but she managed a smile when she saw Coop enter the room.

"Hey," she said as Coop took a seat next to her.

"Hey, girl," Coop replied. "I have some wonderful news…"

An hour later, as Coop stood in the bathroom, he stared at the bottle of narcotic painkillers he held in his hand. It was time to follow-through on the promise he had made after Cara's pictures appeared on CMZ.

It was a promise that he made when all hope seemed lost. Feeling desperate, Coop had sworn that if fate intervened and made everything go away for her that he would give up the pills for good. Going forward, he would only take over-the-counter pain relievers to manage the pain and ice regularly.

While the pain in his arm certainly justified using them, which he had been doing as directed since the surgery, he knew that the temptation to fall back under their tortuous spell would always be there.

Sometimes, Coop thought, life is painful. It can manifest in many different ways, but it can also be used to make you stronger. It can be a reminder that you should always cherish the painless moments and embrace the healing when the painful ones arrive.

Coop took the cap off of the bottle, dumped the contents into the toilet, and flushed them down. This time, God-willing, forever.

Cara was waiting for him in the bedroom when he returned. Her eyes were vibrant and, for the first time in two days, she looked like herself. An enormous weight had been lifted off her, off both of them.

"You ready for lunch?" she asked, smiling.

"I'm so hungry I could eat the north end of a south-bound goat," he replied.

"I'll take that as a yes," she laughed.

"Yes, ma'am."

"Have I told you recently how much I love you?" she asked, wrapping her arms around him.

"Yes, but I'm always willing to hear it again," he replied, smiling.

"Good, because I plan on spending the rest of our lives telling you," Cara said before softly kissing him on the lips.

"Nothing," Coop replied.

Cara smiled and kissed him again before whispering into his ear.

"Nothing…"

91

Detective Jason Knox ran down the hallway of Cleveland Police's 1st District Headquarters. He had just received the call back from the Buffalo Police Department that he had been waiting for and needed to inform his commander as to what they said.

"I've seen that look before," Mick said. "I'm guessing that the news from Buffalo wasn't very good?"

"Not if your name is Lance Barnes," Jason confirmed.

"I was afraid of that," Mick replied.

"BPD said that they found him tied to his bed, naked, with multiple stab wounds to his chest. They're guessing that he had been dead for weeks."

"Weeks? That must've been a pretty awful scene," Mick replied. "Nobody reported him missing? No family or co-workers?"

"Nope. Lance was single, mid-forties, and lived alone. Neighbors told BPD that he was a bit of a recluse," Jason said, shaking his head. "Apparently, he ran a small mail order business from his house by himself, and they said that if he had any family they never saw them."

"What about a girlfriend?"

"That's where it gets interesting. The neighbors said that up until a few weeks ago that they had never even seen another car in his driveway that wasn't delivering pizza," Jason replied. "That's when a few of them said that they started to see a woman hanging around."

"Did they happen to say if her name was Dolly Barnes?" Mick asked.

"Nobody that BPD spoke to knew her name, but they did confirm that the woman in the driver's license I faxed was the same one at his house," Jason said. "Do you think that she and Phil Worthington are pulling some sort of Bonnie and Clyde act?"

"No, I'm pretty sure that they aren't," Mick replied.

"Why's that?" Jason asked, puzzled.

"Because before you came in I just got off the phone with Gatlinburg PD," Mick replied. "Phil Worthington was found dead in Dolly's room at the Midtown Lodge. Stab wound to the chest. No sign of his truck or belongings anywhere."

Almost 500 miles away, just west of Nashville, Dolly sat on a bench outside of a rest stop along Interstate 40 while she waited for the cab that she had called to pick her up. Phil's truck sat in the parking spot where Dolly had left it, with all but one of his bags still inside.

On her lap was a worn leather duffel bag, the contents of which Dolly knew would enable her to create yet another version of herself. While a good chunk of the money would buy her a reliable car at the first used car lot the taxi could find, there would still be more than enough left over to get her to Red Rock Canyon.

She pictured the glowing sky in her mind as the taxi pulled in to the rest stop parking lot. After seeing her wave, the driver pulled up and got out of the cab.

"Are you Dolly Worthington?" he asked as he popped the trunk.

"Yes," she said, smiling at the sound of her newest identity. "That's me…"

92

Two weeks later, Hannah LaMarca sat at her chair inside the studio at Cleveland's Channel One News. She took in a deep breath as the producer counted her down, exhaled as she had one last look at her notes, and then directed her gaze into the camera.

"For the better part of 2006, the city of Cleveland has been living with the uncertainty of whether or not a serial killer has been living amongst us. The Edgewater Park Killer case has captured the attention of not only our wonderful city, but also the nation," she said, reading from the teleprompter.

"When the body of Stoya Fedorov washed ashore earlier this year at Edgewater Park, there were many questions to which there were no answers. That uncertainty only increased as two more victims, also young women, appeared along that same coastline."

"The entire city breathed a collective sigh of relief when Ernie Page admitted to killing Stoya Fedorov shortly before taking his own life. We were all told, by the chief of police himself, that the monster known as the EPK would no longer be a threat to the residents of this city."

"In a Channel One exclusive," Hannah said, taking a pause for effect. "I am here to tell you tonight that the very detectives who confronted Ernie Page on the docks of Edgewater Park Marina did not share the same beliefs as their chief. Commander Mick McCarthy and Detective Jason Knox recently spoke with me in their first televised interview regarding the case, and here's their story…"

The on-air feed cut away to a segment that Hannah had filmed earlier in the week with Jason and Mick. She had suggested that they tape the interview at Edgewater Park, and as they stood along the rough autumn waters of Lake Erie, the detectives told their saga. Mick and Jason told Hannah ahead of time that everything was fair game, with only a few exceptions.

The discussion of any evidence that could possibly jeopardize the ongoing investigation into the shady real estate deals involving Salvatore Furio and Arliss Gold was off-limits, which meant that for the time being, HoJo's legacy would remain untarnished.

"What about HoJo's connection to Vance Gold? Can we discuss that, at least?" Hannah had asked prior to the interview.

"I wish," Jason replied. "Unfortunately, everything we have on him is circumstantial, at best, and most of that we got from a felon and a dead guy."

"Not to mention," Mick added, "It'll just make us look like we're destroying the reputation of a fallen officer."

They covered every other facet of the case, or at least those that they knew the viewers would care about, and did so in a direct and honest fashion. The interview, which was comprised of almost an hour of footage, was edited down to a fifteen-minute segment that the station had been advertising for a week.

Mick spoke of the early days of the investigation, when Stoya's body was discovered, and the immense pressure put on him by Chief Horace Johnston as more victims appeared.

Jason recounted his first encounter with Ernie Page at the Rides-4-Less used car dealership after witnessing him meet with Tick at Edgewater, the subsequent sting that followed, and the shootout with Vladimir Popov's crew at the motel brothel.

They even admitted that they did not believe that Ernie Page was the EPK and recalled the internal struggle that they faced knowing that a serial killer was still walking the streets after his death, despite HoJo's insistence that the case was closed.

Next came the discovery of Vivian Tong's body, which further cemented their belief that the EPK was still on the loose. They spoke of her connection to Vance Gold, Buddy's Speakeasy, and even warned of the growing epidemic of sex traffickers preying on young girls in the Cleveland area.

Mick told the story of how he found his boss, Chief Horace Johnston, dead in his car outside of Buddy's Speakeasy. He brought up the note that was found with HoJo's body, made out to Detective Knox, which up until this point had not been released to the public.

As explosive as that information may have been for most of the viewing audience, it was what they discussed next that certainly would be the talk amongst Clevelanders for weeks to come.

"Tell us more about Phil Worthington," Hannah had asked.

Up until this point, the only information that had been released about Phil was that he had been found dead in a Tennessee motel. For the past two weeks, Cleveland news outlets had been running the story of a local man who had apparently become the latest victim of a woman whom authorities were referring to as "Deadly Dolly", a middle-aged female fugitive believed to be responsible for the deaths of at least three men over the past year.

"Phil Worthington was a husband and a father," Mick replied.

"He was a retired truck driver who ran a successful fishing charter out of this very marina. On the surface, he was a pretty normal guy who had unfortunately endured some devastating losses in his life."

"Viewers at home are probably wondering right now what Phil Worthington's connection to the EPK case is. Can you elaborate?" Hannah asked.

"The connection is," Jason replied. "That Phil Worthington was the EPK."

For the next five minutes, viewers were presented with evidence to support his claim that Phil had taken it upon himself to bring justice to his daughter, Jane. They learned how police believed he had lured and killed Nina and Svetlana, who he blamed for luring his daughter into a world of drugs and prostitution, and dumped their bodies in Lake Erie shortly after the discovery of Stoya Fedorov.

Mick, while purposely omitting the speculation that HoJo was connected to Vance, explained that the chief was likely murdered by Phil as retribution for allowing so many drugs to hit the streets.

Jason followed that up with a revelation about Phil's last known victim, Vance Gold. Prior to opening Buddy's Speakeasy, Jason conveyed that Vance had been the head of a major drug and prostitution ring in Cleveland for years. He surmised that once Phil had discovered that his daughter died while working for Vance, likely getting that information from Nina and Svetlana before killing them, that the owner of Buddy's Speakeasy inevitably became his prime target.

Mick added that Phil likely only had one more target in mind, but that the potential victim was currently in police custody, and that his identity would remain a secret for the time being.

"Wrong place at the wrong time," Mick answered when asked about how Phil Worthington, the man that police believed to be the EPK, ended up as the latest victim of "Deadly Dolly". Still on the run, sightings of the newest member of the FBI's most wanted list had been reported in almost every state since Phil's death.

As the taped segment faded out, her producer gave Hannah the countdown, once again, before going live. So many questions had been answered, but it was the one that the detectives had been unable to give an explanation for that the young news reporter would close with.

"As newly appointed Chief of Police Anthony Lawson finds himself inheriting a post-EPK city of Cleveland, one question that the detectives were not able to answer was in regards to Vivian Tong," Hannah said. "What they did say was that the investigation into the death of Tong, who had gained legal status as a United States citizen after immigrating to Cleveland from Hong Kong, was ongoing."

Hannah let out a long sigh of relief after the producer informed her that they had cut to commercial, and she hoped that Jason and Mick would be happy with the way it turned out – especially the last part about Vivian Tong.

After taping their interview at Edgewater, Jason and Mick had informed her that they had yet to find any evidence linking Phil Worthington to the murder of Vivian Tong. Despite the fact that she had the letters EPK carved into her and that her body was discovered at Edgewater Park, there was no reason to believe that Phil would have had any reason to kill her. It just did not add up.

"Do you think it was a copycat?" Hannah had asked as they walked back to their cars.

"Could be," Mick replied. "We're still looking into the possibility that the man using the alias of Eugene Lankford is our primary suspect."

"Unless we can find some sort of evidence to the contrary," Jason added. "There's a good chance that whoever killed Vivian Tong is still out there, maybe even walking among us. All we can do is hope that we get Eugene Lankford, or whoever this guy is, into custody before he carries on the EPK's torch."

93

"I saw Jason on TV last night," Grace Brooks said to Cara, whom she had just picked up from the Westcott. They were on their way to pick Coop up from an early evening physical therapy session with the team's medical staff. "Tell him he did a great job next time you see him."

"I'll let him know for sure," Cara replied. "I'm just glad that there's some sense of normalcy in his life now that his family is back in their own house."

"How about you and Coop? Things getting back to normal?" Grace asked. "I haven't seen either of you since you got back from Florida."

"Normal?" Cara laughed. "I'm not even sure what that word means anymore."

"That was a tough thing you went through down there with CMZ. I'm really sorry you had to go through that, Cara."

"I appreciate that. It could've been a lot worse, I suppose. Thankfully, the rest of the trip was absolutely amazing."

"Good, you guys needed that."

"Hey, how's your MMA training going?" Cara asked changing the subject.

"Pretty good, but I still have a long way to go."

"I know I wouldn't want to get in a ring with you," Cara laughed.

"I don't know, Cara. I think you're pretty feisty! You'd probably do just fine."

"It's a silly argument though, because I could never give up all the junk food in order to train properly. I don't know how you do it."

"I'd be lying if I said that I didn't fantasize about Hostess cupcakes. Not just one, but I'm talking about like a baker's dozen," Grace mused.

"What keeps you from just breaking down and doing it?" Cara asked.

"I guess there are a few reasons, but the biggest one is my belief that I would only be shortchanging myself later in exchange for a brief moment of gluttony. I'm not going to lie, I do a lot of meditating and reflection to help keep me strong."

"I've been trying to be a little more reflective myself," Cara stated.

"Oh yeah?"

"When all that stuff happened with CMZ, I really was a mess. I felt so lost; not to mention violated."

"Who could blame you, Cara?" Grace interjected. "Nobody should ever have to feel like that."

"I agree, but I still did. The crazy part was that I kept thinking about something Clarence told me when I was a nervous wreck during Coop's surgery, and it really helped calm me down a bit."

"Let me guess - God's there. He's always there…" Grace said while mimicking Clarence's deep voice.

"That's exactly what he said! How'd you know that?"

"Well, because I've heard it quite a bit myself from him. Especially when I was going through my whole ordeal with the excessive use of force accusation," Grace added.

"I have a feeling that Clarence helps a lot of people in that way," Cara stated. "And you know what? I've decided that he's absolutely right."

94

Detective Jason Knox approached the front door cautiously as he wasn't sure how the occupant of the bungalow would react to his presence. Mick, who normally would have been right there with him, had left the day before for a long-overdue vacation to Las Vegas.

"Are you sure you want to be out of town when the interview airs tonight?" Jason had asked when he dropped Mick off at the airport. "Hannah said it's going to be a big deal. You might even get some dates out of this, big guy!"

"That's exactly the reason I'm getting the hell out of here, Knox," Mick replied. "I know if I hang around Cleveland I'll have to beat the women off with a stick."

"Hey, in all seriousness, have a good time out there. You deserve this time away, Mick."

"I appreciate that, Knox. It's been a long time coming. I can't wait to sip drinks by the casino pool all day and park my fat ass at a blackjack table all night. Hell, I might even rent a car and do some sightseeing while I'm out there," Mick replied.

"The possibilities are endless, Commander McCarthy…"

"So are the buffet lines," Mick chuckled.

"Anything you need me to do in regards to the Vivian Tong case while you're gone?" Jason asked.

"You and I both know that Vivian Tong's killer is in the wind, Knox," Mick replied. "Whoever it was, he was a damn good opportunist though."

"Not going to argue with you on that one," Jason agreed. "He sure had us spinning our wheels thinking Vivian was killed by the EPK."

"I'll tell you what, if you find the artist formerly known as Eugene Lankford, I will personally drive my big ass straight back here from Vegas," Mick said as he exited the vehicle. He poked his head back in through the open passenger window and added, "Other than that, I don't give a crap what you do while I'm gone."

Jason smiled at the thought of Mick sipping a daiquiri by the pool in Vegas as he knocked on the door of the bungalow. He knew that the occupant was home and he was also pretty certain that she saw him walking up to the house, but he just wasn't certain how long it would take Ethel Levine to make it to the front door.

One of the first things that Jason did after Phil Worthington's death was announced was to send a landscaping crew over to cut her grass and clean up her mulch beds in preparation for the upcoming winter months. He had also arranged to have Meals-on-Wheels routinely take food to her since he knew that the one person who would have done those things just so happened to be the same man that was gone.

One of the hardest realities that Jason had to face after learning more about the man who turned out to be the EPK, whether he liked it or not, was the realization that Phil Worthington was in a way also a victim.

While Phil chose to turn his rage and insurmountable feeling of guilt after the loss of his daughter into more death and pain for others, he also proved that when faced with unimaginable grief, that there is no telling what a human being is capable of becoming.

"Hello, Detective," Ethel greeted as she opened the door. "I've been wondering if you were going to stop by."

"You have? I wasn't so sure you would want to see me," Jason replied.

"Why would you say that?" Ethel asked, puzzled.

"Well, after everything that happened with your neighbor, I just wasn't sure how I'd be received. I know that Mr. Worthington was very important to you."

"You're right, Detective. I cared for Phil and his family as if they were my own," Ethel replied. "What they say he did to those people, well, that's not the man that I knew. I just don't know what to make of it all."

"I'm sure that it's been very hard on you, Mrs. Levine."

"It has, but you know what? Phil must've known that something was going to happen because he must've arranged for people to bring me food and even do the yard work that he would've done. Isn't that something?"

It was a cruel irony, Jason thought, and for a moment he considered correcting her. However, as he looked upon the frail woman in front of him he knew that for her to heal she needed to believe that it was Phil who had arranged the landscapers and the meals.

"Well, that really is something, Mrs. Levine. He must've cared for you very much," Jason said.

"Yes, I think so too," Ethel said. "Can I ask a favor of you while you're here, Detective?"

"Sure, what can I do for you?"

"I have a light bulb in my kitchen that needs replacing and I can't reach it. Would you mind changing it for me?"

"I'd be happy to, Mrs. Levine," Jason said. "You lead the way."

Epilogue

Cooper Madison stood in front of his team on the steps of the dugout and asked for their attention. When Coop spoke, the team usually listened, but as he stood before them with an ice bag tightly wrapped around his throwing elbow, they were even more attentive than usual.

Many, if not all, of the players knew just how long it took him to get back on a Major League mound after his Tommy John surgery back in 2006, and they hoped that his arm would still be ready for the upcoming playoffs.

"Listen up, y'all," Coop announced. "I know with the postseason comin' up that this isn't the best time for me to be out with an injury, but Doc says that if I rest and ice over the next week that I might still be good to go come playoff time."

Coop studied their faces, hoping to gauge their reaction to the news. While his arm had nowhere near the power it did before his Tommy John surgery, the team had still relied upon it heavily throughout the course of the past season, and he wanted to make sure that they kept their spirits up.

"What if you're not, though?" asked Billy Monlux, the starting shortstop. "Who's gonna throw for us?"

"Well, shoot, there's lots of guys that can throw, Billy," Coop replied. "I'm not the only arm out here. It's a team effort."

"Hey, are you guys gonna chit-chat all day in the dugout or are you going to get your butts out here and practice?" Mark Patterson, the team's manager, yelled from his spot behind the pitcher's mound.

Coop, noticing that one of the players had ignored the manager's order to get on the field, decided to stay behind and check on him as the others ran out to warm-up. It was the team's catcher, Luke, and he had tears in his eyes.

"What's the matter, Luke?" Coop asked, taking a seat next to him.

"We're gonna lose now," Luke replied, his voice trembling.

"Hey now, you can't think that way. Heck, you're the catcher, Luke. The field general. Guys look up to you," Coop said, a mixture of admonishment and encouragement.

"I know, but none of the other dads throw batting practice as good as you do," Luke pleaded to his father.

Coop, unsure if he loved or hated the fact that his 9-year-old son was as competitive as he was at that age, laughed.

"Well, that may be true, but it's just BP," Coop replied, putting his arm around his son. "I'll make a deal with you, okay? I'll promise to do everything in my power so that I'm ready to throw BP before our first playoff game if you promise to wipe those tears from your face and get out there with your teammates. Deal?"

"Deal," Luke replied as he wiped the remnants of his tears on the sleeve of his shirt.

"Atta boy," Coop said as he leaned in and gave his son a quick kiss on top of his mop of shaggy blonde hair.

A few minutes later, as Luke joined his team out on the field, a woman's voice came from just outside the dugout. Coop didn't need to turn around to know that it was his wife, but he did anyways.

"So, how'd he take the news?" Cara Madison asked.

"As expected, I suppose," Coop replied. "He's got a lot of his momma in him, you know."

"You say that like it's a bad thing," Cara laughed.

"No, ma'am. I'm only talking about the good stuff."

"Well, I like to think that he has the best of us both," Cara said as she walked through the narrow gate and into the dugout. Coop greeted her, as usual, with a long hug and a brief kiss.

"I'm not gonna argue with you there," Coop replied, putting his arm around her as they watched their son jog a warm-up lap alongside his teammates.

Luke Jeffrey Madison was tall for his age and his long, unruly hair often matched his personality. He was every bit as athletic as one would imagine the son of a former professional athlete to be, and also as precocious and stubborn as his mother.

"Have I told you recently how much I love you?" Coop asked.

"Yes, but don't let that stop you from reminding me again."

"Well, Mrs. Madison, you should know by now that nothing will ever stop me from letting you know..."

"Nothing?" Cara asked as she looked into Coop's eyes.

"Nothing..."

ABOUT THE AUTHOR

Dan Largent resides in Olmsted Township, Ohio with his wife, April, and three children, Brooke, Grace, and Luke.

His bestselling debut novel, BEFORE WE EVER SPOKE, was released in June of 2018 to rave reviews from readers and critics alike.

Dan has appeared on TV and radio programs across the country to discuss his books and share his unique journey.

43725870R00250

Made in the USA
Lexington, KY
01 July 2019